— Concern from the Editor—

The Department of ██████ requested a copy of the manuscript for *The Orson Welles' Conspiracy* for their review. This mysterious and clandestine government agency simply ***could not*** have known the contents of my father's safety deposit box or the packages Peter ██████ sent me posthumously. Nor could they have known I was publishing this exposé of the greatest conspiracy theory no one has ever even ***conceived*** of.

This mysterious Department has requested ***and*** required me, as the book's editor, to make numerous changes to the manuscript for reasons of "national security" under the treat of imprisonment in a so-called black site. Except for the obvious redactions, what ***other*** changes have been made under duress to both the screenplay and the transcription will forever be unknown to the Reader. But know this, my father is ***not*** an unreliable narrator nor is he a liar. He ***did not*** fabricate either the screenplay or the "forgotten" reel-to-reel tapes containing two infamous interviews with Orson Welles by Peter ██████.

This is a posthumous publication as my father, Orson Welles, and Peter ██████ are all deceased, unfortunately. As the executor of my father's estate, I firmly believe the screenplay should be published as written and the interviews should be transcribed as recorded.

Legal opinion of the publisher's lawyers is that the requests of ***both*** the author's estate and Department of ██████ ***must*** be considered and respected. Unfortunately, one takes precedence or the other: the government of the United States of America over mine, of course.

The book you now hold in your greedy, needy little hands has been ***redacted*** by the mysterious and clandestine The Department of ██████. May they rot in the circle of Hell reserved for censors of the First Amendment!

-Robert Dwight Brown, *editor*

FACT:
The Church of Scientology® was founded in December 1953 by American pulp science-fiction writer L. Ron Hubbard. Belief in "auditing" "thetans" with "E-meters", as apposed to psychiatry is common, as is belief in a space opera starring Lord Xenu of the Galactic Confederacy who brought billions of souls in DC-8 space-planes to Earth to imprison them in Earth's volcanoes with the intent of blowing them up with hydrogen bombs. Its membership includes Hollywood celebrities such as actor John Travolta, late musician Isaac Hayes, journalist Greta Van Susteran, and actor Tom Cruise.

FACT:
William Francis Brown and his son Robert Dwight Brown, a heavily medicated paranoid schizophrenic, believe not only the existence of the lost Orson Welles motion picture *Invasion From Mars*, also in the reality of the invasion of Virginia and Washington DC by the Martians on October 30, 1938 and the subsequent "Orson Welles' Conspiracy", the continual "Interplanetary Cold War" and the implemented"Martian Triangle" that imprisons humans on Earth until a classified time specified in the Tranquility Treaty of 1969.

All descriptions of documents, secret rituals, rival space opera belief systems, by both L. Ron Hubbard® and Robert Dwight Brown®, in this book ***are*** accurate.

The Orson Welles' Conspiracy

Or: On October 30, 1938, The Night of the "Panic Broadcast", Were The Radio Reports of A Martian Invasion REAL?!? & If So Why Was The Event Erased From History?!? Answer: A Conspiracy Between Pres. Roosevelt & William Randolph Hearst & A Young Orson Welles!!!

ROBERT DWIGHT
BROWN
—EDITOR—

Allonymous Books

Allonymous Books
A Division of Chi Xi Stigma Publishing Company, LLC

ISBN 13: 978-1-931608-34-3: *The Orson Welles' Conspiracy*
ISBN 13: 978-1-931608-35-0: *The H.G. Welles' Conspiracy*

"Based on a True Story"

All characters appearing in this work are fictitious, especially those based on real people. Any resemblance to real persons, living or dead, is not coincidental, but somewhat intentional. The events described herein actually happened insofar as one acknowledges the hallucinations of a paranoid schizophrenic can be referenced as actual events and real persons, living or dead, as actual people and that the cat is the reincarnation of J. Edgar Hoover, the dust-bunnies under the couch are CIA operatives, and the Cabbage Patch Kid, whose adoptive name is Alistair Benny, is the legitimate heir to the British crown.

"I would like to thank all of the photographers of the photographs I have included in this work. Most, if not all, of your names have been lost to, not only history, but the immeasurable depths of the Internet. Not even the all-powerful, all-knowing Google can assist me in identifying and crediting you all for your work."– Robert Dwight Brown, *editor*

TABLE OF CONTENTS

"Americans have been trained by media to go into Pavolovian giggles at the mention of 'conspiracy' because for an American to believe in a conspiracy he must also believe in flying saucers or, craziest of all, that more than one person was involved in the JFK murder."

-GORE VIDAL-

"It's not paranoia if they're really out to get you."

-21ST CENTURY AMERICAN PROVERB-

ORSON WELLES
H for Hoax

Hoaxes require intuitive forethought with a premeditated and conscious effort to deceive. The skills of a confidence man, master forger, counterfeiter, [redacted], fortune teller, parlor magician, stage actor, and career politician are necessary to effectively perpetrate the hoax. Hoaxes, as a matter of definition, also require a victim, known to the above professions by such colorful and poetic names such as "mark", "dupe", or "pigeon". Each victim has "dupable" personality traits that "mark" him as a susceptible "pigeon", which include an over eagerness to believe, being easily susceptible to suggestion, a willingness to suspend their disbelief, or an innate need to trust. What explanation could justify hoaxes? The gullibility of an overly optimistic academia whose customarily reticent nature is overridden by the enthusiasm to accept proof of their personally and professionally held theories and beliefs that are so strongly held that evidence to the contrary of the hoax, is so willingly dismissed? Or the trustfulness of a naïve public whose rural and uneducated character suspends any disbelief and readily accepts the nature of the hoax at face value? Neither of these explanations can justify all hoaxes.

But there are certain commonalities that hoaxes share with these nefarious occupations:

- Confidence men begin their "long con" long before the mark ever meets him and essentially and effectively ends the "con" when the mark truly believes that the idea has been their's all along. The con-man knows intuitively that he will be believed cause of (not in spire of) the believability and/or absurdity of his ideas.
- The forger and counterfeiter agonize over the slightest imperfection of the color or texture of the paper, or canvas, the ink or paint, the chemicals used to age and otherwise affect the product, and every stroke of their pen or brush or engraving in their silver plate. The product's authenticity is of utmost importance and fooling experts is prized. The process is as laborious as it is nefarious.
- [redacted]
- A fortune teller, as well as the hoaxer, feeds off of the eagerness of their victims to believe. Through the use a crystal ball, Tarot cards, or a manipulatable seance table, the fortune teller provides the susceptible with the precise story they are most willing to accept as true in exchange for both money and faith. And their faith costs them dearly.
- The parlor magician uses misdirection and preparation to make their audience believe they have seen what they haven't actually seen, though they claim to have seen until their dying day. The lady isn't sawed in half. The milk jug isn't hinged where you think. Preparation/misdirection.
- The stage actor uses suspension of disbelief– the audience's willingness to lay aside their logical and rational intellect to believe every word occurring on a stage only a few feet away.

- The career politician spends a lifetime pandering to his constituency, wielding their preconceived notions, emotions, and beliefs into a cudgel to beat their constituents into voting for them. The voter believes this politician will act in their interests, leaving them, the majority of the time, satisfied and completely unaware they were "marked" as a "pigeon" and "duped" for their vote.

Orson Welles, the famed theater, radio, and film director, wore all of these hats and many, many more. As a director and actor, his audiences willingly suspended their disbeliefs to believe the fictitious action onstage is genuine emotion. Having trained at the knee of Harry Houdini, he had mastered misdirection. Though his mentor loathed fortune-telling, he would embrace these deceptions to weave his fantastical "stories". If anyone were more inclined towards mastering the art of hoaxery, it was a young Orson Welles.

Very seldom is the hoaxer actually willing to take the public spotlight. Most tend to shy away from the glare of scrutiny. But on October 31, 1938, only hours after frightening the entire nation with his "The War of the Worlds" radio-dramatization, the radio-personality and practical joker extraordinaire, Orson Welles stood before the press on Halloween morning with a prepared statement, an explanation of his hoax. "Despite my deep regret over any misapprehension which our broadcast last night created among some listeners, I am even the more bewildered over this misunderstanding in the light of an analysis of the broadcast itself. It seems to me that there are four factors which should have in any event maintained the illusion of fiction in the broadcast. The first was that the broadcast was performed as if occurring in the future and as if it were then related by a survivor of a past occurrence. The date of the fanciful invasion of this planet by Martians was clearly given as 1939 and was so announced at the outset of the broadcast. The second element was the fact that the broadcast took place at our regular weekly *Mercury Theatre* period and had been so announced in all the papers. For seventeen consecutive weeks we have been broadcasting radio drama. Sixteen of these seventeen broadcasts have been fiction and have been presented as such. Only one in the series was a true story, the broadcast of 'Hell on Ice' by Commander Elsberg, and was identified as a true story within the framework of radio drama. The third element was the fact that at the very outset of the broadcast and twice during its enactment listeners were told that this was a play, that it was an adaptation of an old novel by HG Wells. Furthermore, at the conclusion a detailed statement to this effect was made. The fourth factor seems to be to have been the more pertinent of all. That is the familiarity of the fable within the American idiom of Mars and Martians. For many decades 'The Man from Mars' has been almost a synonym for fantasy… this fantasy, as such, has been used in radio programs many times. In these broadcasts, conflict between citizens of Mars and other planets has been a familiarly accepted fairy-tale. The same make-believe is familiar to newspaper readers through a comic strip that uses the same device."[1]

From the *New York Times* to the *Boston Daily Globe* and to the *Daily News,* the front pages across the nation bellowed variations on the same headline: "Radio Listeners in Panic, Taking War Drama as Fact"! But with one simple press conference, Orson Welles was forgiven and all the lawsuits soon forgotten. By quoting from and editorializing on the October 31, 1938 edition of the *New York Times,* let us examine infamous "The War of the Worlds" radio-drama and its effect on the nation in greater detail, shall we?

> **A wave of mass hysteria seized thousands of radio listeners between 8:15 and 9:30 o'clock last night when a broadcast of a dramatization of H. G. Wells's fantasy, "The War of the Worlds," led thousands to believe that an interplanetary conflict had started with invading Martians spreading wide death and destruction in New Jersey and New York.**
>
> **The broadcast, which disrupted households, interrupted religious services, created traffic jams and clogged communications systems, was made by Orson Welles, who as the radio character, "The Shadow," used to give "the creeps" to**

1 Quoted from a prepared speech by Orson Welles to reporters on the morning of October 31, 1938.

he New York Times

-Class Matter, York, N. Y. NEW YORK, MONDAY, OCTOBER 31, 1938. PP

Radio Listeners in Panic, Taking War Drama as Fact

Many Flee Homes to Escape 'Gas Raid From Mars'—Phone Calls Swamp Police at Broadcast of Wells Fantasy

A wave of mass hysteria seized thousands of radio listeners throughout the nation between 8:15 and 9:30 o'clock last night when a broadcast of a dramatization of H. G. Wells's fantasy, "The War of the Worlds," led thousands to believe that an interplanetary conflict had started with invading Martians spreading wide death and destruction in New Jersey and New York.

The broadcast, which disrupted households, interrupted religious services, created traffic jams and clogged communications systems, was made by Orson Welles, who as the radio character, "The Shadow," used to give "the creeps" to countless child listeners. This time at least a score of adults required medical treatment for shock and hysteria.

In Newark, in a single block at Heddon Terrace and Hawthorne Avenue, more than twenty families rushed out of their houses with wet handkerchiefs and towels over their faces to flee from what they believed was to be a gas raid. Some began moving household furniture.

Throughout New York families left their homes, some to flee to near-by parks. Thousands of persons called the police, newspapers and radio stations here and in other cities of the United States and Canada seeking advice on protective measures against the raids.

The program was produced by Mr. Welles and the Mercury Theatre on the Air over station WABC and the Columbia Broadcasting System's coast-to-coast network, from 8 to 9 o'clock.

The radio play, as presented, was to simulate a regular radio program with a "break-in" for the material of the play. The radio listeners, apparently, missed or did not listen to the introduction, which was: "The Columbia Broadcasting System and its affiliated stations present Orson Welles and the Mercury Theatre on the Air in 'The War of the Worlds' by H. G. Wells."

They also failed to associate the program with the newspaper listing of the program, announced as "Today: 8:00-9:00—Play: H. G. Wells's 'War of the Worlds'—WABC." They ignored three additional announcements made during the broadcast emphasizing its fictional nature

Mr. Welles opened the program with a description of the series of

Continued on Page Four

EAD STANDS PAT S A NEW DEALER IN BID FOR SENATE

mocratic Candidate Opposes y Except Minor Changes in Labor and Security Laws

HOLDS THEORY OF TVA

nts Budget Balanced, but ot if This Means 'Misery,' He Tells The Times

Text of Representative Mead's ply is printed on Page 6.

From a Staff Correspondent

UFFALO, N. Y., Oct. 30.—Rep- ntatives James M. Mead, Demo- ic candidate for the short-term atorial seat in the election Nov. oday answered in a statement six questions on campaign es propounded by THE NEW K TIMES to the four New York inees of the two major parties n editorial Oct. 20.

. Mead's answer, in the main, a broad and little qualified de- e of the New Deal legislation h he, as a member of the se of Representatives, had a in formulating and passing. e principles of the Social Se- y and National Labor Relations he defended stoutly, seeing only for revisions to extend benefits of the former, a cor- on of technical defects and a ening of administration.

incipal opposition to the Social rity Act he saw inspired by e who fear that it will "become important a monument to the ocratic party and to men like ident Roosevelt and Senator ner."

poses "Pay-as-You-Go" Policy

unqualifiedly opposed a revi- of the law to make social se- y payments on a "pay-as-you- basis.

ich policy," he declared, ld destroy the reserve funds h are the protection of the fu-

OUSTED JEWS FIN REFUGE IN POLAN AFTER BORDER ST

Exiles Go to Relatives' Ho or to Camps Maintained Distribution Committee

REVEAL CRUELTY OF T

Others Sent Back to Germ Pending Parleys on Issue the Two Governments

Wireless to THE NEW YORK TIMES.

WARSAW, Poland, Oct. 30.— evacuation from frontier area thousands of Polish Jews—8,000 cording to official reports 12,000 according to an estimate the Jewish Relief Committee- ported from Germany began to after they had been massed frontier stations up and down border for twenty-six hours. T terrible ordeal is nearing its en

Polish authorities have permi officials of the Joint Distribu Committee to send the victim relatives' homes in Poland o special camps the committee m tains. The refugees spent a sl less night in barracks, crowded tion buildings or empty fre cars; many spent the night in open in the no man's land betw the frontiers.

The Joint Distribution Comm supplied food and will also pay cially reduced railway fares into interior.

It is believed that the evacua will last another day or so. M refugees desire to remain in frontier area pending the outc of the Warsaw-Berlin negotiati which may result in the repea the deportation order, enab them to return to their homes Germany.

Suffering Is Described

Reports from various points al the frontier describe the terr suffering. The worst situa existed at the Zbaszyn fron station on the Paris-Berlin-W saw-Moscow line. There ne

B. C. VLADECK DIES; CITY COUNCILMAN

American Labor Party Chief Here Was Manager of The Jewish Daily Forward

B. Charney Vladeck, American Labor party member of the City Council and general manager of The Jewish Daily Forward, died at Mount Sinai Hospital last night at 8:15. He was 52 years old.

DALADIER PREPARES TO RULE SEVERELY

Calls Cabinet Meeting to Talk Over Decrees to Promote Recovery in Industry

By P. J. PHILIP

Wireless to THE NEW YORK TIMES.

PARIS, Oct. 30.—With his own Radical Socialist party solidly behind him and with the Communists definitely shaken from his ranks, countless child listeners. This time at least a score of adults required medical treatment for shock and hysteria.

In Newark, in a single block at Heddon Terrace and Hawthorne Avenue, more than twenty families rushed out of their houses with wet handkerchiefs and towels over their faces to flee from what they believed was to be a gas raid. Some began moving household furniture.

Throughout New York families left their homes, some to flee to near-by parks. Thousands of persons called the police, newspapers and radio stations here and in other cities of the United States and Canada seeking advice on protective measures against the raids.

The program was produced by Mr. Welles and the Mercury Theatre on the Air over station WABC and the Columbia Broadcasting System's coast-to-coast network, from 8 to 9 o'clock.

The radio play, as presented, was to simulate a regular radio program with a "break-in" for the material of the play. The radio listeners, apparently, missed or did not listen to the introduction, which...

Promptly at eight o'clock on October 30, 1938, Dan Seymour, the *Mercury Theatre's* announcer, took to the air with the following announcement, that was promptly ignored by most of the listening audience, "The Columbia Broadcasting System and its affiliated stations present Orson Welles and *The Mercury Theatre on the Air* in *The War of the Worlds* by HG Wells."

[The audience] failed to associate the program with newspaper listening of the program, announced as "Today: 8:00-9:00—Play: HG Wells' 'War of the Worlds'—WABC." They ignored three additional announcements made during the broadcast emphasizing its fictional nature.

Mr. Welles opened the program with a description of the series of which it is a part:

"Ladies and gentlemen:" Dan Seymour continued, "the director of the *Mercury Theatre* and star of these broadcasts, Orson Welles!"

"We know now that in the early years of the twentieth century," Orson Welles began paraphrasing the opening paragraph of HG Wells' novel, quoting a number of sentences word-for-word. "This world was being watched closely by intelligences greater than man's and yet as mortal as his own. We know now that as human beings busied themselves about their various concerns they were scrutinized and studied, perhaps almost as narrowly as man with a microscope might scrutinize the transient creatures that swarm and multiply in a drop of water. With infinite complacence people went to and fro over the earth about their little affairs, serene in the assurance of their dominion over this small spinning fragment of solar driftwood which by chance or design man has inherited out of the dark mystery of Time and Space. Yet across an immense ethereal gulf, minds that to our minds as our as to the beasts of the jungle, intellects vast, cool and unsympathetic, regarded earth with envious eyes and slowly and surely drew their plans against us. In the thirty ninth year of the twentieth century came the great disillusionment."[2]

HG Wells meets his misspelled namesake Orson Welles after the latter's notoriety with his famous story, now infamous radio-play!

Within a minute of uttering his brilliant speech,

2 Koch, Howard, *The Panic Broadcast*, 33, 36, based on the opening paragraphs of HG Wells The War of the Worlds

in the minds of the listening public, the fictitious nature of the broadcast would soon come to a close. When Orson Welles concluded his speech with the following words, the broadcast would become all too real, "It was near the end of October. Business was better. The war scare was over. More men were back at work. Sales were picking up. On this particular evening, October 30, the Crossley service estimated that thirty-two million people were listening in on radios."[3]

According to Brian Holmsten and Alex Lubertozzi, editors of *The Complete War of the Worlds*, "*The Mercury Theatre on the Air*, produced by twenty-three-year-old Orson Welles and the elder, Bucharest-born, former grain merchant John Houseman, posted a miserable 3.6 Crossley rating, compared to *Chase and Sanborn's* 34.7 rating."[4]

Charlie McCarthy and his dummy, the ventriloquist Edgar Bergen!

Orson Welles, the boy wonder, the genius of New York theatre, and supposed star of the air-waves, fought a losing battle with a dummy. How absurd, in Orson's mind, was a ventriloquist broadcasting over the radio and consistently beating his program of literary-quality work week in and week out? None of the thirty-odd million listeners of Edgar Bergen seemed to care that they had no way of knowing whether or not Edgar Bergen's lips moved when the Charlie McCarthy dummy quipped a hilarious one-liner.

For millions of listeners the magic of the radio was miraculous, almost like having a telephone to God. One did not need to see Edgar Bergen not moving his lips to truly believe he was not moving his lips. When Gus Wentz unscrewed the backing of his radio-set looking "into the back of the radio to try to see the 'little people' in there"[5], he actually believed magical leprechaun-like little people lived within the cabinet. and when the mayor of Richland Center, Wisconsin, in response to FDR's invitation to the entire nation to "tell me your troubles", wrote the President, "An old friend said to me this morning, 'I almost wept during the President's talk last night, it seemed he was sitting by my side talking in plain simple words to me'"[6].

But those rural and uneducated and urban and educated who did tune into *The Mercury Theatre* were greeted with:

> A weather report was given, prosaically. An announcer remarked that the program would be continued from a hotel, with dance music. For a few moments a dance program was given in the usual manner. Then there was a "break-in" with a "flash" about a professor at an observatory noting a series of gas explosions on the planet Mars.
>
> News bulletins and scene broadcasts followed, reporting, with the technique in which the radio had reported actual events, the landing of a "meteor" near Princeton N. J., "killing" 1,500 persons, the discovery that the "meteor" was

3 Ibid, 36

4 Holmsten, Brian and Alex Lubertozzi, *The Complete War of the Worlds* (Naperville, Illinois: Sourcebooks, 2001),4

5 Barfield, Ray, *Oral interview in Listening to Radio, 1920-1950* (Westport, Conn.: Praeger, 1996), 16-17

6 Brewer, F.L. Richland Center, Wisconic, to FDR March 13, 1933 printed in Lawrence W. Levine & Cornelia R. Levine's *The People & The President* (Boston, Massachusetts: Beacon Press, 2002), 3

a "metal cylinder" containing strange creatures from Mars armed with "death rays" to open hostilities against the inhabitants of the earth.

When the comedic banter of Bergen and McCarthy paused for a musical interlude with Nelson Eddy singing "Neopolitan Love Song" at eight-twelve, four million listeners spun the dial looking for anything more interesting and less ear-grating; only to discover something considerably more horrifying. While many would find Professor Ralph Linton of Columbia University lecturing on "How Civilizations Grow", the Calvary Baptist Church Choir's beautiful renditions of gospel hymns, or a Bach cantata would be heard on the various other stations. The Bach cantata was much like The "War of the Worlds"' fictional Ramon Requello's beautiful interpretation of "La Cumparsita" broadcast at almost exactly the same time.

Most of the radio-listening public went temporarily insane at the moment Carl Phillips voice cracked saying, "Ladies and gentlemen, it's indescribable. I can hardly force myself to keep looking at it. It's awful... The monster or whatever it is can hardly move. It seems weighed down by... possibly gravity or something. The thing's rising up. The crowd falls back now. They've seen plenty. This is the most extraordinary experience. Ladies and gentlemen, I can't find words..." [7]

Princeton professor Hadley Cantril and his research staff, in the 1940 book, *Invasion From Mars*, an exhaustive study of the causes of the panic reactions of the nation that evening, estimated that six million people listened to the "War of the Worlds" broadcast. Cantril reported, "In answer to the AIPO question, 'At the time you were listening, did you think this broadcast was a play or a real news report?' 28 per cent indicated that they believed the broadcast was a news bulletin. Seventy per cent of those who thought they were listening to a news report were frightened or disturbed. This would mean that about 1,700,000 heard the broadcast as a news bulletin and that about 1,200,000 were excited by it."[8]

Unlike the Hindenburg's fiery crash that lasted for moments before most were known to have survived, the CBS reports went from nearly disturbing to categorically horrifying. Nothing in the collective consciousness of the listeners had prepared themselves for what they were hearing. Few would remember Dan Seymour's announcement at the end of the "invasion" half-way through the broadcast, just after the Martians' collapsed into the Hudson River, "You are listening to a CBS presentation of Orson Welles and the *Mercury Theatre on the Air* in an original dramatization of *The War of the Worlds* by HG Welles. The performance will continue after a brief intermission. This is the Columbia Broadcasting System."[9]

Despite the fantastic nature of the reported "occurrences," the program, coming after the recent war scare in Europe and a period in which the radio frequently had interrupted regularly scheduled programs to report developments in the Czechoslovak situation, caused fright and panic throughout the area of the broadcast.

Five weeks prior on September 25, 1938, while adapting Sherlock Holmes for his radio program, a news bulletin on the Munich crisis interrupted his broadcast, no doubt irritating the proud Orson, but that night the germ of an idea was planted in Orson's mind. He would use news bulletins as a dramatic technique to add suspense to "The War of the Worlds", an adaptation he had been planning for weeks.

Over the course of the next five days, tension around the world would come to a head over the Munich crisis. People in all industrialized nations of the world would huddle around their radios for any news. France had mobilized their troops, the Communist Soviet Union threatened to come to the aid of Czechoslovakia, and Great Britain said they too would act if France was forced to take action. Adolph Hitler, in the first of many "stare-downs", blinked and agreed to negotiate with England, France, and Italy. The four powers met

7 Koch, Howard, *The Panic Broadcast*, 50
8 Cantril, Hadley, *The Invasion From Mars*, Transaction Publishers, New Brunswick, 57,58
9 Koch, Howard, *The Panic Broadcast*, 67

Neville Chamberlain, Edouard Daladier, Adolf Hitler, and Benito Mussolini at the Munich Conference, September 30, 1938

in Munich and after eight hours of heated talks, news came of the Prime Minister of Britain Neville Chamberlain's, and Edouard Daladier, the French premier's, historically tarnished Munich Pact. The pact signed on Friday, September 30 averted World War II, for the time being, by handing the territory-greedy German Chancellor a significant portion of Czechoslovakia.

The citizenry of the industrialized nations across the world were glued to their radio-sets in anticipation of the regularly occurring program interruptions bringing news of the Munich crisis; only then did the world breathe a collective sigh of relief when an interruption brought news of the signing of the Pact. On that day, radio proved itself to be a valuable ally to the common people of the world and a source of accurate news reports. Reports that sped through the air to radios worldwide, almost from the moment the Pact was signed. No longer did the people have to wait until the next morning or for the evening edition of the newspaper to learn about events from around the globe. So trusted were these reports that few across the nation could even conceive of such a thing as a fake news report.

Peter [illegible], award-winning director of *The Last Picture Show* and *Paper Moon*, film historian, friend and biographer of Orson Welles, would ask the esteemed personality, "Is it a true story that when Pearl Harbor was announced, nobody believed it because?"

Orson answered in his deep baritone, "Dead right. Particularly since I had a patriotic broadcast that morning and was interrupted in the middle of it. I was on the full network, reading from Walt Whitman about how beautiful America was, when they said Pearl Harbor's attacked– now, doesn't that sound like me trying to do that again? They interrupted the show to say that there had been an attack. Roosevelt sent me a wire about it. I've forgotten what– I don't have it. Something like 'crying wolf' and that kind of thing. Not the same day– he was too busy!- but about ten days later."[10] Orson would never be able to escape the notoriety and infamy that he would earn with his "War of the Worlds" radio-hoax.

The Japanese attack on Pearl Harbor interrupted Orson Welles' patriotic rendition of Walt Whitman!

Telephone lines were tied up with calls from listeners or persons who had heard of the broadcasts. Many sought first to verify the reports.

In what may be considered a stroke of prophetic script-writing, or merely a coincidence, the fictional

10 Welles, Orson, and Peter [illegible], edited by Jonathan Rosenbaum, *This is Orson Welles* (Da Capo Press, 1998), 20

Professor Pearson also had difficulty getting through to CBS studios to give an eyewitness report of the Martians' victory at the small Wilmuth Farm in Grovers Mill, "Of the creatures in the rocket cylinder at Grover's Mill, I can give you no authoritative information- either as to their nature, their origin, or their purposes here on Earth. Of their destructive instrument I might venture some conjectural explanation. For want of a better term, I shall refer to the mysterious weapon as a heat ray. It's all too evident that these creatures have scientific knowledge far in advance of our own."[11]

> **But large numbers, obviously in a state of terror, asked how they could follow the broadcast's advice and flee from the city, whether they would be safer from the "gas raid" in the cellar or on the roof, how they could safeguard their children, and many of the questions which had been worrying residents of London and Paris during the tense days before the Munich agreement.**

Countless eyewitness accounts poured in during the aftermath of the broadcast. For the poor and uneducated, Mrs. Joslin's report was typical, "I was terribly frightened. I wanted to pack and take my child in my arms and gather up my friends and get in the car and just go north as far as we could. But whet I did was just set by one window, prayin', listenin' and scared stiff and my husband by the other snifflin' and lookin' out to see if people were runnin'. Then when the announcer said 'evacuate the city,' I ran and called my boarder and started with my child to rush down the stairs, not waitin' to ketch my hat or anything. When I got to the foot of the stairs I just couldn't get out, I don't know why. Meantime my husband he tried other stations and found them still runnin'. He couldn't smell any gas or see people runnin', so he called me back and told me it was just a play. So I set down, still ready to go at any minute till I heard Orson Welles say, 'Folks, I hope we ain't alarmed you. This is just a play!' Then I was just set."[12]

For Mrs. Delaney, a rich and educated woman from a New York suburb, "I never hugged my radio so closely as I did last night. I held a crucifix in my hand and prayed while looking out of my open window for falling meteors. I also wanted to get a faint whiff of the gas so that I would know when to close my window and hermetically seal my room with waterproof cement or anything else I could get hold of. My plan was to stay in the room and hope that I would not suffocate before the gas blew away. When the monsters were wading across the Hudson River and coming into New York, I wanted to run up on my roof and see what they looked like, but I could not leave my radio while it was telling me of their whereabouts."[13]

William Dock, 76, shot many of the creatures from Mars during their "invasion" with his trusty shotgun! In the morning, he read in the paper that everything had been a hoax created by Orson Welles! What about all of the Martians he had shot dead? What about that?

Or imagine you are nowhere near the Tri-State area. The head of the location department at Warner Brothers studio told of his experience, "My wife and I were driving through the redwood forest in northern California when the broadcast came over our car radio. At first it was just New Jersey, but soon the things were landing all over, even in California. There was no escape. All we could think

11 Koch, Howard, *The Panic Broadcast*, 54
12 Cantril, Hadley, *The Invasion From Mars: A Study in the Psychology of Panic* (Princeton, New Jersey, Princeton University Press, 1941), 49
13 Ibid, 49-50

of was to try to get back to LA to see our children once more. And be with them when it happened. We went right by gas stations but I forgot we were low in gas. In the middle of the forest our gas ran out. There was nothing to do. We just sat there holding hands expecting any minute to see those Martian monsters appear over the tops of the trees. When Orson said it was a Hallowe'en prank, it was like being reprieved on the way to the gas chamber." [14]

But the reprieves came slowly over the course of the evening. Newspaper fact checkers scrambled to authenticate the reports streaming through the doorways and screaming over the telephones.

> **So many calls came to newspapers and so many newspapers found it advisable to check on the reports despite their fantastic content that The Associated Press sent out the following at 8:48 P. M.:**
>
> **"Note to Editors: Queries to newspapers from radio listeners throughout the United States tonight, regarding a reported meteor fall which killed a number of New Jerseyites, are the result of a studio dramatization. The A.P."**

A *New York Tribune* reporter, Dorothy Thompson, wrote the next day, "Hitler managed to scare all of Europe to its knees a month ago, but he at least had an army and air force to back up his shrieking words."[15] And the Associated Press reported, "An offer to volunteer in stopping an invasion from Mars came among hundreds of telephone inquiries to police and newspapers during the radio dramatization of HG Wells' story. One excited man call Oakland police and shouted, 'My God! Where can I volunteer my services? We've got to stop this awful thing-'"[16] The *Trenton Evening Times* wrote, "Radio Dispatchers Frank Kramer and Francis Parr said they were swamped with telephone calls requesting information on antidotes for poison gas and the treatment of persons overcome by the deadly fumes. One Hamilton Township woman vowed she had stuffed all the doors and windows with paper and wet rags, but that the fumes were already seeping into her living room."[17]

> **Similarly police teletype systems carried notices to all stationhouses, and police short-wave radio stations notified police radio cars that the event was imaginary.**
>
> **Message From the Police**
>
> **The New York police sent out the following:**
>
> **"To all receivers: Station WABC informs us that the broadcast just concluded over that station was a dramatization of a play. No cause for alarm."**
>
> **The New Jersey State Police teletyped the following:**
>
> **"Note to all receivers--WABC broadcast as drama re this section being attacked by residents of Mars. Imaginary affair."**
>
> **From one New York theatre a manager reported that a throng of playgoers had rushed from his theatre as a result of the broadcast. He said that the wives of two men in the audience, having heard the broadcast, called the theatre and insisted that their husbands be paged. This spread the "news" to others in the audience.**
>
> **The switchboard of The New York Times was overwhelmed by the calls. A total of 875 were received. One man who called from Dayton, Ohio, asked, "What time will it be the end of the world?" A caller from the suburbs said he had had a houseful of guests and all had rushed out to the yard for safety.**
>
> **Warren Dean, a member of the American Legion living in Manhattan, who**

14 Koch, Howard, *The Panic Broadcast*, 89
15 Holmsten, Brian and Alex Lubertozzi, *The Complete War of the Worlds*, 52
16 Ibid, 53
17 Ibid, 51

telephoned to verify the "reports," expressed indignation which was typical of that of many callers.

"I've heard a lot of radio programs, but I've never heard anything as rotten as that," Mr. Dean said. "It was too realistic for comfort. They broke into a dance program with a news flash. Everybody in my house was agitated by the news. It went on just like press radio news."

How unscrupulous, dishonest, and crooked could Orson Welles be to put to the airwaves fictitious news reports? And who could possibly write such a fraudulent and deceptive script? The answer: Howard Koch, a young playwright, whose first professional job was writing the radio scripts for the *Mercury Theatre*. On October 24th, John Houseman gave an *Amazing Stories* pulp magazine to Howard with instructions to adapt *The War of the Worlds* using news bulletins. After reading the HG Wells classic, Koch realized, "I could use practically nothing but the author's idea of a Martian invasion and their machines. In short, I was being asked to do an almost entirely original hour-length play in six days. I called Houseman, pleading to have the assignment changed to another subject. He talked to Orson and called back. The answer was a firm no, this was Orson's favorite project."[18] Orson insisted on otherworldly realism, meaning Koch would spend the next six days in a "one-week nightmare of scenes written and rewritten between frantic telephones calls and pages speeding back and forth to the studio."[19] Only Davidson Taylor, a distinguished executive for the CBS network, and CBS attorneys "contended that the ["War of the Worlds"] script was too believable and that its realism would have to diminished before the show could go on the air." "Langley Field" was substituted for "Langham Field", "New Jersey National Guard" for "State Militia", and "Hotel Biltmore" was broadcast as the "Park Plaza". But little did these substitutions work their way into the consciousness of the listeners; so real were the news reports interrupting music programs that no one noticed these legally necessary but ultimately clever word choices.

At 9 o'clock a woman walked into the West Forty-seventh Street police station dragging two children, all carrying extra clothing. She said she was ready to leave the city. Police persuaded her to stay. A garbled version of the reports reached the Dixie Bus terminal, causing officials there to prepare to change their schedule on confirmation of "news" of an accident at Princeton on their New Jersey route. Miss Dorothy Brown at the terminal sought verification, however, when the caller refused to talk with the dispatcher, explaining to her that "the world is coming to an end and I have a lot to do."

18 Koch, Howard, *The Panic Broadcast*, 13
19 Ibid, 15

Was it a stretch of the imagination to believe the creators of the "War of the Worlds" radio-dramatization could foresee a truly frightened public? For any form of popular entertainment, whether it be motion pictures, radio, or the stage to be successful, the audience must put aside their rational minds, accept what they see or hear as actually real, and, simply, go along for the ride. Samuel Taylor Coleridge said, "That willing suspension of disbelief for the moment, which constitutes poetic faith."[20] Konstantin Stanislavski, creator of the Stanislavski Method for producing realistic characters, called the process of the suspension of disbelief "the majic if", the process in which the actor, after deeply analyzing his character's motivations, discovers their character's "Objective" in each scene and the "Super Objective" in the entire play. Only then can the actor realistically portray his character to an audience. Did Carl Frank, in his portrayal of reporter Carl Phillips, dig so deep into his character's motivation that he effectively recreated Herb Morrison reporting the fiery crash of the Hidenburg on a New Jersey runway?

But the another question must be asked: was the "War of the Worlds" radio-dramatization the only instance of public panic from an audience? Not according to Johan Zyblerstein, who in his seminal 1934 study of such an event, *King Kong: A "Newsreel" of Confusion*, reports, "From the farms of Quaker-Pennsylvania to the Appalachian mountains, the rural, uneducated, and largely illiterate audiences of the Midwest and South received their only news from the pulpit and from their cinemas in the form of William Randolph *Hearst Metrotone Newsreels*. Reports from sources such as these were accepted as the only readily available source of news from around the world. News that could be viewed in their local motion picture houses only days after the events occurred. So brilliantly edited and spiritedly narrated were the newsreels, that many were viewed as a source of entertainment as well as a resource for news.

"Then in 1933, these rural communities received into their second-run motion picture cinemas, a strange, low-budget talkie entitled *King Kong*. The film was a Beauty-And-The-Beast fable telling the story of an innocent but gusty Hollywood starlet's bizarre unrequited love with a fearsome, gargantuan fifty-foot ape, whose species has been lost to the records of science on a mysterious and uncharted South-Pacific island whose very existence was known only to its primitive, cannibalistic inhabitants. Is it surprising to discover that many in the viewing audience mistook this adventure fantasy, part-horror film as a newsreel? They seemed to accept the story of a enormous ape's journey from an island concealed in perpetual fog and mist to the bright, urban lights of Broadway, where such a spectacle could realistically be exploited as a Vaudevillian attraction, and to its eventual demise after falling to its death from the even greater spectacle of the Empire State Building.

"Many, who had never traveled more than a few miles from their birthplace, would marvel at the newsreel reports of the Egyptian pyramids, battle scenes of war from around the world, and adventure footage of scaling the highest peaks of the Himalayas. Is it so beyond the imagination of us, who sit in the Vaudeville theater watching Harry Houdini knowing full well that we are in sound mind and body, that there is no actual supernatural magic involved in his escaping while immersed in a pad-locked milk can. We remain bewildered by the fact that before our very eyes, we could see could not possibly be. Can we believe that the magic of Hollywood could actually cause panic?"[21]

Cinema audiences in 1933 mistook King Kong *for a news-reel or a documentary and panicked, planting the seeds of an idea that would five years later give birth to "The Orson Welles' Conspiracy"!*

20 *Biographia Lieraria*, chapter 14, 1817
21 Zyblerstein, Johan, *King Kong: A Documentary of Confusion* (Albany, New York: Huffman & Hatcher, 1934), 4-6

If audiences can mistake an "adventure-fantasy, part-horror" film with a newsreel, can Orson Welles be forgiven for irresponsibly mixing fiction and "fact"?

We must also ask, how susceptible could an entire audience of radio listeners be, when all could go mad at the exact same moment? From across the New Jersey flats, all the way to the island of Manhattan, an entire collective of people went, however briefly, insane.

> **Harlem was shaken by the "news." Thirty men and women rushed into the West 123d Street police station and twelve into the West 135th Street station saying they had their household goods packed and were all ready to leave Harlem if the police would tell them where to go to be "evacuated." One man insisted he had heard "the President's voice" over the radio advising all citizens to leave the cities.**
>
> **While, noticeably, the president never took to the airwaves that evening, this particular listener was not the only one to mistake one government official for another. "I believed the broadcast as soon as I heard the professor from Princeton and the officials in Washington. I knew it was an awfully dangerous situation when all those military men were there and the Secretary of State spoke."[22] As the long-play recording so brilliantly records, it was actually the "Secretary of the Interior" that cautioned the people of the nation. Instead of hearing what was actually said, the listener believed what he heard and nevertheless heard what fit with his preconceptions.**

The parlor churches in the Negro district, congregations of the smaller sects meeting on the ground floors of brownstone houses, took the "news" in stride as less faithful parishioners rushed in with said "news", seeking spiritual consolation. Evening services became "end of the world" prayer meetings in some.

One man ran into the Wadsworth Avenue Police Station in Washington Heights, white with terror, shouting that enemy planes were crossing the Hudson River and asking what he should do. A man came in to the West 152d Street Station, seeking traffic directions. The broadcast became a rumor that spread through the district and many persons stood on street corners hoping for a sight of the "battle" in the skies.

In Queens, the principal question asked of the switchboard operators at Police Headquarters was whether "the wave of poison gas will reach as far as Queens." Many said they were all packed up and ready to leave Queens when told to do so.

Samuel Tishman of 100 Riverside Drive was one of the multitude that fled into the street after hearing part of the program. He declared that hundreds of persons evacuated their homes fearing that the "city was being bombed." "I came home at 9:15 PM just in time to receive a telephone call from my nephew who was frantic with fear. He told me the city was about to be bombed from the air and advised me to get out of the building at once. I turned on the radio and heard the broadcast which corroborated what my nephew had said, grabbed my hat and coat and a few personal belongings and

The congregation of a parlor church in the Negro district huddle together as the Martians invade their city just outside their doors!

22 Koch, Howard, *The Panic Broadcast*, 110

ran to the elevator. When I got to the street there were hundreds of people milling around in panic. Most of us ran toward Broadway and it was not until we stopped taxi drivers who had heard the entire broadcast on their radios that we knew what it was all about. It was the most asinine stunt I ever heard of."

"I heard that broadcast and almost had a heart attack," said Louis Winkler of 1322 Clay Avenue, the Bronx. "I didn't tune it in until the program was half over, but when I heard the names and titles of Federal, State and municipal officials and when the 'Secretary of the Interior' was introduced, I was convinced it was the [real] McCoy. I ran out into the street with scores of others, and found people running in all directions. The whole thing came over as a news broadcast and in my mind it was a pretty crummy thing to do."

When the "Secretary of the Interior" took to the airwaves, with the following: "Citizens of the nation: I shall not try to conceal the gravity of the situation that confronts the country, nor the concern of your government in protecting the lives and property of its people. However, I wish to impress upon you– private citizens and public officials, all of you– the urgent need of calm and resourceful action. Fortunately, this formidable enemy is still confined to a comparatively small area, and we may place our faith in the military forces to keep them there. In the meantime, placing our faith in God, we must continue the performance of our duties each and every one of us, so that we may confront this destructive adversary with a nation united, courageous, and consecrated to the preservation of human supremacy on this earth. I thank you."[23]

Can anyone with a copy of the long-play record of the broadcast possibly mistake the similarity between the voice of the Secretary of the Interior and the voice of Franklin Delano Roosevelt, heard by millions on his regular Fireside Chats? Did Orson Welles instruct Kenneth Delmar to impersonate the president with his vocal tone and inflection? Are there depths that Orson Welles would not stoop to frighten his listening public!

President Roosevelt's "Fireside Chats" were welcomed into the homes of every American! Every American knew his voice when they heard it October 30, 1938! But the newspaper headlines would trumpet "FAKE! RADIO 'WAR' STIRS TERROR THROUGH US"!

> The Telegraph Bureau switchboard at police headquarters in Manhattan, operated by thirteen men, was so swamped with calls from apprehensive citizens inquiring about the broadcast that police business was seriously interfered with.
>
> Headquarters, unable to reach the radio station by telephone, sent a radio patrol car there to ascertain the reason for the reaction to the program. When the explanation was given, a police message was sent to all precincts in the five boroughs advising the commands of the cause.

In special report to *The New York Times* on page four, headlined, "Geologists Hunt 'Meteor' in Vain" proved that the "fictional" Professor Pierson was not the only Princeton University professor tramping about Grover's Mill that fateful night.

23 Koch, Howard, *The Panic Broadcast*, 58

> Scholastic calm deserted Princeton University briefly tonight following widespread misunderstanding of the WABC radio program announcing the arrival of Martians to subdue the earth.
>
> Dr. Arthur F. Buddington, chairman of the Department of Geology, and Dr. Harry Hess, Professor of Geology, received the first alarming reports in a form indicating that a meteor had fallen near Dutch Neck, some five miles away. They armed themselves with the necessary equipment and set out to find a specimen. All they found was a group of sightseers, searching like themselves for the meteor.

These two standard bearers of academia were, evidently, so convinced that the reports of the Martian invasion were mistaken for an actual meteorite impact in Grover's Mill, that they hurried, blindly, into the dark night, "armed with a geologist's hammer and a flashlight," and were forever memorialized in the preceding newspaper account.

> The Columbia Broadcasting System issued a statement saying that the adaptation of Mr. Wells's novel which was broadcast "followed the original closely, but to make the imaginary details more interesting to American listeners the adapter, Orson Welles, substituted an American locale for the English scenes of the story."

Orson Welles, weary from lack of sleep, stood before a throng of reporters on the front steps of the CBS studios at 485 Madison Avenue and spoke to a venomous throng of reporters, "Do you want me to speak now?.. I'm sorry. We are deeply shocked and deeply regretful about the, uh, results of last night's broadcast. It came as rather a great surprise that a story, a fine HG Wells classic, would bring such a reaction."

> Pointing out that the fictional character of the broadcast had been announced four times and had been previously publicized...
>
> "Nevertheless, the program apparently was produced with such vividness that some listeners who may have heard only fragments thought the broadcast was fact, not fiction. Hundreds of telephone calls reaching CBS stations, city authorities, newspaper offices and police headquarters in various cities testified to the mistaken belief.
>
> "Naturally, it was neither Columbia's nor the Mercury Theatre's intention to mislead any one, and when it became evident that a part of the audience had been disturbed by the performance five announcements were read over the network later in the evening to reassure those listeners."

The mob of reporters berated Orson with pointed questions about the "Panic Broadcast" and Orson appeared the entire time "looking like an early Christian saint".

REPORTER: Were you aware of the terror such a broadcast would stir up?

ORSON WELLES: Definitely not. The technique I used was not original with me. It was not even new. I anticipated nothing unusual.

REPORTER: Would you do the show over again?

ORSON: I won't say that I won't follow this technique again, as it is a legitimate dramatic form.

REPORTER: When were you first aware of the trouble caused?

ORSON: Immediately after the broadcast was finished when people told me of the large number of phone calls received.

Reporters, photographers, and film cameras would swarm CBS studios at an impromptu press conference a day after the "invasion" from Mars!

REPORTER: Should you have toned down the language of the drama?
ORSON: No, you don't play murder in soft words.[24]

> **Expressing profound regret that his dramatic efforts should cause such consternation, Mr. Welles said: "I don't think we will choose anything like this again." He hesitated about presenting it, he disclosed, because "it was our thought that perhaps people might be bored or annoyed at hearing a tale so improbable."**

But I am here to tell you, my faithful readers, that this *New York Times* report, the infamous story of the radio-dramatized "The War of the Worlds" broadcast, and the entire contents of this chapter are an outrageous lie. A lie and hoax perpetrated by the government of the United States of America and Orson Welles to cover up the Truth. The Truth that there was, indeed, an invasion from Mars that night. That the radio-broadcasts heard by millions of listeners were quite authentic. That there was a government cover-up with a cover-story so laughable that no one, in eighty-five years, has even thought of questioning it. This is the heart of the "Orson Welles' Conspiracy"!

> **Americans have been trained by media to go into Pavolovian giggles at the mention of conspiracy because for an American to believe in a conspiracy he must also believe in flying saucers or, craziest of all, that more than one person was involved in the JFK murder. - Gore Vidal**

Conspiracy theories are, for the most part, absurd, preposterous, and perhaps even laughable. Who in their right mind can even listen to the ridiculous ranting of conspiracy theorists on all manner of subjects without chuckling, rolling your eyes, or at least breaking a smile? A faked Apollo moon landing, the Roswell UFO crash, and the granddaddy of the all– the assassination of President John Fitzgerald Kennedy

24 Quoted from the press conference held on October, 31, 1938

by then Vice-President Lyndon Banes Johnson, or the Central Intelligence Agency,
or Fidel Castro, or J. Edgar Hoover and his Federal Bureau of Investigation, etcetera, *ad nauseam.*

A thorough lack of empirical evidence and mounting evidence to the contrary do little to dissuade the conspiracy theorist from his beliefs. It is the very lack of empirical evidence that fuels those beliefs. The very proof that will vindicate his beliefs is classified top-secret and therefore is immune to repeated filings in the name of the Freedom of Information Act. This Act is believed by many conspiracy theorists to be the paper-strewn gateway to the Holy Grail of their theories.

When the information finally reaches their greedy little hands, they discover to their dismay and consternation that the evidence they have sought their entire lives has been heavily censored with numerous blacked-out sections.

and furthermore

These mysterious sections are, in fact, the very cause of their alarm. What has been blacked-out? And why? Their overactive imagination fills in the blanks (or blacked out sections), only adds fuel to their ever increasingly paranoid fantasies.

All of the evidence presented to the contrary, in vain attempts to disprove their beliefs, is nothing more than an elaborate fiction created by unseen conspirators in furtherance of the conspiracy to hide the truth from the people of the United States of America.

"Fake news" is a new catch-all buzzword for the 21st Century conspiracy theorist, who through their own personal "research" on the Internet are now "experts" in any given field, despite– nay! in spite– of any lack of formal training. Conspiracy theories went viral during the global COVID-19 pandemic, to such a point of absurdity that scientists were dismissed as quacks and quacks were hailed as scientists. Vaccines were dismissed as poison while literal poison was injected as medical treatments. Elections have been stolen despite– nay! in spite– no proof of electoral fraud. Forest-fires, earthquakes, eclipses, and other natural phenomena humanity has coexisted with for thousands of years are now nefarious plots of political rivals or religious minorities. When the President of the United States and members of Congress trumpet the conspiracy theories as reality and reality as conspiracy theories, we as a nation have truly "jumped the shark".

Exposing the logical fallacies in their belief systems does little to dissuade the believer from his belief. This is the heart of the conspiracy theory and a major reason why the government has actually hidden the truth from the people. Few in the general populace, who to some lesser extent distrust their government, will believe the conspiracy theorist, no matter the proof mainstream scientist will present.

This is at the heart of our consternation concerning "The Orson Welles' Conspiracy". My father knew what he heard with his own ears over the radio that warm October evening. The radio reports of , the monstrous alien creatures, the horrifying heat-rays, the Tri-pod walking machines, and the were harrowing. My father knew what he heard on the radio was real, despite the false confession of a young, enigmatic Orson Welles on Halloween morning. The media bought Welles' fabrication, completely and irrefutably. But my father believed. He believed there was a Martians invasion that night. He believed that Orson Welles had to be part of a government conspiracy to hide the truth of an "Invasion from Mars". Eventually, my father faith was confirmed as the truth by Orson Welles himself. My father, just off a turnip truck, was hired by RKO executives to be Orson Welles scriptwriter on a feature film adaptation of Orson's "War of the Worlds" radio-dramatization. Over their bourbon-fueled days and coffee-fueled nights writing their *Invasion From Mars* screenplay (perhaps too bourbon-fueled considering the story related), My father learned about

. My father experienced the nuclear fallout when RKO executives discovered the contents of their secret shooting-script and the true nature of their plans for the motion picture version of Orson Welles' *War of the Worlds* film. My father saw his apartment ransacked and his reputation in Hollywood ruined because of the secrets he and Orson Welles exposed with their screenplay.

All of the evidence of the truth that I will present in this book will be dismissed utterly. As opposed to the thorough lack of substantiation presented by Orson Welles' laughable explanation that everything millions of people heard on the radio was, in fact, a radio-dramatization. An invasion from Mars was quietly swept under the carpet by a ten-minute "confession". No amount of proof that I present in neither this book, nor any "facts" to the contrary that the government may present in its own defense will persuade the people to believe.

I only have my name and reputation, which is my father's name and reputation.

Through a strange convergence of timing, my father had become intimately involved in the "Orson Welles' Conspiracy" in more than one way and at more than one time in his life: in 1938, 1942, 1947, 1969, and 1985. Every time he thought he had escaped the conspiracy, he and Orson Welles were sought out by various presidential administrations to spin a diverse web of lies and deceit to hide the facts of an invasion from Mars and a continual "Interplanetary Cold War".

William Francis Brown, my father and a man also with three names, swore his first oath in 1942 before and God Almighty as his witness that he would never reveal the truth about the events that occurred on the evening of Sunday, October 30, 1938, the night Martians invaded the United States of America. The first oath sworn between Orson Welles and was born in the small hours of Halloween morning on a sound-stage at CBS studios in New York City. Orson Welles was well-known as a boy genius, a radio-producer extraordinaire, a slight-of-hand magician, and a prodigy of the New York theatre scene. He alone orchestrated a vast government conspiracy at the behest William Randolph Hearst and Franklin Delano Roosevelt, two stanch adversaries who were for a time weary allies.

Orson Welles' story was so grossly believable that no one, at the time nor in the decades since, has dared believe anything other than what young Orson said. What millions of radio listeners heard on their radio-sets was nothing but a fanciful radio-dramatization of HG Well's *The War of the Worlds* in the form of an evening of dance music interrupted by fictional news broadcasts.

Not even the most paranoid of schizophrenics has even conceived of the possibility that Martians actually landed on the east coast of the United States on Halloween Eve 1938. The poor deluded psychotics paper their walls with aluminum foil. They construct protective aluminum foil helmets, in the vain attempts to protect their minds from the continuous assault by telepathic government agents. The thin sheets of foil can, in their delusions, guard against the extrasensory attacks by the government and the attempts at extracting their increasingly paranoid thoughts. Schizophrenics, I am proud to say, are blissfully oblivious to conspiracies such as the "Orson Welles' Conspiracy".

No writer, even with the wildest of imaginations or stroke of creative genius, could envisage such as a thing as this conspiracy. The events sparked by a failed invasion from the planet Mars would become the most famous conspiracy theory never heard of. The "Orson Welles' Conspiracy" like all other conspiracies, is absurd, preposterous, and laughable, except for the fact that it is true.

Orson Welles is particularly famous for winning a very heated battle with newspaper tycoon William Randolph Hearst and the executives at RKO studios over his motion pictures *Citizen Kane*. If he had been successful with his equally heated, but far more unheard of battle over his *War of the Worlds* feature film, my father's name and reputation as a young screenwriter would have become as sullied and synonymous with Orson Welles' name.

To have my father's good name and his character forever associated with a vast government conspiracy is unimaginable. His oath to ██████████ and his loyalty to Orson Welles is simply not his primary motivating factor in helping keep this secret for the entirety of his life. It is and always will be laughter. I, under no circumstances, can allow my father to become a laughing stock– at any price. Putting my family name on this the cover of this volume will be the greatest test of my firm belief in the "Orson Welles' Conspiracy".

The transcriptions of reel-to-reel tapes (that have mysteriously come into my possession) and a screenplay written by my father will prove my hypothesis and answer the question, "Did Orson Welles and the United States government hide the truth of a Martian invasion on October 30, 1938?" In this book, I will break a seventy-five year silence by bringing you the truth of "The Orson Welles' Conspiracy".

How did Neville Chamberlain's colossal blunder during the "Orson Welles' Conspiracy" lead to a Martian alliance with Adolph Hitler's Germany? UK Prime-minister Winston Churchill (left) along with US President Franklin Delano Roosevelt and Soviet General Secretary Joseph Stalin meet to discuss how to prevent a second World War from becoming an Interplanetary War! Don't believe me? Read on, Cupcake...

THE DAY THE EARTH MISUNDERSTOOD

In the late 1990's, I began my futile quest to reach Peter ████████, the one living person whom I believed had been the closest to Orson Welles. I had read his 1992 collection of conversations between himself, a famous filmmaker, and the even more infamous filmmaker Orson Welles. But how does one go about reaching out to a filmmaker? These were the days before the Internet Movie Database and its "professional" subscription. As a layman living in a small Colorado city, I had no clue how to contact someone in Hollywood. I went to our local library's reference section and looked through the Los Angeles phone book. I began to make phone calls. Not a single receptionist was even remotely helpful in identifying Peter's agent, manager, publicist, or pool cleaner. I did find one agency that had previously represented Peter, and they gave me his "new" contact, but that information turned out to be "old" information, so I was back to square one. Then, in a year that I can't quite remember, but on Mischief Night (this I clearly remember) I received a phone call from the "right" person.

I explained my situation: I had found my father's screenplay for a "lost" Orson Welles' Invasion From Mars *screenplay in a safety deposit box and wanted (nay–* needed*) someone to authenticate a screenplay that claims to have been written by my father and Orson Welles based on "HG Wells and a True Story". I was provided an address to mail the screenplay and I put it in the mail. Correction– I put a Xeroxed copy in the mail. I wasn't about to mail my father's personal copy over a thousand miles away with no assurances it would ever be sent back to me.*

As the days turned into weeks and the weeks turned into months and the months turned into years (far too many years), I lost nearly all hope of getting a response from Mr. ████████. In January of 2022, I read The Hollywood Reporter *reporting his death. Then I lost all hope of ever finding out if the screenplay my father wrote was authentic. Then many months later a package arrived on Mischief Night. Of course, it did! There was no return address. It must have been mailed on a wing-and-a-prayer. I eagerly opened the box. Inside were numerous boxes of reel-to-reel tapes. What was recorded on these tapes? A letter had been included in the box that answered all my questions and my hopes and dreams.*

– Robert Dwight Brown

Dear Mr. Brown,

I hope all is well with you. If you are reading this letter, then I have passed away. I kept these reel-to-reel tapes in my possession for over forty years, but they will be no use to me when I'm gone. I have instructed my manager that in the unfortunate case that I am no longer counted among the living that these particular and peculiar reel-to-reel tapes should be mailed to an address I have had on file to twenty-five years: yours. I can only hope you're still at home.

These two interviews, conducted on Halloween Eves 1978 and '79, were exorcised from my collection of interviews and reflections, mainly because of the fantastical nature of the interview. Orson told me on the phone, earlier in the month, that the time had come to talk about "The War of the Worlds" in great detail. He waited until October 30th to finally sit down for the interview. However, Orson thought the entire conversation might leave a bad taste in the mouths of all concerned because it was the fortieth anniversary of the infamous night Martians invaded America, at least on the radio.

I mentally gathered together questions relating to "The War of the Worlds" broadcast, questions I had been imploring Orson to answer all these many years that I had been interviewing him at various locations around Southern California. With a handful of note cards and portable reel-to-reel recorder firmly in hand, I drove to Orson Welles' home. There I found him, in his study, typing questions for a series of interviews he would be conducting for a proposed television talk-show; I believed at the time he was setting himself up for a third act as a Merv Griffith-type. I knew that Orson would relish the opportunity to simply converse with some of the most famous people in the world. Only Orson would be able to draw the best stories out of people. So, while he busied himself with his typewriter, I set up my equipment. When I finished, he sat quietly in his chair and the interview began.

One reason I exorcised this interview from my biography of Orson was because I felt that night and every night since that I was the butt of a fantastic, fantastical practical joke, arguably the greatest of his career. He toyed with me throughout the course of the conversation; toyed with me like a cat does a mouse. He was masterful in his pacing and the suspense he created. The story he related to me was like no other in our long and storied friendship. I had no basis of comparison for the tale he told and I remember sounding like a gibbering fool.

I was thankful to Orson for playing his greatest practical joke on me. I told very few people about the prank, because I didn't want to spoil the memory of it or make my friend seem like a raving loon. I cherished the memory. The reel-to-reels, however, though in my physical possession were his intellectual property. I would not, could not publish it without his expressed permission, We both knew that it had no place alongside the other, more appropriate interviews conducted prior to and after this particular evening.

Orson Welles and Peter enjoy some brewskis while recording the reel-to-reel tapes transcribed within our book!

Over the years I have pulled the the reel-to-reel tapes out of mothballs to listen to its power and ponder the great "What If". Though I'm sure it was merely a coincidence, but the interview played out surprisingly like *Citizen Kane*. *Citizen Kane* was famous for its backward flashback nature and our interview that anniversary evening so many years ago had a similar chronological narrative. Orson had a tendency to jump between the events of October 30, 1938 and events during the early years of the 1940's without any sense of rhyme or reason. The story bobbed and weaved around, flowing from one subject to the next with relative ease. His improvisational skills were heightened that night, because how was he able to keep all of the elements of his greatest prank all together rather seamlessly? Just like *Citizen Kane*.

Then, in the later years of the twentieth-century, you mailed me the startling evidence of a screenplay written by your father for Orson Welles sometime between 1941 and '42. A screenplay of a "lost" RKO Radio-Pictures feature film that was never made or, more accurately, a movie Orson, in these very interviews, claims to have made. I have read your father's screenplay every Mischief Night since, wondering and pondering what to do with the reel-to-reel tapes. I have waisted precious years by not sending them to you earlier, but I could not let those tapes out of my possession until my possession was no longer meaningful.

Does Orson Welles expose the truth (in either your father's screenplay or in our interview together) of a *Battle Over* The War of the Worlds? Or has this consummate prankster and bullshit artist gotten one over on me and you through your father? To quote the narrator of famous cartoon advertisement after a small boy asks, "How many licks does it take to get to Tootsie Roll center of Tootsie Pop?" **"The world may never know!"**

Sincerely,

THE BATTLE OVER
The War of the Worlds

ORSON WELLES: I see you been saving all of your questions, written nicely on your note cards, for the evening when I'd finally open up about "The War of the Worlds" broadcast.

PETER : I've been anticipating this moment for a long time. But if the cards are too formal for this occasion I can...

ORSON: No, no. I don't mind. But trust me, those cards aren't going to matter a few moments. You simply cannot be prepared for what I am going to talk about this evening. This is going to prove to be a long and winding road.

PETER: [*Still organizing his notes*] Did you chose today's date on purpose? I'm sure you did, it being Halloween Eve and all. It couldn't be a coincidence.

ORSON: Yes, we are on the wicked anniversary of said date. I knew waiting until October 30th would be in quite bad taste, you understand. This is the best date that I can think of. This is a date that will, as it has for the past forty years, lived in infamy. You may not like what you hear or truly understand what I'm about to tell you, but the time has come. Clotho, Lachesis, Atropos have delivered you into my hands and like the eternal puppet-master, I'm going to play with your strings.

PETER: Let's get started, shall we?

ORSON: So formal. No, no. Please, forgive me, Peter. I'm just trying to postpone the inevitable.

PETER: We don't have to speak about "War of the Worlds". We can talk about anything you want. You know I enjoy your company and your stories, no matter their subject.

ORSON: In hindsight, I never should have invited you to interview here at my home. But I, finally, after forty years, want to talk about *The War of the Worlds* in all its gory... em, glorious details. [*Taking a deep breath*] Ask away.

PETER: What part did your love of Mischief Night play in the entire "War of the Worlds" plan?

ORSON: As you are aware, I am mightily fond of pranks. I simply adore making peoples' tongues wag about something I was able to pull off. But seldom does one get to live out a prank through the eyes of the pranked. *Hearst Metrotone* did a newsreel about the subject of Mischief Night and its relationship to my so-called radio-dramatization. I remember attending a matinée for the express purpose of watching this particular newsreel about my "War of the Worlds" radio-dramatization, as opposed to *Time on the March* or the others.

PETER: Why was watching Hearst's newsreel so important?

ORSON: Concerning the events of earlier that week and all that went on behind the scenes, as it were, I was most curious to see how Hearst would spin the whole affair.

PETER: Because of how radio could deceive millions of people in just a few minutes? How he believed that newspapers were the only source of accurate news.

ORSON: Not precisely, but that explanation will do for now.

PETER: It has never occurred to me how William Randolph Hearst would have reacted to *The War of Worlds* causing such wide-spread panic.

ORSON: He appeared stunned as I was that I pulled off "The War of the Worlds" so flawlessly. Just as I was stunned by the power and impact of his newsreel recounting the events of that Mischief Night. Even if it was a complete fiction instead of about real events.

PETER: I beg your pardon?

ORSON: If I may, I'd like to recreate that initial newsreel moment for you.

PETER: By all means.

ORSON: [*His impressive voice booms mimicking the vocalizations of Newsreel narrators of yore*] "Mischief night! The evening before Halloween. A night known to children and teenage hooligans across the country as Mischief Night. To the police and newspaper reporters, it is more ominously called Devil's Night. A night where anyone dressed in every manner of scary costume, even in the quietest of suburban neighborhoods, can get away with practically anything prankish in nature. A night when all these high-jinks will be either forgotten and forgiven.

"It was on this night, 1938, that Orson Welles played a prank on not only his neighborhood– the radio audience of his *Mercury Theater on the air*, but every state in the union. And because he broadcast his prank on this particular evening, it would be quickly forgiven, but not easily forgotten!

"On this infamous evening, Orson Welles and his *Mercury Theatre on the air* choose to adapt the famed Briton HG Wells' famous science-fiction novel *The War of the Worlds* into a radio-dramatization fit for American ears on William Paley's Columbia Broadcast System. Those who tuned in to listen to the young Mr. Welles, instead of Edgar Bergan and his ventriloquist dummy Charley McCarthy, heard what appeared at first listen to be seemingly realistic news broadcasts continually interrupting an evening of dance music. Five weeks prior on September 25, 1938, while adapting Sherlock Holmes for his radio program, a news bulletin on the Munich crisis interrupted his broadcast, no doubt irritating the proud Orson, but that night the germ of an idea was planted in Orson's mind. He would use news bulletins as a dramatic technique to add suspense to 'The War of the Worlds', an adaptation he had been planning for weeks.

"Over the course of the next five days, tension around the world would come to a head over the Munich crisis. People in all industrialized nations of the world would huddle around their radio-sets for any news. France had mobilized their troops, the Communist Soviet Union threatened to come to the aid of Czechoslovakia, and Great Britain said they too would act if France was forced to take action. Adolph Hitler, in the first of many 'stare-downs', blinked and agreed to negotiate with England, France, and Italy. The four powers met in Munich and after eight hours of heated talks, news came of the Prime Minister of Britain, Neville Chamberlain's, and Edouard Daladier's, the French premier's, historically tarnished Munich Pact. The pact signed on Friday, September 30 averted World War II, for the time being, by handing the territory-greedy German Chancellor a significant portion of Czechoslovakia. The citizenry of the industrialized nations across the world were glued to their radio-sets in anticipation of the regularly occurring program interruptions bringing news of the Munich crisis; only then did the world breathe a collective sigh of relief when an interruption brought news of the signing of the Pact.

"On that day, radio proved itself to be a valuable ally to the common people of the world

UK Prime Minister Arthur Neville Chamberlain (left) signs the Munich Agreement as Martin Bormann, Hitler's secretary, smirks because Adolph Hitler got a sweet-heart deal!

and a source of accurate news reports. Reports that sped through the air to radios worldwide, almost from the moment the Pact was signed. No longer did the people have to wait until the next morning or for the evening edition of the newspaper to learn about events from around the globe. So trusted were these reports that few across the nation could even conceive of such a thing as a fake news report. Orson considered other such fare for dramatization, Sir Arthur Conan Doyle's *Lost World*, where lost recordings made during an expedition to a volcanic plateau hidden deep in the Amazon rain-forest would be aired 'in their entirety'. Would these 'recordings' have created such a stir as 'The War of the Worlds' broadcast had made?

"We will never know.

"Orson instead insisted that 'The War of the Worlds' be dramatized first, if the script could be made ready in time as a Mischief Night prank that would ultimately drive millions upon millions of the hard-working and the Blue Collar populace, from coast to coast, to lose their collective minds. Innocent citizens of the Tri-State area fled their homes and overflowed telephone lines in vain hopes of escaping the fictitious Martians' rampage across the state, lumbering towards New York City in their destructive tri-pods. The general public from outside the Tri-State area, listening on affiliated stations, had nothing to fear until Orson Welles' clever script reported at the height of dramatic tension that Martian cylinders were falling outside of Buffalo, within Chicago's city limits, and near St. Louis. All timed and spaced out like a planned military invasion. At this moment, the panic spread nationwide.

"Was it a stretch of the imagination to believe the creators of "The War of the Worlds" radio-dramatization could foresee a truly frightened public? For any form of popular entertainment, whether it be motion pictures, radio, or the stage to be successful, the audience must put aside their rational minds, accept what they see or hear as actually real, and, simply, go along for the ride.

"Did Carl Frank, in his portrayal of 'reporter' Carl Phillips, dig so deep into his character's motivation that he effectively recreated Herb Morrison when he reported the fiery crash of the Hidenburg on a New Jersey runway? Was 'The War of the Worlds' radio-dramatization the only instance of public panic from an audience? Can Orson Welles be forgiven for irresponsibly mixing fiction and 'fact'? Unlike the Hindenburg's fiery crash broadcast into the living rooms of average Americans, where the tension lasted only a few moments before most were known to have survived, however, the reports broadcast on CBS went from nearly disturbing to categorically horrifying. Nothing in the collective consciousness of the listeners had prepared themselves for what they were hearing. Countless eyewitness accounts poured in during the aftermath of the broadcast.

"We must also ask, how susceptible could an entire audience of radio listeners be, when all could go mad at the exact same moment? From across the New Jersey flats, all the way to the island of Manhattan, an entire collective of people went, however briefly, insane."

The LZ 129 Hindenburg descending on fire!

PETER: —*Whew*— Is that verbatim?

ORSON: More or less. That's how I remember it, though. I have a pretty good memory for lines.

PETER: "Pretty good"? You are notorious for having an eidetic memory.

ORSON: Thank you for using the correct terminology. I hate the phrase "photographic memory", because that isn't at all how memories like mine operate. I am able to recall a great deal with very little exposure to the material, but it isn't like I see a photograph of the script or replay a memory like it's a motion picture in my mind. It *has* been decades since I saw and heard that newsreel, but that is exactly how I remember it being. I was stirred to my very soul listening to that newsreel recount the events of that night. I was very moved by it. It pains me greatly to hear any criticism of my work. Even work that I shouldn't be able to take full credit for.

PETER: Are you trying to say that "The War of the Worlds" wasn't your idea?

ORSON: You misunderstand. "The War of the Worlds" radio-dramatization was entirely my idea. That's the problem. I'm the only one that the people and the government can rest the sole blame on. It was my idea and my idea alone. It was the red-headed step-child of my cursed imagination. The only creative child that I wish I could go back in time and abort.

PETER: But it gave you a career.

ORSON: A motion picture career, yes. That is the only

reason why I did it. I wanted out of New York in the worst way. I had a career there. I could have had a great career there for the rest of my life. I could have been happy in New York. But I wanted Hollywood. I wanted the director's chair. I wanted the key to the entire city. And I got it. All because I came up with the idea for "The War of the Worlds" radio-dramatization. If I hadn't come up with it, the world would be a completely different place. Probably a greener and much more happy place. Every history book in the world would have to be rewritten if I hadn't done "The War of the Worlds".

PETER: Come now, Orson. Even "The War of the Worlds" didn't change the history of the world. True, it made people look at radio differently. But not even you can take credit for changing the history of the world.

"Martian landing site" historical marker commemorating the 1938 very real invasion from Mars that panicked America!

ORSON: This is exactly why I don't really want to talk about it, because you won't believe the true story. The story that must be told. You can't grasp the true nature of "The War of the Worlds" radio-dramatization and what it means to history. My actions that night irrevocably changed the entire course of the western world.

PETER: Is this why you have been reticent about talking about "The War of the Worlds". You've been avoiding talking to me on this subject in particular. Do you feel that much grief and regret over the panic you caused?

ORSON: But I didn't cause the panic. I assuaged the panic. If it wasn't for that radio-dramatization hastily recorded in the small hours, if it wasn't for me going in front of the reporters and the cameras Halloween morning and addressing the public, there would have been a panic across the entire globe. A panic that would have left millions dead and dying in the streets. I feel great relief that my actions saved lives. My grief and regret are born from the fact that people went about their daily concerns oblivious to the true nature of the universe. A nature that is more ominous than anything HG Wells could have possibly imagined. The Brit was certainly a modern-day prophet. He foresaw everything that happened that night and to a certain extent everything that has been whispered about during dark nights in the Oval Office and the Kremlin. HG Wells' true genius with his *War of the Worlds* novel will never be known, just as the true genius of my "War of the Worlds" radio-dramatization will also never be realized. Unless I change things with this conversation. I wanted so desperately to set things straight with a *War of the Worlds* feature. But I never had the chance.

PETER: I wanted to talk to you about *The War of the Worlds* film that never got made. I didn't think we'd get there so quickly. Let me get my notes.

ORSON: Take your time.

PETER: Here we go. [*Reading*] Prior to shooting *Citizen Kane*, did RKO pictures pressure you into filming *The War of the Worlds* as your first feature?

ORSON: Obviously, the executives at RKO felt we should strike while the iron was hot, as they say, and obviously I had no intention at the time of making it. Not under those circumstances. You see, Peter, it was too fresh in my memory. I didn't know all of the facts, just yet. I'd been piecing things together through interviews. I made friends with a German "exchange student" who had become enamored of a starlet while he was spying on the Hollywood industry for Germany. Gunter was an accomplished stage actor back in Austria having played Falstaff in a German translation of Shakespeare. I have never understood translating Shakespeare into a foreign language, something has to be lost in the translation. But Shakespeare was something we had in common, and I used this to my advantage. He played an American better than most Americans.

PETER: You befriended a Nazi spy?

ORSON: Yes and no. You will find this a rote response this evening. You see, there was this famous story going around about Nazi spies getting caught within days of arriving on the east coast because they knew nothing about American culture and our accents and besides their counterfeit currency was perfect except for the fact that it was all printed in German. But that was a ruse by the Germans to sneak accomplished actors-turned-spies into our midst. However, I used my influence with this young starlet to start a relationship with this Nazi Spy and eventually used the German *Abwehr* for my own purposes in the construction of my *War of the Worlds* screenplay. [*Chuckles*]

PETER: Orson?

A trial of Nazi saboteurs conducted by a special seven-man military commission! Was Orson's Gunter among the saboteurs? Who knows?

ORSON: I'm so sorry, Peter. I'm getting regretful in my old age. I so desperately wanted to pull off that story, but I can't. I had pranked old Kaltenborn with a Nazi-Martian story and I so wanted to pull off one on you, but I just can't get through it without chuckling. It is a sad state of affairs when one can't get through a prank without...

PETER: There was no Nazi spy?

ORSON: Of course not, my friend. Gunter was nothing more than an foreign student-intern who's family escaped from Austria shortly after Hitler's invasion. The Nazi spy element is a remnant of that old Kaltenborn prank, that I was hoping to weave in and weave out of this story I'm relating this evening. I have no need for that spy element anymore because, well, I knew everything that happened that night because I was there the entire time. I was so intimately involved. It was my *War of the Worlds* after all. While I remained dear, dear friends with the President for the rest of his life, I ultimately rationalized the blame for "The War of the Worlds" radio fiasco entirely on Franklin.

PETER: You blamed the President of the United States of America? Why? Because he didn't stop your broadcast? Because he didn't stop that panic? I don't see what that has to do with anything.

ORSON: It has everything to do with the price of tea in China! For God's sake. I saved the man's political career. His decisions that night were criminal to say the very least. They call me the greatest charlatan that has ever lived because of what I did with "The War of the Worlds" radio-dramatization, but he is an even greater swindler than PT Barnum. Hell, I shouldn't have gone after William Randolph Hearst with *Citizen Kane*. I should have gone after Franklin Delano Roosevelt. Damn it. World War II would never have happened if I didn't do the damned "War of the Worlds" recording. If I hadn't released that accursed wax recording onto the people of this nation, the entire world would have united around the President and ushered in a one world government. A New World Order.

PETER: That's a little incongruous. Just a moment ago, you said the people would have impeached the president and now you're saying the entire world would have rallied around FDR? Even Hilter?

ORSON: Especially Hilter! Don't you see. The documents Gunter's little starlet mistress delivered to me exposed the entire conspiracy. [*Chuckles again*]. (Sorry, I'm mixing my stories here. I really am getting long in the tooth. I can't keep track of what really happened and what's a prank. But I digress.) Let's move on, shall we?

PETER: Orson?

ORSON: You see, if it wasn't for "The War of the Worlds" radio-dramatization there wouldn't be any conspiracy theories. Not a single one.

PETER: What do you mean? No conspiracies? Can you elaborate on that?

ORSON: Beginning that night, people began to question what they heard on the radio, what they read in the newspaper, and eventually, in the coming decades, what they saw on television. Before that night, everything that was said in news reports and by the government was never questioned. The thought never entered into the

US President John Fitzgerald Kennedy moments before being shot by lone-gunman, Lee Harvey Oswald on November 22, 1963!

collective consciousness of the people of this nation to question their authority figures until the "Panic Broadcast". God, I hate that expression for it, but it is fitting. "Panic Broadcast." Hell. People would not have questioned JFK's assassination if I hadn't done "The War of the Worlds". It just wouldn't have happened. They would have believed that Lee Harvey Oswald acted alone and shot the President from that book depository. And Oswald's assassination would have been seen as the act of a lone and be grieved dying man wishing to avenge his president's murder. But no. Because of me, people instantly began questioning the government's story. They saw holes in the story that just fueled the fire. Without me, the holes would have been filled in with details that supported the government's position. But because of me, those holes were filled with outrageous theories of government conspiracies that continue to this day. And it all began with "The War of the Worlds". If I hadn't done what I did, everything would be different. JFK would probably still be alive.

PETER: You don't actually believe you had anything to do with the assassination of President Kennedy.

ORSON: Of course not. Not directly anyway. What I have pieced together from my Nazi secret agent [*chuckles*] back in 1941 and what I've learned through my contacts in the CIA and KGB [*chuckles*] have led me to believe that of all of the outlandish conspiracy theories that can be traced to "The War of the Worlds" radio-dramatization, but the JFK assassination isn't one of them. What I have been able to piece together is this... Lee Harvey Oswald actually acted alone in the assassination of JFK. It has nothing to do with "The War of the Worlds" or the events that it spawned. But do I have regrets over it. Yes, I do.

PETER: Okay. This entire line of questioning has gotten a little off track. My mind is reeling. I never realized the guilt you feel over "The War of the Worlds".

ORSON: The guilt. The blame. The responsibility.

PETER: Is this why you don't want to talk about this?

ORSON: I have been talking about this, but I really do not want to talk about it. Not because of my guilt or the blame that I feel or my responsibility in the whole cursed thing. It is because spirits and omens are flying around us this Mischief Night. This is the essence of Mischief Night. They are all around us on the night before Halloween. With both of us sitting before the fire, we should be able to see them out of the corner of our eye. You can't see ghosts and demons by looking straight at them; they vanish like a fart in a whirlwind, but catch them in your peripheral vision and you can see them quite clearly. They are taunting me; mocking me. They know the secrets of the universe and either cannot or will not share them with us. I hate to wax philosophical here, but these particular spirits have been taunting me on Mischief Night, October 30th, every year since 1939 when I first hid away in my apartment in New York City trying so desperately to escape the attention of any reporters desperate for any comment of the first anniversary of "The War of the Worlds" brouhaha. I left my receiver off the hook. Kept the shades drawn and the lights out. All except for a single candle lit on the mantle.

The spirits of Mischief Night, disguised as innocent school children, haunt Orson Welles' on every Halloween Eve since 1938!

When I finally chanced to walk down to the corner store, I wore the most ghastly amount of theatrical make-up with a crepe-hair beard and ringlets, and the shining achievement of this fastidious endeavor, a Orthodox-Jewish hat. I chanced on the notion that any reporter stalking my apartment wouldn't dare approach a fifty-year-old, slightly graying old Hassidic man on his way to the market. And yet, while returning to my apartment with a loaf of bread, bottle of milk, and a chocolate bar, someone recognized me in the ridiculous getup. Not a reporter mind you, but an imp, right there out of the corner of my eye standing under a street light. He laughed at me and said, "We know what you did", then vanished. He knew that I mocked Mischief Night. He and the denizens of Hell all know what I did a year previously and have readied a place in Dante's Inferno for me. A special reservation for one in the ninth circle of Hell. The circle set aside especially for the betrayers. The coldest and iciest of the circles. Cold, like most Mischief Nights in New York. Cold that evening in 1939 as I walked down the street to my apartment and cold the year previously when I betrayed the nation. I betrayed the confidence of the entire populace of the United States of America that night. I stomped on the ideals set forth by the Founding Fathers. I crushed the hopes and dreams of the radio listeners, who believed, they all truly believed that Martians were invading their countryside intent on destroying them all. I stole away forever the innocence of Americans who would gather around their radio-sets and listen to an evening of entertainment or learn of world events on the news broadcasts. From that day on, they would all question the reality of what they were hearing. In the backs of their minds, they would all question the genuine news reports. That little voice that speaks to us in the quiet moments would whisper to them putting fears into their sub-consciousness, fear that would continually creep into the waking thoughts. All because of me.

PETER: You really can't believe all this, Orson. It was after all Mischief Night. A night where all is forgiven.

ORSON: All is forgiven, but not forgotten. Americans have never forgotten what I did to them. But the sad thing is, none of them even have the foggiest notion of my true act of betrayal. I wanted to open this particular can of worms. You see, I'm not going to take you behind the scenes, Peter, into the studio that night and I'm not going to tell you what really was going on at CBS that night. It was really boring. What I am going to tell you is that an evening of dance music preempted *Mercury Theater on the air.* I was completely oblivious to the panic that was going on.

PETER: How could you? You were in the middle of a performance of "The War of the Worlds".

ORSON: Not quite. I was in rehearsals for *Danton's Death*. That was all that was really going on inside the studios that night. Rehearsals. During those few hours that panic gripped the populous, I can't really tell you what was going on outside of the studios, because I wasn't there at the "time". I didn't know the true story of the panic until hours later. I just didn't know the details then. I would piece together certain things, of course over the course of the evening. I do have a writer's imagination and any writer's imagination tends to run wild when one lets it loose to rampage, rape, and pillage. I can give to you all the supposition and hyperbole you can possibly imagine, but I just didn't know the intimate details, but I would quite quickly.

PETER: I'm ready to hear the story.

ORSON: I'm afraid you're not. Not really ready. But that doesn't matter. Your questions are a little useless know, but I'll let you ask a few anyway.

PETER: When did you decide to use the technique of faking news reports in the context of a radio-drama.

ORSON: The idea of faking news reports, as you put it, in the context of a radio-drama, occurred at around forty-seven minutes past midnight the following Monday morning.

PETER: I don't understand.

ORSON: Listen and learn and, by all means, pay very close attention. Let me back up several weeks. This may help a little. We were doing a Sherlock Holmes story that Sunday, if I remember correctly it was September 24th or 25th, somewhere around then. When world events interrupted my broadcast to report news of a crisis concerning Hitler's encroachment on Czechoslovakia. I didn't learn we were interrupted until after the broadcast and when I learned I was furious. How dare CBS interrupt my show to report on news from half-way around the world. News that could have waited until after my show or even the next morning in one of Hearst's rags. I was stark-raving furious over it. Davidson Taylor, the VP in charge of operations tried to quiet my furor, but I wouldn't have any of it. But over the next five days, I, too, because reliant on radio broadcasts to learn about what was, to my mind and the minds of most people around the world the beginnings of a second Great War. A war that would engulf the entire world, a second world war as it were. But the idea to fake news reports never even crossed my mind. I couldn't make the leap of faith necessary to reach that brainstorm.

PETER: Then when did "The War of the Worlds" begin to take shape in your mind.

ORSON: Twelve-forty-seven in the AM. But I'll get to that later. What I had been planning for months, but never got the script just right, was an adaptation of Sir Arthur Conan Doyle's *The Lost World.* I had this brilliant idea of "finding" lost reel-to-reel recordings floating in a crate down some tropical river. When listened to, these tapes recorded the harrowing final

Orson Welles' failed concept for a meta-radio-dramatization!

moments of an expedition to a mysterious plateau, probably in Africa or the Amazon, I couldn't really decide. The tapes would capture the words of the few survivors as they fought for survival amongst cavemen and dinosaurs and other mysterious creatures lost to records of science and history. The tapes would be realistic and hopefully harrowing. I wanted to broadcast it on Mischief Night. The intrepid scientists brought a Tyrannosaurus back to be displayed at Radio City Music Hall, then it escaped and rampaged through New York. I thought the broadcast would frighten the listening audience into thinking this was all real, that a dinosaur was rumbling down Broadway while they listened in horror, in the relative safety of their homes. But the script never really came together. Howard Koch just couldn't make it work right, draft after lousy draft. Mind you, most of the pages were quite good, but as a whole it just didn't work. And I didn't really know just how to badger Howard to get the damn thing finished right. We couldn't get the scene with the Tyrannosaurus rampaging through the streets of New York to sound anything less than cheap melodrama. Also it reeked too much of *King Kong* for me to get it past Standards and Practices. So the Monday before, I decided to put on "Rebecca". It was a nice little ghost story. But no where near as attention graping as the "Lost World" tapes would have been.

PETER: Wasn't "Rebecca" broadcast weeks later? Oh, is this why you turned to "The War of the Worlds"? You decided during the week to postpone "Rebecca" in favor of "Worlds"?

ORSON: I'll get to that. Let me play the director for a moment and paint a picture for you, okay?

PETER: Okay.

ORSON: "Rebecca" was, in fact, scheduled for that Sunday, Mischief Night. But a decision was made by Davidson Taylor, one that I was completely unaware of; a decision that made me more furious than being interrupted over the Munich Crisis.

PETER: A decision to broadcast "The War of the Worlds" instead?

ORSON: You're getting ahead of yourself here. No, the decision was to preempt me entirely. *The Mercury Theatre on the air* wasn't supposed to air at all that night. I didn't learn this fact until moments before I planned to go on the air with "Rebecca".

PETER: Oh, I see. You planned to do "Rebecca" but at the last moment switched in midstream. Didn't you tell me? Yes, I distinctly remember you telling me that when you did soap operas, you would run into a studio from another studio where you just finished another character and were briefly told what kind of character you were playing and you made up the performance on the spot. Chinese Mandarin, sixty years old. What a hoot.

ORSON: Nice little digression, but way off track here. We were being preempted. The script wasn't being changed or shuffled around. We were being preempted. We weren't going on the air at all.

PETER: I don't understand.

ORSON: Sit back and listen. I'm about to screw with your preconceived ideas a little. We had been preempted by Guy Lombardo and his orchestra. You see, Bill Paley had invited President Roosevelt to the ballroom at the Hotel Annaoplis in Washington

Guy Lombardo and his orchestra preforming at Washington DC's Hotel Annapolis in support of FDR "March of Dimes" campaign and inadvertently becoming the inspiration of Ramon Raquello in Orson Welles' "War of the Worlds" radio-dramatization!

DC for an evening of dance music in support of FDR's "March of Dimes" campaign. William Randolph Hearst bullied his way onto the program with promises a large cash donation in exchange for Marion Davies being allowed to be the Mistress of Ceremonies. He had some fool notion that Ms. Davies might have a second act to her career in radio, all despite his loathing of the medium. He thought radio was nothing but vaudevillians and talentless hacks. I was furious when I learned that we had been preempted for something as ridiculous as an evening of dance music.

PETER: Are you trying to tell me that the evening of dance music was real?

ORSON: Exactly. Why was Bill Paley kowtowing to someone like William Randolph Hearst, a man whose very reputation I couldn't abide even then? I decided to have a little revenge on the pricks, the whole lot of them. I had my entire staff of voice actors with me that evening and I planned, in the next few moments, the greatest prank radio had ever heard of.

PETER: And that the news interruptions were all part of "The War of the Worlds" prank?

ORSON: Exactly... wrong. You don't understand. The prank that I had planned was perfect, just not that perfect. Like I said earlier, the idea for "The War of the Worlds" radio-dramatization didn't occur to me until around twelve-forty-seven in the morning, several hours later. What I planned with Kenny Delmar was pure genius. No one would have even known I pranked the entire listening public. An hour or two into the evening of dance music, Kenny and I snuck out of rehearsals while the others were smoking on their coffee break. We went to the broadcast room and switched the signal from the remote feed at the hotel back to the studio and played a wax recording.

PETER: A wax recording of "The War of the Worlds" radio-drama? That is rather brilliant. You didn't need your entire cast to pull off the prank live. Using a prerecorded wax record, you could intermittently interrupt the signal from the remote playing the evening of dance music and switch the broadcast to scenes from "The War of the Worlds", then switch back to the evening of dance music without Bill Paley being any the wiser. You switched back and forth from an actual evening of dance music to reports from Grover's Mill, New Jersey. You and Frank Readick set up the story at the Princeton Observatory, before switching back to the dance music. Do you think Davidson would have been aware of what you were doing at this point.

ORSON: Davidson is never aware of anything. But this isn't what...

PETER: You have Frank interview Ray Collins concerning the cylindrical meteorite crash on his farm, and then meteorite obliterates the farm with its heat rays. Frank sounded not unlike Herbert Morrison did when he was an eyewitness to the Hindenburg disaster, which was obviously your masterful direction. Then, as the professor of astronomy, you report your observations from the relative safety of a nearby farmstead. You no longer have any reason to go back to the evening of dance music and you let your prerecorded wax recording play on and on and on. Kenny Delmar updates the audience as the Captain of the signal corps, then only moments later, quite brilliantly impersonates FDR warning the people of the dire situation the nation is in being invaded by Martians. Then Ray harrowingly reports of the Martian machines wading through the Hudson into New York City.

ORSON: You're letting your exquisite imagination run away with you...

PETER: Bill Paley would have been oblivious to "The War of the Worlds" being broadcast over his air and obviously Davidson didn't catch on to what you were doing until it was too late. It is quite foolproof it really is. Pure Genius.

ORSON: Precisely... not. I may have been called a genius since I was knee high to a grasshopper, but I'm just not that bright. My idea was a little more tame, but despite it's timidity Kenny was panicking over pulling it off. He didn't want to go through with the prank. He thought we were going to get into trouble. I didn't realize the kind of trouble we would get into with this recording. Boy, the world just crapped all over me because of my practical joke. I tried to convince Kenny, that there was no way, we would get into trouble. It was foolproof. Kenny also didn't think it was funny. It was damn funny. Want me to describe it to you?

PETER: Yes, of course. I love hearing about your famous practical jokes.

ORSON: We were going to switch the broadcast signal from the remote unit at the hotel back to the studio and play a wax-recording. I wish you had been there

The Mercury Theater on the air actors performing the "Invasion From Mars" were: Orson Welles, William Alland, Ray Collins, Kenneth Delmar, Carl Frank, William Herz, Frank Readick, Stefan Schnabel, Howard Smith, Paul Stewart, and Richard Wilson at 12:57 AM, not live on the air at the "scheduled" 9:00 PM Eastern Standard Time.

with me as a co-conspirator, because your eloquent hypothesis would have been the superior prank. I was thinking small, smaller than I should given my reputation. We played this wax-recording. What was recorded on the wax-recording was a simple mimicry of an evening of entertainment that lasted all of a minute or two.

PETER: Then how did you prank an entire nation with but a few minutes of material?

ORSON: The real prank came after the minute or two. The recording become warped and the voices were grossly distorted. People listening at home would think the speakers are conking out on them. Add a dozen seconds of white noise and then silence and they'll all think their radios have bit the big one.

PETER: That is pretty funny, Orson. But what does it have to do with "The War of the Worlds"?

ORSON: I'll get to that in a moment. Imagine millions of people across the country calling their radio repairmen to make an emergency house call. Millions of phone calls clogging switchboards across the country. Chaos for fifteen minutes, then we switch the signal back. The radios miraculously work again. It was foolproof.

PETER: Wouldn't listeners just have to change the channel to discover their speakers were working correctly.

An imagined radio-repairman confounded by Orson Welles' prank!

ORSON: Kenny thought the same thing, but I was intent on acting the fool. Single-mindedly so. After fifteen minutes of interrupting the evening of dance music, I went on the air with, "This is Orson Welles, ladies and gentlemen. This was just a radio version of dressing up in a sheet and jumping out of a bush and saying, 'Boo!' I couldn't soap all your windows and steal all your garden gates by tomorrow night, so I did the next best thing. I made you think all your radios were broken for fifteen minutes. So if your doorbell rings and nobody's there that's no Martian, it's Halloween." That's what sealed my fate.

PETER: That was the extent of your prank? What about "The War of the Worlds" broadcast? What was the world listening to if it wasn't you?

ORSON: For the entire evening, I thought the people were listening to Paley's evening of damnable cocktail music. That's what I thought right up until the moment the military came bursting through the doors of the studio and held everyone at gun point.

PETER: All because of the panic caused by "The War of the Worlds" broadcast?

ORSON: Up until that point, I didn't know there was a "War of the Worlds" going on. I didn't know what was going on outside the studios. I didn't know there was a panic. I was oblivious to it all.

PETER: Davidson didn't alert you to the panic that was overtaking the entire nation? Why didn't Davidson try to stop the broadcast if millions of people were panicking?

ORSON: All I could think of was the military were simply overreacting to my little Mischief Night prank with the radio distortion. Poor Kenny Delmar thought the same thing. All he could say over and over again was, "We're in so much trouble. We're in so much trouble. We're in so much trouble." The Captain, whose name I can't quite remember, got into Davidson Taylor's face and demanded to know who played the practical joke in the nation.

PETER: I've never asked you, but were you genuinely afraid you were going to go to jail over "The War of the Worlds" broadcast?

ORSON: I was afraid of far worse. You don't have to be a paranoid schizophrenic to be paranoid when starring down the barrel of a gun, especially one wielded by the military. But I would soon learn the truth. The truth that I was oblivious to because I had locked myself into the studio to rehearse *Danton's Death*. *Danton's Death* was a fiasco in the making and I knew it. It had over 350 light cues. Three-hundred-and-fifty! For pity's sake! I hadn't the time to make it work, and it never came together. Not after burning the midnight oil, night after night after night. It just never came together. But "The War of the Worlds" radio-drama. Ha! That script came together in less than four hours. That's what I'm trying to tell you. I wrote and recorded "The War of the Worlds" radio-drama in less than four hours. I wrote, rehearsed, directed, performed, and recorded entire "War of the Worlds" episode in less than four hours. An entirely original episode, all because as part of my involvement in a government conspiracy, I was forbidden to use any of the actual broadcast available on the teletype.

PETER: The teletypists had transcribed the broadcasts that evening? I thought they only recorded transcriptions of news broadcasts and the like, not fictional broadcasts.

ORSON: Yes, the teletypists transcribed the evening events. But I couldn't use a single blessed word from the teletype. Virginia had to become New Jersey, Grove Hill became Grover's Mill, real Princeton professor Arthur Buddington became fake Princeton professor Richard Pierson, the Vice-President, John Nance, became the "Secretary of the interior", etcetera *ad nausem*. While Davidson Taylor and The Captain were arguing over whether I played a massive prank on the entire nation, as The Captain maintained, or as Davidson insisted, there was a Martian invasion that night.

PETER: An "invasion" that night? I don't understand.

ORSON: Davidson had somehow convinced himself that the news-reports broadcast over the radio that night were real; that there was an actual invasion from the planet Mars that night. He insisted that the broadcasts heard by the people across the entire nation were real and quite authentic. He persevered with the asinine belief that hundreds of men, women, children, and fighting men had, in fact, died. That the news reports broadcast over CBS where real. The military insisted it had to have been all Hans Von Kaltenborn's idea of a joke at the expense of Bill Paley and the Columbia Broadcast Service. It was all absurd. The military even, very briefly, tried to pin this on me. And all I had done was put my little distortion prank out on the air.

PETER: This is mind-boggling. "The War of the Worlds" was a prank by Hans Von Kaltenborn, the respected newsman? Now, you're pranking me, Orson. I cannot believe this.

ORSON: I didn't know what to believe either. You see the teletype I read seemed real, you have to understand. The teletype was as real as it could be. Everything that was recorded on the teletype seemed to be an authentic capturing of a moment in history; a moment when Martians invaded America on a quiet autumn evening. But as I proved with my own "War of the Worlds" recording that I paraded in front of reporters that next Halloween morning, a Martian invasion could be faked. The world believed, they bought hook-line-and-sinker that I faked a Martian invasion that night. But I did not prank the entire nation. I can say that rather emphatically. I did not fake a Martian invasion.

PETER: You're trying to tell me that "The War of the Worlds" was a prank, a practical joke, by one of CBS's most distinguished newsmen? He was Walter Cronkite before there was a Walter Cronkite. Why would he do it? This doesn't make any sense at all, Orson. It really doesn't.

ORSON: It could have been Hans Von Kaltenborn. He did get into a world of trouble a few months previous for airing a fictionalized report about another meteorite crash in the Alps. This prank I am more than willing to take credit for. Kaltenborn had strenuously objected to my being hired by Bill Paley. He thought that my *Voodoo MacBeth* had taken the beauty of Shakespeare and debased it for the savage masses. Because of the cast and my audience, I took this as bigoted and plotted my revenge. I impersonated a Nazi defector who had proof of a Martian invasion of Germany.

Orson's Voodoo Macbeth *earned him the opportunity to make The Mercury Theater on the air! Then* War of the Worlds *earned him the keys to Hollywood to make* Citizen Kane*!*

PETER: That is how "The War of the Worlds" began?

ORSON: Not exactly. I wanted the worst possible revenge of Hans Van Kaltenborn for trying to sabotage my employment at CBS. I was already outgrowing theater and I was already looking towards Hollywood. I knew if my radio-show could get a sponsor that would be the next step towards my goal of the director's chair on a major motion picture. But I couldn't let Kaltenborn derail my fledgling position at CBS.

PETER: You were going to prank Kaltenborn?

ORSON: I went to my property people at the *Mercury Theater* and told them I was working on a new play for Federal Theatre Project. Ironically, they thought I was adapting HG Well's science-fiction novel *The War of the Worlds* for the stage.

PETER: This is how "The War of the Worlds" began. I had no idea.

ORSON: What I needed were communications from Nazi officers to the *Abwehr* detailing a landing of a Martian machine in the Alps mountains. The communiqués had to be in German, just in case immigrants from the Little Germany neighborhood on the Lower East Side came to see my show. There had to be accurate English translations for us stubbornly monolingual Americans. Photographs would have to be created or at least doctored to show the first contact between the Martians and the Nazis; the subsequent negotiations for peace between Mars and Earth; and then more photographs of the autopsies of the Martians who were slaughtered by the murderous Nazi bastards. The *Mercury Theatre* thought I was trying to make a political statement against the Socialist threat posed by Hilter; that I was using my position in the Federal Theatre Project to spur on a national debate over fascism in Europe. They loved the concept of my *War of the Worlds* stage-play, because of what they thought it promised.

PETER: Why would the props need to be in such detail if they were only going to be seen by the actors on the stage?

ORSON: My property people also wondered the same exact thing. On the spur of the moment, I came up with the excuse that there would be a museum set up in the lobby of the theater where the "evidence" of the Martian invasion would be displayed for all the audience to see, up close and very personal. I wanted them to be lured in before the play even began. That I wanted their suspension of disbelief to be suspended before they ever sat down in their seats. My staff bought the entire gag. It was quite priceless, really.

PETER: How does this relate to Hans Von Kaltenborn?

ORSON: I wanted to prank old Kaltenborn. I wanted to ruin, maybe not his reputation, but his personal view of his reputation. Through a series of "long distance" calls between Berlin and New York, I pretended to be a Nazi defector, who wanted the world to know the truth about a Martian invasion of Germany and promised to send proof in the form of the communiqués and photographs.

PETER: How did you call from Germany?

ORSON: One of the girls on the CBS switchboard had already taken quite a shine to me, so I had her patch in a call from my apartment and she just told Kaltenborn it was patched from Berlin. Hans didn't suspect a thing. I'm particularly good with accents, so it wasn't as difficult a process as one might presume to pull one over on old Kaltenborn. With transcripts of our interviews and the faked documents in hand, he went before Bill Paley. Hans insisted his sources inside the German government were authentic, and went on the air with the reports, and then when I exposed the ruse, the old man was quite embarrassed. He was reprimanded by Paley himself and put on some kind of probation.

Esteemed CBS radio-newsman, Hans Von Kaltenborn, going on the air with his tranche of "Martian" photographs and documents made by the property department at the behest of Orson Welles!

PETER: There really is no length you will not go to for a prank.

ORSON: None, whatsoever. So at the time the military busted in my door and held me at gunpoint, it made perfect sense that this all could have been a retaliatory prank to get back at CBS and ultimately me. For most of the summer, he continued to insist "until [his] dying day" that the story was factual. He even had the documents I manufactured studied by the OSS. He had a contact at the OSS who provided him with the verification that the photographs and documents were, in fact, authentic, and he broadcast it on CBS to much acclaim, then much censure.

PETER: Wait, a minute. The "props" you had made for your fake "War of the Worlds" stage-play were authenticated by the government? That certainly raises the bar on the occupation of prop-making, doesn't it?

ORSON: Yes. Isn't that a kick in the head. Kaltenborn had actual verification from the OSS that my– I mean– his reports were authentic, but Paley still wasn't buying it. The story was too outrageous to believe. Who in their right mind would believe Martians invaded and there was a "war" between "worlds"? Kaltenborn was headed for the gallows because of that one measly report. He would ultimately fall on his sword because of the supreme embarrassment he felt. Because of my reputation (and because I kind of bragged about it), he knew that I was the one responsible for single-handedly ruining his own reputation as an esteemed newsman and threatening his livelihood. More than any other individual, I know why The Captain could have reasonably believed this was all some elaborate ruse orchestrated by Hans Von Kaltenborn to get back at Columbia for his censure. But I, more than any other individual, knew the truth of the entire situation, from my faking Nazi documents and photographs for a supposed "War of the Worlds" stage-play to the faking of news broadcasts for my "War of the Worlds" radio-drama. Only I was capable of pranking the nation with a faked Martian invasion. Yet, until that very night, the greatest length I went for a prank was hiring of a bunch of out of work actors to dress like police officers and try to arrest poor Kenny Delmar... who peed himself. It was great. You know I love a great practical joke and I wish that I could claim "The War of the Worlds" radio-drama as my own, which of course I have for the past few decades. I wish I could, but I really can't.

PETER: Do you feel any regret over claiming the prank as your own?

ORSON: Of course not. Briefly. Very briefly. For an infinitesimally short amount of time, actually I thought that if it was Hans Von Kaltenborn, it would have hurt CBS and hurt the nation to know that a good upstanding newsman resorted to such lengths to get back at William Paley. It would have hurt a lot more people than a radio-dramatization that got a little out of hand. CBS executives, thinking only of their stockholders, looked at the bottom line and decided that having me as the scapegoat was a hell of a lot more attractive than exposing Hans Von Kaltenborn as the ring-leader of the entire affair.

PETER: I cannot believe that Hans Von Kaltenborn was behind the entire "War of the Worlds" prank.

ORSON: Nor should you believe this. The Captain proved to be a charlatan, trying to pass the buck away from the true masterminds of that night's events. And if I've learned anything. It's that you can't trust what anyone associated with the government tells you.

PETER: That doesn't seem logical.

ORSON: What wasn't logical was Davidson continued to insist it was all real.

PETER: You mean, you actually believed Davidson Taylor's story that Martians actually invaded America?

ORSON: During the course of said evening, I gleamed information from the argument between Davidson and The Captain. Davidson was so utterly convinced that the entire affair was real that when threatened with arrest, he didn't budge. Not even an inch. It was amazing to look at this man, a man I disliked in the greatest way possible and yet, I felt a sense of awe. And when I read the teletype of that evenings news broadcasts, I couldn't help but feel they were real. Hans Von Kaltenborn would have had to have had almost the entire staff at CBS under his conspiratorial wing. Announcers. Technicians. The ladies at the switchboard. Even the politician who went on the air. It would have been a conspiracy of enormous magnitude. But an actual Invasion From Mars, that was laughable. To even consider the idea that Martians actually invaded the United States of America and led a rampage towards Washington was preposterous. I didn't know what to think, until while reading the teletype, I exclaimed, "This is goddamn brilliant shit, Davidson. It reads like great radio. It has everything. Drama, conflict, characters you can care about, and frightening monsters. Forget "Rebecca", I want to adapt this son of a gun." And like I said before, my fate was sealed.

PETER: You would turn Hans Von Kaltenborn's prank into a radio-drama.

ORSON: Sure, I had the teletype. I had the actors there in the studio. Hell, if audiences across the world, even in the more civilized countries, thought *King Kong*... actually thought *King Kong* was a documentary of some long, lost Polynesian island. You have to understand that modern audiences are entirely susceptible to the power of suggestion. They are extremely willing, on a subconscious level, to suspend their disbelief. You see it in theater all the time. People moved to tears, moved to laughter, moved to anger... All by the actions of actors on a stage. It's really something. It really is. And despite the fact that none of Mr. Hearst's newspapers ever reported the story of a forty-foot tall ape climbing such a recognizable landmark as the Empire State building, people allowed themselves to believe the absurd. In the darkness of a cinema, with it's constant newsreels describing world events almost as they happen, they believed. And if they were willing to believe that a giant ape, did in fact, die in New York City, then they could easily believe that what they heard on the radio tonight was nothing but a cleverly executed radio drama. Then they would believe that Hans Von Kaltenborn's prank was in actuality an adaptation of HG Wells' classic *The War of the Worlds*.

PETER: Remarkable. Truly outstanding story. A little outlandish. I have a feeling this is another of your infamous practical jokes. But I am willing to suspend my own disbelief to believe that Hans Von Kaltenborn pranked the nation and you took credit for it. I can't believe I actually went along one of your practical jokes. My side of the conversation must seem laughably naïve. Granted it was masterful in its execution, but that twist at the end is a little far-fetched and perhaps even laughable. Sorry, Orson. I have to be honest with you. Our friendship has always been based on honesty, even though you are pulling my leg with this one.

ORSON: Laugh all you want. I know the truth. After negotiating with Hearst over my possible future endeavors, his first promise was a sponsor for the *Mercury Theater*. My future in Hollywood was secured when he would give me not only the director's chair, but the key to the entire bloody city. Then and only then did Howard Koch sit down to create from shear nothingness an original "The War of the Worlds"-style radio-dramatization. We couldn't use a single blessed word from the teletype, but Howard came through like the trooper that he is, beautifully. Hans Von Kaltenborn's supposed prank lasted over three-and-a-half hours. And by morning, Hearst had his wax recording of "The War of the Worlds" radio-drama and I stood before the entire nation playing the part of the wounded actor whose radio-dramatization got a little out of hand.

PETER: You have such guilt over "The War of the Worlds" wasn't your brilliant idea. I'm going to go along with you for a moment, a moment I may regret when you finally mock me for my naïvety. Do you feel such guilt because it was Hans Von Kaltenborn all along? Because you took credit for someone else's prank?

ORSON: Of course not. I have no guilt over that, because that didn't happen.

PETER: I don't understand.

ORSON: My guilt comes from the fact that I believed Davidson Taylor's story. That I conspired with William Randolph Hearst of all people to cover up the fact that... never mind.

PETER: No, no. Go on. Go on.

ORSON: I don't want to talk about it. I really can't. I made promises that I wouldn't speak about it. I swore on the Bible. I swore on the Bible. Jiminy Cricket! Don't you understand. That's why Franklin Delano Roosevelt and William Randolph Hearst rained down a world of hurt on me over my *War of the Worlds* feature. It was my movie and I had every right to tell the story. Every right! I was as much a part of the conspiracy as they were. They had no right to destroy it. To destroy me! Go on, Peter, go on and ask me about my *War of the Worlds* movie. I'm now ready to talk about that. I'm ready.

PETER: I'm not...

RADIO WAVES FROM OUTER SPACE!

COAST TO COAST AM

ART BELL: There is a caller I want to put on the air shortly, very shortly; only in a matter of minutes will this caller prove, beyond any shadow of doubt, that all conspiracy theories are an outrageous lie. Blasphemy I know. But this caller is not a died-in-the-wool skeptic with his head buried in the sand of ignorance. Oh, no. This caller is a believer unlike all others. But all other conspiracies pale in comparison to this one. The "Greatest Conspiracy". The conspiracy theory to end all conspiracy theories. Tonight is the anniversary of a landmark day in human history, a day on which we saw our greatest victory over an unseen enemy only a handful of government officials had the necessary clearance to even know existed. I have a fax from the gentleman, here that puts it in very eloquent words, "...A lie and hoax committed by the government to cover-up the truth. The truth that there was, indeed, an invasion from Mars on October 30, 1938. That hundreds of men, women, and children did, in fact, die that night. And that the radio-broadcasts heard by millions of listeners were quite authentic." Wow! Now! That is some really heavy, really weird stuff. Unbelievable. Weird. But truly fantastic. The details I have are a little sketchy, but my guest will, no doubt, shed considerable light on this fascinating story. But before I get to that, let me take some callers on the Wild Card line for anyone to call in on, particularly if it involves the Alien Agenda. For those of you wishing to call in, it's 702-727-1295. Let's get to a few of those. From KOTN-AM in Pine Bluff, Arkansas.

ARKANSAS: I've been listening to your show for over a year now.

ART: Thanks a lot.

ARKANSAS: I'd like to thank you for your story from last week concerning the connection between Amelia Earhart's disappearance over the Pacific and the rash of

Foo Fighter reports from that era.

ART: That was an extremely fascinating show.

ARKANSAS: Any very informative. There is no longer any doubt in my mind that Ms. Earhart was chosen for alien abduction because of her knowledge of state-of-the-art technology.

ART: Well, state-of-the-art for the 1930's that is. Thanks. And if you have an interest in alien conspiracies, you will love the next segment of tonight's show. It'll blow the lid off the Alien Agenda.

ARKANSAS: Cool, I'll keep glued to the radio.

ART: Ah, a fellow Nevadan on KXNT-AM 840.

NEVADA: Hi, Mr. Bell… I'm a junior in high school and during astronomy class,we watched the moon landing from back in '69. Since I was born in after the fact, this was the first time I got to see it on television.

ART: And what was your opinion of the broadcast?

NEVADA: Well, now I'm convinced that it was filmed on a Hollywood soundstage, maybe like they say in Nevada, maybe not. I don't know. But probably in Nevada somewhere.

ART: What conclusions have your drawn from the footage to make you think this way?

NEVADA: Well, first, there are no stars in the background.

ART: And what do you see when you look into the night sky here in Nevada?

NEVADA: My point exactly. Even in the bright lights of Las Vegas, if you get far enough away from the strip, you can see stars in the sky. But in the darkness and thin atmosphere of the moon, there should be one hell of a star show going on. Countless stars unlike anything you can see on Earth.

ART: Interesting. Interesting.

NEVADA: And, let me add if I may.

ART: You may.

NEVADA: If the boots of the astronauts make little clouds of dust poof off the ground and linger around for a while, then shouldn't the landing craft have caused a great big cloud of dust hang around like a thick fog? Unless the craft was already on the ground, in a soundstage, somewhere.

ART: Did you challenge your teacher with the truths about the moon landing or should I say moon landing hoax.

NEVADA: Mr. Harris claims that there would have been a full-earth out for those standing on the surface of the moon, so there wouldn't be any stars visible because of the reflection of sunlight from the earth. I got a D on my report.

ART: It is sad, really sad, to see academically intelligent people in the teaching profession, who claim to be open minded and free-thinkers, are so blind the truth staring them in the face.

NEVADA: I know, but what can I do? I'm only seventeen.

ART: Believe. You must believe. It is that simple. You may only be seventeen now and the world seems to be run by close-minded adults from a bygone era, but remember one day the world will be run by the hopefully open-minded of your generation. We can only hope. In the sixties, we couldn't wait for the time when our generation would be running things, but as we have seen with Baby Boomers in public office. They kowtow to the party line, the same bipartisan party line that has kept these secrets secret. And

Buzz Aldrin (left) and Neil Armstrong, filming the moon landing hoax on a Hollywood sound stage in April 1969.

the skeptics, they never change as well. Until an alien ship lands on the lawn on the White House, they will never see the truth.

NEVADA: Thank you. And I'll keep believing.

ART: No, thank you. And for trivia buffs out there. If you listen to that moon landing again, listen closely, "One small step for man, one giant leap for mankind,"are not the first words spoken by Neil Armstrong. A couple more calls before we get to the Call of the Century. One from KFOR-AM 1240 in Lincoln, Kansas.

KANSAS: Is this a secure line?

ART: As secure as cordless phones and land lines can be in an age of rampant government wire taps and short wave radios.

KANSAS: [Censored] I forgot about that. [Censored] Just a minute. Sorry. I'm back. My call does, indeed, concern the Alien Agenda, like you asked about.

ART: What concerns you most about the Alien Agenda, Lincoln, Kansas.

KANSAS: Satellite technology mostly. There is no reason that aliens need to travel all the way across the greatest of space all the way to our little planet to learn about us. We are broadcasting the day-to-day events from every corner of the world. All into the depths of space. Even now, some alien on his own planet is listening to our very conversation.

ART: Quite true. But this has been an ongoing part of the Alien Agenda for quite a few years now. While we have SETI, the Search for Extraterrestrial Intelligence, searching the skies looking for alien radio signals, the aliens of the Agenda, only need to tune their dials to CNN to get all the world's news in every convenient package.

KANSAS: Yes! Yes! My point exactly. We have no shame in broadcasting the most intimate details of our lives over the air waves. How do you think these aliens of no doubt vast intelligence, perceive us as a species. News broadcasts are one thing, but I hate to think that aliens are judging our entire race based on prime time programming like *Murphy Brown* and *Northern Exposure*. I shudder to think what they think about us. Are we the Arkansas of the universe?

ART: I think our caller from Arkansas would have a little trouble with that.

KANSAS: I'm sorry, but you see my point. They only see the worst that humanity has to offer. We have absolutely no shame in broadcasting the most intimate details of our lives over the air waves. They merely have to watch what we recklessly beam into space. They have all the information they need on us to lead an all out invasion of our planet. Hell, every science-fiction movie ever broadcast on HBO or on the Sci-Fi channel would be an excellent tutorial of humanity.

ART: Yes. Yes. Yes. Someone has seen the light. Lincoln, Kansas, tonight is your night. Tonight, you will feel vindicated. Please, please I get you, stay tuned to our show tonight. The final call from Colorado on KCSJ-AM 590.

COLORADO: I'm listening to your show for the first time and I'm very intrigued by what I've heard. So I thought maybe you could help me out a little bit.

ART: I hope to help all seekers of the truth.

COLORADO: You, see, uh, I have this overwhelming feeling, I don't know exactly what it is, you see, but it is a feeling, that I'm sure of. Yes, a feeling that Hollywood agents, sort of like the government agents you have warned us about. Well, at first, I was afraid these agents working for the Alien Agenda. If you will allow me to paraphrase you a little, well, I was afraid they'd hack into my computer which is of course hooked to the ARPANET (you see I'm something of a computer whiz. I've been connected since my parents bought me a personal computer years ago) and they'd be able to see what I've been writing. And what I've been writing is really, really revolutionary stuff, let me tell you, it'll revolutionize Hollywood completely. I'm talking *Citizen Kane* type stuff here. I can't go into detail about my screenplay, because this is a public program and people are listening to me and they'd be able to steal my story away from me, just like the Hollywood agents are trying to do. So, anyway, at first I unplugged myself from the ARPANET, but that didn't help. So I deleted the screenplay from my computer in a hopefully successful means of defeating them. And I began writing my movie down in longhand on pages of pages of legal pads. So I shredded them all. And now, well, now, if the government has the kind of technology, that my friends have said you said the government has, technology that can listen to our very thoughts. Then maybe it isn't that far of a reach to think that that Hollywood, that multi-billion dollar corporations, might have access to similar technology. Huh? Huh? Am I right? Well, so now, whenever I leave the house, I have the feeling, the overwhelming feeling, that they are using satellites or CIA psychics are trying to steal my story from inside my own brain. What can be done to protect my story if Hollywood agents can steal every idea that I have from inside the head. I don't know what to do, or where to turn. Please, Mr. Bell, help me.

ART: You are paranoid, buddy. Get some help. Professional help. You need it, desperately... Before we go to another commercial break, let me tease you with the following history lesson on a event all radio-personalities are weaned on. *[coughs]*

On October 30, 1938, one of the greatest hoaxes ever committed on the fine, upstanding, and honest people of the United States of America was perpetrated. On that infamous night, Orson Welles, and his *Mercury Theatre on the air* "The War of the Worlds" for a radio-play. Using seemingly realistic news broadcasts and program interruptions over a backdrop of an evening of dance music, he drove millions of radio listeners, much like yourselves tuning in to hear your favorite radio programs, drove them however briefly-insane. I'm going to read this to you, I have it here somewhere, ah-yes, here it is. A facsimile copy I was faxed from a librarian at the Manhattan public library earlier afternoon. It's a really fascinating read, it really is. I'll give you just the headline, "Radio Listeners in Panic, Taking War Drama as Fact". Try and find a copy of it on microfiche at your local public library. It's really worth the effort to read. It's great. You see because Orson Welles was known to most radio listeners of his day as the voice of the "The Shadow". The Shadow knows who gives the creeps with countless children listening in. "The creeps", indeed. I found... more accurately a intern from a nearby community college found for me... some soundbytes of a few of the eyewitnesses, or should I say "earwitnesses"- pardon the pun. Let me cue them up in a second… Here we go.

RADIO INTERVIEW 1: I turned the radio to get Orson Welles, but the announcement that a meteor had fallen sounded so much like the usual news announcements that I never dreamt it was Welles. I thought my clock was probably fast.

RADIO INTERVIEW 2: At first I was very interested in the fall of the meteor. It isn't often that they find a big one just when it falls. But when it started to unscrew and monsters came out, I said to myself, "They've taken one of those *Amazing Stories* and are acting it out." It just couldn't be real. It was just like some of the stories I read in *Amazing Stories*, but it was even more exciting.

RADIO INTERVIEW 3: The next day when I read that it was a Halloween prank. It was like being reprieved on the way to the gas chamber.

ART: "A Halloween Prank" indeed. One more quick sound-byte. Martin Luther King, Jr.:

MARTIN LUTHER KING, JR: The truth shall set us free!

[Commercial break]

ART: Yes, my faithful listeners, the truth will set us free. Welcome back to "Coast to Coast AM with Art Bell", speaking from KNYE 95.1 in Pahrump, Nevada. My guest this hour will answer the question never before uttered by human lips and as ridiculous as it may sound, "Did the United States government hide the truth of an invasion from Mars on October 30, 1938? And what role, if any, did Orson Welles and his *Mercury Theatre on the air* play in the cover-up? Please introduce yourself to the listening audience, Mister?

WILLIAM BROWN: Brown, William Francis Brown. But please, call me, Willie.

ART: Welcome to "Coast to Coast AM", Willie Brown.

WILLIE: Thank you. I have spent the majority of my adult life trying desperately to come to terms with the cold October 30th evening sixty years ago this very night that I was both an ear and eyewitness to. The fact that this story, this conspiracy would cross my life's path not once, not twice, but multiple times over the last fifty-plus years is as close to fate as I can imagine it. The first time was, of course, that Mischief Night so long ago, when as a young boy of fourteen, I didn't even know the name Orson Welles. I knew nothing of his *Mercury Theatre on the air*. I knew nothing of his reputation as a practical joker. But the next day, I would know everything there was to know about Orson Welles and his newfound reputation as the hoaxer of a nation with his otherworldly radio-adaptation of "The War of the Worlds". An adaptation that I knew was a lie, an outrageous lie and a conspiracy against the good people of this nation.

ART: What made you so sure that there was a conspiracy against the great people of this nation?

WILLIE: I had summered with my sister Caroline and her husband on the shores of Virginia sound, much to the consternation of my mother who had practically disowned my sister for the double sin of marrying a crippled Catholic. But I enjoyed the summer with my sister and her husband so much that I wanted to spend at least the fall semester on Virginia. My father thought it would do me some good before I returned to Colorado, finished high-school, and took my rightful place in the steel-mill that fueled the economy of my little hometown.

ART: Did you begin the evening as most people listening to the radio that evening by listening to Edgar Burgen and Charlie McCarthy?

WILLIE: Not exactly. My brother-in-law was a devout Catholic, so we were listening to Father Coughlin's broadcast on another station. Father Coughlin began his broadcast as he had every other Sunday evening, not by preaching religious sermons, but railing against political interests that he felt was bringing down the good name of our country. My brother-in-law had nothing but good things to say about Father Coughlin and despite my repeated protests, we sat listening to Father Coughlin. I thought it was particularly ridiculous to spend a Sunday morning at mass and spend the same Sunday evening listening to the preaching of Father Coughlin, but I was a visitor in my sister's house, so I sat patiently for the end of the program. But fifteen minutes or so after eight, the phone rang and after spending a few moments talking to someone, my sister turned the dial to CBS.

ART: Like I imagine thousands, hundreds of thousands, or perhaps even millions of people did the same thing.

WILLIE: After five or ten harrowing minutes, my mother was able to get a line connected with my sister. She too was listening to on the radio all the way back in Colorado. Mother had read the radio listing in the newspaper to my younger brother Bob. She had asked what he wanted to hear most, *The Chase and Sanburn Hour with Edgar Bergen and Charlie McCarthy*, *The Mercury Theatre on the air*'s "Rebecca", some obscure local radio public affairs show, or God-Forbid, Father Charles Edward Coughlin. Mother only added the last one because she knew Bob wouldn't choose it. We were Protestant and Father Coughlin was, even to a child's ears, a radical Roman Catholic. My Irish-Protestant mother was a woman who spoke with piss and vinegar and spit venom at all passing Catholics. She didn't believe all Catholics were truly evil, just Father Coughlin and the Pope. I'm sure that my mother mumbled a prayer under her breath, which after fifty years of hindsight and because I know my mother well enough to know she said a prayer for forgiveness for disliking Catholics so much. But she would go on disliking Catholics, including my brother-in-law, the crippled Catholic. In the end, Father Coughlin would not have been tolerated back in my mother's home, it was Charlie McCarthy hands down. I can picture my brother sitting there and listening to the antics of a ventriloquist and his dummy. And how I envied him, he wasn't listening to Father Coughlin. He was far too young to understand the irony of a ventriloquist was actually a famous radio personality.

ART: It is rather odd, but then I could add for clarity that there were live audiences watching the radio-broadcasts of those old radio performers. To that limited audience, at least, he was a true ventriloquist.

WILLIE: But that might have been lost on my brother... and me.

ART: Am I thoroughly enjoying our conversation, Mr. Brown, but I'd like to get back for a moment to the exact moment you changed the channel to get Orson Welles.

Excuse me, CBS.

WILLIE: Most people, as you know, turned the dial just as the first musical interlude came.

ART: Is that what some of us old-time radio-types call the "Nelson Eddy Tuneout"?

WILLIE: I've never heard it put quite that way, Mr. Bell, but it is quite common, in hindsight, to believe that people turned their dials to catch the harrowing beginnings of the CBS broadcast, because we today are turned off by Nelson Eddy's operetta-type pieces done in that keening singing-mounting voice of his. While I listened to Father Coughlin ramble on and ramble about this political thing or another, my mother was in raptures listening to Nelson Eddy. It was probably closer to Dorothy Lamour's rendition of... something...came on that prompted my mother to change the channel to CBS. And half-an-hour later, to call my sister on Virginia to see if we were in fact being invaded. My sister, came running into the living room and changed the channel to CBS, much to the protest of my brother-in-law. But what we heard on the radio was so harrowing, Martians invading the Virginia sound not even a mile east, down the beach.

ART: Virginia? Didn't Orson Welles' 'War of the Worlds' take place in New Jersey.

WILLIE: I've never been able to explain the existence of Orson Welles' "War of the Worlds" recording fully, Mr. Bell. I really can't. After all the years of research into the truth of that night. All I can tell you is that I've listened to that recording by Orson Welles. While both feature the subject of a Martian invasion, they are not the same. Not the same at all. Orson Welles' recording seems far too polished and not nearly as harrowing as what I heard. I can't explain it fully, I can't. The invasion on the recording only lasts a half-an-hour before digressing into a post-apocalyptic horror where Professor Pierson converses with someone only referred to as the "stranger". The invasion I heard seemed to last an eternity, but at three-and-a-half hours, far longer than Mr. Welles' supposed radio-play, I was shocked that it did not match my memory by any stretch of the imagination. New Jersey was substituted for Virginia and a farmhouse in Grover's Mill became the landing point of the Martians instead Grove Hill, only miles from my sister's house. When the *New York Times* would report, the next morning of panic in New Jersey, I couldn't believe my ears. The panic had been across Virginia. I listened to reports of destruction from the beach all the way to New York City herself. I couldn't believe that all of the newspapers in the area were reporting this was a hoax. I know that I heard on the radio. People across the nation knew what they were listening to was real, I couldn't believe my ears. This is when I began to distrust our government.

ART: Are you trying to tell me there was a conspiracy to cover-up the truth.

WILLIE: Yes.

ART: And what truth is that, Mr. Brown.

WILLIE: That what I, my sister, my brother-in-law, and my family back in Colorado listened to was real.

ART: And not a radio-dramatization as the popular imagination believes?

WILLIE: Certainly not a radio-dramatization. All I know is that invasion had to be real. Nothing else is even remotely possibly from my point-of-view. Martians had to have landed on Virginia sound and invaded the political capital of the world, Washington DC. Martians killed hundreds of men, women, children, and fighting men. I was an earwitness, and to a lesser extent, an eyewitness. I don't know what kind of conspiracy it was or what heights it reached or the depths it sunk, I have my theories, but what I can say without reservation, what I heard was real.

ART: It must have been exciting.

WILLIE: Nobody knew what to think or say. I just sat there, Indian-style on the rug by the fireplace. The news was something that seemed so far away. I heard the events of the Munich crisis only a few weeks earlier. Those broadcasts had my sister and her husband glued to the radio set at all hours, listening for the latest news bulletin, even when it finally interrupted Charlie McCarthy, much to my displeasure. But for the news to be in my backyard just a mile or so up the beach.

ART: So you listened to the Martian invasion in it's entirety on the radio.

WILLIE: Not exactly. After realizing that the end of the world was coming so close to home, my sister was forced to return the channel to Father Coughlin who must have heard about the invasion from Mars, because he had stepped down from his political soapbox and began a sermon to quiet the fear in his audience, a sermon tinged with Martian intrigue.

ART: I was able to find a wax recording of his speech Mr. Brown.

WILLIE: Oh, truly wonderful. Excellent. I can't wait to hear it again after all this many years

From A Recording of FATHER COUGHLIN: No one would have believed, in the nineteen centuries since the Crucifixion and Resurrection of our Lord and Savior, that the End Times would be fulfilled, not through the flaming arrows of the angels and demons of Biblical Prophecy, but through science, intellectual study, and monsters which science can rationally explain. So I ask: is this world being watched keenly and closely by intelligences greater that man's and yet as mortal as his own? As we busy ourselves about our various, secular concerns, are we being scrutinized and studied, perhaps almost as narrowly as a man with a microscope might scrutinize the transient creatures that swarm and multiply in a drop of water? With infinite complacency men go to and fro over this globe about their little affairs, serene in their assurance of their empire over matter! Is it not possible that the infusoria under the microscope do the same? Are Angels and Demons that have visited this world since the dawn of Creation creatures of faith or creatures of science, extraterrestrials from far-flung worlds? Has no one given thought to the older worlds of space as sources of Biblical danger, or thought of them only to dismiss the idea of life- God's Creation- upon them as impossible, improbable, or, heaven forbid, blasphemous? Is it blasphemous to believe that the Star of Bethlehem that led the wise men to that humble abode was in actually a conjuncture of the planets Saturn and Jupiter in the night sky? Is it blasphemous to believe that God would not use the laws of nature and physics, that He created, to fulfill his Word and Prophecy? It is curious to recall some of the mental habits of those departed days. At most terrestrial men fancied there might be other men upon Mars, or the Moon, perhaps inferior to themselves, after all the Son of Man was born on this round little globe, and ready to welcome a missionary enterprise to spread the Word of God! Yet across the gulf of space, minds that are to our as ours are to those of the beasts that perish, intellects vast and cool and unsympathetic, do they regard this earth with envious eyes? As I have said, we have been blessed with a Lord and Savior that has forgiven the sins of Man not the sins of Martians or Venusians. Do they draw their plans against us? Is this the great disillusionment? That the planet Mars revolves about the sun, not as Church Fathers had once believed about the earth. At a distance of million of miles, the light and heat it receives from the sun is barely half that of that received by this world. Is it unforeseeable that God placed our planet at a mean distance of 93 million miles in a Belt of Life, so that we might be given a world that is perfectly suited for said life? Is it, if the nebular hypothesis has any merit, older than our world? And long before this earth ceased to be molten, did life upon its surface begin its course? It is scarcely one seventh of the volume of the earth and must have accelerated its cooling to the temperature of which life could, very well, begin. Is God such a vain God that he would only put life on one simple little blue planet circling one simple little yellow star. In a galaxy that is filled with billions of stars and a universe filled with billions of galaxies, it is vain of man, and so blinded by his vanity, that no man of God has expressed any idea that intelligent life might have developed there far, or indeed at all, beyond its earthly level? Nor is it generally understood that since Mars is older than our earth, with scarcely a quarter of the superficial area and remoter than the sun, it necessarily followed that it is not only more distant from time's beginning but nearer its end. Are the End Times for that planet nearer than our own? Would a Kind and Forgiving God permit a species to evolve that is so intelligent, destructive, and evil that it shows no thanks and reverence to its Creator and God? Would a Righteous and Just God allow that world to destroy itself in order that another flawed yet faithful world might find forgiveness in the words and prophecies of John the Divine? That this faith filled world through the trials and tribulations of Revelation, should find a Millennium of Peace with its Lord and Savior. But I ask, would one world's slow and agonizing death force its inhabitants to covet the life and beauty of our own? Can the prophecies of Revelation that have been interpreted and reinterpreted over the centuries find its fulfillment not in a manner befitting faith, but in a manner befitting science? Do the inhabitants of Mars know of our faith in one God and the mystery of the Holy Trinity? Do they know of our faith in an eternity beyond this life? Do they have a God or gods that they find faith and solace in? Or are their hearts hardened by their brightened intellects and enlarged powers? Are they jealous, looking across the gulf of space with instruments similar to our own and intelligences such as we have scarcely dreamed of? Do they see us at its nearest distance of only 35 million miles sunward of them a morning star of hope, our warmer planet, green with vegetation and grey with water, with a cloudy atmosphere eloquent of fertility? Do glimpses through our drifting cloud wisps of broad stretches of populous country and narrow, navy-crowded seas? And do we men, the creatures that inhabit this earth, are we at least as alien and lowly as are the monkeys and lemurs to us? Does the intellectual side of man already admit that life is an incessant struggle for existence, and would it seem that this too is the belief of the minds upon Mars? Their world is far gone in its cooling and this world is still crowded with life, but crowded only with what they regard as inferior animals. Have their gods, if they should have the faith to believe, have their gods given them the commandment, *"The fear of you and the dread of you shall be upon every beast of the earth, and upon every fowl of the air, upon all that moveth upon the earth, and upon all the fishes of the sea: into your hand are they delivered"*! Are we to be sacrificed by a Vengeful God to besmitten from the earth by the hand of the Martians who carry warfare, like their namesake the Greek God Mars, sunward their only escape from the destruction that, generation after generation, creeps upon them. And before we judge them too harshly, we must remember what ruthless and utter destruction our own species has wrought, not only upon animals, such as the vanished bison and the dodo, but upon its inferior races. The Tasmanians, in spite of their humanlikeness, were entirely swept out of existence in a war of extermination waged by European immigrants, in a space of fifty years. Are we such apostles of mercy as to complain if the Martians warred in the same spirit?"

ART: That is a frightening sermon.

WILLIE: After that powerful sermon, Father Coughlin urged his listening audience to turn their dials to CBS because only CBS appeared to be broadcasting the news reports that were streaming into their New York studio. We turned the dial back to CBS as they continued to broadcast news about the invasion. I kept an ear tuned to the radio, while my eyes scanned the tree line up the beach for any sign of the Martians. Listening to the radio had become,in a matter of minutes, a life-or-death decision. The voice of Father Coughlin, a man my mother could not stand, had played an important role that night. He was for a moment at least, a calming influence on all of us. The true potential of radio was finally sinking in, despite the fear. Listening to my mother play a Scott Joplin song on her piano was one thing, but listening to Scott Joplin play his own song was another thing entirely. By hearing their music and their voices, they seemed like old friends. Edgar Bergan, Charlie McCarthy, the Lone Ranger, the Shadow, even the President of the United States was made a member of the family through his radio fireside chats. Even you, Mr. Bell, through listening to your program over the years, you are in many ways like a friend to my son. A friend from many years ago, that he was able to keep in contact with through your program. It is because of this friendship that he has have with you and your program that I am able to open up and talk about something that has been on my mind for sixty years. And tonight, it's like renewing a friendship all over again.

ART: I try to be a friend to my entire listening audience. There is no one else in the world I'd rather be friend with than my listeners. I have spent my entire career protecting them from ridicule and offered them all an open forum free from censorship. While, to be perfectly honest, I don't necessarily believe everything my callers say to me. I believe they have a right to say what they want to say. And through calm manner, patient questions, and a fair amount of keen insight into my listeners to get their point-of-view across in as clearly and intelligently as possible. I approach my work seriously, Mr. Brown. And I will defend my listeners and their right to freedom of speech to my dying day. Through this medium of radio, I am able to reach, educate, entertain, and possibly even enlighten every one of you listening every night. Only through this tireless approach will the truth many of my listeners ardently believe be finally exposed.

WILLIE: I completely understand your feelings, Mr. Bell. I have spent the entirety of my life, searching for the answers I seek. And while I have been able to find the answers to those questions raised that October evening through a professional relationship with Orson Welles as his screenwriter, I have more questions that need answers. Questions concerning the greatest conspiracy theories of all time. All of them are lies and disinformation put out by the Bilderbergers at their annual conferences to coverup the truth of an "Orson Welles' Conspiracy". A vast, single conspiracy theory that began in the infancy of civilization and continues to the present day. I know this and more. And the answers are written down by my own hand and stored safely in the safety of a safety deposit box. One day, Mr. Bell, they will be exposed. Not by my hand, but hopefully the hand of my youngest son, Robert. He alone will have the courage to expose the truth of the "Orson Welles' Conspiracy"!

ART: I hate to end our conversation on this note, Mr. Brown but I have bills that have need to be paid and other conspiracies that need to be exposed. ⚛

CITIZEN WELLES

PETER: Do you have any regrets over not having made *The War of the Worlds* into a feature film?

ORSON: Well... I did.

PETER: You regretted not making it?

ORSON: I wouldn't have regretted never having shot it. It was never a priority with me. I was far more interested in *Heart of Darkness*, the life of Christ, or god-forbid... anything else. Anything but *The War of the Worlds*. I would have given my eye-teeth to avoid filming *The War of the Worlds*. Everyone wanted me to film it. George Schaefer begged me to shoot it before I got him fired. Charles Koerner said I had to film it or he would sell my contract. Louis B. Mayer offered to buy my contract if I would film it for MGM. I'm sure Disney would have paid me handsomely to animate it if I could find a way to fit in cute little singing animals into a violent Martian invasion. What I regret most is having shot it.

PETER: I don't understand.

ORSON: I regret having shot it. I was such a coward. They say it isn't the size of the dog in the fight, it's the size of the fight in the dog. But there was just no more fight in this dog.

PETER: What? You gave in and shot a *The War of the Worlds* feature?

ORSON: Yes, I shot the movie. When the heat died down from the god-awful *Citizen Kane* mess and the colossal bungling of the studio with my *Magnificent Ambersons*, the only job Charles Koerner would give me at RKO was *The War of the Worlds* feature. I wanted to move on to anything else. Anything else they would have offered me, even some B-list romantic comedy with wild animals and annoying children. Anything but *The War of the Worlds*. I didn't want to shoot it... yet. Technology hadn't progressed far enough since *King Kong* to make the special effects truly special, radically revolutionary. If I was going to do a space opera, I was going to do

George Schaefer, president of RKO Pictures; Dolores Del Río, actress; and Orson Welles at the premiere of Citizen Kane *at the Palace Theater in New York City on May 1, 1941!*

Louis B. Mayer, co-founder of Metro-Goldwyn-Mayer studios (MGM) threatens to purchase Orson Welles' contract after Citzien Kane, *and force Orson to make the "goddamn Martian motion-picture"!*

a science-fiction film to end all genre pictures.

PETER: Couldn't you have just adapted Howard Koch's radio-script?

ORSON: Absolutely, I could not have just adapted Howard Koch's radio-script. That script had nothing to do with the real story. What would I have done? Would I have just pointed a camera at a radio for two hours and have a mother, father, grandfather, two sons, and a daughter react to what they heard? Koch's "War of the Worlds" was nothing more than a radio-drama. It was intended to be heard, not seen. It was created to be what it was. If I was going to do *The War of the Worlds* as a feature, it had to be a motion picture that would revolutionize the medium. I had a story in mind that would make HG Wells proud, what with Martian invaders and time-travel...

PETER: Time-travel? I beg your pardon?

ORSON: That was a problem that I've always had. I had all these grandiose ideas in my head, but somewhere between the brain and the finger-tips, the information gets muddled. I know intimately what happened that night, but at the same time, I didn't know what happened in all the scenes I wasn't actually in. It was strange to try to imagine your memories as if they were a motional picture.

PETER: For someone with your skill behind the camera, that should be second-nature.

ORSON: I know what was in the teletype despite it having been seized by The Captain.

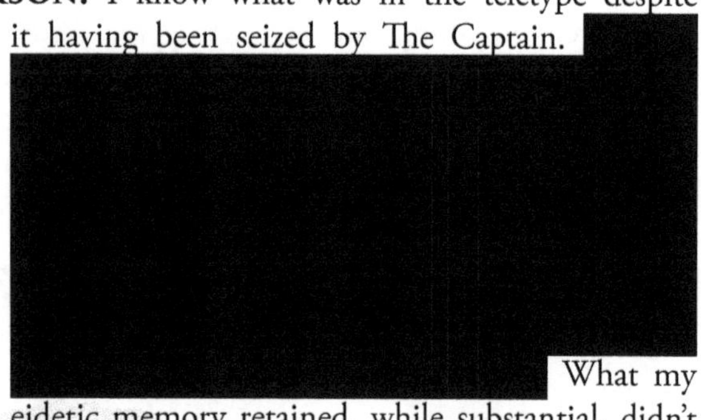

What my eidetic memory retained, while substantial, didn't complete the picture to a necessary degree. What I needed to know was what was going on before, during, and after the fact. I wanted to tell the true story. How can one tell a story that would be fit for an end-of-life memoir when one doesn't know what happened when one wasn't around. But I needed to find out that

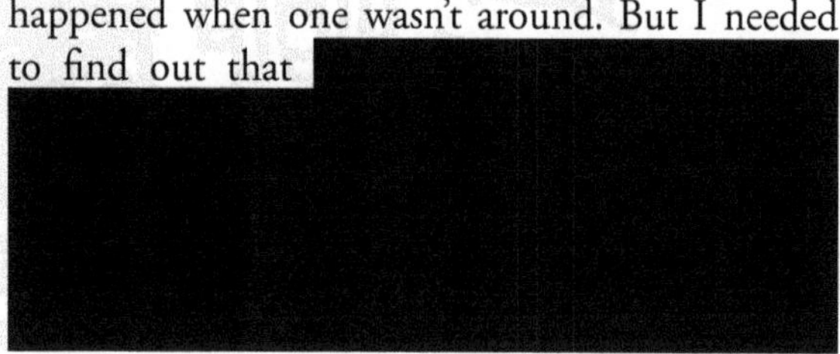

PETER: You wanted your *War of the Worlds* to be about the panic caused by your radio-dramatization? That is certainly a novel approach. I wouldn't have thought of that. It could almost be a documentary if you had the mind to go interview those who you panicked. Or a docudrama, mixing interviews with dramatic recreations. I can see why that appealed to you. You always had a knack for mixing truth and fiction. Your *F for Fake* is a testament to this element of your personality.

ORSON: I wanted my *War of the Worlds* to be about the panic caused by... that cursed teletype. I couldn't get what I read out of my mind. Blasted eidetic memory is a curse of curses. But what I read in that teletype led me to one very certain conclusion. There was a Martian invasion that night and hundreds of men, women, and children died. This is the heart of my regret over the entire affair. If I would have kept my trap shut and not offered the brilliant cover-story to The Captain and William Randolph Hearst, the entire world would have learned of the Martian invasion that night. And the entire course of American history would have to be rewritten with full knowledge that we are not alone in our own solar system, let alone the vastness of the universe. That there are envious eyes that slowly and surely drew their plans against us and continue to draw their plans against us. How was I supposed to write scenes that I wasn't in?

PETER: I...

ORSON: But if I was going to be pressured into making *The War of the Worlds* into a feature, I needed to know the true story of Mischief Night. I needed an ally. That I why I accepted Gunter's request for a dinner date with that to-be-unnamed starlet. I knew instantly that his accent wasn't Iowan, even though it was very, very close. His Iowan accent had just a hint of Luxemburgeese to it. Very, very good. So, I decided to help him.

PETER: Wait, what. I thought the Nazi spy story was a prank. You actually decided to help someone who you have claimed was a Nazi spy? Yet you also deny he was a Nazi spy?

ORSON: Let's not let facts get in the way of a good story, shall we? I would only help him as far as his mission was concerned. He was supposed to learn as much as he could about Hollywood. That was the extent of his mission. I didn't think anything he learned about Hollywood would be particularly valuable, even to Adolph Hitler, who was a complete nut. Hitler so firmly believed that knowing what propaganda Hollywood was doing for the American government would give him an advantage in his own propaganda machine. He thought that Disney making cartoons featuring Donald Duck caricaturing Nazi Germany and Japan with the most offensive stereotypes was how America was going to win the war. But Hitler could never consider the truth. Our propaganda didn't sway the American people to believe what they actually did not believe, it just reaffirmed that we already believed. Nazi propaganda had a similar mission, but tried a whole hell of a lot harder to convince the German people that its message is what the Germans actually believed. Most Germans did not tow the Nazi party's line, yet because of the Nazi propaganda and the eloquent, if somewhat vulgar, speeches by the Nazi leaders they ultimately did the propaganda. These are two completely different mindsets. So I didn't have any problem teaching Gunter techniques a film-school student would learn during the first few weeks and helping him with said starlet. In exchange for my council, I put him on a very specific mission– uncover any information of a Martian invasion of Virginia and anywhere else in the world on October 30, 1938. If the teletype was correct and Edward R. Murrow, did, in fact, broadcast news reports of a Martian invasion of Germany, then there would have had to have been official Nazi reports. The information he returned with was harrowing. Simply harrowing. I had known the conspiracy went all the way to FDR himself, but I didn't know some of the more pertinent details. The Martians invaded not only Virginia, but waged an all out assault on Germany that could have crippled Nazi Germany if we, myself and my American co-conspirators, hadn't interfered. I knew when I finished reading the "Top-Secret: Eyes Only" reports that I had to film my *War of the Worlds* feature.

PETER: You finally decided you would film *The War of the Worlds* as a motion picture?

ORSON: That's why I registered *Invasion From Mars* with the Motion Picture Producers Association and set out on my ingenious plan to convince RKO to film *Invasion From Mars* with reverse psychology. I would insist on not filming it and they would, of course, force me to film it.

PETER: Where is the film? Why hasn't it been released?

ORSON: You have to understand that I was in a particularly arrogant and obstinate mood while working on preproduction on *Invasion*. I wanted to piss people off. Everyone. Franklin Delano

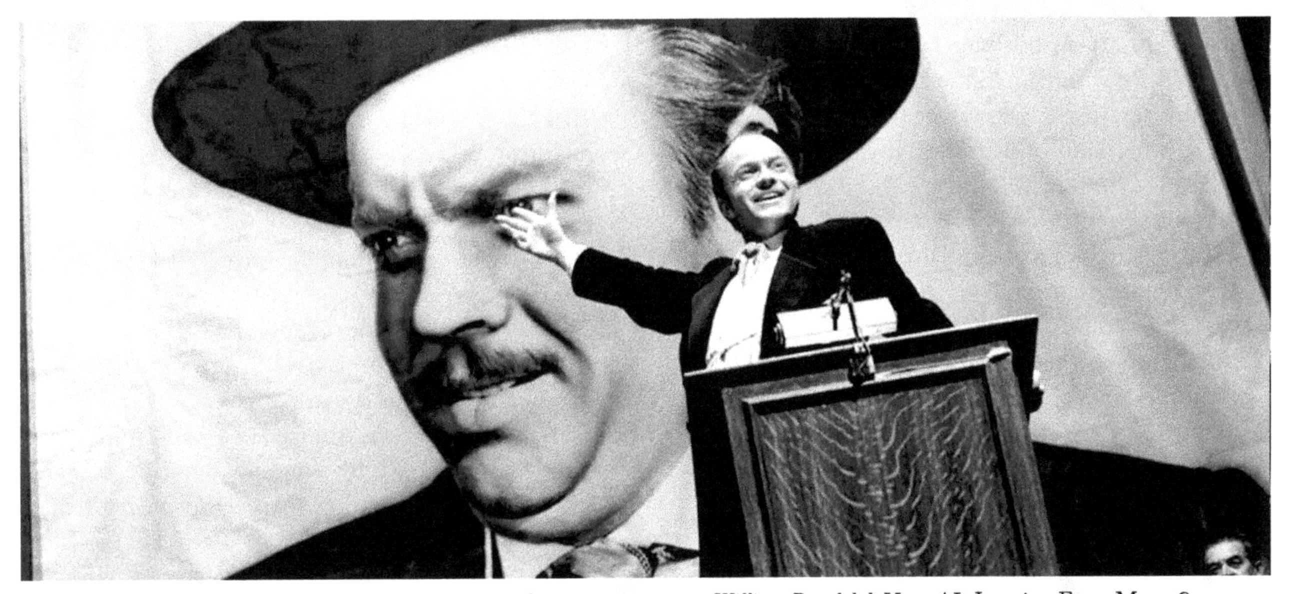

In Citizen Kane, *Charles Foster Kane was a caricature of newspaper magnate William Randolph Hearst! In* Invasion From Mars, *Orson would not cower behind such a satirical technique: William Randolph Hearst would be named William Randolph Hearst, Franklin Delano Roosevelt would be named Franklin Delano Roosevelt, and George Orson Welles would be named ... well... George Orson Welles!*

Roosevelt. William Randolph Hearst. Bill Paley. Davidson Taylor. The Captain. Everyone! I had made Charles Foster Kane an amalgam of four different people, including myself. But with *The War of the Worlds*, I wouldn't even bother to hide behind that technique. Hearst would be Hearst. Roosevelt would be Roosevelt. And Welles would be.. well, me.

PETER: I don't understand.

ORSON: You sound like a broken record. You see, George Schaefer and his successor, Charles Koerner, and the cabal of executives at RKO wanted a simple adaptation of the original radio-script by Howard Koch. But I didn't want to tell that story, particularly after Howard copyrighted the script himself. How arrogant can someone be? If it wasn't for my conspiracy, he wouldn't have ever had the idea for the radio-script. If it wasn't for me, he never would have sat down at the typewriter during the small hours of that cold Halloween earliest of mornings to write a radio-dramatization of HG Wells' *The War of the Words*. And he chose to copyright the script as if it was entirely his concept. It was entirely his *story*, but it was entirely my idea. I wouldn't give Howard the satisfaction of a screen-credit. Not that it would matter when I told the truth like a newsman at a Hearst rag.

PETER: That doesn't bode well for the truth, Orson.

ORSON: I would give RKO Howard's "War of the Worlds" script to mask my true intentions. What they thought I was filming would be completely different from what I was actually filming. And thanks to a visit by John Ford to my set during *Citizen Kane*, I had learned to spot RKO moles on my set. The higher-ups at RKO would never know what kind of film I was making until it was too late. The film would have to be released onto an unsuspecting audience and an unsuspecting government. I wanted to tell the story of a conspiracy from the highest levels of the government all the way down to little old me.

PETER: A conspiracy to cover-up what? A Martian invasion? You can't be serious.

ORSON: Yes, I am so-ever-loving serious. A Martian invasion. I conspired to cover-up the fact there really was an Invasion From Mars that night. *[Long moment of silence.]* People think that *Citizen Kane* ruined me, but it was really because I didn't know when to stop. I aired some very powerful people's very dirty laundry. Turning William Randolph Hearst into Charles Foster Kane was a drop in the ocean compared to what I tried to do with my *Invasion*. But FDR and Hearst had nothing to fear, of course not, no one would have believed my *Invasion From Mars* film anymore than they believed there was an actual Invasion From Mars that night. Fool me once shame on you, fool me twice shame on me. Fool me three times and they'll lock me away on a looney-farm. The people would not have believed my story, even if it was released into motion picture houses. That was the genius of it. However, not even FDR or Hearst would have taken a chance on the public learning any tidbit of truth about the whole affair. If *Citizen Kane* taught me one thing, it is that powerful people will do practically anything to hold onto their power. Anything. Everything. *Kane* was a drop in a proverbial ocean compared with what these powerful men did to stop me. *Kane* didn't exactly ruin my career. It prepared me for the battle I would fight over *Invasion From Mars*, a fight to the death, the death of my career. It was a "War of the Worlds" radio-drama that launched my career and it was *Invasion From Mars* feature that ended it so spectacularly.

PETER: Let me see if I've gotten some of this right. There was an "Invasion From Mars" that Mischief Night. Martians actually invaded American soil. The news broadcasts heard by millions of people were, in fact, real. And not Hans Von Kaltenborn as you tried to brilliantly prank me. You, actually, conspired to cover-up the truth of a Martian invasion by creating "The War of the Worlds" radio-dramatization from scratch at the behest of Hearst and the President. Then a year or so later, after the so-called *Citizen Kane* debacle, you filmed an historically accurate account of the real events of the Martian invasion, including a conspiracy from FDR through Hearst down to you. Is this right?

ORSON: Right on the money, my boy. Right on the money.

PETER: And the battle over *Invasion From Mars* became the battle over your career and the fights you would fight for the rest of your life.

ORSON: On the nose. After over a half-an-hour of long and quite windy winding passages, we are finally, just now, getting to the real meat of this conversation. I cannot believe we actually got to a point were we can actually begin talking. This is where it everything gets interesting.

PETER: I don't even know what I just said. ⚛

January 17, 1942

The Man At The End of (His) Time

Hedda Hopper's HOLLYWOOD

I had an interesting conversation with the young Orson Welles. He couldn't find nary a project at RKO that Charles Koerner would approve after the atrocious *Citizen Kane* ignominy. At twenty-seven years old, could Orson still be considered a "*wunderkind*"? There is another German word that is fitting for my emotional state while sitting at our table: "*schadenfreude*". Oh, such a glorious word that has no direct translation into English, which according to a German dictionary means "pleasure derived by someone from another person's misfortune". Oh, a truer word has never been coined!

Young Mister Orson attempted to entertain me with a few quaint magic-tricks to lighten my lingering darkened mood. I can't stand the boy. I'm not afraid to say that. I just can't stand the arrogance of the "genius".

Joseph Cotton (left) sneaks into an interview between Hedda Hopper and the "boy-genius", Orson Welles! Young Orson, though a bitter smile, has been long-windedly complaining he is being forced to film Invasion From Mars *in a vast conspiracy from Louis B. Mayer to Walt Disney!*

"I'm doing *The War of the Worlds* movie because they won't let me do anything else. That's the God's honest truth. I can't even avoid it by abandoning my contract at RKO and going elsewhere, anywhere else. Mayer, the Warners, even Disney all want *The War of the Worlds.* Any other movie other than *The War of the Worlds*! A musical? Yes, please. A 'screwball' comedy? Sure, I guess. A cartoon? That's exactly what Walt wants from me. Can you imagine the abomination of an animated *War of the Worlds*? Singing Martians? Dancing tri-pods? Dear, God!"

He paused to take a sip on his ice-water.

"Hedda, I'm even willing to go backwards in time to direct a silent film. The new car smell has definitely worn off on 'talkies'. Is there is a growing nostalgia for a modern silent film? I think so. But all anyone in power wants from me is *The War of the Worlds.* Sure, that damned radio-drama made my career. Gave me the keys to Hollywood. But here I am in the Ninth Circle of Hell directing this cursed science-fiction motion picture. I cannot escape this albatross that is tied around my neck."

Curious he used the Dante's Ninth Circle of Hell as a metaphor for the current state of his Hollywood career. Traitors to their Lords and benefactors are doomed to suffer for all Eternally in Judecca, a frozen lake in the Ninth Circle of Hell, which was named by Dante for Judas Iscariot. Judas is history's greatest traitor, who betrayed our Lord and Saviour. Orson is a traitor to William Randolph Hearst. While, the boy may never have considered Mr. Hearst to be his lord, he not only turned traitor, but he failed to observe fidelity to the great man. Hollywood only has one lord and his name isn't Mayer, Warner, or God-forbid Disney. His name is William Randolph Hearst!

But I can't say that I blame the brass at RKO for their decision to reign in the "boy wonder". Orson Welles lied to me when I asked him pointblank if *Citizen Kane* was based on Mr. Hearst. Orson Welles lied to the world when George Schaefer premiered that slanderous film. Orson Welles not only lied about a great man, he painted a characachure merely for comedic effect. Now, I was giving the young man an audience and a forum to promote his next project in my column.

Orson resumed saying, "Why is everyone in Hollywood obsessed with rehashing the past? Can't anyone look towards the future. That's what I tried to do with *Citizen Kane.* Nobody saw it, of course, because of a conspiracy against me and my film."

I bit my tongue when he had the audacity to say that. It was his conspiracy with Schaefer that tried to bring down a great man like Mr. Hearst. Orson continued with that haughty arrogance which is so common with him, "But *The War of the Worlds*, which I'm being forced to make, is going to change the business anyway. I'm going to make sure of it. It's going to blur the lines between entertainment and the documentary. Nobody is going to be able to tell fact from fiction. Hell, nobody is going to be able to look at a Hollywood picture in the same old light after I'm done with my *War of the Worlds.*"

Oh! This *War of the Worlds* picture is a project I hope doesn't see the light of day. If there is a God in Heaven, four out of five movies that this man makes will never see the light of day. Mark my words. Mark my words. Four out of five movies that this man makes will never see the light of day!

Now I'll give him the final words I'll ever record from him: "I hope to revolutionize the space opera made famous by the Flash Gordon serials and Buck Rogers comic strips. My movie will hopefully confuse and confound the viewing public, much like my "War of the Worlds" radio-dramatization, forever blurred the lines between science-fiction and science-fact."

The Invisible NewspaperMan

ORSON: After being less than thrilled with my *Heart of Darkness* screenplay which they said was overly long and not at all written in the Hollywood style and after the "success" I had working with Herman Mankiewicz on *Kane*, RKO assigned me a seventeen year-old whippersnapper of a writer who didn't have a single writing credit to his name. The young man, fresh out of some Colorado steel-mill town, with, get this, a name that means "town" in Spanish. How original is that? You name your town "Town"? But I digress. This young man had come to Hollywood with a gleam in his eye and an ache in his gut to write the great Hollywood epic. He was given a few rewrites on a few no-account B-list movies starring no-account B-list actors, like our previously sitting Governor Ronald Reagan. But by his own admission, not a single word he wrote ended up on the screen and therefore no screen credit.

William Francis Brown, my father, walking down Hollywood Blvd!

PETER: How did a seventeen year-old get writing assignments at RKO?

ORSON: Willie Brown had convinced... he had connived... he had bullshitted his way onto the RKO studio lot and into the writers' room. He claimed to be the protégé of his home-town hero, Damon Runyon. His tall tales about his relationship with Damon Runyon were quite... something. And that's coming from me! *[Laughs heartily.]* Willie maintained they maintained a long-standing game of correspondence horse-racing.

PETER: You mean correspondence chess.

ORSON: No, I mean correspondence...! horse-racing!

PETER: I don't know how that would even work. Correspondence chess makes sense given the letters will contain a move and the return correspondence makes the counter-move. Each player in turn keeps their own chessboard up to date. But correspondence horse-racing? How would that work?

ORSON: It's really a wonderful Runyonesque concept, it really is. Willie would Western Union his paper-route money to New York City with his betting lines encrypted in a code only he and Damon Runyon knew the cypher. Damon would venture into an illicit, underground, back-room, smoke-filled, dimly-lit gambling hall and place the bets, collecting any winnings, if any, and Western Union

Damon Runyon plays correspondence 'horse-racing' with Willie Brown!

them back to Willie Brown.

PETER: You don't think Damon Runyon would actually gamble away a young boy's paper route money, do you?

ORSON: No, I don't believe anything of the sort. I don't think Damon Runyon was a degenerate enough of a gambler to gamble away a young man's paper route money. I think Runyon never actually placed any bets, and would instead send money back, telling Willie he'd won. Sometimes Damon would say Willie lost, but keep the money on hand, only to return it, saying the next time he'd won. Willie would always be one step ahead of the "house" as it were due to Damon's generosity.

PETER: That's quite a story, a story worthy of Damon Runyon and... Orson Wells.

ORSON: Quite. *[Laughs heartily.]* Willie would eventually use the money he'd squirreled away from this correspondence craps to move to Hollywood.

PETER: That's quite a mentor/protégé relationship.

ORSON: I agree. Runyon had apparently taken the long-distance, pen-pal, mentor role rather seriously, critiquing Willie's many short stories. Willie didn't have any aspirations of being the next Earnest Hemmingway, he thought of himself more like a Robert E. Howard or HP Lovecraft or L. Ron Hubbard. Willie would reminisce on sending his stories off to Damon Runyon off looking like Greta Garbo, but they'd come back looking like Mary Kelley.

PETER: That's quite the simile.

ORSON: True. True. But any writer worth his salt wants his manuscripts bloodied with the red ink of true and honest editor. Willie was wise enough despite his youth to have come to that Zen of writing, the knowing that your editor only has your best interests at heart. Damon Runyon wanted Willie Brown's stories to be the best they could possibly be. He knew the Zen of editing by making the writing the best it could possibly be by blooding it. Only hacks think their first draft is their final draft. The true art and joy of writing is in the rewriting.

PETER: Preach, Orson, preach.

ORSON: Mank never reached the Nirvana of that Zen. He thought my bloodying the screenplay of *Citizen Kane* was an assault on and an insult to his talent, when it wasn't anything of the sort. Every time I cut out the fat out of an over bloated scene, his protestations that I was murdering his child made for many a bourbon-fueled row. I wasn't being merciless with my slashes, I was being merciful. Mank may have had a supreme gift for writing the spoken word, but alcohol had idled his mind and made him into a glorious hack. What writer couldn't see that I only had the best of intentions by savaging it with the quick slashes of my editor's pen? It's become cliché that the pen is mightier than the sword, but it's even truer that the editor's pen is a straight-razor intent on disemboweling a ordinary story in order to make it truly infamous!

PETER: That's a rather brilliant, if somewhat nauseating, turn of phrase, Orson.

ORSON: I have been wise enough to have come to this Zen. So had Damon Runyon. And a wet-behind-the ears writer from Colorado had at the age of seventeen entered the writer's Nirvana. Despite every single word he wrote ending up on the cutting room floor, he continued to be Zen and tend his creative garden, knowing one day his crops would come in. He had no doubt he would see his words spoken by the lips the greatest actors and actresses in Hollywood. But me, I hadn't yet reached his Nirvana yet, but I would. I most certainly would over the course of making my *Invasion From Mars* feature enter into purest of Hollywood Nirvana. But at the time, in my own arrogance, I thought assigning me this eager yet uncredited writer was not quite the show of good faith I was hoping from Charles Koerner. My first task for the seventeen-year-old, who dared to call himself a Hollywood screenwriter, was writing the *War of the Worlds* screenplay I would submit to RKO, while I worked on the real *Invasion*

From Mars screenplay. William Brown turned in a strikingly accurate interpretation of what the world believed to be Howard Koch's original "War of the Worlds" radio-script. William's script was so faithful to the radio-drama that it gave the studio brass everything they could possibly want from a *War of the Worlds* feature. I'm just sorry that his work would be in vain. Not a word he would write on that particular screenplay would find its way onto the screen. I had another story to tell.

PETER: Which was your continuing assertion that there was a Martian invasion that night. Seems far-fetched even for you.

ORSON: Aaaannnnndddd as the fates would have it, not a word that I would write on my *Invasion From Mars* screenplay would end up on the screen either. I just couldn't figure it out from the "Top-Secret: Eyes Only" documents. There were significant passages redacted. I didn't know if the Secretary of State was the bad guy or if it was the Vice-President. There were conflicting reports. Was Dwight D. Eisenhower with the President or was it General George Patton? I didn't know if

or if

Through five or six different drafts, I didn't know my ass from my elbow. I just couldn't get the damn story to work. And while I was working on my *Invasion From Mars* screenplay and with the studio pacified with their fake script, I put young William to tinkering with my *Heart of Darkness* concept. He came up with some really great ideas. Like moving the setting to some Far East country and casting me as a great hulking beast of a man. Much like I am now, Peter. The young man was a visionary. I'm glad Francis Ford Coppola is presently filming *Apocalypse Now* because I never was able to. Francis is certainly one of the remarkable new crop of film makers that is going to change this town like I was unable to. All the power to him.

PETER: Your ideas do sound similar, even if they are separated by decades.

ORSON: There are only so many ways one can approach a story, Peter. There are only a handful of truly original ideas in the world. I'd be truly amazed anyone actually has an original idea. You'd think the well would have run dry by now. But that was the thing about all of the scripts I assigned Willie Brown to write, on the books and off. They were truly original. Radically original. Willie Brown was also a world-class bullshitter. I never knew when a story came out of his mouth if it was true or not. Every story had the hint of truth, just exaggerated to a ridiculous degree. Over many a pint of beer in a pub down the road, he would spin these whoppers of tall tales about his youth and time abroad seeing the world.

PETER: Sounds like someone I know, Orson.

ORSON: I never believed any of his stories were true, but they were fascinating none the less. I felt an affinity for the boy because most people don't believe some of the stories I told of my youth.

PETER: I can relate, Orson.

ORSON: Mine were true; his were bullshit. But I enjoyed them all, because of the fact they were bullshit. That was the pleasure of working with the kid. He truly knew how to take fact and spin it into wondrous bullshit. It was after one of our late night conversations about a trip to Paris when he was twelve, a story filled with outlandish lies, that I knew I had to turn my screenplay over to him. If he could take a hint of truth and turn it into bullshit, then he could take the government's bullshit and

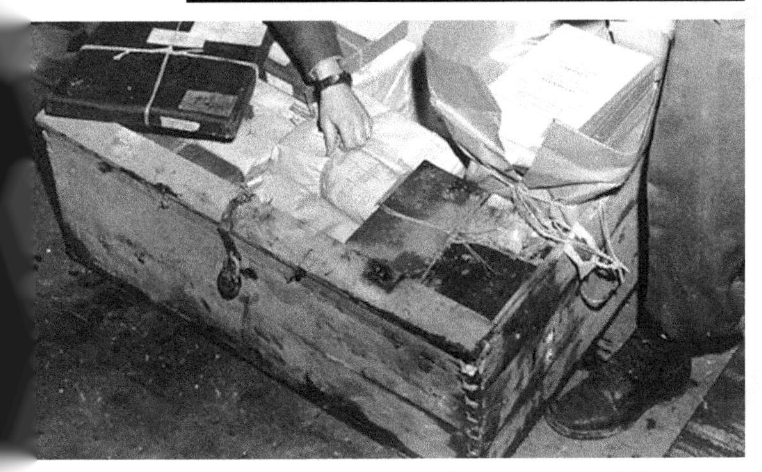

The tranche of German documents Gunter sent Orson Welles!

turn it into the truth. I gave him the documents, which I had kept a closely guarded secret and gave him a week to come up with the script. I didn't have much time, RKO already had a script they had approved and they wanted the first camera tests to happen any day now.

PETER: That must have put a lot of pressure on you and the young writer.

ORSON: Pressure I could handle. It was putting this particular screenplay into this young man's hands that worried me.

PETER: Because he was untested and you were unsure he could do the job?

ORSON: Of course not. I was unsure of myself, because I knew that nobody would release the final film. After what I was planned, just like Hedda Hopper said, I'd be lucky to have one of five of my films ever released into the motion picture houses. I knew *Invasion From Mars* would be stillborn. Never to see the light of day. And I was giving this young man hope. Hope that his words would end up on the screen. It's the hope of every writer out in middle America who yearns to come to Tinseltown and get his words up on the screen. It is the greatest dream that a writer with Tinseltown in his eyes has. It is what gets him up in the morning and what puts him to sleep at night. The dream that his words will be spoken by actors and actresses and heard in the motion picture houses and will actually move people to laughter or to tears. It is a great dream and a dream that as of yet, young Willie Brown had yet to have realized.

PETER: This is a terrible business we have chosen. To suffer rejection is commonplace and success is so rare and often fleeting.

ORSON: So poetic and so true. Willie came to Hollywood instead of entering the steel mill, like his father wanted him to do. He said that if it wasn't for *Invasion From Mars* he would have to return to his boyhood home and go to work in the accursed steel mill like his father wanted to and settle down with a family and live a normal American life. I felt a great pang in my heart, because I knew all the hard work he was putting into this screenplay would be for naught. That he would end up living a normal life back in Colorado. That he would probably he very happy with a nuclear family and his regular job and the bullshit yarns he would spin. But there would be this one regret, for that one dream he had would vanish like a fart in a whirlwind before his very eyes. All because of me. He was working his butt off for me and nothing would come of it. Just a train ticket back to the mountains of Colorado. This is what pained me most. I knew, beyond a shadow of doubt that Franklin Delano Roosevelt and William Randolph Hearst would never allow this movie to see the light of day and unlike with *Citizen Kane* the brass at RKO would eat the hundreds of thousands of dollars they would spend on this film. The first of the many films of mine that will never, ever see the light of day.

The steel mill my father would be destined to spend 40 years working in!

PETER: You knew in 1942 that your life's work would never be seen.

ORSON: I made a great first film. It was a film that I would never live up to, no matter how hard I tried. I have no doubt I made better films than *Kane* since then. *Invasion From Mars* was, in fact, the first of my films actually better than *Citizen Kane.* After all, this one didn't have the stink of alcohol that permeated *Kane.*

PETER: Is that an veiled attack on Herman Mankiewicz?

ORSON: It's not veiled in the slightest. He tried everything he could to take credit away from me for my work on *Kane.* But when the proverbial shit hit the proverbial fan, he did everything in his power to rest the blame squarely on my shoulders. All of a sudden, it was my idea to go after Hearst; it was my idea to be so vicious and cruel; it was my idea to put Hearst's pet name for his mistress' privates onto the lips of Charles Foster Kane. I hate Mank with a purple passion for his backstabbing. That is why *Invasion* is such a better film. It was written in a much happier mood by much happier people. The screenplay Willie turned in to me was brilliant. I didn't know where the truth began and where the fiction ended. Which was perfect. It was far, far more linear than Kane was, which is not my style at all, but that was okay with me. It even began with a newsreel, which I didn't care for particularly because Kane started with a newsreel. It would be expected of me to use fake newsreel footage again, so the newsreel wouldn't make it into the second draft. The murder of Guy Lombardo by Marion Davies was a complete shock to the system. It came as a complete surprise and I love surprises. I don't remember anything about a murder, but if it was a fanciful fabrication on William's part, it was genius. But sometimes, as any director knows, genius sometimes ends up on the cutting-room floor. Willie was trying to find a reason for Hearst to acquiesce to the President after a long-drawn out game of oneupsmanship and blackmail between the two powerful men, but then it occurred to me that Hearst would go along with the conspiracy just to ruin radio's reputation, so snip-snip onto the cutting room floor sent the scene. The time-travel plot, however, was pure unadulterated genius. It was born out of a *Deus ex machina* I couldn't figure a way out of. My script just ended with such an outlandish god coming from the machine, that I couldn't turn in that draft. It would have been *too* absurd. There needed to be a way out of the *Deus ex machina*. Anyway. But the time-travel invented by Willie allowed me my fondness for taking a script out of order, but because of the time-travel gimmick, the script could be technically linear, while being ridiculously loose with the order of events all because of time-travel. The entire script was genius. It was actually as close to a popular film as I would be capable of making.

PETER: But you so enjoy existing outside of mainstream Hollywood.

ORSON: That is more out of a necessity than a career choice. I would enjoy making a popular film, if the Hollywood brass would allow me to do it. To actually bring a film like that to completion without their grimy little fingers all over the negatives. *The War of the Worlds* was and still could be a sensation like *Star Wars* has proven to be. Who would have thought that a space-opera, a science-fiction film would take the archetypes of Joseph Campbell and spin them into popular entertainment for the masses. *Star Wars* was the success I had hoped for for my *War of the Worlds*. My problem was I was being forced to make this movie in 1942 with 1940's technology. If I had the opportunity to make this film now, having experienced the brilliance of young George Lucas; if the subjects of the conspiracy had been long dead for decades, with their influence and power long abated; if I hadn't been hamstrung by the Hollywood system my entire career, then perhaps my *Invasion From Mars* would have been, to use the modern phrase, a Hollywood blockbuster. But since my time at RKO and in Hollywood was coming to a close, I knew this was probably my last chance to make a popular film. So I set out that night trying to figure out how to make this movie now that I had a movie to make.

PETER: What was your first move? Finding a cinematographer like Gregg Toland, or even Toland himself? Or contracting Willis O'Brien for the model animation?

ORSON: The first thing I wanted was a cast of complete unknowns. I didn't want to use my *Mercury* actors and actresses because they were associated with me too prominently. Every actor in this movie couldn't have had a single screen credit, not even a b-list credit. I wanted theater people fresh off the turnip truck from part's unknown. There is a certain kind of talent that theater people have that Hollywood actors don't. Hollywood actors dread long takes. I adore long takes. If I could have filmed *Heart of Darkness*, it would have looked like one long take. But cameras only have so much film and you can't do a feather wipe every ten minutes. It looks like crap. Theater people on the other hand do entire performances in one long take. There is no yelling "cut" and starting over and over and over again. You just can't if there is an audience sitting in the theater with your. I wanted the camera to be the audience on this film, just observing the action like a theater audience would. If there was a mistake five minutes into the take and if the take wasn't completely blown, it was up to the actors to wing it. Fix it on the fly, like you have to do in live theater.

PETER: Like when after a long night of shooting *Citizen Kane*, Joseph Cotton was so exhausted that during a crucial moment misspoke, you just chuckled and let the scene play on. You ended up keeping it in the film.

ORSON: I never said, "Cut." That is the beauty of Hollywood. Unless the director says "Cut", everyone just keeps going– the actors, the camera, lights, sound, even craft services [*chuckles*], everyone just keeps going. That is when the magic of Hollywood actually mimics the magic of Broadway. You just fix it by keeping going. You find a way to move the story on. That is the magic I wanted to capture on my *Invasion.* The magic of theater that I so sorely missed. Even though I had fallen head-over-heels in love with film by this point in my life, I still had feelings for my lost love, the theater. I didn't want to go back theater, mind you. I was now married to film and didn't want an annulment. I would live the rest of my life in love with film. It may not have been my first love,

PETER: Theater was your first true love.

ORSON: Theater was my first mistress. Painting was my high-school sweetheart, if we're going to keep continuity with the metaphors. Film was the strongest, longest lasting love of my life. But, I digress. The magic of theater that is lost in film comes from the not knowing.

PETER: Not knowing what?

ORSON: The not knowing if your cue line is going to be there and if it isn't what in the blue Hell are you going to do? What if you're Lenny caught alone on stage playing the scene where you have to kill Curly's wife, but she misses her entrance because she is in her dressing room sneaking an extra goddamn cigarette, and you're forced to make shit up for five minutes. Can you imagine the horror? You look out into the audience and there the director and producer are white-knuckled, gripping the arm rests with a death-grip. There you are one stage all by yourself sitting on a bale of hay. You can't leave the stage because the action of the play cannot move forward until you kill Curly's wife and she isn't making her goddamn entrance! You have no idea she is sneaking an extra smoke, but you know that the scene must continue. You're bellowing, "I wish I had someone to talk to. I wish I had someone to talk to. Oh! Why don't I have someone to talk to." You are frantic hoping that the actor's offstage, the actor playing Candy, who is your best friend, will find Curly's wife and throw that bitch on stage. But you must continue with the play, so you begin at the beginning saying "George says, 'Lennie, for God's sake, don't drink so much. Lennie, you hear me! You gonna be sick like you was last night.'" And "George says, 'God damn it, we could just as well of rode clear to the ranch. That bus driver didn't know what he was talking about. "Just a little stretch down the highway," he says, "Just a little stretch"— damn near four miles.'" And "George tells me, 'You crazy fool! Thought you could get away with it, didn't you? Don't you think I could see your feer was wet where you went into the water to get it? Blubbering like a baby. Jesus Christ, a big guy like you! Aw, Lennie, I ain't takin' it away just for meanness. That mouse ain't fresh. Besides you broke it petting' it. You get a mouse that's fresh and I'll let you keep it a little while.'" You keep repeating George's lines until Candy finally finds the bitch and pushes her on stage. You actually wish you could go all Method and actually kill her on stage for leaving you floundering for five-*goddamn* minutes (the audience would never know, would they?). The thought crosses your mind that you might just get away with murder. This is the Hell and Heaven of theater. Or in *Midsummer Night's Night* what if, god-forbid, Titania is in the lady's room dying from an appendicitis. The show must go on with the actor playing Oberon playing *both* Oberon and Titania while paramedics are tending to Titania.

Lon Chaney Jr. and Burgess Meredith star in the 1939 production of John Steinbeck's Of Mice and Men*!*

PETER: It does, doesn't it?

ORSON: Theater people know this truth. It is this truth that drives them all. The not knowing. So if the actors auditioning for *Invasion* had theater experience out in Any Town, US: community theater experience, high-school, or even their church's Christmas pageant, they were hired. As a bonus, it kept the cost of the movie down.

And since I was convinced RKO would eat the entire budget, I wasn't malicious enough to wish bankruptcy on them. Even though they deserved to lose every penny for trying to take *Kane* away from me, for succeeding in recutting *Ambersons*, and successfully erasing from history my *Invasion From Mars* feature. Telling the truth, the whole truth, and nothing but the truth in a Hollywood feature was the most startling innovation of my entire career, but I fully intended on bucking all of the Hollywood's conventions because no one outside of a few executives at RKO and government officials would ever see the finished cut.

PETER: What other innovations did you have planned for *Invasion*? Like your use of sound or deep focus was in *Citizen Kane*?

ORSON: I knew that I wanted to use color for the first time. With *Heart of Darkness* I wanted the starkness that black and white gives you. With *Kane* I wanted a newsreel quality throughout the entire film. But with *Invasion* I wanted color. I love black and white. Even today, I prefer black and white over color. There is more you can do with shadows and mood in black and white that you just can't do in color. Color is too much like reality. You see things as they really are. That's not movie making. Movie making is taking something that's not real and making it look real. I know that doesn't make sense, but it's true. Theater uses color because it's real. I had dinner with Willie and his family, in Colorado, years later and one of his children remarked, as only children can, that he didn't think color was invented until *The Wizard of Oz*; that the colors of the sunset, the vivid paintings in the museums, and leaves turning in the autumn didn't get their color until after they invented Technicolor for *The Wizard of Oz*.

Conspiracy theory: was color invented with the release of The Wizard of Oz*? Were all the flora and fauna, the mountains, the sky, and great works of art "colorized" by scientists and artists in the years since? Yes!*

PETER: That's a remarkable kid.

ORSON: Truly remarkable. Color is such an important part of life. And life is theater. You can't take away the colors on the stage. You can try with various grays and bland make-up, but you can't truly erase color from the stage. But movies are more natural in black and white. More real. That's the real benefit of film.

PETER: What's a benefit of theater?

ORSON: Oh, the fact that the actors are really there with you in the theater. They aren't off making another movie while you sit in the cinema. The actors are there with you during the performance. That is the benefit of the magic of theater that the movie experience cannot possibly recreate. This is why black and white is so important. Theater can't be in black and white. It has to be in color. So film should be in black and white because it can. But I knew that color would be very important to *Invasion*.

PETER: Why was color so important if you don't think color is necessary in film.

ORSON: Because in this film it was. Red plants. Green fire. I was telling, what I believed to be a true story, and reality is in color. But the reality I needed to create with *Invasion From Mars* was not a natural reality. The events recounted by *Invasion* were anything but natural, so it needed to be an unnatural color, like Technicolor. Not a naturalistic color like today's films. With the three color process, the reds are redder and the greens greener and the blues bluer. Watch *Gone With the Wind* and you'll see that the colors are not entirely real. They are more colorful than nature. More real. In *Invasion*, the audience had to see the world in a vivid brightness that would shock them. Remember, color was still a relatively foreign element in film, especially in 1942. The cold October night in 1938 when the government tried to stay hidden in the black and white shadows of history, was a night that I would expose to the entire world in the brilliant light of Technicolor. They were all very important ideas. To be working with a color pallet for the first and hopefully last time, was quite a thrill. I had to make color as important to *Invasion* as, like you said, sound was for *Kane*. ❀

October 31, 1995

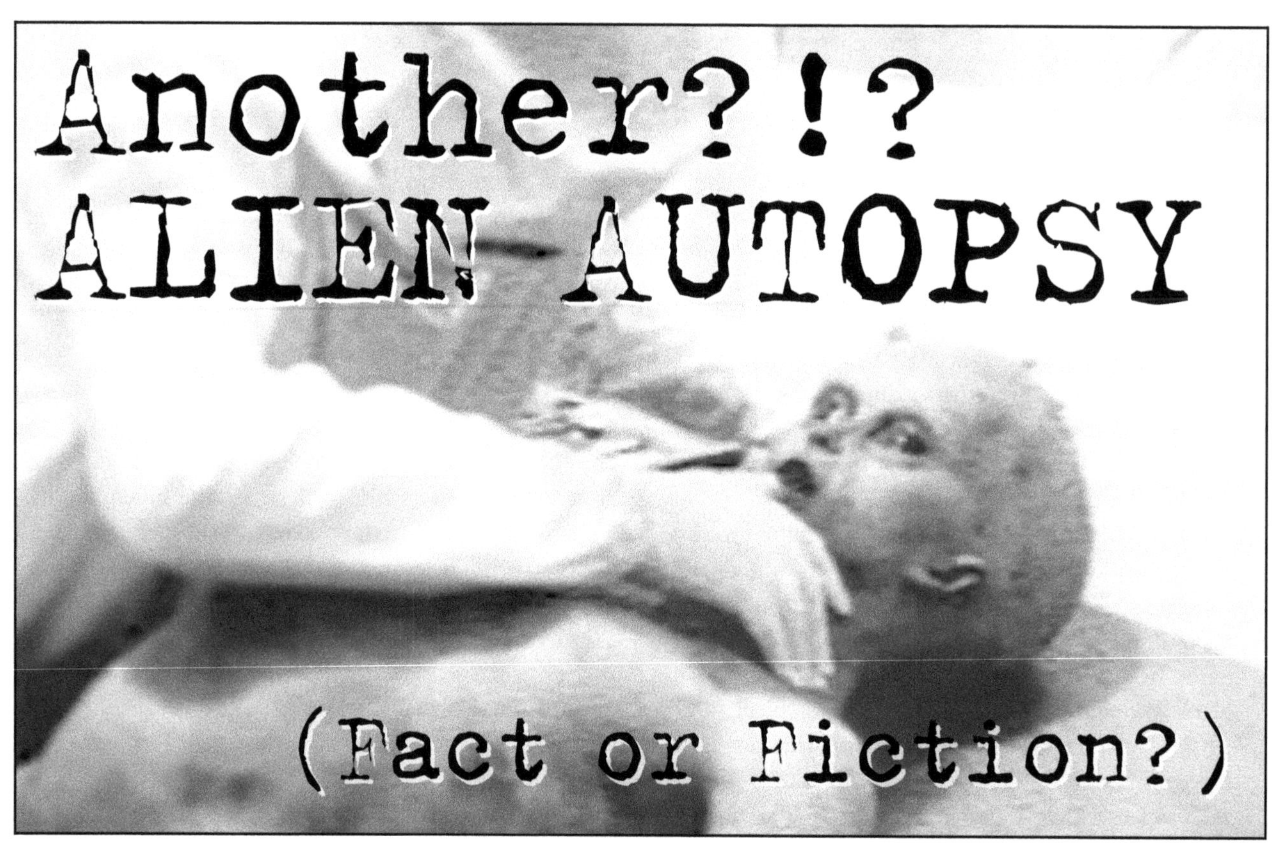

This is an "alien", but it is not a Martian-alien.

Yesterevening, an alien autopsy video was broadcast, uncensored, on television. No, not that alien autopsy video! Another alien autopsy video! Another alien autopsy video?

Yes, quite.

But the first televised alien autopsy bore a resemblance to the little Grey aliens made famous by Steven Spielberg's *Close Encounters of the Third Kind* or Whitley Streiber's *Communion* book series. Oh, no. This *new* footage was instantly discredited by *both* the mainstream media *and* those within the conspiracy community, despite, or in spite of, the fact our footage predated FOX's by nine years! Not from 1947, but 1938!

Supposedly.

Since the newspaper isn't the best medium for distributing video, unlike television or the nascent Internet, I'm forced by this limitation to describe the alien autopsy footage in words:

The room is slightly out of focus. Then it comes into focus. The room is being recorded on a black and white military camera.

The morgue, in an unidentified county, in an unidentified state, is stark in its whiteness. There is a stainless steel table in the center of the room with what appears to be a dead Martian body laying on it. I don't know why I say Martian. The little gray men are certainly not from Mars but according to experts and conspiracy theorists hail from the Zeta Reticuli star system. Is it because the "Martian" strangely and like the

Martians described in HG Wells' seminal sci-fiction classic, *The War of the Worlds*? Damn, that man was a freaking genius!

Near the table, on a wheeled tray are a number of ghastly looking implements used during an autopsy. Near the door is a clock that reads 1:18 in the small hours of the morning.

In the room is the coroner, dressed impeccably in white. In one corner of the room standing out of the way is a military officer, a young man dressed in a white-dress shirt and black tie, and an academic man wearing a plaid suit. These three stay out of focus for length of the autopsy.

A military officer of unknown rank says, "Doctor, make no haste in performing this autopsy. I must remind you that your first priority is to determine the cause of death."

The coroner says, "This is a remarkable find. In all of human history, this is the first scientific examination of an extraterrestrial corpse. I should like to take my time to preform a proper autopsy."

The Military Officer says, "You'll have plenty of time to make a complete examination on the dozens of other Martian dead. But the Army needs to know what killed these... things, so we can prepare appropriate counter measures."

The coroner moves over to the left side of the slab. He pulls the tray over to his left.

He turns and looks at the camera.

The coroner says, "I will be utilizing this military camera for documentation of this autopsy for use by the District of Columbia's Coroner's Office and the United States government and it's military. I will begin the autopsy with a report of my initial external examination. Due to it's apparent alien origin, it is impossible to determine it's age or sex, despite or because of its lack of sexual organs. It's height is 86 inches, at seven feet two inches. Body weighs approximately 625 lbs. It is in actuality heavier than it appears, as if the creature is unaccustomed to Earth's greater gravity. The body has been previously washed. There are no apparent external injuries present."

The coroner, having examined hundreds, if not thousands, of human bodies in his career takes to the autopsy with some vigor. He handles the body without fear of losing precious scientific knowledge. He handles, cuts, and moves parts of the body freely.

He reports on the external and very alien appearance of the body.

The coroner says, "The body is of an alien origin. The creature's skin appears to be a dark green; wet and leathery in appearance. There are three arms, two extending from its apparent shoulders and one, slightly smaller arm, protruding from its chest. The arms from the shoulder to the elbow are very flexible, like the tentacle of an octopus. At the elbow, the arm branches into three separate tentacles and at what appears to be the wrist, each of the three tentacles branch into three smaller tentacles which may function as fingers. Whether these tentacles are invertebrate or vertebrate, we must await further internal examination. They don't feel at all rubbery, but very solid; perhaps suggesting a skeletal and musculature similar to man's. The legs appears to be similarly constructed as the arms, except they are stockier in construction with flaps of skin holding the tentacles together forming a tripodal means of locomotion."

He examines the head.

The coroner says, "There appears to be Three eyes, continuing the tripodal nature of his evolution. The solid black eyes are oval shaped and wrap around the head to the back of the cranium, giving the alien 360 degrees of vision."

He peals back the black membrane covering the eyes.

The coroner says, "There appears to be a black membrane covering the eyes. No apparent iris or cornea present. There are no external ears or internal ear canals."

He moves his attention to the mouth.

The coroner says, "The mouth is rimless with a V-shaped upper lip. Lifting the upper lip there are a dozen very sharp canine-like teeth along with several plate-like teeth near the back of the jaw. There appears to be a thick green substance, perhaps saliva."

He collects a sample of saliva in a dish.

He motions for the camera to move with him.

The coroner says, "Moving for a coronal mastoid incision across the head."

He cuts into the flesh with a scalpel and then pulls back the scalp exposing the cranium. He examines the interior of the scalp for any evidence of trauma.

The coroner says, "There is no evidence of trauma to the cranium."

He grabs a bone saw and removes the skull from around the brain, exposing it. He removes the brain, walks over to the scale, and weighs it.

The coroner says, "Brain weights approximately 600% more than the human brain despite being of three times the size of a human brain. Removing a slice of brain for further examination."

The coroner places the brain sample in a small dish.

The coroner moves back to the alien and begins a deep incision in the chest.

The coroner says, "Moving onto the *thoracoabdominal* incision.

The film abruptly ends...

Of course it freaking does.

CONSPIRACY! FROM 20,000 LEAGUES

ORSON: To say that my *Invasion From Mars* strained my relationship with Franklin Delano Roosevelt would be an understatement. To Hearst, this was just par for the course; nothing more, nothing less was expected of me. But that was such a long way off, considering that I had to get the screenplay Willie wrote into the hands of actors, the actors before the cameras, the cameras capturing images onto film, and the film edited into the final motion-picture. There were so many obstacles in my way to that ultimate goal of an *Invasion From Mars* feature film actually being filmed, while creating the illusion that I was actually filming a *War of the Worlds* feature.

PETER: *Invasion From Mars*? *The War of the Worlds*? Which is which?

ORSON: I had learned from John Ford how to spot spies on my set, so that was one weapon in my armory. But I don't believe in conspiracies. All of these conspiracy theorists who believe that President Kennedy was assassinated in a plot orchestrated between J. Edgar Hoover, Lyndon Banes Johnson, and Fidel Castro are cuckoo-birds. To keep a conspiracy going requires, not only a lot of disinformation, but the trust and confidence of dozens, if not hundreds of people, to keep the secret. Gossiping hens in a suburban cul-de-sac know intimately how difficult it is to keep a secret actually secret. It would have taken only one member of my crew to go crying to mommy, I mean, Charles Koerner and the entire *War of the Worlds* conspiracy would unravel like pulling a loose string on a sweater. How plausible is it that a vast conspiracy to murder a sitting US President involving the director of the FBI, the Vice-President, and the Communist leader of Cuba could escape someone having a crisis of conscience and spilling the beans? How plausible is it that nobody on their deathbed would confess to their priest or an eagle-eyed news reporter the sins that they committed as part of a vast government conspiracy? That is the problem I have with conspiracy theories and the raving loons who spout them as the truth. I intimately know the

Only the sanest of conspiracy realists believe that Lee Harvey Oswald acts as a "lone-gunman" in his assignation of President Kennedy!

John Ford, Oscar-winning film director, mentored a young Orson Welles as it concerns spies put on Kane's *set by RKO's George Schaefer!*

loyalty that is required to effectively perpetrate a hoax.

PETER: Like the "War of the Worlds" radio-dramatization?

ORSON: Oh, we're back here are we? Round and round on a carousel with that damned endless calliope music ringing in our ears as it spins faster and faster, and never are we able to get off. Since we're on this ride, I have to relate the story.

PETER: The story of what?

ORSON: The behind the scenes of the night we recorded the "War of the Worlds" radio-dramatization.

PETER: I was hoping we would get to that, but I wasn't sure how to redirect the conversation once we got on the feature film tangent.

ORSON: Peter, you don't have to be the shy boy at the Prom standing with his back against the wall of the gymnasium trying to get up the nerve to ask the pretty and popular girl to dance. You are the interviewer and I am the subject of the interview. Ask all of the questions you want.

PETER: How integral was Howard Koch to the process of creating the script. I remember reading in his book [*The Panic Broadcast*] that you were asking him to create an original invasion story from scratch. That he only had a week to write an original invasion from Mars.

ORSON: That is total horse-hockey.

PETER: He didn't have a week? He had longer? Much longer?

ORSON: He only had a few short hours write an original invasion from Mars. Those that have idolized my radio-drama, listening to a vinyl record of the recording every October 30th, believe that we changed "Langley Field" to "Langham Field", "New Jersey National Guard" to "State Militia", and "Waldorf Astoria" to "Park Plaza Hotel". But this is wishful thinking. We actually changed every detail, no matter how small. The only change we made that could be related to simple transposition of letters was converting "Grove Hill", Virginia, to "Grover's Mill", New Jersey. Everything else from that confounded teletype could not be used in the slightest. In the "War of the Worlds" radio-dramatization, the Martians had to land in New Jersey and attack New York City, instead of actually landing in Virginia and nearly incinerating the White House.

PETER: Was this because Standards and Practices thought that an attack on the White House would be to dramatic and frighten too many listeners with the death of their President?

ORSON: It wasn't Standards and Practices holding the censorship axe over my neck, it was the OSS

PETER: Why would the precursor of the CIA have any interest in a simple radio-dramatization?

ORSON: Because it was well within their job description, being the Office of Strategic Services and all. I don't think they were called the OSS that night, but that is who they were in essence, just under a different name, which even my eidetic memory is at a loss to remember after forty-years. They may not have had guns trained on the back of our heads, but it sure felt like it.

PETER: All because you broadcast "The War of the Worlds" as part of your weekly *Mercury Theater on the air* and caused such wide-spread panic? That seems to be an overreaction.

ORSON: Considering what actually happened that night, this was an underreaction. They were surprisingly calm considering the events the teletype so perfectly recorded of that night's broadcast. You cannot believe how Howard begged me... nay, pleaded with me to let him see the teletypes of that evening's reporting by Hans Van Kaltenborn and Edward R. Murrow that were broadcast across the network of the Columbia Broadcast System. Howard wanted to know what actually happened that evening so he could have some basis to create the completely original invasion story.

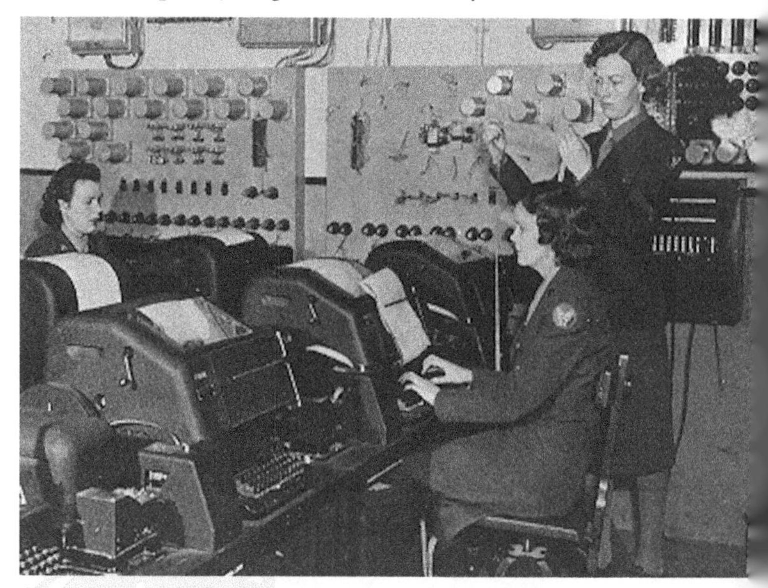

The teletypists at CBS studios producing a transcript of the very real news-broadcasts that panicked America on October 30, 1938!

PETER: Being able to use nothing from HG Wells because your radio-drama need to be set in America is completely understandable.

ORSON: Sometimes it seems like we're having

completely different conversations. That is an error on my part, because I haven't been clear enough. I am not able to be as communicative because I have sealed these memories in the most secure and impenetrable memory vaults in my brain. Having an eidetic memory paints my recollections with the beauty and splendor of a motion picture. But these are memories I have striven to leave on the editing room floor of my memory, so I don't remember them as clearly as I should. I will need to communicate with you better.

PETER: You are as talkative as you've ever been, Orson.

ORSON: But I shouldn't be. I swore an oath before God and the President of the United States that I would keep the secrets that I left burning in a mental metal waste-paper basket. Secrets held by that lone teletype. Howard wanted that teletype because he wanted he wanted to plagiarize it, but I couldn't let that teletype out of my hands. If even a single word of that teletype made it into Howard's "War of the Worlds", then someone somewhere would realize that there was an invasion from Mars that night and that it wasn't a simple radio-dramatization of HG Wells' *The War of the Worlds*. That teletype was a baneful temptation to show to the press. If I had done just that, the world would be such a different place. But just before going out to meet with the press that cold Halloween morning, I burnt the teletype in a waste-paper basket. I am getting ahead of myself, but I must admit it was cathartic.

PETER: There is little doubt that your meeting with the press to explain your actions by broadcasting your "War of the Worlds" program had to be cathartic.

ORSON: No, burning the only evidence of what actually happened the previous evening was cathartic. Once that evidence was gone, the only "evidence" was the wax-recording of the "War of the Worlds" radio-script Howard so brilliantly pulled out of his backside; the wax-recording the *Mercury Theater on the air*, so brilliantly performed in the cold, lonely hours just before the dawn. This is why the conspiracy worked. I had the loyalty of my actors. They had been with me as the *Mercury Theater*, then followed me onto the air with the *Mercury Theater on the air,* then many of them journeyed across the breadth of the nation to the opposite coast to make *Citizen Kane*. The *Mercury Theater* were the faithful Mormons, I was their prophet, not unlike Brigham Young, and Hollywood was our promised land. My conspirators were faithful lemmings following their leader over the cliffs and into the sea. They were willing to do anything and everything I asked of them. I asked them to never, ever talk about even with their most trusted confidantes. This is why the conspiracy to cover-up a Martian invasion was so successful.

PETER: Not this Martian invasion nonsense, Orson. I know you are trying to prank me with this story, but it is getting a little long in the tooth. You cannot expect me to believe that Martians actually invaded America, attacked and murdered hundreds of Americans, and you, Orson Welles, conspired with the government to cover-up the truth. It is a great story. It is a great prank. It is the ultimate prank to pull on your close and dear friend on the fortieth anniversary of your most famous prank on the nation, but I'd rather we stick with the facts of that night. How did "The War of the Worlds" radio-broadcast come about that evening? This is the story that I want to hear. I want to hear you how you told Kenny Delmar to sound like Franklin Delano Roosevelt when Standards and Practices said it couldn't be the President in the script. You had to have known that even though the character was announced as the "Secretary of the Interior", the people would hear the voice of the President and believe there was an actual invasion from Mars going on. I want to learn more about how simply changing"Langley Field" to "Langham Field", "New Jersey National Guard" to "State Militia", and the "Waldorf Astoria" to the "Park Plaza Hotel" convinced the radio-listeners that what you were relating in your "War of the Worlds" radio-dramatization were real newsbroadcasts. These are the stories I'd like to hear. Not this invasion from Mars nonsense.

ORSON: Then you might as well turn off your little reel-to-reel recorder and call this a "good-night". You can think what you will of our conversation. You may think this is a prank upon you, and you have no reason to believe otherwise, but I want to tell my story the way I want to tell it. I want that tape that is spinning around and around etching this conversation in its strange analog hieroglyphics onto the magnetic-tape. If I could stand before the press and take credit for an invasion I had nothing to do with, then you can be my friend and allow me to spin the most wondrous bullshit tonight. Why don't you come down the rabbit-hole with me, Peter? Let's see Wonderland.

PETER: [*Hesitates*] I'll buy into this, Orson, just to see how far you are willing to go for a prank.

ORSON: [*Correcting*] How far I am willing to, for once in my life, to tell the honest-to-God truth.

PETER: Shoot your pigeon full of bullshit buckshot, Orson Welles. Shoot away.

ORSON: Finally! We've accomplished something this evening. Sort of like I tried to accomplish that cold October evening forty-years ago.

PETER: Down the rabbit-hole we go...

ORSON: [*Obviously grinning like the Cheshire Cat*] The first thing I had to figure out was how was I supposed to keep secrets from the very people who could not be entrusted with the secrets found on the teletype. How does one go about pulling the wool over the eyes of the very cast who I was expected to conspire to hide the truth of an invasion from Mars? My cast was well aware we did not broadcast a "War of the Worlds" radio-drama during our regularly scheduled time-slot. They knew *The Mercury Theater on the air* was preempted by an evening of dance music. They knew we were rehearsing *Danton's Death* in the CBS studio to save on taxi fees. What they didn't know was there was an invasion from Mars that night. How do I get them to write, rehearse, and record a radio-dramatization of "HG Wells' *War of the Worlds*" in the middle of the night with nary of explanation of the whys and the wherefores?

PETER: And how did you accomplish this magnanimous feat?

ORSON: I knew what I wanted and needed to get out of this. It didn't have to be perfect, it just had to be plausible. Once Howard had a semblance of a story, my cast knew that I wanted to record a "War of the Worlds" radio-drama. They bought my line about striking while the iron was hot; they believed that I was inspired by Archibald MacLeish's "Air Raid" radio-drama. You, see I was cast in said radio-drama just eleven days earlier along with Ray Collins amongst others. Why I would want to create an invasion from Mars using news interruptions of an evening of dance music, so shortly after the hyper-realistic "Air Raid", well, they dismissed me as a plagiarist. But why I didn't want to wait until the next Friday to broadcast this live on the air, instead of merely recording my radio-drama in the middle of the night left them mightily confused.

PETER: They were willing lemmings running over a cliff, all because you wanted to record a "War of the Worlds" radio-drama in the middle of the night?

ORSON: I was their Svengali. They would do everything that I asked of them, no matter how absurd it was. The more absurd the project was, the more willing they were to follow my lead. They would work all night, without sleep, without cigarettes, without many of the necessities of life, all so I could create the art they knew their Svengali wanted created. This is the power I wielded during *Voodoo MacBeth*, during our run on CBS, and on the set of *Citizen Kane*. My cast on *Kane* was well aware we were mercilessly lampooning William Randolph Hearst. They knew the kind of man Hearst was and the influence he held in Hollywood. They knew there would be consequences for my career– their careers– in Hollywood, but still they helped me produce *Citizen Kane* of their own free-will.

Orson Welles (left), Archibald MacLeish and William Robson performing the radio drama "Air Raid" on October 19, 1938!

PETER: So the *Mercury Theater on the air* was willing to go along with the madness of recording a radio-drama of HG Well's *The War of the Worlds* in the middle of the night, instead of waiting to broadcast it live?

ORSON: Correct. They bought my improvised line that Standards and Practices needed the time to review such an idea so it could not cause the wide spread panic that I knew it would. I told my cast, the S and P weren't willing to accept a script for their review, because they were incapable of imagining the realism of such a script. Their little minds needed to experience the story as it would be broadcast, with a cast and crew performing "The War of the Worlds". I told them to be rest assured that the wax-recording would pacify Standards and Practices and we would be able to broadcast this story at a certain point in the future, but I needed that wax recording as part of my "master plan".

PETER: And they acquiesced?

ORSON: Most certainly. A Svengali has quite a mysterious hold over his actors and singers. In the studio that Halloween Eve, Frank Readick would channel Herbert Morrison describing the Hindenburg disaster live on the air, in the person of "Carl Phillips". And like you said earlier, I told Kenny Delmar to mimic Franklin Roosevelt. But here is the thing, Howard's script was only a half-and-hour's worth of invasion. It was incredibly difficult to get the teletype out of my head and instruct Howard how to write an original invasion before the press beat our doors down looking for proof in the form of a wax-recording. That damned teletype just continued to echo in my brain like a song you just cannot get unstuck from your mind, so I was of little help to poor Howard when it concerned where to go with the Martian invasion. And there we were with only a half-an-hour of a "War of the Worlds". What we recorded was good. My sound people were able to whip the most perfect sounds effects. My cast was able to make it sound so real. We played what we recorded for Hearst and it sent shivers up my spine, because it was just so effective. But we were stuck. I needed an hour to fill and I didn't have it. I couldn't figure out how to pad the story without resorting to mindless filler and fluff. Then Howard popped his head up from where he had been sleeping in the corner and said why didn't we just get away from news broadcasts gimmick and tell the story of a survivor relating the story from the future. Sure it wasn't exactly an entire evening of news broadcasts, but that was the point wasn't it? So the recorders were turned on and Carl Frank and I used our estimable skills to improvise the rest of the script. We just turned on the recorders and winged it. A half-and-hour of pure, unadulterated, improvisational bullshit. And there you have it, "The War of the Worlds".

PETER: That's nice and all Orson. But before we plunge further down the rabbit hole, why didn't your cast expose the conspiracy that next morning when you went before the reporters. They would have discovered when they got back to their apartments that morning with the *New York Times* sitting before their door. They would know that the nation believed there was a broadcast of "The War of the Worlds", they would know they were not broadcasting live on the air that night. They would have put two-and-two together and realized there had to have been a "actual" invasion from Mars last night. They would have realized that they were part of a government conspiracy to cover up the truth. Why wouldn't they just expose you?

ORSON: [*Dramatically*] Svengali!

PETER: *Deus ex machina*!

ORSON: That's cruel.

PETER: That's the truth! Okay, I can understand some of your cast being loyal to you, seeing that they followed you all the way to Hollywood. But there was no love lost between you and Howard Koch. Why didn't Howard just expose all of this in his book [*The Panic Broadcast*] when he had the chance. Instead, he just continued to tow the party-line like as it was true?

ORSON: You have to understand the government had been looking over our shoulders for years. Even after the move to Hollywood, we, and I mean myself, Kenny Delmar, Ray Collins, and many, many others would come home to find our apartments ransacked. Even Howard Koch, who remained all the way back in New York, suffered these ransack attacks. Those that recorded that evening's events in their dairies discovered them to have had their pages ripped out. The intruders left Howard's early drafts of *The Panic Broadcast* still burning in waste-paper baskets, so they would be found by him when he came home. It's a wonder they didn't burn his house down. In order for his book to be published, Howard would suffer the ignominy of relating the cover-story of the conspiracy we all so masterful weaved that infamous cold, windy October evening. That is why Willie Brown and I were so secretive. We weren't just hiding our screenplay from the brass at RKO, we were hiding them from, not only, the OSS, but the White House itself. Nobody could know what we where doing or why. We thought we were safe at a distance of over twenty-five thousand miles, in that temperate paradise constructed by the Griffiths, Zukors, Mayers, Selznicks, Cohns, and Warners: Hollywoodland. We thought that the government couldn't care less about a science-fiction satire that RKO was funding. How could the so-called intelligence officers of the OSS, the precursor to the CIA care about a film that was, as far as everyone was concerned, was nothing more than an adaptation of

the "War of the Worlds" radio-drama script written by Howard Koch and broadcast on CBS (that is an awful lot of abbreviations). We thought they would be pacified by our continuing to assert the entire invasion from Mars that panicked America was nothing more than a radio-dramatization. We had little fear of reprisal from the governments stooges. The assassination of JFK wouldn't happen for another twenty-years, so we didn't have any concept of such rampant paranoia. We thought that only those Americans who were Communists or Nazis felt fear from their government. How could a film director and his screenwriter have conceived of the lengths the government's agents would go to keep their secret secret? Sure we both had a writer's wild imagination, but nothing we thought would happen happened. And nothing we found wouldn't happen actually hadn't happened. It is what we didn't even think of that was so mercilessly thrown at us. I thought what William Randolph Hearst did to stop my *Citizen Kane* was the ultimate affront to decency, but he only threw over-paid lawyers and two bitter, aging gossip columnists at me. I don't remember DeMille or Ford having these kind of hindrances piled in front of them.

PETER: You were given *carte blanch* to make any movie you wanted with complete authority over script and edit. You were given powers that even DeMille and Ford never acquired and they had made millions for Hollywood. You made millions panic because of a radio-drama and they gave you the keys to the city and crown to the kingdom. You had to have known that William Randolph Hearst would do everything within his power, and he wielded a ton of it, all to destroy you. You had to sleep in the bed you made.

ORSON: But I didn't have to like it; accept it yes, like it no. If fact I loathed the position I put myself in. If I would have done the "life of Christ", maybe I'd have been hailed for producing another Biblical epic in a long line of Hollywood epics. I wish I would have had the courage of my convictions and write my "life of Christ" epic in Shakespearean verse.

PETER: Shakespearean verse?

ORSON: If Archibald MacLeish could go on the radio the same week as my so-called "War of the Worlds" radio-dramatization with his verse-play, then why couldn't I write the *Gospel According To Shakespeare*? I would have had my Biblical Hollywood epic written in classical Jacobean English, *iambic pentameter*, and rhyming couplets.

PETER: You actually considered writing your "life of Christ" in Shakespearean verse?

ORSON: What's in a name? That which we call Shakespeare- by any other name would smell just as sweet? I think Oxford wrote Shakespeare. If you don't agree, there are some awfully funny coincidences to explain away... I'm not alone in my feelings. Freud was adamant about it. Olivier and Gielgud, arguably the greatest Shakespearian actors of my generation, believed as I do. Mark Twain, for criminy sakes wrote a book about it! Emerson? Whitman! How could you possibly not?

PETER: Your argument is that Edward de Vere took the *nom-de-plum* William Shakespeare and presented plays as such? Why? Is it because as a member of the aristocracy, an Earl of Oxford couldn't been seen writing something as common as plays?

Edward de Vere, 17th Earl of Oxford, was the author of Hamlet, Romeo & Juliet, MacBeth, King Lear, Richard III, and Othello!

ORSON: *Nom-de-plum*? Heavens, no. I'm not suggesting anything of the sort. Not a "pen-name". Mercy. Not even a pseudonym. An allonym. This is a completely different literary creature all together. A wicked little fraud and deceit utilized by many of the greatest philosophers, wordsmiths, statesmen, and, yes, apostles. This is what allonymous is all about.

PETER: I'm not quite sure I know what "allonymous" is?

ORSON: An orthonym is writing under your given name. A homonym is sharing your own legal given name with another much more famous author. A pseudonym is writing under a fictional name not your own and anonymous is writing under no name. Allonymous writing is writing under an actual historical person's name.

PETER: Why would anyone want to publish under someone else's name? Isn't that akin to plagiarism?

ORSON: Heavens, no. It's the exact opposite of plagiarism. Plagiarism is taking someone else's words and claiming they are your own. Allonymous is taking *your* words and claiming they are *someone else's* words. They can't be any more different.

PETER: Then it's more akin to forgery.

ORSON: Forgery? Again, you can't be more wrong. Forgery is taking, say, the Mona Lisa and painting another Mona Lisa and passing yours off as the original Mona Lisa. Allonymous is painting something new and exciting and saying, "Look! This could be an entirely new Leonardo DaVinci. Prove me wrong."

PETER: Then in my opinion, it's worse than plagiarism and forgery.

ORSON: Oh, ye of little faith! It is grand and glorious. And it is far more common than one would think. After Plato's death, his students continued writing philosophical tracts in his name. No one in their time or for hundreds, nay, thousands of years, thought this was in any way deceitful. They were carrying on Plato's own tradition by continuing his thought... in his name. This is writing allonymously. Alexander Hamilton, one of the founding fathers of our country, wrote with a couple of compatriots, the *Federalist Papers* under the name of the Roman official Publius. This gave the *Papers* and, ultimately the young nation, an air of historicity it desperately needed. Are these great men frauds and their words fraudulent?

PETER: I'm not quite sure, given your argument.

ORSON: Was William-Henry Ireland a forger for publishing *Vortigern and Rowena* and *William the Conqueror* as authentic Shakespeare? If Shakespeare didn't actually write Shakespeare, how can we fault Ireland for writing "Shakespeare"? There were many plays written during Shakespeare's own lifetime that people of his day thought were actually written by Shakespeare. There was no doubt whatsoever in the minds of audiences and critics that these suspect plays were written by William Shakespeare. These plays are now considered "apocryphal" because scholars say they may not have been actually written by the pen of William Shakespeare of Stratford-upon-Avon. Ironically, there is some scholarly movement lately concerning *Two Noble Kinsmen* and *Edward III*, which says that these two once apocryphal plays are actually part of the legitimate Shakespearean canon. Hilarious. Who is to say, who wrote what? Scholars? Bah. Did Moses write the Torah or was it some Hebrew priest hundreds of years after the fact? Did Matthew write Gospel of Matthew? Or Luke Luke? Many scholars… hmmph… think a disciple of Paul actually wrote at least one of the letters attributed to Paul. Is the Word of God any less the word of God because of the writer? Is Shakespeare any less Shakespearean if written by Edward de Vere? The words are the words are the words.

William-Henry Ireland forged hundreds of documents and passed them off as William Shakespeare originals!

PETER: I can see your point.

ORSON: The point is, I don't even know the point I was trying to make. Some people have a stick up their butt about authenticity. Is Hamlet any less magnificent if written by the Earl? Or a woman as some others suppose. Scholars claim that if Shakespeare didn't write Shakespeare then all is for naught. The plays are brilliant no matter their authorship. Shakespeare or de Vere? Apocryphal or canon? It does not matter. I have a little story to tell.

PETER: Do tell.

ORSON: An old world antique bookstore owner came to me, of all people, to look at a copy of an early 17th Century quarto a collector claimed was play called *The Gospel According To Shakespeare* by William Shakespeare. Now, this wasn't the title of the play itself. The play was called *The Divine Tragedy of Jesus the Christ*, but the play was subtitled by the publisher of the quarto, *The Gospel According to Shakespeare*. To my untrained eye, it was authentic.

PETER: Why would an old world antique bookstore owner come to you of all people for authentication?

ORSON: Maybe it was my reputation because of my work with the Federation Theater Project.

PETER: Or your "reputation" as a conman.

An old world antique bookstore owner gave Orson Welles a copy of a "lost" Shakespeare play based on the Christ's Passion week!

ORSON: *[ignoring the slight.]* I don't think it was an actual 17th century manuscript. That I know for sure. It may have been a later reprint of an earlier manuscript, I don't know. It seemed to be derived from foul papers, this I knew.

PETER: Foul papers?

ORSON: Shakespeare, or de Vere, never published his own plays. They were published by others from different types of play scripts. Some were prompt-books given to actors, but this proved hinky because most prompt-books cut many of the other actors' lines out of other actor's copies. The actor had their lines and their cues and that was it. The publisher needed several copies of prompt-books to reconstruct a complete play. Other scripts were foul papers, or rough drafts by the playwright that may not have the revisions made during and after production included in them. All this made getting a complete version of any Shakespearean plays difficult during the first few folios. *The Gospel According to Shakespeare* appeared to be foul papers because it looked to have been drawn from a rough draft of a Shakespearean play, perhaps from early in the rehearsal period. The author may have been pressured by time to finish the play for its benefactor. I can imagine old Edward huddled around a candle in the cold of the London winter trying to get the play finished in time for Lent. He was just running out of time. Turn all of the parables into iambic pentameter? That'll take too long. They're stories. Just keep them in prose. Prose isn't bad. Falstaff, the greatest character in Shakespeare never spoke in poetry. There were other apparent short-cuts made indicating it was, in fact, foul papers. The stage directions, for instance, were taken practically verbatim from the King James version, as if the author just threw up his hands to the actors and said, "For Christ's sake, just do what the Bible says you're supposed to do." Hell, that sounds like it would be spoken from the pulpit not the prompt.

PETER: At what point in your career did this rare-book collector come to you?

ORSON: A little after my *Macbeth* was a success. My name was wagging on everybody's tongue. This was the first time in my career that that would happen. The first, but unfortunately, not the last.

PETER: Ah, the voodoo *Macbeth*.

The three witches prophecy the death of the titular MacBeth, just as Hedda Hopper prophesied Orson's Hollywood fate!

ORSON: Oh, how a loathe that phrase. *Voodoo* MacBeth! Well, yes. It was shortly after I was Broadway's darling and only a few short years before I became Hollywood's pariah. As a lover of everything Shakespeare, it had always struck me as odd that ol' William never tackled the life of Christ. If there is no other life in all of history that was more important to have written a play about, I'm at a loss for what it could be. The Passion of Jesus written in iambic pentameter! A passion play by the hand that wrote *Hamlet!* Imagine. Why in the hell didn't Shakespeare or de Vere or whoever, write the Passion of Jesus? If I hadn't held that quarto in my greedy little hands, I would have wanted to write a Shakespearean passion play myself and publish it allonymously as William Shakespeare.

PETER: What if you did actually did write it? It would prove within your character.

ORSON: Touché. But I'm not sure I'd have the mettle to tackle meter in such an undertaking. Transposing *Macbeth* to Haiti is one thing, scaring the entire nation with a radio-drama is a second thing, but writing a new Shakespeare play in iambic pentameter and passing it off as authentic is another thing entirely. No one in nearly 400 years has written a play in Shakespearean-style verse. There has to be a reason for this. It simply may not be possible given the evolution of the English language. For a Jacobean Englishman to write iambic Jacobean English in pentameter, is certainly one great accomplishment. But for a playwright in the intervening centuries? Impossible. What if what I wrote was bad Shakespeare? I don't think my psyche could handle the criticism. Who could? I tell you, I think counterfeiters and forgers have the hardest art.

PETER: Art? Don't you mean crime?

ORSON: No. Of course, it's an art. You spend your entire careers perfecting your craft to impossible standards, mastering mimicry, and you can't even take credit for your work. You don't put your own name on it. You put someone else's name on it. Allonymously! We've come full circle. If you're great, nobody will ever be the wiser. If you're terrible, you're exposed as a fraud and hoaxer and damned to the ninth circle of Hell with all of the other traitors. Ah, for the anonymity of the forger. I could write iambic pentameter if I had the desire, but it would be bad Shakespeare.

PETER: And what if it was great Shakespeare?

ORSON: I'd have to take immediate credit for the actual authorship. Whoever wrote *The Gospel According to Shakespeare* should have taken credit for it. I know I would have. I would have stood on that stage in front of my full house and said, "Shakespeare? Bah. The Bard was a hack. He ran a proverbial iambic gin mill churning out masterpieces of the English language. *I* wrote the Passion of Jesus in *Shakespearean* verse! *He* never tackled the subject. *He* was probably scared to tears to write something as epic as the Passion of Jesus the Christ! It wasn't even that hard. I wrote it in what? Twenty-six days. Hell, forget Shakespeare. Praise me! I am the rightful heir to the legacy of Shakespeare!" But I didn't write it. Allonymously or not. How I wished it was authentic. From the pen of Shakespeare-upon-Avon or the Earl of Oxford, I could care less. It was such a fascinating and superb play. I should have produced it right then and there, while I was still on Broadway.

PETER: If only you had known then what you later discovered with the "War of the Worlds" radio broadcast, just how effective a little slight-of-hand is in the marketing and promotion of a production, a staging of *The Gospel According to Shakespeare* would have been a gold mine. A long lost play by William Shakespeare, can you imagine? Even as a forgery, it would have played for years.

ORSON: But I didn't know then what I know now. I don't even know now what I knew then! I wouldn't have had the career I had if I had known what I know whenever I knew it.

PETER: Wow, my head is spinning.

ORSON: Your head? My mouth. But I never saw them again; the quarto and the rare book dealer vanished like a fart in a whirlwind. I wondered in the years since if that wasn't a ghostly apparition of the Bard manifesting himself, desiring some belated recognition for their passionate work on the Passion of Jesus.

PETER: What impressions did you get from the play. Could it have been authentic? Or was it a masterful forgery?

ORSON: From what I remember, it was a little short for a Shakespearean play and obviously obsessed with rhyming couplets. This marked the play as early in Shakespeare's career, but the King James Version of the *Holy Bible* wasn't published until 1611, very late in his career.

PETER: But if Shakespeare didn't write Shakespeare?

ORSON: Oh, ye of great faith. I will play the Devil's Advocate against myself. Given that ol' Oxford died seven years before King James published his "authorized" version of the Bible, how can this Shakespearean play be written by a dead man before the source material was even published? It still makes no matter; Oxford, no doubt, had a copy of Tyndale's *Holy Bible*, which His Majesty authoritatively plagiarized throughout the KJV. So this passion play could have been written early in the career of said playwright, Shakespeare or de Vere, take your pick, or it could have been written late in their career and perhaps even after their own death, which de Vere would have had to have accomplished given a few glaring timeline difficulties. Every play from *Timon of Athens* and on would have had to be been written before de Vere died in 1604 and produced patiently and posthumously at regular intervals for nearly a decade. Holy hell, I'm blowing holes in my own theories here. Stop me, Peter, before I go any further.

PETER: Shouldn't we get back to the *War of the Worlds* feature you claim to have written the screenplay for.

ORSON: Fine, spoil the tangent.

PETER: It was a pleasant digression from this prank you'll pulling on me this evening.

ORSON: If Charles Koerner would have allowed me to film the "Life of Christ" in Shakespearean verse, then perhaps *The War of the Worlds* feature film wouldn't have ruined my career. If I had filmed a Biblical epic, and I could have, I do have an Eidetic memory and could have perfectly recalled that old bookseller's foul-papers in their entirety. It could have been so easy. *If* I had filmed a Biblical epic, maybe my career would not have been what it turned to be. And what it turned out to be was a trip through Dante's *Inferno*. If I had a Hollywood epic on my résumé, then maybe Hedda Hooper's prophecy wouldn't have come true. But I wasn't allowed to film *The Gospel According to Shakespeare*, I had to film *The War of the Worlds* as my next feature. So there I was dreaming of scheming with my partner-in-crime, a young Willie Brown. The conspiracy hadn't grown beyond to the two of at this point. Willie had just turned in a brilliant adaptation of the script Howard Koch had cobbled together in the small hours of Halloween morning. I would let the RKO lawyers try and get him to sign over the film rights to the "War of the Worlds" radio-dramatization. Howard had the audacity to copyright a script he really didn't have the right to copyright. It was a "work-for-hire" at the very least, and a conspiracy with the highest levels of the government at the most. While the lawyers and brass at RKO were preoccupied with wrangling with Howard back in New York, it would give me and Willie the precious time we needed to craft our own *War of the Worlds*.

PETER: Wait a minute! When did all this take place?

ORSON: I don't know. It was around February of... what would it have been... 1941 or '42.

PETER: That's not possible. I just found the hole in this little web you are spinning this evening, Orson. You were in South America during this time-period. There was no possible way on earth that you could have shot a *War of the Worlds* feature for Charles Koerner. You were all over South America. You shot footage of Carnival in Rio. You were a good-will ambassador for the Northern Hemisphere, working for Nelson Rockefeller and the OCIAA. You did radio there. Hell, you accepted an award for *Citizen Kane* in Buenos Aires. You were in Fortaleza shooting the Jangadeiros sequence, then Recife, then Salvador, Bahia. You shot footage for *It's All True* all over the continent. Are telling me *It's All True* was all a lie?

ORSON: Peter... I would never...

PETER: You were south of the equator for over half-a-year. *Ambersons* was recut precisely because you weren't in the country. You weren't on the continent. Hell, you weren't even on this side of the world. Now, you're telling me that instead of spending all that time in South America, you were actually in California shooting *The War of the Worlds*. That doesn't make any sense. Why did you give up the recuts of *Ambersons*?

ORSON: I... I... I...

PETER: Was it because you were so focused on getting *The War of the Worlds* going so you sacrificed your cut of *Ambersons* on a sacrificial pyre in order to keep Charles Koerner occupied and away from you?

ORSON: Sure?

Is this a photograph of Orson Welles in Brazil during 1941–42 or its is from Mardi Gras in New Orleans, Louisiana during a break in filming Invasion From Mars?

PETER: Why invent a bloviated story about the film trip to South America? We've discussed many times during our conversations about your trip to South America. Conversations just like this one. Sacred conversations recorded for posterity. Are you telling me all of the those conversations, all those stories, are lies?

ORSON: Yes?

PETER: Why would you lie to me about all of them? Don't tell me it was to protect the conspiracy about a *War of the Worlds* feature. At this point, I don't think I could handle any more lies, Orson. Please. What is the purpose of tonight?

ORSON: It is to finally to tell the truth! To come clean about one of the worse periods in American history. Actually two of the worst periods in our history. October 30, 1938 and the year 1942, when I shot my *Invasion From Mars* feature and the entire world went black because of it.

PETER: So if the world thought you were in South America during this stretch of time that would explain away *The War of the Worlds* feature, wouldn't it? And what of the footage you shot while in South

America. You couldn't have known there would be a government conspiracy to stop your *War of the Worlds* feature. Who faked the footage and why? Are you going to tell me all the South American footage was stock footage. That you didn't step a single foot in Brazil. Don't tell me that was a cover-story made up by the government to cover-up the filming of *The War of the Worlds*.

Is this a forged photograph of a superimposed Orson Welles created by the US government to falsify the Brazilian production, therefore giving Orson's résumé an "alibi" during 1941–1942? No!

ORSON: Then I won't. But it's the truth. And you explained it all so much more succinctly than I could. You know I tend to ramble. And as for the stories of South America. As fate would have it, they actually did happen. Just not in the time period history records. I did shoot *It's All True* and that's all true. It really is. It was after the *Invasion From Mars* debacle that I needed an escape. So I escaped to the furthest, most far flung place I could think of. I didn't lie to you, Peter. I've never, I would never lie to you. Only the dates were fudged a bit. Remember, these were the war years. The nation's attention was entirely focused across the Atlantic and in the Pacific theater. Nobody gave two squirts of soul owl shit about what and when a Hollywood film-maker was traipsing across South America.

PETER: After tonight, I don't know what to believe.

ORSON: Then just believe. Make a leap of faith. Faith in me as your friend that I wouldn't– won't– lead you astray. Make that leap, Peter. Keep your faith in me.

PETER: I will. But please, don't make a mockery out of our friendship.

ORSON: I won't, Peter. I swear on my eyes of my first-born son.

PETER: You don't have a first-born son, Orson. *[Chuckles.]*

ORSON: *[Laughs heartily.]* There's my Peter. Let's more on, shall we? With Koerner and the brass focused on *Ambersons*, Willie and I have all the precious little time we could be afforded to craft out own *Invasion From Mars* feature.

PETER: Again, I'll bite. The film in which you claim to tell the "true" story of that cold, windy October evening; the evening on which millions of radio listeners panicked, not because of your "War of the Worlds" radio-dramatization, but after hearing news reports of an actual invasion from Mars; the evening which you conspired with the President and Hearst to cover-up the truth?

ORSON: On the nose, Peter, on the nose. Willie and I needed to get away from the prying eyes of Hollywood so we could set about feverishly writing an entire Hollywood screenplay in only a long weekend. So, Willie and I were ensconced in Mank's old bungalow in Victorville.

PETER: At Campbell's Guest House? The same bungalow that Herman Mankiewicz wrote *Citizen Kane*? Why did you choose to hide in the most obvious place imaginable?

ORSON: Because it was the most obvious place imaginable. "Hiding in plain sight", isn't that the idiom.

PETER: But shouldn't you have been preparing test shoots? The "fake" script you had Willie Brown adapt was in the hands of Charles Koerner and the rest of the brass at RKO Weren't they expecting you to begin prepping for a production any day now?

ORSON: I forgot to tell you that I had connected a long-distance call to Howard and whispered in his ear like a little devil sitting on his shoulder. I told him that he had every right to ask for ridiculous sums of money to sign over the rights. This was his

The infamous bungalow where not only Citizen Kane *was written but* Invasion From Mars *was penned as well!*

right as the copyrighted writer of the "War of the Worlds" radio-dramatization; it was his right to secure a future for his wife and children; it was his right to insist the movie be titled *Howard Koch's War of the Worlds.*

PETER: You're devious.

ORSON: You expect any less from me?

PETER: Certainly not.

ORSON: The brass at RKO have never dealt with anyone like Howard Koch. He was also educated as a lawyer. They'd spar for several weeks, buying me and Willie Brown all the precious seconds we could buy ourselves. It was a series of bourbon-fueled days and black coffee-fueled nights. Unlike Mank, Willie was not a professional alcoholic. The bourbon loosened his mind and allowed him to write some of the most ingenious, yet absolutely ridiculous plots and subplots. He was able to take an eidetic, yet half-remembered, memory and spin it into the most wondrous bullshit of a subplot. Each and every new draft caused the story to spin into exponentially ludicrous directions. I had no idea how the Martian invasion was defeated. There was nothing in my experiences that night to give me in a hint of what happened to the Martian invaders. Because of this hindrance, Willie ended one of the later drafts with a *Deus ex machina* that was completely absurd. I told him I didn't want such affront to literary decency in my *War of the Worlds*, so in the very next day in the very next draft, he drew further inspiration for the works of HG Wells, by bringing time-travel into the story.

PETER: Time-travel? You can't be serious.

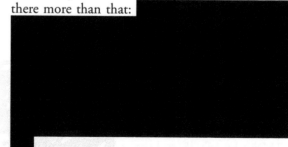

Did HG Wells serve as the inspiration for a deus ex machina*?*

ORSON: I am ever so serious. Our audience would be expecting some inspiration from HG Wells in a film then called *The War of the Worlds*, but weaving in inspiration from *The Time-Machine* would surely get Sir Herbert's solicitor to send an angry letter to RKO's lawyers. It was bad enough that HG Wells had his good name sullied by an association with his misspelled namesake that infamous evening in 1938, but we had the gall to further disgrace the esteemed British novelist with a time-travel plot so intimately associated with his other most famous novel.

PETER: Why include such obvious fiction in a screenplay that you are asserting tells "truth" of a real, authentic, and historical invasion from Mars?

ORSON: Truth is relative, Peter. Why should any event, real or fictitious, not be permitted a few creative rewrites? How many true stories are told in Hollywood that are inerrantly free of fiction? Names are often changed; multiple people are combined into single characters; locations are moved; and the order of events altered; all of these are done in the hope of producing riveting cinema. So if Willie wrote some obvious fiction in our *War of the Worlds*, I felt it might just lessen the wrath that would be wrought towards us for exposing the truth of an invasion from Mars. I had no intention of convincing the nation that an invasion from Mars happened that cold and windy Halloween Eve in 1938. I just wanted to thumb my nose at the authorities one more time, whether they be the brass at RKO, Hearst again and again and again, and even the President, who would have become my close friend by this point in time. I knew what I accomplished with the cover-story so absurd, so laughable that no one in the few short years between the "War of the Worlds" radio-drama and the *War of the Worlds* feature film believed anything other than my most ludicrously concocted conspiracy. In the last forty years, no one has suspected anything of the nature.

PETER: That is an understatement.

ORSON: No one, no matter how unmedicatedly schizophrenic, has even conceived of the idea that Martians invaded Virginia on October 30, 1938; that our planetary neighbors nearly conquered the nation- nay faith- nearly conquered the world. But there more than that:

PETER: And yet you are claiming it is true. That the invasion from Mars is "true", then why include a time-travel subplot that is so obviously "untrue".

ORSON: There is simply no way of knowing what happened when I wasn't there. I never left New York City, yet I was able to become embroiled in a conspiracy that included President Roosevelt and William Randolph Hearst, but it just wasn't cinematic. The story that I recalled from only a few years earlier was so hazy and dreamlike.

PETER: That could explain so many things, Orson. Were you drinking?

ORSON: We were preempted. Davidson Taylor had the audacity of preempt my *Mercury Theater on the air* with an evening of dance music being broadcast from the Hotel Annapolis in Washington, DC. So I had little recourse but imbibe a bit.

PETER: This could all be the remembrances of an alcoholic stupor, Orson.

ORSON: I drank a little from a flask; okay, I drank a lot from my flask. It wasn't like I had invented LSD and went on a hallucinatory trip.

PETER: Perhaps, your time-travelling friend picked up some tabs from Timothy Leary in the summer of '68 and then traveled backwards in time to slip you a mickey.

ORSON: Hardy-har-har, Peter. The memories of that night are hazy only because I don't know what really happened outside CBS studios that night, except for what was in the teletype. That I remember clearly. In our screenplay, I was able put words onto the lips of Hans Van Kaltenborn, Edward R. Murrow, and everyone else who was broadcast over the aerial that night. That much I did know. That much I could confidently put into our screenplay. But what I wasn't so confident with was what happened off the air, what happened off the air in the ballroom at the Hotel Annapolis, or what happened in the "Top-Secrecy" of the White House. This is what I didn't know and this is what concerned me the most. I had my suspicions because of the "Eyes-Only" documents I was able to get from that starlet Gunter was so infatuated with. These were details I could piece together much like Marion Davies' jigsaw puzzles.

Marion Davies, the mistress of William Randolph Hearts was obsessed with solving elaborate jigsaw puzzles, while living at San Simeon!

PETER: Still pouring salt into that old wound even after all these years, Orson?

ORSON: [*Ignoring the comment*] But I didn't have the box the jigsaw puzzle came in so I couldn't see the entire picture. I had all the pieces, I just didn't know where they went. This is where the bullshitting extraordinaire Willie Brown came into the scene. He was able to see the picture from just the pieces. He was able to piece the puzzle together to make our screenplay in and of itself such wondrous bullshit. Here I was learning at the feet of the master. People consider me to be such the consummate bullshit artist because of the stories of my youth, but mine were true however. The philosophy espoused by Willie Brown was utterly brilliant and inspirational: to tell a remembrance exactly as it occurred was disingenuous to the drama inherent in the telling of any good story. What happened in the moment is but the first draft of the event. The memories we form in the very moments afterward begins the process of revising the memory. Every subsequent recollection inherently involves a rewrite and every rewrite revises the memory or edit that recollection until we achieve the final draft of memory. If others happen to remember with any less of the inherent drama, it is because they do not have the imagination necessary.

PETER: That is "wondrous bullshit".

ORSON: That is the Zen of bullshit according to Willie Brown. The beauty of spouting bullshit is being at peace with bloviating and hyperbole. The polished bullshitter simply does not care what the opinion of the listener is, nor should they. A certain serenity overcomes the bullshit artist with every telling of a cock-and-bull story. It is a philosophy worth living and we lived it for a few weeks of bourbon-fueled days and black coffee-fueled nights while Willie and I ensconced ourselves in Mank's old bungalow in Victorville.

PETER: We've come full-circle... again.

ORSON: Indeed, we have. Let's move then, shall we?

PETER: Let's.

From the Desk of
WILLIAM FRANCIS
BROWN

October 30, 1997
Morning

To my son, Bob,

I swore an oath before a young Orson Welles, President Franklin Delano Roosevelt, and God with the intention of never revealing the truth about the events that occurred on the evening of Sunday, October 30, 1938, the night Martians invaded the United States of America.

The secret of what transpired during the small hours, that saw Orson Welles, the boy genius, radio producer extraordinaire, slight-of-hand magician, and prodigy of the New York theatre scene orchestrate a vast government conspiracy with a cover-story that was so grossly believable that no one, at the time or in the decades since, has dared believe that what was heard by millions of radio listeners was anything but a radio-dramatization of HG Wells' "The War of the Worlds".

Not even the most paranoid of schizophrenics has even conceived of the possibility that Martians actually landed on the East Coast of the United States on Halloween Eve 1938. These poor deluded schizophrenics who wallpaper their walls with aluminum foil, with which they also construct protective helmets from, in the vain attempts of protecting their minds from the continuous assaults by the government's supposed extrasensory perceiving agents and their attempts at extracting their thoughts are blissfully oblivious to paranoias like this.

No fiction writer, even with the wildest of imaginations or stroke of creative genius could envisage of such a thing as this occurring. That the events sparked by this failed invasion from the planet Mars would become the most famous conspiracy theory never heard of... "The Orson Welles' Conspiracy".

"The Orson Welles' Conspiracy" and all other conspiracies are, for the most part absurd, preposterous, perhaps even laughable. Who in their right mind can even listen to the ridiculous rantings of conspiracy theorists on all manner of subject without chuckling or at least breaking a smile? A faked Apollo moon landing, the Majestic 12 and their Project Blue book, the Roswell UFO crash, the New World Order, Yale University's Skull & Bones fraternity, Area 51, the Philadelphia Experiment, the Bilderbergers, the Great Pacific Tsunamic free energy suppression, and the granddaddy of the them all- the assassination of President John Fitzgerald Kennedy by the then Vice-President Lyndon B. Johnson or the Central Intelligence Agency or Fidel Castro or J. Edgar Hoover and his Federal Bureau of Investigation, etcerera ad nausium.

They are all absurd, illogical, preposterous, outrageous, implausible, and laughable. A thorough lack of empirical evidence and mounting evidence to the contrary do little to dissuade the conspiracy theorist from his beliefs; it is the very lack of empirical evidence that fuels his beliefs that the very evidence which will vindicate this beliefs is classified top-secret and thus immune to his repeated filings in the name of the Freedom of Information Act, believed by many conspiracy theorists to be the paper-strewn gateway to the Holy Grail of their theories.

But when the information finally reaches their greedy little hands, they discover to their dismay and consternation that the evidence they have sought their entire lives has been heavily redacted and therefore only adds fuel to their ever increasingly paranoid fantasies. And all the evidence present to the contrary in vain attempts to disprove their wholehearted beliefs is nothing more than an elaborate fiction created in furtherance of the conspiracy to hide the truth from the people of the United States of America.

Nor does exposing the logical fallacies in their belief system do little to dissuade the believer from his belief. This is the heart of the conspiracy theory and a major reason why the government has actually hidden the truth from the people. Few of the general populous, who to some lesser extent distrust their government, will believe the conspiracy theorist no matter the proof that is present.

This, also, is at the heart of my consternation, concerning "The Orson Welles' Conspiracy". I know what I heard with my own ears: the crashed "meteorite", the monstrous alien creatures, its horrifying heat-ray, the Tri-pod walking machines, the black fog, the red plants.

This is evidence of the truth to the contrary of the thorough lack of empirical evidence presented by Orson Welles' laughable conspiracy concerning the invasion from Mars that the entire nation bought hook-line-and-sinker and continues to believe such claptrap to this day.

However, no amount of empirical evidence that I present in this series of letters, nor the mounting evidence to the contrary the government may present in its defense, will persuade the people to believe my story.

I only have my name and reputation. Orson Welles is particularly famous for winning a most heated battle with William Randolph Hearst and the executives at RKO studios over his motion picture Citizen Kane, but if he has been successful with his equally heated but far more unheard of battle over his War of the Worlds feature film, my name and reputation as a young screenwriter would have become sullied and synonymous with Orson Welles' equally famous War of the Worlds radio-dramatization.

To have my family's good name and my character forever associated with a vast government conspiracy is unimaginable. My oath to Orson Welles and the 32nd President of these United States, Franklin Delano Roosevelt, is simply not my primary motivating factor in helping keep this secret for seventy years. It is and always will be laughter; I, under no circumstance, can allow myself to become a laughing stock, at any price. Putting my name on the cover of this volume will be the greatest test of my firm belief in what Orson Welles did that cold October evening so long ago.

Sincerely, your father,

William Francis Brown

William Francis Brown

Creatures of the Black Coffee

ORSON: Who could possibly turn in ten radically different drafts in twenty-one days? Only someone with Willie's perjurious imagination, that's who! He was the most phenomenal writing partner one could possibly have.

PETER: What made the young man so special?

ORSON: Writers tend to be given the shortest of shrifts in Hollywood. Directors want to change the script to fit their own particular vision of the film. Actors beg and extort to get more lines, more prominent scenes, more close-ups, more opportunities to secure that allusive Oscar, etc. *ad nauseum.* Writers are the ones who typically originate the story. They've already spent months, if not years, of blood, sweet, and tears to get the screenplay polished. They spend months trying to get the script into the hands of the person who can best pass the script along to the next person, until someone at some studio is willing to buy it for pennies on the dollar. Then the brass of a variety levels of shininess, tell the writer which changes he has to make to the script. They are of the opinion that their opinion is the only one that matters. They look at a screenplay, having no concept of how the writer has conceived all of this brilliance out of thin air. They don't possess a creative bone in their body. They probably believe the creative process is akin to witchcraft and they, as the holders of the keys to the Kingdom of Heaven, are the only ones have the God-given right to screw with every word the writer wrote. They have to cleanse the screenplay of the witchcraft of genius by absolving it of its very creativity in the Church of the Holy Hays.

PETER: Isn't that a bit over-dramatic?

ORSON: The priests of pedanticalness agonize over the script to find something, anything that will prove their own brilliance and will allow them to move another rung up the brass ladder. Their notes on this scene or that scene do not serve the screenplay or the production, only their over-inflated sense of self-worth. They can't seem to make any sense out of what you're reading. The script calls for a woman to wears a blue scarf to dinner at the Ritz and a yellow hat to the horse race the next day, "But that, that doesn't make any sense. Where'd she get the yellow hat? And why a blue scarf? Those don't match." It's a black-and-white film, you imbeciles! It doesn't matter what the color of sour owl shit is!

PETER: Orson!

Will H. Hays, once seen as the savior of Hollywood, would institute the "Hays Code" to hamstring creativity in the name of morality!

ORSON: And it's white and runny with black specs in it. That's what the color sour owl shit is!

PETER: Orson!

ORSON: My dear God, executives need to put their imprint, their asinine stamp on everything that comes across their desk. If something from their own imbecilic intellect doesn't end up on the page or the screen, then their own ego is crushed and they will stop at nothing to crush you and your's. And yet, these MENSA-wannabes, have the most difficult times understanding the most basic elements of storytelling. How can one of these "executives" read a script where a woman sees a shooting star, makes a wish to be married happily-ever-after, and meets the perfect man in a screenplay called *When You Wish Upon A Star,* and yet cry out in infantile indignation, "That doesn't make any sense! Wait! I'm getting an idea. Yes! That's it! What it needs is a giant mutated spider!" And you end up with a romantic-comedy where Rock Hudson saves Doris Day in a climatic battle with a giant-bloody-spider! That doesn't make any sense!

PETER: That's an exaggeration of the process... only slightly. Everyone in the process has a right to their opinion, Hollywood is a collaborative place. Movie-making requires many more people than just the writer. The writer only began the process. And the process has many steps. A producer has to feel confident in raising the capital. The studio has to feel confident in buying advertising. And shouldn't the director has a say in telling of a story he is going to spend months, if not years of his life on?

ORSON: But where does it all end, Peter. You're saying the writer gave birth to the child only to abandon it at that orphanage of bastard children called Hollywood. So you're saying, he no longer has a right to contribute to the life of that child? That any old evil executive can adopt said child and give the child to any tyrannical director to slave away washing and cleaning the metaphorical mansion, making millions?

PETER: I take back what I said a moment ago. This is what is over-dramatic. But isn't that exactly what you did to Mank on *Citizen Kane?* You even took his name off of the birth-certificate.

ORSON: Willie certainly took his, our frustrations out when he pulled the RKO executives into the script, making them look like the donkey's ass.

PETER: You're just going to ignore me.

ORSON: I'm not ignoring you. Haven't you been involved in the Hollywood "process" long enough to have your own frustrations about the "system"?

PETER: Certainly.

ORSON: You know that the writer has no right to express his frustrations about the process while being so intimately involved in the process.

PETER: Of course. You can certainly take your ball and go home, but you won't make it to the Major League Baseball game that is a Hollywood premiere or the World Series that is the Oscars! What other recourse does a writer have? This is how the game has been played since the days of yore.

ORSON: Willie found a brilliant and creative way to take his, our frustrations out when he pulled the RKO executives into the script. I laughed out-loud at the scene, knowing that might actually be the scene that gets the script pulled and not our vast conspiracy to expose FDR and WR.

PETER: What was the scene in question?

ORSON: Let me set the stage a bit. In first eight or nine drafts, Willie insisted that we have a news-reel to establish to the audience that history of the "War of the Worlds" radio-dramatization. He wanted a news-reel to tell the "real" story of what happened that night to set the stage for the rest of the movie. If we told the "truth" as the audience believed it, it would allow us all the freedom in the world to tell the actual truth. I hated the idea of the using a news-reel, because I had used the technique in *Citizen Kane*, and I was loath to repeat myself in this film. Willie insisted that the news-reel was essential. I insisted that it had only been a handful of years, so the memory of my scaring the entire nation with a radio-drama was still fresh in the minds of the audience. I hated to think that Charles Koerner would agree with me on this point. So, I tasked Willie to come up with another idea, any idea that wasn't a news-reel.

PETER: And what did he come up with?

ORSON: The notes that I had made on the most recent draft centered around the *Deus ex machina* at the end of the movie. We had Nikola Tesla appear at the end of the movie and explain what happened to the Martians and how the movie would resolve itself. I was reluctant to use the technique without first establishing the *Deus ex machina* earlier in the script and weaving it so thoroughly into the plot that it was no longer a *Deus ex machina.* Willie Brown was a night-owl in *extremis.* He could almost be considered a vampire, he had the trademarked pale-white skin and almost albino-blonde hair. He tended to get ready for bed just as the sun was rising. He would see the sun begin to crest over the horizon and say, "Dear God, it's time for bed." This, however, made our time ensconced in Victorville so productive.

PETER: How so?

ORSON: I would wake up at the butt-crack of dawn and there, on my desk, would be sitting the latest draft of the screenplay. Since I knew, he wouldn't wake up until two or three in the afternoon...

PETER: My.

ORSON: I knew that I had several hours to review the draft in quiet serenity, before he would wake up, take a shower, drink his first coffee of the day, all the while readying himself for the war-of-words that would result before, during, and after he read my notes. Because of my tendency to write extensive notes, obsessive notes, and passionate notes, he called me a "Note-Nazi". Every time I detailed a note with an emphatic flourish of arm waves, a note he couldn't disagree more with, he would exclaim "*Heil Hilter*" with the snap of his arm.

PETER: Oh, my.

ORSON: You have to remember that this was before the world knew what unimaginable evil Hitler would be remembered and condemned for by history. We both got a kick out of Nazi humor. Everyone did. Dr. Seuss drew the most outrageous political cartoons, and yet they are only outrageous through the rose-coloured glasses of the progressive 1970's. Even though we were at war with Germany, no lowly American citizen was yet aware of the Holocaust. All Willie and I really knew about Hitler was limited to Charlie Chaplin's *The Great Dictator* and a Donald Duck cartoon screened for staff at RKO Pictures.[1]

Dr. Seuss, before creating the Cat in the Hat, was an American propagandist during the height of World War II.

PETER: Really? You didn't educate yourself about the war beyond a couple of Hollywood films, and one short film at that?

ORSON: You have to remember I gave a patriotic speech the morning "that will live on in infamy". I knew what most people knew from dramatic news-reels, overly-dramatic Hearst newspapers, and near-constant radio-news interruptions, which continued on even after my debacle with "War of the Worlds". Of course, I knew what other people knew. Everyone knew the news. But there are certain truths that only satire can reveal. That is why, of the war years, I choose to remember Charlie Chaplin and Donald Duck.

PETER: I see.

ORSON: We had to have had as much fun with the world at war and we were having as much fun with our own, albeit much smaller scale war with RKO. When you are under the gun, as it were, with the brass threatening our careers with their own vitriolic orders, we needed to relish our own propaganda. Each and every scene were we could lampoon our enemies, or our perceived enemies, was blissfully cathartic. That is why the scene Willie wrote lampooning the RKO executives brought, not only a smile to my face, but a guffaw that escaped my lips, almost waking the sleeping screenwriter in the bungalow next door.

PETER: We are finally back on track.

ORSON: Even, if we made a few unplanned detours, Peter, we will get to our destination. This I can assure you.

PETER: I'm not even sure I remember our destination.

ORSON: Don't fear. I most assuredly do. The scene was quite brilliant. I hated the news-reel concept and told Willie that he needed to solve the news-reel problem and the *Deus ex machina* problem at the same exact time. We got into a heated argument over this and I stomped off for bed. I'm sure he soothed the wounds inflicted by my words with a couple of fingers of bourbon, neat. Then, he got to work on the scene. When I awoke the next

1 *Der Fuehrer's Face*, a Walt Disney cartoon directed by Jack Kinney

To anyone who saw Nikola Tesla's electrical demonstrations at the World's Fair, no one would be surprised if he invented a time-machine!

morning to Willie quietly praying under this breath as he slipped silently into slumber, I walked over to my desk and pulled out the script. He had solved the *Deus ex machina* with Nikola Tesla by drawing in another HG Wells' story, *The Time Machine.* The second scene, which had previously been the confounded news-reel, was now a scene between Orson Welles and Orson Welles.

PETER: I don't understand.

ORSON: Willie had the Orson Welles from 1938 time-travel into the future and learn at the teat of Orson Welles from 1942, who was editing scenes from his *Invasion From Mars.*

PETER: You shot a scene in the movie about the editing of the very same film? That is rather odd.

ORSON: It was brilliant. Who better to explain the importance of going along with the vast government conspiracy than having the 1938 Orson Welles converse with the Orson Welles from 1942. The slightly older and more world-weary Orson Welles could use his eidetic memory to tell the time-traveling Orson Welles each and every step to make and each and every word to say in order to orchestrate the vast government conspiracy.

PETER: My head hurts.

ORSON: My mouth hurts from my constant grinning as I read this scene. It was brilliant. It was absurd. It was brilliantly absurd. And then the very next scene was straight out of *Citizen Kane* and I couldn't be happier.

PETER: That doesn't make any sense.

ORSON: In *Citizen Kane*, I followed the news-reel with a scene of reporters who had just seen the news-reel and wonder what in the darkness of the screening room wondered what "Rosebud" could possibly be. In *Invasion From Mars,* Willie followed the scene from the future with a scene of RKO executives watching the previous scene in the screening room.

PETER: What?

ORSON: The RKO executives just finished watching the scene between Orson Welles and Orson Welles and of course, they don't understand why Orson Welles spoke to Orson Welles and why there were two Orson Welleses in the scene.

PETER: That makes two of us.

ORSON: It was a vicious lampoon of the endless battles the genius must wage with the imbecile. And it is the imbecile who has the power, but thankfully they are wonderfully unequipped to win a true battle of wills.

PETER: Ouch.

ORSON: You've been in Hollywood long enough to loath the process. I may have lampooned the President in my *Invasion* and William Randolph Hearst a second time, in three films, yet these few pages roasting the RKO brass had me more worried than any other scene in the entire screenplay. Who were Franklin Deleno Roosevelt and William Randolph Hearst really, when one had to battle the nameless and worthless executives at RKO Radio Pictures.

Befuddled RKO executives watching the scene of Orson Welles from 1938 in the editing room with Orson Welles from 1942!

PETER: That was kind of vicious.

ORSON: I don't really care anymore. If only I had told my past self to not get involved in this conspiracy– to run, run as far away from the conspiracy as humanly possible, perhaps I could have lived out my life in the bright lights of Broadway instead of eking out a meager existence, nearly forgotten, in Hollywood.

PETER: You don't believe that, do you?

ORSON: Willie Brown was the lucky one. He was the one that got to escape the unnumbered circle of Hell that is Hollywood. He was the one that was able to labor the rest of his life in a steel-mill under scorching heat and a backbreaking workload. He was the one that had a family that loved him and put up with the bullshit stories he would tell. He was the one who had the life worth living. How I envied him his paradise in Colorado.

PETER: You cannot believe that.

ORSON: I have. I do. But I remember those days in Victorville as some of the happiest of my career. While I had to fight through the penny-pinching of George Schaefer and the arrogance of William Randolph Hearst to get my movie made, the futility of *Citizen Kane* began with when I had to fight through the drunken stupor of Mank, just to get a workable script. I was the one that had to take hundreds of pages of overwritten dreck to find a passable script after weeks of fevered editing. But with Willie Brown, we may have had our own fights, because with each and every draft, he felt it was finished. There wasn't anything that could be changed. To Willie, the last draft he had written would have to be the final draft. But, as with the *Deus ex machina*, he would see the errors in the script that now seemed to leap out at him, and while he had no idea of how to fix the script, but he would inevitably find the solution. The problem of the *Deus ex machina* in one draft, allowed him to bring in a time machine and the *Time Machine* plot allowed him to solve another problem. There just wasn't enough Orson Welles in the script. This didn't bother me in the slightest, because I didn't want to be the focal-point in the screenplay. I know the role I played in the conspiracy that William Randolph Hearst somewhat affectionately called "The Orson Welles' Conspiracy". And the time-travel plotline allowed the script to seem to jump about in time, which I adore. *Citizen Kane* was certainly considered a jumbled temporal mess.

PETER: Kind of like this conversation.

ORSON: This is one thing that I have learned since *Kane* has been brought out of mothballs and had the bright lights of film school shined upon it. For the few people who saw the movie during its short time in the cinemas, the jumping around in time as too new, too radical, too I don't know. But I adore the technique. In *Invasion From Mars*, the time-travel device allows the story to seem to jump around in time, although the script is obsessively linear. With the exception of the second and third scenes, the scene between Orson Welles and Orson Welles and the scene between Orson Welles and the RKO executives, of course.

Did Nikola Tesla invent a time-machine to serve as a deus ex machina!

PETER: That is an awful lot of Orson Welles in two short scenes.

ORSON: You have no idea. But the movie proper begins with the scene between Davidson Taylor and myself; the scene in which he explains to me that *The Mercury Theater on the air* had been preempted. After this scene, the film is relentlessly linear, and only seems to be a "jumbled temporal mess" because of the brilliance of the time-travel technique. When the film was first screened to Charles Koerner and the other brass at RKO Pictures, they hated the "jumbled temporal mess" as much as Willie Brown had prophesied they would in the third scene of a screenplay written miles away and months earlier in Victorville. It was quite amusing that RKO executives in both fiction and reality would not understand the time-travel mechanic. Charles Koerner made my day, my year, my entire career up until that point, when he asked, "Why are there two Orson Welles in the scene? I don't understand."

Willie Brown was just as prophetic with his screenplay as HG Wells was with his novel, albeit on a much smaller and less important scale.

PETER: Are we back to whole "actual" invasion from Mars shtick again, Orson?

ORSON: *Au contraire, mon frère.* We are still in Victorville feverishly writing on the *Invasion From Mars* screenplay while the brass at RKO are pacified with their own personal copies of the *War of the Worlds* screenplay. But it wasn't all tea and roses in Victorville. While Willie would eventually acquiesce to my demands of a rewrite, he would fight tooth-and-nail that each and every draft was the final draft. He thought we were wasting time working on a script that was already finished. He reminded me that there was a ticking clock. We needed to get back to the studio to work on the movie itself. Willie didn't know that I was reluctant to go back to Hollywood. That all I really desired was to actually work on the screenplay until my dying day. I never wanted to leave Victorville. He was too young to understand that the men we were conspiring against in Hollywood in order to make the cursed movie in the first place would be a cake-walk compared to the men we would anger in the government. Charles Koerner would simply fire me. Louis B. Mayer would then hire me for pennies on the dollar and force me actually make a movie from the *War of the Worlds* screenplay he would easily pick up out of Koerner's trash. I would go from being the prince welcomed into the kingdom of Tinseltown to the pauper few would ever acknowledge again. I had deceived young Willie Brown into thinking that this was his ticket to writing the great Biblical epics for Cecil B. DeMille or the westerns of John Ford. It would be one thing to be blacklisted from Hollywood having made a film as important as *Citizen Kane* has proven to be, it is another thing entirely to never have a single word you wrote ever appear on the silver screen. I can't imagine Willie Brown returning to his father with his tail tucked between his legs, while being led on a leash to a steel-mill you know you will spend the rest of your life working in. I can't imagine the feeling of castration a bullshit artist like Willie Brown would experience being unable and unwilling to tell tales of his adventures in Hollywood to his wife, his children, his co-workers, and random old acquaintances he bumped into at the shopping mall. I was willing to fall on my sword to end the charade of a career in Hollywood, but I wasn't willing to take young Willie with me. While he slept his days away in Victorville, I was trying figure out a way to get Willie Brown off this voyage of the damned and onto another so that when the shit finally hit the fan, he was safely working on another film. Any other film. This is where the *Gospel According the Shakespeare* should rear its ugly head again. And just in time.

PETER: I feel the sensation of a "jumbled temporal mess" in our conversation, Orson.

ORSON: But, when I called Charles and told him that I had an idea for DeMille, that he should do a Technicolor remake of his silent film *The King of Kings*. I would pitch the idea of bringing *The King of Kings* back, not only in sound, but Shakespearean verse. It would be a Biblical epic and a classical film all wrapped up in one. DeMille would have his screenwriter to bring *The King of Kings* to the silver screen again. I wasn't stuck on the title and if it got Willie Brown off of my sinking ship and onto dry land, then all would be worth the effort.

Would a Shakespearean King of Kings *by Cecile B. DeMille save Willie Brown from returning home and working in the a steel mill?*

PETER: Wasn't DeMille with Paramount? Why would RKO want to sell an idea to Paramount?

ORSON: In its own unique way, Hollywood may have been more like baseball than any other business in the country. They both shared the idea on ownership. Actors and actresses were groomed to be Hollywood stars, just as athletes were groomed to be baseball players. Where baseball players were indentured servants to the owners of their team, they were only free when traded to another team. It wasn't uncommon for studios to take their actors, actresses, directors, and writers and let them be borrowed for a film instead of outright stealing talent. I can't remember any instance as radical as the Red Sox trading Babe Ruth to the Yankees, but there must have be one case to make my analogy work. Charles was already fed up with my antics on the lot long before he even took the job as the head honcho. He would be more than willing to trade a young and uncredited screenwriter to Paramount along with an as yet unwritten screenplay, one that I could easily pull out of my eidetic backside in a weekend. All that it cost me was to call an end to my unscheduled and unapproved vacation in Victorville. Charles wanted his director back on his lot working on his *War of the Worlds* feature. He would move mountains in exchange for my cooperation. Which he wouldn't get, of course, but he didn't need to know that, would he?

PETER: Of course, not. Why would he or I think any different?

ORSON: All that concerned me was that Willie Brown would be safely with his name on another screenplay, working for another director at another studio. Willie needed to be as far away from me as humanly possible, when the thermal-nuclear warhead that was *Invasion From Mars* blew me and RKO Radio Pictures to smithereens. Unfortunately...

PETER: Unfortunately, what?

ORSON: DeMille wouldn't commit to the movie, because he loathed the idea of doing a remake of a "perfectly fine motion picture". Without DeMille on board, Paramount wouldn't trade for an uncredited writer, no matter how exciting the project was. Over a series of heated telephone calls, I decided to push for *Gospel According to Shakespeare* to be my next feature, but Charles wanted me off their lot in the worse possible way... permanently. So, I phoned Charles asking him to sell my contract to Louis B. Mayer, so I could make my life of Christ feature for the lion, but Louis was only interested in *The War of the Worlds*, which as far as Louis was aware, I was already doing that film for RKO. Meanwhile, the accountants at RKO, those miserly scrooges, wouldn't pay for the bungalow in Victorville any longer. Without the peace and quiet of the bungalow, I wouldn't have the peace and quiet to stream my eidetic consciousness into a typewriter to produce the *Gospel According to Shakespeare* screenplay. And despite Willie's predilection for bullshit, he couldn't bullshit his way through Shakespearean verse. With the Victorville bungalow in foreclosure, Koerner called me into his office and told me that Willie Brown was being cut. RKO didn't need him any longer. They had their *War of the Worlds* screenplay, and while it was a faithful adaptation of Howard Koch's "War of the Worlds" radio-dramatization, it wasn't "anything special". In fact, it was rather "pedestrian". So, they were going to release him from his contract. I begged and pleaded with Charles to keep Willie on the life of Christ feature, for Christ's sake, but Charles wouldn't budge. Willie had been released. He was going to have to return to his father and work in that steel-mill for this rest of his life. That was if I couldn't come up with another solution.

PETER: What solution could that have been?

ORSON: Give Willie a job on *Invasion From Mars* under an assumed name. Willie would report for duty as the script-supervisor as Harry Lime.

PETER: Your character from *The Third Man*?

ORSON: I was always partial to the name. I considered using it as a *nom de plume* throughout my youth. I even convinced Carol Reed to convince Graham Greene to give that name to my character in *The Third Man*. It was such a better name than the one my character had in the early drafts.

PETER: You're just going to let this bit of Hollywood trivia hang there with nary an explanation?

ORSON: Yep. I had hoped that Willie would break a little smile seeing "Harry Lime" up on the silver screen years after he resigned himself to his life in Colorado. An inside-inside-joke. Maybe he would tell his young wife that he was "Harry Lime" on the set on *The War of the Worlds*. Maybe he wouldn't. And maybe his bride would dismiss this as just another one of Willie Brown's whoppers of stories. I could imagine him sitting in their car after the movie and her smiling politely as he spun such wondrous bullshit of his adventures in Hollywood. She may believe him, or she may not, but would patiently listen to his "story". Little would she know that it was all true. He couldn't possibly make up a story any more filled to the brim with bullshit than the adventure Orson Welles and Harry Lime experienced once the cameras began to roll on *Invasion From Mars*, or *The War of the Worlds* as far as Charles Koerner was concerned.

PETER: We're finally getting to the meat of the story. ⚛

From the Desk of
WILLIAM FRANCIS
BROWN

October 30, 1997
Evening

To my son, Bob,

You may be asking yourself, then why did I break my sixty-year silence on such a public forum as "Coast to Coast AM with Art Bell"? Why not day-time television's numerous talk-shows hosted by the likes of Montel Williams, Jenny Jones, Maury Povich, Ricki Lake or the hundreds of others whose carbon-copy talk-shows were promptly cancelled by the finicky finger of fate. Perhaps CNN's prime-time staple Larry King Live with his part-entertainment, part-pseudonews interviews? All of these shows have had a penchant for exploiting a gullible viewing audience with subjects and guests which have taken a particularly unorthodox views of the nature of the world in general. Surely these forums would have readily accepted "The Orson Welles' Conspiracy" with open arms. These talk-show personalities acknowledge such outlandish personalities such as the self-styled, albeit world-famous psychic-mediums Sylvia Brown and John Edward. Every generation has had its own psychic-of-the-moment: Edgar Casey, Madam Blavatsky, Arthur Ford, Jeanne Dixon, Uri Geller, Shirley MacLaine, and James Van Praagh. Larry King, without any secondary guests of opposing opinions, allows psychics, such as Edward and Brown, to use their deceptively charismatic personalities to convince telephone callers that they commune with their deceased loved-ones and, in the case of Sylvia Brown, that her spirit guide Francine gives her insight into the secrets and mysteries of the unseen universe. Even supposedly hard-journalistic broadcasts such as Nightline with Ted Koppel broadcast a report on the United States military's use of the paranormal telepathic espionage technique known to the susceptible as "Remote Viewing". Larry King devoted an hour to the broadcast of a forum of purported experts debating the UFO phenomenon. That hokum such as this can find its way onto the nation's airways, without constant dissent, is baffling and quite disturbing.

So why "Coast to Coast AM with Art Bell"? I, personally, have no use for a man who had made a living exploiting his listening audience's regrettable interest in unidentified flying objects, time travel, occult knowledge, the protosciences of a biogenesis, astrobiology, neurotheology, and xenoarchaeology, pseudo-sciences of biblical scientific foresight, Christian Science, creation science, baraminology, flood geology, intelligent design, critical race theory, cryptozoology, Dianetics, the Duesberg hypothesis, megalithic yard, modern geocentrism, neuro-linguistic programming, perpetual motion, phrenology, physiognomy, remote viewing, spiritualism, the paranormal and most unfortunately, conspiracy theories. Pertaining to the definitions of some of the terms above, I haven't the foggiest!

This Art Bell is a charlatan and his callers are cranks, his guests are quacks, and his listeners are fools. His broadcasts are the subject of constant ridicule, unremitting skepticism, continual disapproval, unvarying condemnation, and relentless criticism. Bell defends his interviews with the callers by a foolish belief that by not criticizing them, they will be immune to such ridicule. On the contrary, by not screening his calls, Mr. Bell opens himself to various ridiculous claims.

One such caller, an amateur astronomer named Chuck Shramek, who no doubt had the most honest of intensions, exposed himself to frightful ridicule. Don Ecker of UFO Magazine reported, "It was November of 1996 and the huge story of the day was the Hale Bopp Comet. A beautiful and fiery display in the heavens, Hale Bopp was wowing all. One evening in November the Art Bell program received a call from Shramek. An amateur astronomer, Shramek had been 'imaging' the comet with his 10" SC telescope and a CCD camera. In the photo Shramek took there appeared to be another body close to the comet that had a 'ring like' form around this mysterious body. Shramek called it a 'Saturn Like Object'. He emailed it to Bell who quickly placed it on his website. The storm broke! Shramek was attacked across the board from all corners of the skeptical world. Alan Hale, co-discoverer of the Hale Bopp Comet, accused Shramek of 'promoting government conspiracies, promoting the work of fringe writers that include Richard Hoagland and Zecharia Sitchin.'" Mr. Shramek's innocent call about an unidentified "Saturn-Like Object" in his photograph of a comet began a firestorm of events that would end in the deaths of thirty-nine people with Art Bell at the eye of the maelstrom.

The very next night, "Coast to Coast AM" welcomed a repeated guest, Courtney Brown, the tenured Associate Professor of Political Science at Atlanta, Georgia's Emery University, to comment on the Hale-Bopp comet and its companion. Brown's Farsight Institute's professional remote viewers reported that by targeting the comet they identified an object which was artificial in nature and no doubt under intelligent control. Whitley Streiber, author of the alien abduction themed New York Time's non-fiction bestseller Communion and a friend and colleague of Art Bell, went on the Larry King Show with a photograph of the purported Hale-Bop "companion" UFO. The University of Hawaii stated that the photograph posted on Art Bell's website of the Hale-Bopp companion was, in fact, a digitally doctored photograph taken from their observatory.

This all would be laughable in its absurdity, except for the fact that a UFO religion led by Marshall Applewhite and Bonnie Nettles took the reports of the Comet Hale-Bopp companion "arrival is joyously very significant to us at 'Heaven's Gate'. The joy is that our Older Member in the Evolutionary Level Above Human(the 'Kingdom of Heaven') has made it clear to us that Hale-Bopp's approach is the 'marker' we've been waiting for -- the time for the arrival of the spacecraft from the Level Above Human to take us home to 'Their World' -- in the literal Heavens. Our 22 years of classroom here on planet Earth is finally coming to conclusion - 'graduation' from the Human Evolutionary Level. We are happily prepared to leave 'this world' and go with Ti's crew." Thirty nine members of the cult, dressed in matching sweat-suits and wearing brand-new sneakers, committed mass suicide based on the unfortunate and na�ve reports of Art Bell. But he continues to protect himself by calling his show "absolute entertainment".

Laughable.

However, Art Bell would cross the threshold, going from mere observer to actual participant, and into the pantheon of conspiracy theories at approximately 1:00 AM Eastern Standard Time on Friday morning, September 12, 1997 when Bell, himself, became the focal point for his own government conspiracy theory; a theory that involves aliens, government agents, electromagnetic pulses, errant satellites, and a former employee of the United States Air Force operating facility at Groom Lake, Nevada, formerly known as Air Force Flight Test Center, Detachment 3 and now known to skeptics and believers alike as Dreamland, the Farm, and most notoriously, Area 51.

Area 51 is, in reality, simply a designation taken from older maps of the Nevada Test Site, the locality of the US Department of Energy's nuclear weapons tests. This infamous military base, which the United States government fails to unequivocally acknowledge nor emphatically deny, is according to conjecture, used conjunctively to warehouse, scrutinize, and possibly "reverse engineer" crashed spacecraft of distinctly extraterrestrial origin and the scientific study of their living and/or deceased alien crew. The roads leading to Area 51 are littered with signs warning that "photography is prohibited" and to those under suspicion of trespass "use of deadly force is authorized" as pertaining to the 1950 McCarran Internal Security Act.

While many believers sight this as proof of a vast government conspiracy, they fail to recognize the simple fact that all government military bases, unequivocally acknowledged or emphatically denied, have similar discretions.

There is a question both the skeptic and believer must consider, is the large air base's location at the southwest corner of Groom Dry Lake, analkali bed, only few miles away from Puhrump, Nevada, the home of the "Coast to Coast AM with Art Bell" radio studio, a mere coincidence in this government conspiracy theory? And that the only eyewitness to said events of the morning of September 12, 1997 was a reporter for the less than reputable Penthouse adult men's magazine? All these are the ingredients for a classic, albeit ridiculous, conspiracy theory. This following is a transcript from the most harrowing part of supposed Area 51 broadcast:

ART BELL: On my Area 51 line 1, you're on the air, hello.

CALLER FROM AREA 51: Hello, Art?

ART: Yes.

51: *[sounding frightened]* I don't have a whole lot of time.

ART: Well, look, let's begin by finding out whether you're using this line properly or not.

51: Ok, in Area 51?

ART: Yes. Were you an employee or are you now?

51: I… I'm a former employee.

ART: A former employee?

51: I... I was let go on a medical discharge about a week ago and, and… [chokes] I kind of been running across the country. Damn, I don't know where to start, they're, they're gonna, they'll triangulate on this position really, really soon.

ART: So you can't spend a lot of time on the phone, so give us something quick.

51: *[voice broken with apparently suppressed crying]* OK, um, um, OK, what we're thinking of as aliens, Art, they're, uh, they're extra-dimensional beings, that, an earlier precursor of the space program they made contact with. They are not what they claim to be. They've infiltrated a lot of aspects of... of... of the military establishment, particularly the Area 51. The disasters that are coming... they... the military, I'm sorry, the government knows about them. And there's a lot of safe areas in this world that they could begin moving the population to now, Art.

In Penthouse Magazine (August 1998), Mark Ehrman made visual contact with Art Bell. Art Bell, however, made auditory contact with an employee of infamous secret military base Area 51.

ART: So they're not doing, not doing anything.

51: They are not. They want those major population centers wiped out so that the few that are left will be more easily controllable…

ART: *[fragment]* …discharged…

51: *[sobbing, then fragment]* I say we g…

Orchestrated not unlike Orson Welles' infamous radio-broadcast of "The War of the Worlds", this publicity stunt brought instantaneous mainstream attention to a radio program, which in spite of all attempts at spinning the Comet Hale-Bopp/Heaven's Gate fiasco into something less detrimental continued to be looked at with skeptical and scornful eyes. Those behind this hoax no doubt believed this publicity stunt would persuade and influence listeners toward their cause, the cause of furthering their hateful agenda, the persecution and harassment by the United States government. Despite drawing millions of listeners each and every night, "Coast to Coast AM" continued to have only a thoroughly niche audience.

Those outside looking in, viewed Art Bell as charlatan and agitator, who exploits this listeners for his own profit and gain. The mainstream media echoed these sentiments because the hoax was laughable in its execution. The lone eyewitness to the event was Mark Ehrman, a reporter for Penthouse magazine researching for an article entitled "Making Visual Contact with Art Bell", a man undoubtedly na□ve about the inner-workings of a radio-studio and caught completely unaware of the nature of what he was hearing and ignorant of the complexities of the publicity stunt.

Just as the call was reaching an utterly absurd and unrealistic climax, the hysterical and melodramatic caller stopped in mid-sentence. There was for twenty-five seconds, a situation in which all radio personalities dread: "dead air". This is a technique some believe was originated by Orson Welles fifty-nine years earlier to an analogous effect. Bell then rebroadcast a cued portion of a previous interview with Mark Fuhrman about, of all things, marijuana busts.

The interview continued unedited for thirty minutes, its only purpose, filling time; time that unnerved the listening audience making them increasingly uncomfortable wondering with their wild, fanatical imaginations what could have possibly gone awry with the phone call and what could have possibly happened to the unfortunate caller from Area 51.

Had the government traced the telephone call to a rural pay-phone and triangulated his position with global-positioning satellites, then eliminated the caller utilizing Ronald Reagan's "Star Wars" orbital laser technology? The sheer number of implausible ideas swirling around the minds of the increasingly paranoid listeners must have been staggering.

Then as abruptly as the segment ended, the "technical problems" were miraculously resolved. Art Bell returned to the air waves and reported to his agitated audience, who now hung on his every words hoping his explanation agreed with their outrageous imaginings, that the caller had screamed in what Bell took to be genuine terror or fright. This scream, which would have without a shadow of a doubt produced a fit of uncontrollable laughter in the listeners, had not been broadcast to the listeners, as it apparently occurred shortly after the line was disconnected from an unknown yet malicious source (a source mostly likely to have been the disconnect button on Art Bell's console). The transcript continues with a caller from Michigan commenting on the harrowing call; a caller who to my ear at least, sounds remarkably rehearsed.

[At 2:29:43 elapsed time the show resumes]

ART: In some way... Something knocked us off the air and we're on a back-up system now.

CALLER FROM MICHIGAN: It's the... The government, er...

ART: I don't know.

MICHIGAN: It has to be something now.

ART: Well, did you hear... Now you tell me, because you were listening.

MICHIGAN: That was awful strange.

ART: There was a really weird guy on the air when it went off?

MICHIGAN: Yeah, real weird out.

ART: Like, a going, sort of, soft of, sounding paranoid.

MICHIGAN: Yeah.

ART: Schizophrenic.

MICHIGAN: Like crying and everything.

ART: Yeah... yeah... yeah... and how far into the conversation was it when it went off?

MICHIGAN: Just a couple, about fifteen, twenty seconds. I'd say.

ART: Oh, you guys, you really missed a call then. And I've got a feeling that someone didn't want you guys to hear it.

MICHIGAN: Yeah.

[Art chuckles]

MICHIGAN: Cause it's really strange, then all of a sudden I'm hearing Mark Fuhrman when... when...

ART: Well, the network, of course, the network went immediately to a back up tape, while we tried to figure out what blew up here.

MICHIGAN: Uh-huh.

ART: So that's what you heard happen.

MICHIGAN: Uh-huh.

ART: And now we're on a back up link system.

MICHIGAN: Uh-huh.

ART: Boy, I'm telling you.

MICHIGAN: Am I on the air now?

ART: You're on the air right now. Well... you better be... yes.

MICHIGAN: Uh...

ART: And where are you, by the way.

MICHIGAN: I'm in Michigan.

ART: Michigan?

MICHIGAN: Yeah, I called the other night. And I wanted to ask two things.

ART: Real quick.

MICHIGAN: I, uh, wanted to say one thing and I wanted to ask another.

ART: Real quick.

MICHIGAN: I wanted to know if you'd play that "remote viewing" one when you were in... while you go to Egypt.

ART: Yes.

MICHIGAN: And also, I wanted to know, and all this stuff about... like... huh... Area 51... if it's like the government is trying to put it all out there like that... so... like some other place isn't being watched so much.

ART: In other words, it's some big decoy. And we'll apparently be back after the news.

[News break]

ART: We lost all transmit capabilities, on this end, here in Nevada. The transmitter went belly up, suddenly, for some unknown reason. I've never seen it do this in all the years, all the years that we've been on the air. I've never seen the transmitter in this way, just simply fail. And massively fail like a massive heart attack of some kind. And so we've gone to a back-up system to get the system to get the system to you, right on, and I'm presuming that it's getting to you right now. Totally bizarre folks. Totally bizarre.

Several inquires must be made concerning the baffling event recounted here: Why would any government agency, no matter how paranoid and secretive, go through the trouble of expending the effort and expense of altering a GE-1 satellite's spatial attitude with the purpose of silencing an obviously troubled and delusional man's incoherent rant concerning "extra-dimensional" alien entities inhabiting the government's conspiracy theory hotbed known as Area 51, broadcast on a radio talk-show with the sullied reputation of "Coast to Coast AM"? How can a caller from Kingston, Nevada (itself near Area 51) and an RF engineer employed at Hughes Aerospace in Tucson, himself an expert on EMP shielding both suffered "cloud bounce" from the electromagnetic pulse causing their home telephone lines to go dead and their personal computers and digital watches wiped clean, yet they were able to call into the Puhrump, Nevada studio of Art Bell, himself a victim of the surprisingly selective pulse?

Why, in the name of goodness and reason, after a successful power outage had silenced the paranoid caller and nullified any possible conspiracy theories, would someone alleging to be with "Area 51 security" expose the details of his classified employment with a secret government operating facility the very same government neither acknowledges nor denies by stating on public airwaves that his job is to "close" in Groom Lake security?

Why would he explain that the "Coast to Coast AM" network had been "pulsed" by an orbital electromagnetic pulse targeted solely on the Puhrump, Nevada radio-studio? And why would he inform Art Bell that he "would not hear from the caller again"?

Conspiracy theory nuts, those who listened to the broadcast as it occurred and the millions of others who downloaded the broadcast over the Internet, would claim disinformation as the only rational explanation for the elaborate silencing of the former employee of Area 51 and the security officer's subsequent telephone call.

I offer a counter explanation: lunacy. That and an Orson Welles worthy publicity stunt. So why did I confess my involvement in a vast government conspiracy on such a public forum and breeding ground for such claptrap as "Coast to CoastAM with Art Bell"? I didn't make the decision to call him, my son did.

You, my son, was absolutely convinced Art Bell would be my savior. Art Bell, you told me repeatedly in numerous long-distance telephone calls, would offer me a forum where I would be completely free from public ridicule and I would escape certain scorn and derision. I would be embraced by reassurance, and, most assuredly, I would not be made a laughing stock. (You know you father far toowell) So, in hindsight, I should never have dialed 1-702-727-1222, the telephone number given to first time callers into KNYE 95.1 FM, the home of "Coast to Coast AM with Art Bell". But having just that, I should have hung up the phone the moment he put me on the air. However, hearing my son's voice on the radio recounting his schizophrenic hallucinations and paranoid delusions after nearly sixty years brought me crashing back to reality. The origins of my son's paranoid fantasies were, in actuality, born with "The Orson Welles' Conspiracy".

Sincerely, your father,

William Francis Brown

William Francis Brown

Spies! From Office Space

The ballroom at the real Hotel Annapolis that Orson Welles' recreated on a false set on his sound-stage to fool RKO executives!

Was William Dock, 76, the basis for Farmer Wilmuth in the "fake" radio-dramatization that Howard Koch's script made famous?

ORSON: I had a couple dozen sets, not only designed, but built for *The War of the Worlds* that I never had any intention of filming on. The *Invasion From Mars* script that Willie and I labored on was blessedly short on scenes, unlike the set-building I overindulged with on *Citizen Kane*. For *Invasion,* I had my studio at CBS, the ballroom at the Hotel Annapolis, and of course the oval-office in the White House; and certainly miscellaneous offices and hallways, which could and would be interchangeable. But I had the carpenters busy building sets for scenes for *The War of the Worlds*, including, but certainly not limited to, the observatory at Princeton, the Wilmuth farm near Grover's Mill, the ballroom at the Park Plaza Hotel, and the rooftop at the CBS studios, and the desolate streets in the post-invasion apocalypse with Pearson and the Stranger. There was an ulterior motive to my building these sets, it kept the spies for the brass at RKO occupied; everyone, except for an essential few, thought we were filming a simple adaptation of Howard Koch's "War of the Worlds" radio-script. I still feel bad for the actors who were cast as "Professor Richard Pierson", "Carl Philips", "Farmer Wilmuth", the "Secretary of the Interior" and all of the others. While they would act in front of the cameras on the aforementioned sets, the cameras were actually rolling film for a feature that was actually filmed solely to pacify the brass and not for general release in the cinemas.

PETER: You certainly were covering your bases in this little conspiracy of yours.

ORSON: Little conspiracy? It was a vast conspiracy; a conspiracy worthy of the United States government. I felt like a vaudevillian plate-spinner trying to keep so many plates in the air and not crashing down upon my head. As I've said, I had Willie Brown write an adaptation of Koch's "War of the

HOWARD KOCH
THE PANIC BROADCAST
THE WHOLE STORY OF
ORSON WELLES'
LEGENDARY RADIO SHOW
INVASION FROM MARS
THE COMPLETE SCRIPT, WITH MANY PHOTOGRAPHS, CARTOONS AND NEWSPAPER ARTICLES OF THE ASTOUNDING AFTERMATH!
AN INTRODUCTORY INTERVIEW WITH
ARTHUR C. CLARKE

Willie Brown based his decoy screenplay on Howard Hoch's "War of the Worlds" radio-script published in 1970! Which was, of course, not *the "whole story" of Orson' Welles' legendary radio show! The book you hold in your greedy hands is the "whole story" of the vast government conspiracy!*

Worlds" radio-script, I built the sets required for such a film, and cast of the necessary actors and actresses. While all this busy-work was busily being worked, Willie and I wrote the *Invasion From Mars* script in Herman Mankiewicz bungalow in Victorville. Once back on the studio lot, we re-purposed the sets built for the fake film to work for the actual film, and cast an entirely different group of actors, who were listed on the call-sheet of *War of the Worlds* simply as extras.

PETER: Why are you calling the film *Invasion From Mars* instead of *The War of the Worlds*? What prompted the change?

ORSON: I called the film I was actually filming *Invasion From Mars* and the fake film was not actually filming *The War of the Worlds*. It helped to keep Willie and me sane while trying to keep the two productions separate. While Willie was technically only my screenwriter, he was so much more; he was my partner-in-crime, my co-conspirator and my confidant. If it wasn't for Willie's presence and participation as "Harry Lime", Charles Koerner and the rest of the brass would have easily caught on to my subterfuge and had me drummed out of Hollywood unceremoniously. As for the titles *Invasion From Mars* and *The War of the Worlds*, the brass simply believed that the two were interchangeable.

PETER: And none of either cast caught on?

ORSON: Of course not. I cast contracted actors in the lead rolls and amateur actors from surrounding community theaters as extras for *The War of the Worlds*. The very same community theater actors were then cast as the principle characters on *Invasion From Mars*.

PETER: And they never suspected a thing?

ORSON: Of course not. The amateur actors were so pleased to have lines, and in some cases, pages upon pages of lines on a major RKO feature film. They never complained and more so, never suspected anything was amiss. They thought they were being filmed by the second unit.

PETER: Orson Welles directing the second unit? How in the world did you pull that feat off?

ORSON: They assumed I was such a controlling, power-mad director, that I *insisted* on filming the second unit scenes. All of the scenes in *Invasion From Mars* fit into the idea we were filming *The War of the Worlds* so interlockingly like a jigsaw puzzle.

PETER: *[Sighs.]* Surely, they would have caught on to the shear amount of script you were filming. You were effectively shooting two complete films simultaneously. Even if one of the films was, as you claimed, only to keep the RKO brass occupied. That could not have passed the smell test.

ORSON: How many pages did Mank write on *Kane* that I had to whittle to make a producible script? How many scenes are routinely filmed that never make it into the finished cut? How many actors over the years have complained that they ended up on the cutting-room floor? It's become cliché. With this new LaserDisc home video format finally on the market, I'm sure it's only a matter of time before Hollywood begins mining their vaults for all of these unnecessary scenes to release "director's cuts" of practically every film ever released.

PETER: Surely, they wouldn't tinker with Hollywood

Herman Mankiewicz toiling away on the script to The American, *which Orson Welles' butchered as (and stole credit to)* Citizen Kane!

history.

ORSON: Surely, they would. I can see it now. Those LaserDisc sleeves emblazoned with "the version the director (never) intended you to see", "30 minutes of unseen footage restored", or even "45 seconds you never saw in theaters." It is only a matter of time, Peter. Only a matter of time.

PETER: *[Audibly sighs.]*

ORSON: All of those scenes that may have been forgotten about by the studio brass, discarded by director's onto the cutting-room floor by ruthless editors. But they have never once been lost, discarded, or forgotten by those who were featured in those scenes. Their only scenes. What about all of the B and C-list actors who brought their friends and family to the big Hollywood premieres, but walked out of the cinema with their heads hung, because it was only at that moment did they realize they ended up on the cutting-room floor. Their friends and family try to console the inconsolable. Even major A-list actors discover they are victims of the infamous cutting room. This is the Hollywood system. Everyone who was an extra on *War of the Worlds* and a featured player in *Invasion From Mars*, just assumed I was filming everything and would do my editing in the editing room. Even green community theater actors knew this truth of the Hollywood system.

PETER: You used the Hollywood system to game the Hollywood system. That's kind of brilliant.

ORSON: Any less would not be worthy of me. And when the film never made it into theaters, no one would ever believe the wild stories they would tell of the film they acted in; a film that no one at RKO would ever acknowledge.

PETER: Why would they never mention they acted on a *War of the Worlds* feature? Surely there would be some stories floating around Hollywood about a *War of the Worlds* film.

ORSON: You know Hollywood as well as I do, Peter. Films self-destruct all the time. Some never go beyond the screenplay or ever get in front of the cameras. Those that do, sometimes they run out of time or money. Some lose principle actors to alcohol or affairs or other productions. Some are utterly ruined in the editing room. Others are completed but sit on the shelf collecting dust for years or even decades. There were and are any number of reasons why films are never completed or fail to reach the cinemas. How many of my own films have been abandoned for all of these reasons and more? How many of these Hollywood films have become public knowledge? Despite my own fame in Hollywood, how many of my failed films are known outside the infinitesimal collective of cinemaphiles, who are obsessed with me. The memory of a *War of the Worlds* film simply vanished, just like Uncle Henry's farm in *The Wizard of Oz.* My film vanished like a fart in a whirlwind... all the way to Oz! Only the Munchkins have ever screened a copy of my finished film!

The infamous cyclone snatching Dorothy away from her farm in Kansas! Little does Orson Welles know the only surviving print of his Invasion From Mars *will be likewise spirited away to a super secret government vault with the Ark of the Covenant!*

PETER: Orson! Such hyperbole!

ORSON: It was a perfect plan.

PETER: Your plan involved casting actors in and hiring an entire crew for a *War of the Worlds* feature; a film damn near everyone in Hollywood is expecting you to make; and you anticipated that no one would blab about it. [*Sarcastically*] Sounds like the perfect plan.

ORSON: Since nobody has even whispered about the film until tonight... [*mimicking Peter's sarcasm*] sounds like the perfect plan. But the conspiracy between me and Willie wasn't to keep knowledge of the film from the people of the United States, that was the government's conspiracy. The "Willie Brown Conspiracy", as it were, was to film *The Invasion From Mars* under the nose of the brass at RKO Pictures, all while their respective noses were buried so far up my backside that they never realized their *War of the Worlds* feature was not getting made. If knowledge of the actual invasion from Mars leaked in the days and weeks after our *Invasion From Mars* feature film was completed, it was nary a concern of mine. I knew the government would stop at nothing to keep the knowledge exposed by *The Invasion From Mars* from disseminating to the public. Why should I care less who knew about the film once it was completed? It was getting the film completed that proved to be the problem!

PETER: Without the executives at RKO finding out about your subterfuge?

ORSON: Exactly. I had the executives convinced. Now all I needed was to keep my cast, I mean both casts, from blowing my cover. You see, as far as the cast and crew of *War of the Worlds* was concerned, I had gone off on a bender and Harry Lime was there to save the production from eminent disaster. Harry had to rally the cast and crew together so they could keep my "condition" a secret to spare their director the ignominy of being drummed out of Hollywood. Harry would direct the film in order to keep the production going.

PETER: What? *War of the Worlds* was actually shot by the Harry Lime, essentially the second-unit director, while *Invasion From Mars* was the first-unit?

ORSON: That's one way of looking at it. All that mattered to all involved, Harry Lime, the cast, and myself included was that if I was fired, the production would fold and everyone would be let go and that certainly wasn't in the best interest of those involved on *The War of the Worlds*. We needed to get the film finished.

PETER: And your cast– I mean– cast*s* agreed?

ORSON: Certainly. Do you know how many directors throughout the history of Hollywood were outrageous drunks? They bought into Harry's story that after *Citizen Kane* I was trying to tank the production, to tank my entire career, by falling off the wagon. They believed I was drowning in a

Orson Welles would not only take the pseudonymous director's name for his character in The Third Man, *he would also base the performance on Willie Brown's turn as Harry Lime, the "director" of* The War of Worlds!

Though the vodka in the bottles would have been replaced with water and the whiskey with sun tea, Orson Welles based his own onset inebriated and outlandish behavior on the notorious tea-totaler WC Fields (pictured left, certainly not right)

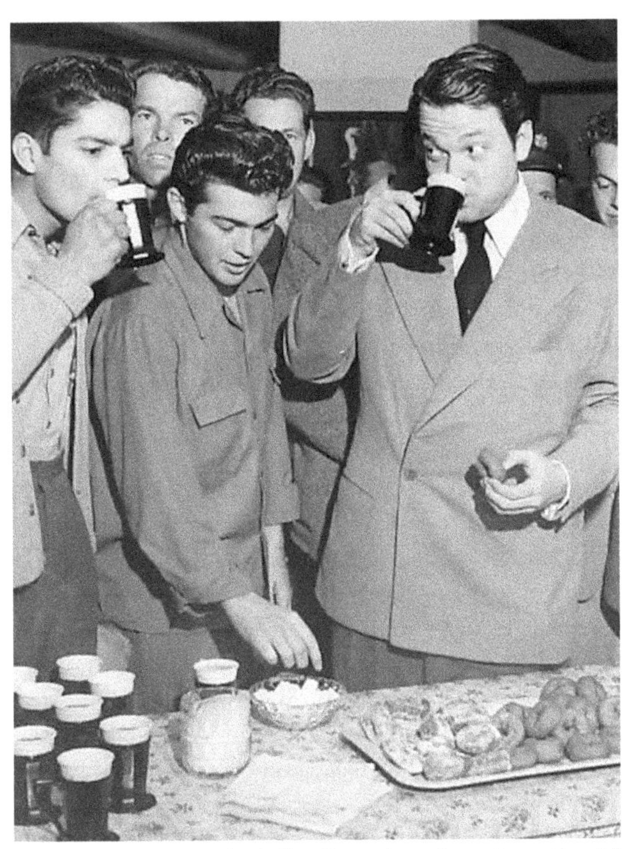

Orson Welles imbibing (spiked) coffee at the craft services table with young actors playing soldiers in his War of the Worlds *feature!*

bottle of booze morning, noon, and night. I would show up on set, stinking of booze and doing my best WC Fields impersonation.

PETER: Ouch.

ORSON: Or Mank.

PETER: Double ouch.

ORSON: I would insist on directing the scene they were in the middle of shooting. The subsequent takes would be monumental failures and Harry would then escort me from the set and finish the scene himself. Much to the relief of all involved. It worked out brilliantly. The brass at RKO got their *War of the Worlds* rushes, which got them off my back and I had the freedom to direct *The Invasion From Mars* in relative peace and quiet.

PETER: And when RKO's spies appeared on the set of *The War of the Worlds*?

ORSON: Relative. My cast and crew covered for me. They were such troopers. I was like a drunk uncle at Christmas dinner. You were worried sick your drunk uncle would ruin the holiday, but your family still adores them. My cast and crew still adored me, all because of Harry Lime's constant praise of their wayward director. They would actually thank me for the opportunity to have a screen credit on an actual Hollywood motion-picture. All this despite them believing I was a terrible drunk.

PETER: How were you able to maintain doing two productions at the same time. Wouldn't the costs have been outrageous. I can't even imagine how one would accomplish such a feat.

ORSON: For every foot of film shot on the set of *Invasion From Mars*, two feet of film would be recorded in the daily tallies as having been shot on *The War of the Worlds*.

PETER: Clever.

ORSON: Charles knew that I shot far too many takes for the tastes of the brass, and because of this, they never questioned the amount of film I was using, or the number of actors required on set. The cast of *Invasion From Mars* had been listed as extras on the *War of the Worlds* call-sheets, so until all the book-keeping has done, not even the accountants would know how many man-hours I was using to get both films made. The accountants wouldn't get wise about the double billing until it was far too late. The brass were strangely so satisfied with the fake rushes that they actually gave me the room I needed to stretch my arms... stretch my arms out to strangle them of course.

PETER: How droll, Orson, how very droll.

ORSON: I would finally have my finished film shot and in the can before anyone realized I had switched the child they were so desperate to be born with a changeling. How Harry Lime and I were finally able to make it into the editing room without the jig being up was a complete mystery. If I had been a religious man, I might have considered it a Mystery of Faith, but there wasn't any faith to be had in our little conspiracy. It was nothing but dumb luck that we found ourselves in the peaceful quiet of the editing room. Films are not made on the sound stage, in front of the cameras, the real genius of filmmaking happens in the editing room. On the set, I can shoot take after take after bloody take from every conceivable and absurd angle. The director is Jackson Polack just throwing paint around; the editor is more like Michelangelo, who sees the David in the block of marble and knows what pieces to remove. I always walked away from filmmaking covered more in paint than I cared for and would spend the next several weeks...

PETER: Orson.

ORSON: Months...

An accountant working at RKO Radio Pictures, who would be none-the-wiser concerning the War of the Worlds *budget until it was too late!*

PETER: Orson.

ORSON: Years having to remove layers upon layers of built up paint to finally reveal the truth masterpiece I created.

PETER: That's a more appropriate metaphor.

ORSON: The accountants wouldn't get wise until it was far too late. I would finally have my finished film shot and in the can before anyone realized I had switched the child they were so desperate to be born with a changeling. How long would it take until the new parents realized that they innocent child they were nurturing was actually a demonic spawn of the Devil who would rend their souls asunder?

PETER: That's not quite an appropriate metaphor, Orson.

ORSON: But once Willie Brown—

PETER: Harry Lime, Orson. If you're intending to maintaining the conspiracy.

ORSON: —Harry? Willie? There's no need to dick around with semantics.

PETER: Orson! Language!

ORSON: It doesn't matter. While we secluded ourselves in the quiet of the editing room, we discovered a new problem. Although all the film canisters were conveniently labeled either *Invasion From Mars* or *The War of the Worlds*, we discovered we weren't as careful as we had thought we had been. We would discovered scenes necessary for *Invasion From Mars* nowhere to be found and scenes from *The War of the Worlds* everywhere to be found. We had mixed up our shooting scripts. So instead of having to go through just one set of canisters, we had to go through them all. Miles upon miles of film that we never thought would ever see the light of day, we were forced to watch *ad naseum*. I had this recurring nightmare that during the Hollywood premiere of *Invasion From Mars*, Howard Koch would be sitting beaming a few rows in the front of me. Then by the time the first reel was done, Howard would realize the horror of the changeling child he saw before him. It knew that I had lied. Lied to the brass at RKO. And worst of all I had lied to him. How dare I? He would now do everything in his power to

The theater fire from Orson Welles' nightly nightmare!

destroy this abomination of a film and me along with it. In my dream, I never saw Howard get up from out of his seat. It wouldn't be until I saw the horror of the film melting on the screen, that I realized Howard was intent on destroying me. Soon the fire that started in the projection room would engulf the theater. The audience would begin trampling each other in vain attempts to escape the conflagration. The sounds of screams and the scent of burning flesh turn the Hollywood premiere of *Invasion From Mars* into a literal Dante's *Inferno.* As I sat in my seat too stunned to move, Howard would walk up behind me with a butcher's knife and slit my lying throat.

PETER: My word, Orson. That's graphic.

Little did George Orwell know that what he was merely speculating about in his seminal novel 1984 *had been lived by Orson Welles in 1942!*

ORSON: I awoke in a cold sweat over this nightmare every single night during our editing of *Invasion From Mars.* Little did I know the hell I would unleash upon poor Willie and myself once the most powerful people in the world saw the film. When I read George Orwell's dystopian masterwork, *1984*, I'm afraid I was a little let down by the entire premise. How could Orwell be so naïve to believe he was writing speculative fiction? Didn't he realize the true power wielded by the President of the United States of America, the most powerful office in the world, and the power of those who pulled the President's strings? If he only knew what the true state of affairs was, he would have burnt his manuscript in the fireplace as being too tame and not nearly imaginative enough. Airstrip One is a veritable Disneyland compared to the nation we live in. The citizens of Oceania are blissfully aware of the unending war, the omnipresent and seemingly omnipotent government surveillance systems, and propagandistic manipulation of the populous. We are not. "War is Peace, Freedom is Slavery, Ignorance is Strength." They see their worship of "Big Brother", the leader of the "Ingsoc" party, not as a hopeless struggle against totalitarianism, but as an acceptance of how life is. A cult of personality is still a cult. But if George knew the truth, as I know it, he would have been thoroughly disappointed by his own Muse, that he would refuse to write another word. What Winston Smith did in the *Minitrue*, by rewriting newspaper articles, so that the historical records always supports the party line, is no different than what I did on that cold October morning in 1938 when I conspired with the government to cover up a Martian invasion. Changing the historical record to serve the needs of the Party. What is worse, Peter, a government that discourages "Freedom as slavery", or a government than enslaves its people through false freedom?

PETER: You don't mean that literally.

ORSON: I do. A people that believe they have the freedom to say anything because it is protected by the Constitution of the United States of America is actually less likely to use their freedom of speech than in a totalitarian regime where you are not allowed to speak. If you can be arrested by the "Thought Police" because of a "thoughtcrime", are you more likely or less likely to have rebellious thoughts? These are witty enough phrases to have entered into our vocabulary, but they ultimately do a disservice to us all. The hippies were able to voice their concerns about the Vietnam war in a chorus of protest, but ultimately who won the movement? The war came to an end in spite their protests. The status quo remains and will always remain. Only rarely does a movement actually change the culture. The Civil Rights movement may seem to be a victory today, but in the future, we will look back on these progressive years as not nearly progressive enough, and perhaps even regressive, just as the Jim Crow laws were slavery in all but name. You are more likely to revolt when you realize you have few rights, than you are if you (so wrongly) believe you have too many rights. If you are allowed to read anything, you are more likely, not less likely, to believe anything the government tells you. That's the trap set by the Founding Fathers. If they give you the right to bear arms, you are less likely to think you might actually need them. The only time you hear of these militias stockpiling an armory is when they believe the government is about to limit their rights. You give people enough freedom, so that you can better control them.

PETER: You're laying it on awfully thick.

ORSON: The Code of Hammurabi, the Ten Commandments, the Magna Carta, all were seen as landmark documents in their own time, each one more progressive than the last. If even the king was subject to the law and individuals had rights, rights to justice and a fair trial, then the peasantry could and would be placated. Has the world changed with any of these? The world only got incrementally better. Very seldom is there a seismic shift in governance. The writers of our Constitution surely didn't believe the Magna Carta was enough, because the Crown still wielded an ungodly amount of power. They settled on a democracy as our force of governance, but was it true Athenian democracy or a constitutionally limited representative democratic republic? How could any of us actually have freedom when we enslaved an entire race of men? Power was reserved for white, Anglo-Saxon Protestant men. The government of our supposed United States of America has used the very Constitution to repress and enslave *everyone*.

PETER: Now that is just reckless hyperbole, Orson.

ORSON: It's not paranoia if the government is actually out to get you. Since 1942, I have a special affinity for paranoid schizophrenics. What must it be like to live your life believing you are being watched by the government. When you come home from work, you wonder how long government spooks have spent in your home, violating your privacy, and installing listening devices to keep track of you. You know some faceless agent of a shadow department agency has rifled around your drawers and cabinets, looking for anything incriminating, looking for evidence of a truth that only you have proof of, but you have no proof they were ever in your home. You cannot confide in your closest and dearest friends, because they will ask you if you are on your medication, or worse, merely pity you. To live in constant fear of people who wield a power so absolute they can come and go at will, do what they please to whom they please, with little– no!– *no* accountability, has to be a special kind of torture. This is the torture I have lived through every day of my life for the past– exactly– forty years. Not only did I sign my own personal deal with the Devil when I swore before God and country that I would not reveal the *Truth* that Martians invaded Virginia and marched on Washington DC that cold, evening in late October, 1938, that the radio-broadcasts heard by *million* of listeners were real– nay– authentic news reports. If I had not conspired with FDR's proxy-puppet William Randolph Hearst to be a part of a vast left-wing conspiracy to deceive the kind, honest, hardworking citizens of this great nation, then maybe the last forty years would have developed differently. Of course, it would have. It would have developed differently.

PETER: Why would the government be so concerned about our knowledge of a Martian invasion?

The Roman Catholic Church under Pope Pius XII would collapse to utter rubble if the truth of the existence of Martians, who are not mentioned in the Holy Bible, had been exposed by Orson Welles!

ORSON: "Why would the government be so concerned about our knowledge of a Martian invasion?" This knowledge would cripple and destroy our fragile human psyche. We would like to believe that when confronted by a literally alien threat, that humanity would rally itself together in unity and solidarity. But that isn't really the case. Entire nation-states would crumble to dust and stock markets would vaporize currency like a fart in a whirlwind. Religions everywhere on earth would have all faith lost in them once their sycophants learned that humans are not a unique creature made by our Creator in His own image. The religious questioned whether the earth was round, whether there were other planets in our solar system, whether the earth was the center of the entire universe or orbited lazily around the sun. If knowledge that our Creator created another sentient creation on our planetary neighbor, then the entire book of Genesis was a bold-faced lie. Why are we so special if *Martians* exist? If we are just one in an entire commonwealth of sentient species in our solar neighborhood, then we are not special, not unique, not created in the image of God. What does God look like if we are humanoid and Martians are literally unearthly creatures? We couldn't both be created in His image. Scientists know that Mars is the older, colder world. If the Martian civilization was at its height when we were still swinging in trees, do we have the image of God wrong? Wouldn't God have made Martians in his own image, before turning his attention to the strange primates slowly descending from the trees to hunt the savannas of Africa? Where would Martians fit into the narrative of the Word of God: The Holy Bible? They don't. They simply don't.

PETER: Didn't Jesus speak of other sheep in his flock?

ORSON: Since when did you become a Jesuit lawyer? We as a species just have to believe we are unique. Why do so many Evangelical Christians dismiss our intimate evolutionary relationships with Neanderthals and *Homo Erectus*? We, as a species, have driven every other *hominid* to utter extinction. We cannot abide sharing this planet with any other form of sentience. We would have been broken the very core of our being if we discovered we were not... *special.*

PETER: That's awfully condescending.

ORSON: That's awfully the Truth! HG Wells was a Goddamn prophet. I may have been part of an "Orson Welles' Conspiracy" but there was another conspiracy before me: an "HG Wells Conspiracy"! What I went through pales in comparison to what Herbert George Wells went through! I don't know much about it but I do know that

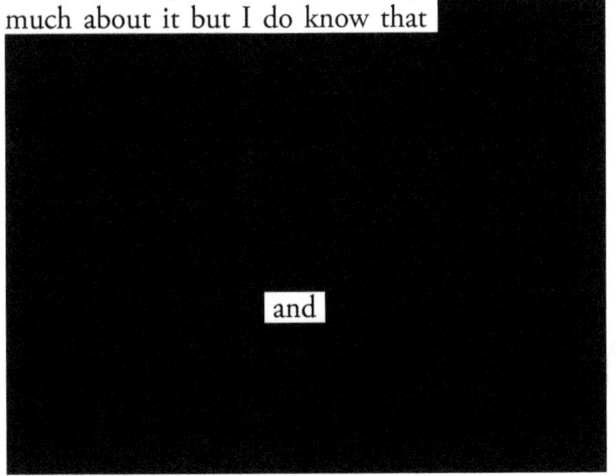

HG Wells, along with his misspelled namesake Orson Welles, discuss the geopolitical realities the older Brit had began to expose in his *seminar 1895 and 1897 journalistic exposés in* Pearson's Magazine*!*

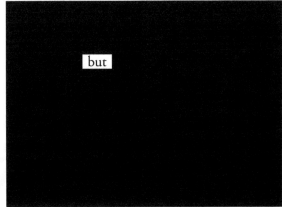

I have made *The War of the Worlds* my own Holy writ. Why devote oneself to the fiction of the Holy Bible, when you can read the historical and factual truth of *The War of the Worlds*. When I played Father Maple in *Moby Dick*, I studied the great sermons of Charles Spurgeon to prepare for the role. Now, if I had my druthers, I would quote *The War of the Worlds* chapter-and-verse: *"No one would have believed in the last years of the nineteenth century (or even the middle years of the twentieth) that this world was being watched keenly and closely by intelligences greater than man's and yet as mortal as his own; that*

as men busied themselves about their various concerns they were scrutinised and studied, perhaps almost as narrowly as a man with a microscope might scrutinise the transient creatures that swarm and multiply in a drop of water. With infinite complacency men went to and fro over this globe about their little affairs, serene in their assurance of their empire over matter. It is possible that the infusoria under the microscope do the same. No one gave a thought to the older worlds of space as sources of human danger, or thought of them only to dismiss the idea of life upon them as impossible or improbable. It is curious to recall some of the mental habits of those departed days. At most terrestrial men fancied there might be other men upon Mars, perhaps inferior to themselves and ready to welcome a missionary enterprise. Yet across the gulf of space, minds that are to our minds as ours are to those of the beasts that perish, intellects vast and cool and unsympathetic, regarded this earth with envious eyes, and slowly and surely drew their plans against us. And early in the twentieth century came the great disillusionment. The planet Mars, I scarcely need remind the reader, revolves about the sun at a mean distance of 140,000,000 miles, and the light and heat it receives from the sun is barely half of that received by this world. It must be, if the nebular hypothesis has any truth, older than our world; and long before this earth ceased to be molten, life upon its surface must have begun its course. The fact that it is scarcely one seventh of the volume of the earth must have accelerated its cooling to the temperature at which life could begin. It has air and water and all that is necessary for the support of animated existence. Yet so vain is man, and so blinded by his vanity, that no writer, up to the very end of the nineteenth century, expressed any idea that intelligent life might have developed there far, or indeed at all, beyond its earthly level. Nor was it generally understood that since Mars is older than our earth, with scarcely a quarter of the superficial area and remoter from the sun, it necessarily follows that it is not only more distant from time's beginning but nearer its end. The secular cooling that must someday overtake our planet has already gone far indeed with our neighbour. Its physical condition is still largely a mystery, but we know now that even in its equatorial region the midday temperature barely approaches that of our coldest winter. Its air is much more attenuated than ours, its oceans have shrunk until they cover but a third of its surface, and as its slow seasons change huge snowcaps gather and melt about either pole and periodically inundate its temperate zones. That last stage of exhaustion, which to us is still incredibly remote, has become a present-day problem for the inhabitants of Mars. The immediate pressure of necessity has brightened their intellects, enlarged their powers, and hardened their hearts. And looking across space with instruments, and intelligences such as we have scarcely dreamed of, they see, at its nearest distance only 35,000,000 of miles sunward of them, a morning star of hope, our own warmer planet, green with vegetation and grey with water, with a cloudy atmosphere eloquent of fertility, with glimpses through its drifting cloud wisps of broad stretches of populous country and narrow, navy-crowded seas. And we men, the creatures who inhabit this earth, must be to them at least as alien and lowly as are the monkeys and lemurs to us. The intellectual side of man already admits that life is an incessant struggle for existence, and it would seem that this too is the belief of the minds upon Mars. Their world is far gone in its cooling and this world is still crowded with life, but crowded only with what they regard as inferior animals. To carry warfare sunward is, indeed, their only escape from the destruction that, generation after generation, creeps upon them. And before we judge of them too harshly we must remember what ruthless and utter destruction our own species has wrought, not only upon animals, such as the vanished bison and the dodo, but upon its inferior races. The Tasmanians, in spite of their human likeness, were entirely swept out of existence in a war of extermination waged by European immigrants, in the space of fifty years. Are we such apostles of mercy as to complain if the Martians warred in the same spirit? The Martians seem to have calculated their descent with amazing subtlety--their mathematical learning is evidently far in excess of ours--and to have carried out their preparations with a well-nigh perfect unanimity. Had our instruments permitted it, we might have seen the gathering trouble far back in the nineteenth century. Men like Schiaparelli watched the red planet--it is odd, by-the-bye, that for countless centuries Mars has been the star of war--but failed to interpret the fluctuating appearances of the markings they mapped so well. All that time the Martians must have been getting ready." [Takes a few deep breathes.] War of the World chapter one verses one to... who the hell knows.

PETER: Orson, are you winded from that long-winded exposition?

ORSON: Quite. *[Breathes heavily into the microphone.]* Now where were we? ⚛

PARANOIA! THE BRAIN EATER

ORSON: As Willie Brown and I slowly pieced the *Invasion From Mars* jigsaw puzzle together from the mess of two jigsaw puzzles being mixed together, we finally had a cohesive and coherent film.

PETER: Again with the jigsaw dig at Marion Davies, Orson?

The actress Dorothy Comingore plays with jigsaw puzzles in what film critics said was Orson Welles thinly veiled attack on Marion Davies!

ORSON: Nothing of the sort. I don't have the foggiest notion as to what you may be referring to... having mixed shooting schedules made the film canisters we needed to unravel an ungodly mess of pieces of a film. It was just the most applicable metaphor I could make at the moment. No disrespect towards Ms. Davies was intended nor desired. I was just thankful to have a finished film to screen for network executives. Charles Koerner was so excited when one of his spies– I mean– stooges– I mean– assistants– no, I actually mean– traitors informed him that *The War of the Worlds* was being editied. The celebration that went on behind closed doors must have rivaled Mardi Gras. Only Harry Lime and myself were not invited, of course. Why celebrate with the founders of the feast? They contributed nothing, quite literally nothing to our film.

PETER: "Literally", Orson? Really? You know my pet-peeve about the use of the word "literally". They contributed financially to your motion picture.

ORSON: Like I said, "nothing"– important. They contributed literally nothing important to our film.

PETER: Except paying for the thousands upon thousands of feet of film used to shoot your movie. And, of course, signing the checks that paid for your actors, assistant directors, second-unit director, location scouts, camera operators...

ORSON: You've made your point.

PETER: Film loaders, lighting technicians, grips, gaffers, best boys, sound designers, set builders...

ORSON: Peter.

PETER: Scenic decorators and dressers, propmasters, costume designers, hair and make-up artists, special effects, stunt-men, craft services...

ORSON: Spies, flunkies, yes-men, hangers-on, royal-pains-in-my-arse...

PETER: Now, you've make your point.

ORSON: RKO contributed, figuratively, a drop of water in the bucket of the ocean of Hollywood financing and quite literally $303,574.81 to make our film. Satisfied?

PETER: Quite.

ORSON: And every single penny of that $303,574.81 was going to be– literally– pissed down the toilet the moment I presented our finished film to Charles Koerner– Ha!

PETER: How did Mr. Koerner react to your screening of *Invasion From Mars*?

ORSON: Oh, Peter. I can't spoil the ending of my little conspiracy just yet. You don't ask Mozart to listen to the final movement during the Overture?

PETER: *[Sighs.]*. This is going to be a long night. You have anything stiff to drink?

ORSON: I thought you'd never ask. *[Overly dramatic and tragic pause. Sound of pouring.]* It was all my fault. If it wasn't for the audacity of my arrogance, I never would have put myself, Willie Brown, my cast and crew, and the entire RKO studio in jeopardy of being labeled forever onward as traitors. How could I have known the lengths that the government would go to keep their secrets, however asinine and implausible these secrets may have been.

PETER: How could you have not known? That is your greatest sin and weakness, Orson. It was, it is, and it will forever be your hubris. How couldn't you have known that poking that sleeping grizzly bear, you would incur the wrath of William Randolph Hearst? You flaunted your hubris on the silver screen. Charles Foster Kane was William Randolph Hearst. Susan Alexander was Marion Davies. Xanadu was San Simeon. *The Examiner* was *The Inquirer. Et cetera. Et cetera. Ad nauseam.* The list of parallels and outright slander is a mile long.

Orson Welles insisted until his dying day that his portrayal of Charles Foster Kane was more based on himself than William Randolph Hearst!

ORSON: Kane was actually a composite of several people including myself. Don't forget, I was far more merciless with myself in my portrayal of Kane than I ever was with Hearst. Hearst never lost his mother like Kane did. I was the one who lost his mother! I am Kane. I... am... Kane! I have always been Kane. *Citizen Kane* told my life story, not Hearst's. My rise. My fall. I have destroyed my life just as easily as Kane destroyed his room in that iconic cinematic moment. *Citizen Kane* was prophecy. The prophecy foretold by Charles Foster Kane was not fulfilled by William Randolph Hearst, but by George Orson Welles!

PETER: I'm truly sorry, Orson.

ORSON: And Susan Alexander was, in fact, based on...

PETER: Stop it, Orson. We've been friends for far too long to whitewash *Citizen Kane*. You knew what you were doing the entire time. You knew the moment Mank showed you *American*, that stupid book he was toiling away on. *Citizen Kane* was the life story of William Randolph Hearst. You weren't hiding anything. You were flaunting your twenty-four year-old hubris in the face of one of the most powerful men in the country. You gave the Hearst's pet name for Marion's– private parts–

When William Randolph Hearst and Marion Davies privately screened a copy of Citizen Kane, *how horrified and indignant were they when they heart his pet name for her most sensitive area uttered by Orson Welles?*

to that damned sled. You were so intent on giving William Randolph Hearst a hotfoot that you were genuinely surprised when you got burned. Third degree burns, Orson. Third degree burns! You felt those burns for your entire career, you were never truly able to escape the effects of that conflagration called *Citizen Kane*. The scars of that battle may have healed somewhat in the last four decades, but you haven't learnt a good Goddamn thing. I'm done. Good-day, Orson. We'll talk again soon.

ORSON: Peter, wait. Don't go. I'm enjoying our conversation far too much to let is end like this. Please, Peter, sit back down. No, no. No! Don't turn off the recorder. I'm sorry. I really am. You know me. When I get going on a good story, I forget myself. Please, sit back down. Let us continue, please. I really need to exorcise my demons and this is the only way I know how. This is my autobiography recorded on your reel-to-reels. You have been the best priest-confessor I've ever known. Please, Peter, forgive me. It is has been far too long since my last confession.

PETER: God... damn... it, Orson. I'll sit back down. I won't touch my recorder. I promise. We'll continue on with your cockamamie story. I owe your that much for the sake of our friendship.

ORSON: Thank you, Peter. You are a saint among sinners.

PETER: Let's get on with this before I change my mind. I just know I'm going to regret this, I swear.

ORSON: *[Overlapping.]* You won't regret this, I swear. Where were we? Oh, yes. *[Pauses.]* Of course, I should have known that when you swear an oath before God and country that there would be repercussions for my act of treason by filming the *Invasion From Mars*. I was so convinced of the absurdity of the "Orson Welles' Conspiracy" that I didn't think anyone would actually buy into it. It was just too absurd, too fictitious a possibly to ever be taken seriously by the common people. Who in their right mind would believe that Martians invaded Virginia and marched on Washington DC? The conspiracy hatched between William Randolph Hearst and myself in the small hours before dawn that Halloween morning was so complete, so effective that not a single newspaper in the whole county– nay– the entire blessed world hinted at an actual invasion. They bought the party line hook, line, and sinker.

The Boston Daily Globe

DIO PL TERRIFIES NATION

PATROL WAGON, AUTO CRASH

Mars Invasion Thought Real

Many Fear World

NEWS FINAL

RADIO 'WAR' IRS TERROR THROUGH U.S.

"War" Victim

"I Didn't Know"

BID FOR SENATE

Democratic Candidate Opposes Any Except Minor Changes in

ew York

Copyright, 1938, by The New York Times Company.

NEW YORK, MONDAY, OCTOBER 31,

dio Listeners in Panic, Taking War Drama as

Many Flee Homes to Escape 'Gas Raid Mars'—Phone Calls Swamp Police Broadcast of Wells Fantasy

A wave of mass hysteria seized | and radio stations here and

The headlines, instead of screaming about a Martian invasion, crucified me instead. **"FAKE RADIO WAR STIRS TERROR THROUGH US" "Radio Listeners in Panic, Taking War Drama as Fact" "RADIO PLAY TERRIFIES NATION" "War of the Worlds" Broadcast Creates Panic In The East" "US PROBES 'INVASION BROADCAST; RADIO PLAY CAUSES WIDE PANIC" "War Skit On Radio Terrifies Nation" "OTTAWA SEEKS WAY TO BAN RADIO 'HORRORS'" "'Mars Invasion' In Radio Hoax Terrifies US"** Every headline that proclaimed a "Martian Invasion" were about me and a radio-dramatization. Peter, tell me were where the headlines screaming about the wanton destruction of the Martian machines? Where were the reports of damage to roadways by the weight of their strides? Where were the screams from the families of the deceased men, women, and child, who died during the albeit short-lived invasion? THERE WEREN'T ANY! Where were the intrepid reporters chasing down all the leads of the actual invasion. Why did every single intrepid reporter ignore all of the honest and impassioned reports of the invasion by citizens of Virginia, by citizens all the way to Washington DC. Thousands witnessed, not only with their ears listening on the radio, but with their very eyes? Every report of an actual invasion, all of them, were readily dismissed in favor of lambasting and lampooning the "boy-wonder", America's favorite new scapegoat. All reports of panic rested solely on the heavy shoulders of one man: me. George Orson Welles. The government had no reason to be upset by my *Invasion From Mars* motion picture. No one, and I mean absolutely no one, would have walked out of a screening of my movie believing that the government had actually covered up a Martian invasion. They all would have walked out of their movie houses believing they had just been pranked by the *Wünderkind*, the boy genius, Orson Welles. Even the most paranoid of schizophrenics would focus their paranoias, not on a vast government conspiracy to cover up an a very real invasion from Mars, but would instead on the belief that I was playing a colossal prank on them *personally*. They would be looking over their shoulders, not for government agents out to destroy them, but living in constant fear of Orson Welles appearing out of nowhere with film cameras to capture the "gotcha" moment when I exposed them as the *only* victims of my prank.

PETER: While I delight in your little prank this evening, certainly nobody else has relished the idea of being the subject of one of your infamous jokes. Why would anyone who saw *Invasion from Mars* actually *believe* you? Why would the government actually care? Ah– there's the rub, Orson. The government wouldn't care! That is the whole in your little story this evening, Orson. The air in the balloon is slowly escaping, the balloon flying around the room, out of control. Not even you could put the air back into this little prank you're pulling, Orson.

ORSON: But... I underestimated the paranoia of those in the highest levels. I underestimated the lengths those in the highest offices in the land would go to insure they kept their grip on that kind of absolute power. Why would FDR order several government agencies to infiltrate RKO studios in order to destroy my motion picture? Why would the President take the chance of the entire conspiracy being exposed in a Hollywood picture? Why would he risk being impeached? Just to silence me? The risk versus reward was skewed far too much in my favor.

PETER: You thought the same exact thing when you broadcast *The War of the Worlds*. Despite having the police show up while you were broadcasting your radio-dramatization, you didn't stop the production. Your audience was terrified they were going to die any moment. They were stuffing wet towels into the cracks of their doorways to stop the Martian's poison-gas from seeping into their homes and killing their families. They were clogging the telephone networks desperate to reach their more distant relatives just to say good-bye. You didn't heed the warnings of Davidson Taylor to pause your production so you could assuage the fears of a listening audience brought to tears by the seemingly real news broadcasts you were distributing through the airwaves. The next morning you went before the reporters and feigned shock and disbelief that you had any knowledge of the terror you caused.

ORSON: But, Peter–

PETER: You thought the exact same thing about William Randolph Hearst and *Citizen Kane*. Your hubris couldn't contemplate that a man of his power and renown would do everything in his power to destroy your picture and ruin your reputation. This was the man's *modus operandi*. He personally called for a President McKinley to be shot and then when the President was assassinated by an anarchist, he shrugged off any and all blame. You thought Hearst was so secluded in his estate, so secluded by his

William Randolph Hearst called for the assassination of President William McKinley almost daily in his newspapers! When the President was, in fact, assassinated, Hearst shrugged off all responsibility! Hmph!

wealth, that he wouldn't notice a simple RKO Radio Pictures production *that was about him*! That slandered him! You didn't think he would throw every incalculable resource at his disposal to destroy you and your little picture? Did you learn nothing from the boycotts by every Hearst newspaper? The lawsuits from his army of attorneys? The rightful and justifiable slander of you by Luella Parsons published in each of his papers? You thought you were far too clever to get into any trouble. That is the albatross that has been hung around your neck since you were a boy, Orson. Your hubris is your perceived cleverness.

ORSON: I didn't thi—

PETER: And now, you claim you filmed a motion picture that exposes the lies, the deceit, the conspiracy to cover up an actual invasion from the planet Mars. I'll bite. For the sake of our little Lincoln-Douglas debates, I'll bite. You broke your oath that you swore before God, country, and Franklin Delano Roosevelt in such a glorious and public fashion as filming an *Invasion From Mars* motion picture. A motion picture you readily claim exposed the President's duplicity in deceiving every citizen of our great nation, by hiding the fact that Martians landed on American soil and invaded Washington DC. The President ordered our military into action to engage this literal alien threat to our country. First hand eyewitness accounts of a Goddamn Martian invasion prompted CBS Radio to broadcast reports of said invasion, causing widespread panic throughout the entire US of A. And after the invasion was– somehow– remarkably– quizzically– quashed after a few short hours, Franklin Delano Roosevelt and William Randolph Hearst entered into a vast government conspiracy with you, for some– odd– surprising– questionable– reason.

ORSON: Peter, I think I've given you the wrong impress—

PETER: What in the Hell did you think was going to happen? If as you claim, you didn't hide their names: Roosevelt was *Roosevelt*, Hearst was *Hearst*, and you were, well, *you*. This was no longer satire. You slandered them. You libeled them. Did you think they'd throw you a ticker-tape parade for being courageous enough to expose them as conspirators? You are an intelligent man, Orson. What were the odds that you would get away with it?

ORSON: I thought it was a sure thing. The chance of being exposed for exposing the cover up of an invasion from Mars was so infinitesimal that even Las Vegas wouldn't make book on it out of fear of losing their shirts, or more accurately, the Mob's shirts. You know, Peter, that I've never really been a gambling man. *[Peter coughs.]* Unlike Mank, who was a compulsive... *[Peter coughs loudly.]* You need a slip of water, Peter?

PETER: I'm fine, Orson. I'm fine.

ORSON: The sleight-of-hand close-up magic that I learned as a young boy at the knee of Harry Houdini has forever barred me from the casinos of the world. *[Peter coughs.]* But I digress. One thing paranoid schizophrenics get laughably wrong concerning their paranoia of government agents is these agents are so skilled in the tactics of espionage that you won't even get a hint that you have been compromised... until it is far, far too late. While Charles Koerner was on vacation at the sanitarium enjoying yogurt enemas and having his brain washed with medication and electricity,

PETER: Wait what? You slipped, my friend. What is this about Charles Koerner and a sanitarium? You've completely failed to mention this.

ORSON: Indeed I have, Peter. Indeed a have. Just a moment. Let me gather my thoughts— Harry's and my paranoia at being discovered had seemingly infected all of those around us. Like the ominous warning found in King Tutankhamun's tomb, "Cursed be he who moves my body. To him shall come fire, water and pestilence". While we had tried to distract Charles Koerner, this network of

Orson Welles performing magic during The Mercury Wonder Show, *a magic-and-variety stage show that entertained US soldiers during World War II!*

little spies, and all of the other various shinyness of brass at RKO, instead we infected the entire studio with a scourge-like paranoia. I always wondered if you think you can catch paranoid schizophrenia as if it were the common cold, are you already schizophrenic?

PETER: That is mightily philosophical, Orson.

ORSON: Charles Koerner was but the first of many to succumb to this curse. The full extent of his nervous breakdown, that would slowly begin to manifest itself over the course of our shoot, would only require a brief respite in a sanitarium. His secretary had grown concerned that of a growing paranoia that his office had been bugged by the OSS. He couldn't go anywhere, do anything that was being scrutinized by our very government. He complained that the President of the United States was listening as he showered and brushed his teeth in the morning, that FDR was listening while he ate his breakfast and read the morning edition, and that Roosevelt was listening while he, well to use a more appropriate term, went tinkle. His word, not mine. He accused passersby on the street of being federal agents under J. Edgar Hoover intent on destroying not only him, but RKO as well. He accosted more than a few business men, whom had happened to be wearing particularly bad suits. By the time his sanity was restored and he returned to the studio lot to resume his position, government had actually bugged every room on the lot, government agents had infiltrated every department in RKO studios, and a few of the more glamorous government spies had been cast in other studio productions. Little did Charles or myself know this would be but the opening salvo in the battle over *War of the Worlds.*

PETER: You do know how to sow insanity, Orson.

ORSON: Soooo, while Charles Koerner was on vacation at the sanitarium enjoying yogurt enemas and having his brain washed with medication and electricity, I continued preparing *Invasion From Mars* for release like nothing was the matter.

PETER: You what?

ORSON: Not even Charles's secretary was aware of the true nature of my film. No other executive, no one on the board of directors, or anyone else at RKO for that matter, had any inclination that the film I continued to prep was not the famed Howard Koch version of *War of the Worlds.* The young editor assigned to piece together a trailer... fascinating thing trailers...

PETER: What is so fascinating about trailers? They're a promotional tool so readily discarded into the waste bin once the film is released.

ORSON: True. True. But what I find so fascinating is they once came *after* the feature, thus the moniker "trailer". Although "coming attraction" would probably be a more accurate descriptor, trailer is what entered the lexicon. Anyway. The first thing I did was pluck Art Gilmore out of radio to be the voice of my trailer for *Invasion From Mars.* He would go on to have quite the career as the "voice of coming attractions", including a second go around with Martians voicing George Pal's *War of the Worlds* trailer, but he was going to be the conspiratorial voice of my *Invasion From Mars.* As much as I hated reusing a mechanic from *Citizen Kane,* there was no way this trailer could be anything other than a newsreel.

PETER: You were seriously planning to make your trailer look like a newsreel? That is a level of audacity I cannot even comprehend, even from you, Orson.

ORSON: Not just any newsreel, a Hearst Metrotone newsreel.

PETER: What?!?

ORSON: If there is one thing to be learned from Jonathan Swift and that glorious construct called Juvenalian satire, nothing is safe, nothing is sacred, not even intellectual property protected by the hallowed institution of the United States Patent and Trademark Office. Being housed under the auspices of that particular office made using the actual title cards and musical themes from Hearst Metrotone newsreels all the more enticing and rewarding.

PETER: Enticing Hearst is more like it. He'd send his legion of lawyers after you again. Again, Orson!

ORSON: There is one thing that modern film-making cannot seem to get right: the newsreel voice. It is almost laughable to see today's voice-actors try to imitate the classic newsreel voice. Their tone and cadence is so hilarious it's pathetic. It is the palest and least sincere form of flattery. But for those of us reared on the newsreel, like Art Gilmore was, my newsreel would sound more than real, it would be truly harrowing. I would ape the opening of Hearst's own *War of the Worlds* newsreel in which he gleefully threw me under the bus. These are the actual words I put onto the eloquent and enunciating lips of Art Gilmore: "Mischief night! The evening before Halloween. A night known to children and teenage hooligans across the country as Mischief Night. To the police and newspaper reporters

it is more ominously named Devil's Night. A night where anyone dressed in every manner of scary costume, even in the quietest of suburban neighborhoods, can get away with practically anything prankish in nature. A night when all these juvenile and asinine highjinks will be either forgotten and forgiven. It was on this night, 1938, that Orson Welles pranked, not only his neighborhood– the radio audience of his *Mercury Theatre on the Air*– but every state in the union. And because he broadcast on this particular evening, his prank would be quickly forgiven but not easily forgotten!" We then cut to actual film footage of me the morning after when in a press conference, "Do you want me to speak now?.. I'm sorry. We are deeply shocked and deeply regretful about the... uh... results of last night's broadcast. It came as rather a great surprise that a story, a fine HG Wells classic, would bring such a reaction." Then a reporter asks, "Were you aware of the terror you were giving with this role? The terror going across the nation?" I let a pregnant pause linger and then answered, "I cannot continue with a charade of a press conference." There are hushed murmurs from the reporters. "Have any of you questioned why we are here this morning? Are you all blind and ignorant of the length and breadth the government would go to to deceive our great nation? What if the radio broadcasts listeners heard last night were real? How would it be humanly possible for a troupe of radio-actors to convince an entire nation of an invasion from Mars using the asinine concept of an radio-adaptation of a British science-fiction novel? Ask yourself again: what if the radio-broadcasts heard last night were real? Do not kowtow. Do not be complicit. Ask the pertinent questions: what if Martians had, in fact, invaded American soil? What if hundreds of men, women, children, and military men died last night? What lengths would a Bolshevik president, a Svengali of yellow journalism, and a radio-producer desperate for celebrity go to to hide this truth from the American people: the truth of an Invasion From Mars!" Then the "newsreel" would play scenes from *Invasion From Mars* in stark, utter, and uncomfortable silence. The newsreel trailer would be, not Juvenalian satire, but the truest, purest fact-reporting.

PETER: Not even you would have released that onto an unsuspecting American public.

ORSON: Have you learned nothing about me during all our years of friendship, Peter. Of course I would have. And I would have if not for conspiracies against me that would be revealed in the coming days and weeks. That newsreel would have been released into the cinema houses if not for the government agents whom had so quickly and efficiently infiltrated RKO studios from the janitorial staff to the board of directors themselves. Even my young editor proved to be an undercover government agent. All while overseeing the literal splicing of film footage and the recording of Art Gilmore's voice-overs, he was reporting back to Franklin Delano Roosevelt my every move, my every intention. President Roosevelt was no doubt given detailed reports of what I ate for lunch and dinner in the commissary and when and in which bathroom I relieved my bowels.

PETER: Orson, that's paranoid.

ORSON: No, that's pragmatic. At what point did FDR learn of my duplicity? When did he learn that I was not, in fact, recording a film-adaptation of Howard Koch's *War of the Worlds* radio-dramatization? I didn't know. I couldn't be sure. I would never truly be sure. I could not pin-point the exact moment he learned. Charles Koerner did not realize until that moment in the screening room, when I presented my final cut of my *Invasion From Mars*, that I had no intention of releasing a simple film adaptation of Howard Koch's *War of the Worlds.* I don't believe Charles Koerner realized the true nature of my crime against the government of the United States

Did J. Edgar Hoover start one of his infamous files on Orson Welles in the aftermath of the infamous radio broadcast? Did Hoover believe that Orson Welles was part of a "commie-plot" to undermine American's faith in radio and stoke fears of America's unpreparedness for war?

of America. I have no doubt he went to the sanitarium convinced this was nothing more than Howard Koch's *War of the Worlds*. When it was nothing of the sort. This was treason of the highest order. I have no doubt that J. Edgar Hoover started an FBI file on me the moment I went before the press that cold Halloween morning after my so-called radio-dramatization. I don't believe even J. Edgar would have been given the necessary clearance to know about the "Orson Welles' Conspiracy". He would have readily opened a file on me just for having had the audacity and influence to frighten an entire populous with a radio-drama. How frightening must have it been to the leading G-man to know that a radio-producer, the voice of the Shadow, could incite such panic in the hearts and minds of the American people. If someone like me could do this, what could someone with actual ill intent accomplish given similar means? Radio had proven it could incite panic. Could radio incite mob-violence? Could radio incite mass-treason? Insurrection? Revolution? Civil war? These were questions I have no doubt that J. Edgar Hoover wanted to know the answers to. Remember Peter, I had a patriotic broadcast the morning of the attack on Pearl Harbor and was interrupted in the middle of it.

PETER: I remember the story well.

ORSON: It was on the full network, reading from Walt Whitman about how beautiful America was, when they said Pearl Harbor's attacked– now, doesn't that sound like me trying to do that again? They interrupted the show to say that there had been an attack. Roosevelt sent me a wire about it. I've forgotten what– I don't have it. Something like 'crying wolf' and that kind of thing Not the same day– he was too busy!– but about ten days later. If *I* had this Svengali effect over a radio audience, why couldn't J. Edgar Hoover also use the power of radio for his own gains? Didn't Joseph McCarthy use the media to spread his vile poison against the working men and women of Hollywood painting them all as Reds? This is the kind of power men like these feared. This is the kind of power that I wielded so easily and effortlessly. If I could go before the press and spew a cockamamie story of a radio-dramatization of an HG Wells' classic and have it accepted as the Gospel according to Orson Welles, so completely and irrevocably silencing any inquiry into an actual invasion from Mars. Then what effect would my *Invasion From Mars* feature have had on an unsuspecting film-going American

President Roosevelt's "Fireside Chats" were welcomed into the homes of every American! Every American knew his voice when they heard it October 30, 1938! But the newspaper headlines would trumpet "FAKE! RADIO 'WAR' STIRS TERROR THROUGH US"!

audience? Could I topple an American Presidency? We now know, Peter, in the later years of the Seventies, we know that a newspaper article about a seemingly insignificant burglary can force the resignation of an American President. Could I have forced Franklin Delano Roosevelt to admit before a radio-audience, not at all like his fireside chats, that he ordered the cover-up of a Martian invasion? That the military spent the Halloween of 1938 and the days following repairing or repressing all of the destruction left in the wake of the Martian machine's march towards Washington DC. Sure, people were looking at the residents of Grover's Mill, New Jersey for any stories relating to the Martian scare instead of combing Grove Hill, Virginia for any trace evidence of an Martian invasion. I gave the government the most precious gift of all... time. They say time heals all wounds, but time even more effectively erases memories. If not for Abraham Zapruder accidentally and illegally recording President Kennedy's assassination, how well would the memories of the witnesses have held up to history? All evidence of a conspiracy to assassinate an American President would have vanished like a fart in a whirlwind. But because of the Zapruder film, we, as an American people, have our doubts. We have gone looking where we were not supposed to look. There a Warren Commission into the assassination of President Kennedy, *because* of, *in spite* of, the Zapruder film. We, as a nation, asked

questions we were never supposed to have asked. President Kennedy could have easily been assassinated by a "lone gunman," but we went looking for evidence of a conspiracy even if there was actually no conspiracy to be found. We have conjured evidence out of thin air! In the days, weeks, and decades since the Mischief Night of 1938, nobody looked for evidence of a Martian invasion, because nobody thought to look for evidence of a Martian invasion. The world isn't the same as it was then. The world was a much larger place before television camera could beam pictures across the globe. In 1938, people sat around their radio-sets *listening* to Munich Crisis unfold. They *listened* to an invasion from Mars. Today, it was have been so much harder to hide the truth, when televised news audiences can *see*. Even in the five short years between my supposed radio-dramatization of *War of the Worlds* and the filming of my *Invasion From Mars*, not all evidence of the Martian invasion would have been removed, repaired, or repressed from the route between Grove Hill, Virginia and Washington DC If after the release of my film, geologists and archeologists went looking for evidence, they would have found it. Easily. It would be staring them as plain as any face on Mount Rushmore. Even today, I have no doubt, evidence could still be found. Hell, archaeologists are still finding the very pot a Pharaoh pissed in four-thousand years later. The evidence is out there, Peter, right this very moment, if only someone, anyone would just look! The truth is out there! But nobody, not seen the most paranoid of schizophrenics, is looking. All because I was masterful in conceiving and executing the "Orson Welles' Conspiracy"!

A family in America's Heartland listening to the Munich crisis unfold!

PETER: Um... I don't know what to say.

ORSON: You don't have to say anything. Just bask in the ignominy of my brilliance.

PETER: Wow... simply... wow...

ORSON: I just wish I knew when Franklin discovered that I violated my oath before God and country and Franklin to keep the Martian invasion "Top-Secret". At what point did Willie and I screw up? The exact when and how has been the key source of my paranoia in the decades since. I ask you, Peter, can you be paranoid, when the government is actually out to get you?

PETER: I...

ORSON: If I could pinpoint the exact moment this little conspiracy between Willie Brown and myself was exposed, I could go to my grave a happy man. But I can't. In the decades since, I have replayed the entire situation through that cursed eidetic memory of mine and I cannot for the life of me figure out the *who* and the *when* and the *how*. Of course, I knew the *if*. There was no question that Franklin did learn about my film. I knew the *where*. It occurred within the walls of RKO's Forty Acrees. And I knew the *what*. Franklin learned that I made a film that exposed the "Orson Welles' Conspiracy". But in those final days of shooting and early days of post-production, I was blissfully unaware that the jig was up. ⚛

THE MAN FROM M.A.R.S.

Martians! American Resistance Syndicate

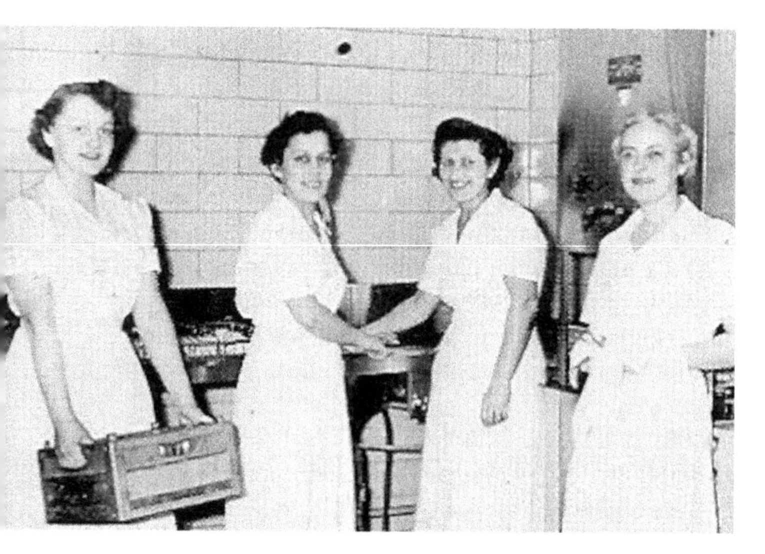

ORSON: Was the lunch-lady in the cafeteria, the one with the hairy mole and equally hairy upper-lip, was she an undercover government agent? And in drag? Were the secretaries or telephone operators actually *femme-fatales* trained by the OSS in the arts of seducing foreigners on foreign soil into betraying their own governments? Were the janitors actually trained assassins? Where the Yes-Men, those executives who kowtowed to the likes of Charles Koerner, actually G-Men? I don't know! I couldn't have known! They were spies and spies are trained to be invisible. I didn't have known my own arse from a hole in the ground! Perhaps they had bugged my arse and I wouldn't have known it!

PETER: You don't seem to know very much, Orson, even after thirty-some-odd-years.

ORSON: Of course, I know *now*. As the teller of this story, particularly one who as survived the story to tell it, you know I lived to tell the tale. Where is the suspense in that? I also know who lived and when the dead died. I alone know who betrayed me, when the plot was hatched, and when it was executed. But the artcraft of the storyteller is to create suspense throughout the entire story. To balance the knowing and the not knowing. When do I expose these secrets that I alone carry with me? What rights do you, Peter, have as to when and if you ever learn the truth of what actually happened? You don't. You don't have any inalienable rights. You have to trust me. You have to trust that I will reveal all by the end of this evening. If I don't, then I have broken my covenant with you, Peter. You will feel betrayed that you have devoted this entire evening listening to my words. And rightfully so. Know this. I lived through the battle over *War of the Worlds* and I fully intend to eulogize the lives of those who died. This is my pact with you. This is my obligation for the dead

PETER: Thank you?... I guess?

ORSON: I do know the exact moment I learned of the infiltration of government agents onto the RKO lot.

PETER: Due tell.

ORSON: In our supreme arrogance, both I and Willie

RKO Radio Pictures
780 North Gower St.
Hollywood

Please return promptly to
STENOGRAPHIC DEPARTMENT
when you have finished with it

THE WAR OF THE WORLDS

Written by
William Francis Brown

Based on the radioplay
by Howard Koch

FINAL

Brown put our names on the screenplays for *Invasion From Mars*. Of course, Willie put his name on the screenplay for *The War of the Worlds* that was adapted from a radio-play by Howard Koch, but the screenplay we wrote in the bungalow in Victorville had our names emblazoned on the first page.

PETER: Orson...

ORSON: I know. I know. We should have used *nom-de-plumes*. Hell, Willie already was walking around the studio lot with one. "Harry Lime". All the actors, assistant directors, second-unit director, location scouts, camera operators, film loaders, lighting technicians, grips, gaffers, best boys, sound designers, set builders, scenic decorators and dressers, propmasters, costume designers, hair and make-up artists, special effects, stunt-men, craft services...

PETER: My that eidetic memory.

ORSON: ...Everyone knew him as Harry Lime. The scarlet playing Marion Davies believed he was a thirty-five-year-old seasoned assistant and second-unit director, and she had no clue he was a just turned eighteen-year-old snot-nosed kid without a single screen credit to his name. Willie always seemed to look like an old man, even then. He had the opposite problem that plagued Baby Face Nelson. Willie could walk into any post-Prohibition bar in town and drink. Without fear. No police officer would ever question Willie's age. His face bespoke maturity, wisdom, and old age. The government sought out William Francis Brown, not Harry Lime. As my closest compatriot, they needed to turn Willie against me. They assumed Willie was the mentor in our relationship. That he was the Herman Mankiewicz to my Orson Welles.

PETER: That analogy makes no sense.

ORSON: The government had no clue he was fresh off the turnip truck; that he had no writing credits to his name. They assumed an older and wiser William Francis Brown would want to reign in his out-of-control protégé. That he could talk some sense into me. Stop me from releasing *Invasion From Mars*. Little did they know, he was the protégé and I was the mentor. But they were forced to speed up their timeline. When Willie returned to his apartment a half-an-hour after Harry Lime rolled off the studio lot, he discovered his apartment in the very process of being ransacked. I have no doubt, they assumed Willie Brown as still on the lot, also having no clue that Harry Lime and Willie Brown were one and the same.

PETER: That's a lot of clueless people embroiled in a conspiracy.

William Francis Brown, my father, walking down Hollywood Blvd!

ORSON: Everyone in a conspiracy is clueless, Orson. That's how conspiracies are protected. If the left hand doesn't know what the right hand is doing, then the conspiracy is safe. Conspiracies are the Three Stooges of plots. For the observer looking it, they are all slapstick and pratfalls. If Willie and I do our jobs correctly, the government should look less like the Untouchables and more like the Keystone Kops. But I digress. The government agents ransacking Willie Brown's apartment were genuine-

ly shocked when Willie walked in the front door, caught red-handed like a peeping Tom searching through a pantie drawer.

PETER: Are you saying Willie Brown had a pantie drawer?

ORSON: Peter, that's not very polite. What's good for J. Edgar Hoover should be good for the gander. Shouldn't it? But Willie Brown's pantie drawer had a much more blasé explanation. "Marion" had an entire drawer at his apartment. That is a level of commitment somewhere between "going-steady" and a putting a rock-on-her-finger. And yes, Willie caught them with their mitts on Marion's unmentionables, which of course, will not be mentioned here.

PETER: Except you're talking about them right now.

ORSON: *[Pauses.]* And the agents had no idea Willie Brown left the lot. They had been given reports of a Harry Lime, amongst many, many others, having driven off the lot, but not a sign of Willie Brown leaving RKO, until the moment he walked in the front door of his apartment. The G-Men pulled their weapons on a unsuspecting screenwriter. Before Willie knew it, they were realigning an overturned chair and forcing him to suddenly sit. They trained a desk-lamp from its normal position over his typewriter to shine a bright-light in his eyes. In the gloom of late California twilight's abrupt transition to the darkest of moonless nights, Willie saw this scene play out in the black-and-white expressionist cinematography, the dramatic, harsh lightning of class *film noir.* From his seated position, with the lowering government agents staring down at him, he saw with the director's keen eye the gross distortion of the "Dutch angle" camera technique. The street lamp from across the street streamed through the Venetian blinds, casting strong, deep black bands across the stark white stucco walls. They were more ominous than vertical jail-cell bars and just as confining. Willie was imprisoned in the safety of his own apartment. Not even the flames from their ignited lighters glowed red and orange given his sudden colorblindness. The glowing coal at the tips of their cigarettes bloomed with the contrasts of bright white, stark blacks, and glorious grays. Their smoke circled the desk lamp and tickled his nostrils. But little did the government agents know that even knowing about the "Orson Welles' Conspiracy" had made Willie so gloriously paranoid that he had bugged his own apartment.

PETER: He what?

ORSON: Listen. I've got it cued.

PETER: You've what?

ORSON: I've got it cued. You are about the see the Man From M.A.R.S. at they height of his powers.

PETER: Man From M.A.R.S.. I assume that is an acronym for something. This being a government conspiracy and all.

ORSON: Of course it is an acronym. "M.A.R.S." stands for "Martians! American Resistance Syndicate."

PETER: Of course it does! But can only two men constitute a syndicate?

ORSON: There were three of us actually... but... but I can't go into that right now. I've ready said more than I should have about that. Damn. Can we end this digression and get to the reel-to-reel?

PETER: You're the man of the hour! Fire away.

[Orson Welles turns on a second reel-to-reel and plays the following:.]

Willie Brown (portrayed by Fred MacMurrey) is viscously interrogated by Government Agent Ecks (played by Edward G. Robinson)!

Willie Brown and his girlfriend stop at gas station in fear of running out of fuel while fleeing the Martian tripods invading America!

AGENT ECKS: What were you doing the night of October, 30, 1938?

WILLIE BROWN: Four years ago? I can't remembered what I did four weeks ago, let alone four years ago.

AGENT ECKS: What were you doing the night of October, 30, 1938? The night Orson Welles broadcast "The War of the Worlds".

WILLIE: Oh... *that* October, 30 1938. "My girlfriend and I stayed in the car for awhile, just driving around. Then we followed the lead of a friend. All of us ran into a grocery store and asked the man if we could go into his cellar. He said, "What's the matter. Are you trying to ruin my business?" So he chased us out. A crowd collected. We rushed to an apartment house and asked the man in the apartment to let us in his cellar. He said, "I don't have any cellar! Get away!" Then people started to rush of the apartment all undressed. We got into the car and listened some more. Suddenly, the announcer was gassed, the station went dead so we tried another station but nothing would come on. Then we went to a gas station and filled up our tank in preparation for just riding as far as we could. The gas station man didn't know anything about it. Then one friend decided he would call up the *Newark Evening News*. He found out it was a play. We listened to the rest of the play then went dancing."

AGENT ECKS: I don't believe you.

WILLIE: Okay... "I wife and I were driving through the redwood forest in northern California when the broadcast came over our car radio. There was no escape. All we could think of was to try to get back to LA to see our children once more. And be with them when it happened. We went right by gas stations but forgot were low on gas. In the middle of the forest our gas ran out. There was nothing to do. We just sat there holding hands expecting any minutes to see those Martian monsters appear over the tops of the trees. When Orson said it was a Hallowe'en prank, it was like being reprieved on the way to the gas chamber."

Willie Brown, driving through California's redwood forest, sees the gloomy glow of the Martian tripods invading California!

AGENT ECKS: Why are you changing your story?

WILLIE: *[Feminizing his voice.]* "I was terribly frightened. I wanted to pack and take my child in my arms, gather up my friends, and get in the car and just go north as far as we could. But what I did was just set by on window, praying, listening, and scared stiff, and my husband by the other sniffling and looking out to see if people were running. Then when the announcer said 'evacuate the city,' I ran and called my boarder and started with my child to rush down the stairs, not waiting to ketch my hat or anything. When I got to the foot of the stairs, I just couldn't go out, I don't know why. Meantime, my husband, he tried other stations and found them still running. He couldn't small any gas or see people running, so he called me back and told me it was just a play. So I set down, still ready to go at any minute until I heard Orson Wells say, 'Folks, I hope we haven't alarmed you. This is just a play!' Then I just set!"

AGENT ECKS: Are you making fun of me?

WILLIE: *[Impersonating another young woman.]* "I kept on saying, 'Where are we going to go? What can we do? What difference does it make whether we get killed now or later?' I was really hysterical. My two girlfriends and I were crying and holding each other and every seemed so unimportant in the face of death. We felt it was terrible we should die so young. I'm always nervous anyway and I guess I was getting everybody we more scared. The boy from downstairs threatened to know me out if I didn't stop acting so hysterical. We tried another small station which had some program on that confirmed our fears. I was sure the end of the world was coming."

AGENT ECKS: Stop this now...

WILLIE: *[Taking on a woman's Bostonian accent.]* "I never hugged my radio so closely as I did that night. I held a crucifix in my hand and prayed while looking out of my open window for falling meteors. I also wanted to get a faint whiff of the gas so that I would know when to close my window and hermetically seal my room with waterproof cement or anything else I could get hold of. My plan was to stay in the room and hope that I would not suffocate before the gas blew away. When the monsters were wading across the Hudson River and coming into New York, I wanted to run up to my roof to see what they looked like, but I could not leave my radio while it was telling me of their whereabouts."

AGENT ECKS: ...or God help me...

WILLIE: *[Returning to his natural voice.]* "They should have announced that it was a play. We listened to the whole thing and they never did. I was very much afraid. When it was over we ran to the doctor's to see if he could help us get away. Everybody was out in the street and somebody told us it was just a play. We always listen to Orson Welles but we didn't imagine this was it. If we hadn't found out it was a play, I don't know what we'd have done."

AGENT ECKS: Damn it, man!

WILLIE: What are you doing in my home?

AGENT ECKS: I'll ask the questions around here! What were you doing the night Martians invaded America?

WILLIE: Wait! What?

AGENT WHY: Sir, you shouldn't be asking that.

AGENT ECKS: What? Oh. Right. What were you doing the night of Octo...

WILLIE: No. No. Wait! That is a question I will answer.

AGENT ECKS: You'll what? You will?

WILLIE: I am more than willing to reveal where I was the night Martians invaded America. But before I go into any great detail, we must get on the same page. Martians *did*, in fact, invade America that night? Right? This is one piece of the puzzle that I need filled in before I can paint the full picture.

AGENT ECKS: I am willing to stipulate...

WILLIE: On the record. *On... the... record.*

AGENT ECKS: I will go on the record that Martians did, in fact, invade America on the night of October 30, 1938.

[Orson pauses the reel-to-reel.]

ORSON: I can image Willie Brown grinning just like the Cheshire Cat. Thanks to his bugs, he has a government official... on the record... confirming the invasion from Mars. That night Willie needed to get as much out of this... few watts shy of a light bulb... government agent as he possibly could. Who do they think they have sitting in their little interrogation chair? There is no way they think he is the fresh off the turnip truck teenager from small-town Colorado that he is in reality. They could, however, conceivably believe, like Mank, he is a long-in-the-tooth, three sheets to the wind, four on the floor, lit like a Christmas tree screenwriter.

PETER: Orson, why all these constant little jabs at Herman Mankiewicz after all these years?

ORSON: Little do the spooks realize they had the one and only heir-apparent to Orson Welles himself sitting in that chair. Now, the story Willie, is about to tell is the biggest, warmest, dankest, fly-attracting, steaming pile of bullshit you will ever encounter in your life, my friend. Willie in this interview is the epitome of the unreliable narrator.

PETER: You have been making a case for yourself as the personification of the unreliable narrator, Orson. Have you not been paying attention to your own bullshit this evening?

ORSON: Hardy-har-har. What I have been trying to do this evening is to be the antithesis of the unreliable narrator. As is the case of all conspiracy theories, the government has made their story so bullet-proof that any dissenting opinion comes across as madness. Franklin Delano Roosevelt, William Randolph Hearst, and I are, in fact, the unreliable narrators of history. I am trying, with every fiber of my being, to come clean. To finally be honest. To be the most reliable narrator I can be. I know I sound like a raving loon, but that is because history itself has become *Tristram Shandy*.

PETER: I apologize, Orson. Please continue.

ORSON: Apology accepted. Now, where was I? Oh, yes. Listen well and learn.

PETER: The anticipation is killing me.

[Orson restarts the reel-to-reel.]

WILLIE: Did you know that in the early years of the twentieth century this world was being watched closely by intelligences greater than man's and yet as mortal as his own? How could we have known that as human beings busied themselves about their various concerns we were scrutinized and studied, perhaps almost as narrowly as a man with a microscope might scrutinize the transient creatures that swarm and multiply in a drop of water. Why did we with infinite complacence go to and fro over the earth about our little affairs, serene in the assurance of our dominion over this small spinning fragment of solar driftwood which by chance or design man has inherited out of the dark mystery of Time and Space. How could we have known that across an immense ethereal gulf, minds that to our minds as our are to the beasts of the jungle, intellects vast, cool, and unsympathetic regarded this earth with envious eyes and slowly and surely drew their plans against us. It was near the end of October. Business was better. The war scare was over. More men were back at work. Sales were picking up. On this particular evening, October 30, the Crossley service estimated that thirty-million people were listening in on radio.

AGENT ECKS: I don't care what was happening on October 30th.

WILLIE: Then why were you asking where I was that night four years ago? I'm quite confused.

AGENT ECKS: What I want really want to know is what you were doing with these documents we have found earlier in the day in a bungalow in Victorville, so we can bring you up on charges of espionage and treason.

WILLIE: Why? What crimes have I committed? What secrets have I exposed? Have you read the screenplay I submitted to Mr. Koerner, president of RKO Pictures? I wrote a perfectly authentic adaptation of Howard Koch's "War of the Worlds" radio script. There is nothing in that screenplay that hasn't already been published in *The Invasion From Mars* by Hadley Cantril. I can't see anything in that screenplay that would scream espionage and treason?

AGENT ECKS: And this! *[Sound of a large screenplay being slammed on the desk.]* This screenplay entitled *Invasion From Mars* has been shot by Orson Welles and was written by a one "William Francis Brown".

WILLIE: You just happened to have a copy of a screenplay handy while ransacking my apartment? That's a quite convenient plot contrivance, isn't it?

AGENT ECKS: Answer my question.

WILLIE: You haven't, technically, asked a question. You have only made statements.

AGENT ECKS: Where did you get the information contained in this screenplay? There are elements of this screenplay that can only be found in the classified "Top Secret" documents we found in that Victorville bungalow.

WILLIE: Wait! Is there... is there anything that I can do to get myself out of this situation? You see... Orson Welles... I'm just a Hollywood screenwriter. I'm just a hired gun... *[Pregnant pause.]*

AGENT ECKS: Answer my question. *[Bangs the table.]*

WILLIE: You... ah... you knew that when Orson Welles was brought to Hollywood, he was the hailed as the Golden Boy. But he didn't have a screen-credit to his name. He hadn't written anything, directed anything that appeared on the screen. He had no experience. None. Zip. Bupkis. George Schaefer, then president of RKO, assigned Herman Mankiewicz to baby-sit the "boy-wonder" and ensure that his first picture wasn't a bust. And after Orson's colossal blundering with *Citizen Kane,* Charles Koerner, my boss here at RKO, needed someone to continue to baby-sit young Orson Welles. Mr. Koerner wanted Orson to film a straight adaptation of his "War of the Worlds" radio-dramatization. If Orson Welles could scare millions of listeners with a radio-drama about an invasion from Mars, then imagine what kind of picture he could make with the hundreds of thousands of dollars and talent behind RKO Pictures?

AGENT ECKS: That makes sense. But it doesn't explain these documents...

WILLIE: You see. I'm quite young looking. I'm much older than I look. It's the benefit of having a baby-face. I have years, decades of experience writing screenplays. That is why I was assigned to baby-sit Orson Welles on a *War of the Worlds* feature.

AGENT ECKS: We've done our homework, Mr. Brown. We have a dossier on you. You don't seem to have any writing credits at all. We cannot find a single motion picture with a screen credit for William Francis Brown.

WILLIE: *[Pregnant pause.]* Haven't you heard of a "script doctor"?

AGENT ECKS: A what? What's that?

WILLIE: We are the most valued, but most under appreciated screenwriters in Hollywood. Once a screenplay has been written, a director hired, and a cast cast, and there are problems with the script, a script doctor is brought in to fix any of the problems the director or cast may be having with it. Sometimes the dialogue is very well written but cannot be properly articulated by even the most accomplished actor or actress. Sometimes there are story problems or plot holes. Other times there are scenes are just too damn expensive to shoot. There are a host of reasons why a script needs to be doctored and that is why every studio has their chosen few who are trusted by to save the studio hundreds of thousands in production costs, if not millions of dollars in lost revenue. This is the very reason why you can't find a screen credit to my name. The brass doesn't want the public to know that any film had a troubled production. It isn't good for business. The original screenwriter could have written god-awful, pot-boiling claptrap and yet I am, as I am wont to do, able to turn it into damn-near Shakespeare. But I don't get any of the glory. I don't win any Oscars. This is my lot in life.

AGENT ECKS: And this is why Mr. Koerner assigned you to work with Orson Welles?

WILLIE: After the meandering, time-jumping, self-aggrandizing, pretentious, and down-right boring experiment that was *Citizen Kane* and his equal failure as a director on *The Magnificent Ambersons,* which could only be saved by taking the final cut away from the "boy-wonder", Mr. Koerner had no choice but assign one of his most cherished script doctors, not just to fix the screenplay after the fact, but before it was even written.

AGENT ECKS: And that is why you wrote the *War of the Worlds* screenplay?

WILLIE: That was before Orson and his new partner-in-crime Harry Lime went off and bastardized *my* brilliant adaptation of Howard Koch's seminal radio-dramatization with that screenplay sitting on my desk.

AGENT ECKS: Are you claiming you had no knowledge of the *Invasion From Mars* screenplay.

WILLIE: None. Until you dropped it so dramatically on my desk, I had no knowledge an *Invasion From Mars* screenplay even existed.

AGENT ECKS: But your name is on the damn thing!

WILLIE: You don't have any idea how Hollywood works, do you? The original screenwriter on the film, no matter how little of his actual work ends up on the screen, is credited on all subsequent versions of the screenplay. I don't have any idea what Orson Welles and Harry Lime were actually up to. I don't any the foggiest clue what is actually in that screenplay sitting there, but I can tell you I didn't write a single word of it. And if what you are claiming if true, that Orson Welles and Harry Lime have stolen "Top-Secret" documents from the government, then I don't think Mr. Lime would be foolish enough to put his own name on the blasted thing.

The "Top-Secret" documents that Willie Brown left carelessly strewn around for Government Agent Ecks to find!

AGENT ECKS: But you had access to the bungalow in Victorville where we found the "Top-Secret" documents. I'm not going to allow a smooth-talking screenwriter to write himself out of this interrogation. You had access to the documents. Your name in on the blasted screenplay. Your explanations... your bullshit... just doesn't hold any water with me. It's just as if we caught you red-handed. If you hadn't interrupted our work here, we would have, no doubt, discovered further evidence of your duplicity. My men are going to spend all night going over every inch of your apartment, and they are going to find the proof, the evidence, that you are a traitor against our great country. I'm going to break you. Instead of spinning web of lies, I am going to get the truth out of you. Even if one of us is driven mad in the process. You are going to be charged with treason and executed for crimes against your country!

[Orson clicks off the reel-to-reel.]

2 Record Set
MF201/2
The complete original radio broadcast.
THE WAR OF THE WORLDS
STARRING Orson Welles And The Mercury Theatre On The Air
DAILY NEWS FINAL
FAKE RADIO 'WAR' STIRS TERROR THROUGH U.S.
"War" Victim
"I Didn't Know"
Exactly as heard on CBS Radio October 30, 1938.
Radio play by HOWARD KOCH suggested by the H.G.WELLS novella.

The very wax recording pressed on vinyl and released to for the world to listen to in the privacy of their own homes forever obscuring the reality of the Martian invasion and the truth of the Orson Welles Conspiracy!

ORSON: Well, I think that I've ran my mouth long enough this evening. Given the lateness of the hour, I think we should continue our interview on another night, preferably one that doesn't reek of the inappropriateness of Mischief Night.

PETER: You're just going to leave me hanging like that? I've got questions that need answers and you are choosing not to answer them? You're just going to take your ball and go home?

ORSON: I... I... I... um... I have to otherwise I might say something that I shouldn't. That I don't have clearance to say.

PETER: You don't have clearance? You've been talking out of your backside all evening. Now you're saying you don't have clearance? From whom?

ORSON: I'm afraid I'm going to say something that I shouldn't you see, it goes beyond the "Orson Welles' Conspiracy. You see the conspiracy never ended. Not in 1938. Not in 1942. It continues to this very day. If I'm not careful I might say

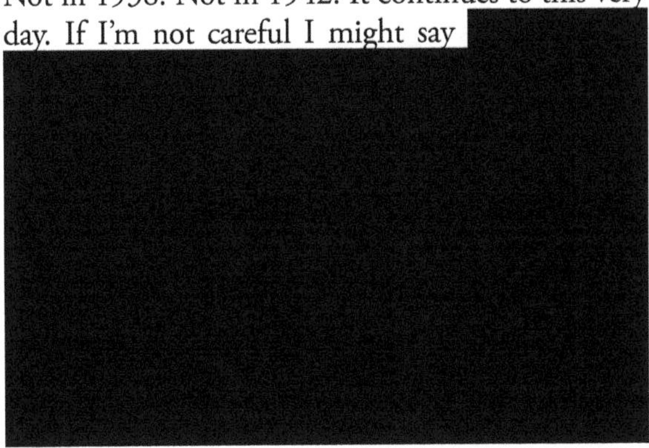

PETER: I don't understand.

ORSON:

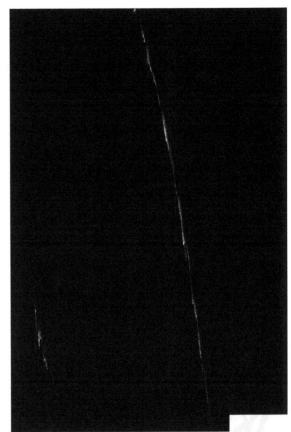

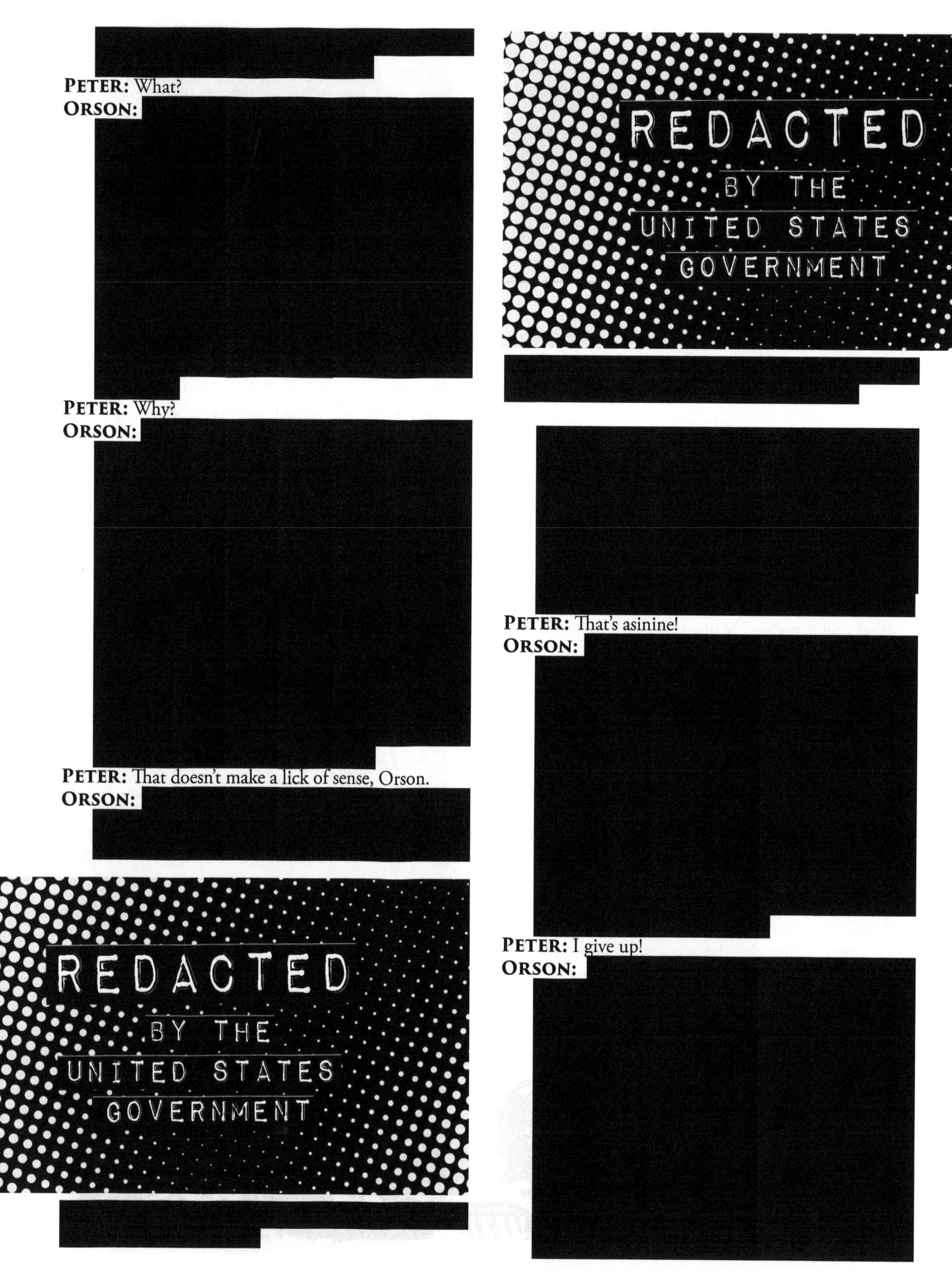

PETER: What?

ORSON:

PETER: Why?

ORSON:

PETER: That doesn't make a lick of sense, Orson.

ORSON:

PETER: That's asinine!

ORSON:

PETER: I give up!

ORSON:

PETER: That's stretching credulity.

ORSON:

PETER: But... but... but.. but.. but...

- How did the interrogation of Willie Brown end?
- Was Willie able to get away from the government agents and if so, did he help finish the film?
- If you filmed the film, that you say you not only filmed but finished, then where is the film?
- Why hasn't it been seen since? Is it locked away in a vault or was it burnt as William Randolph Hearst demanded of *Citizen Kane?*
- Did anyone ever actually see it? And if so, whom?
- Did the editors edit it?
- Did RKO executives screen it?
- How many saw it with their very eyes?
- What about the evidence the government found in the bungalow in Victorville? Did the government ever use this evidence against you in a court of law?
- Did the government realize that Willie Brown had lied to them? Did they return to interrogate him about his lies and complicity in your conspiracy to film your version of events?
- Did the government agents discover that Willie Brown and Harry Lime were one-and-the-same? That it was entirely a ruse to flout them and flaunt your arrogance?
- Did you eventually show the film to RKO President Charles Koerner? What was his reaction?
- Did he rain down hellfire and brimstone upon you? Of course, he did. Of this I have no doubt.
- Or did you find some way of talking yourself out of being fired on the spot? Why weren't you fired?
- Why weren't you sued for stealing studio funds to produce a fraudulent and ultimately failed feature?
- And how exactly did you try to convince Charles Koerner to release a film that we now know was never actually released?
- Why wasn't there the glitz and glamour of a Hollywood premiere at Grauman's Chinese Theatre with a cavalcade of the Who's Who of Hollywood? Was this the steep price you paid for producing the fraudulent feature?
- And once FDR and WRH realized the film was filmed and finished, what did they do? Why weren't you hounded by government agents and Hearst's reporters to the ends of the earth? Surely, Hearst's reporters were more cunning than the agents of Roosevelt.
- What happened to the rest of the "Orson Welles' Conspiracy"?

ORSON: Those are all valid questions, Peter. I just don't...

PETER: What happened to the rest of the "Orson Welles' Conspiracy?

ORSON: Actually, the "Orson Welles' Conspiracy" was the conspiracy between FDR and WR Hearst and myself on October 30, 1938. You want answers about the "Willie Brown Conspiracy" of 1942. The "Willie Brown Conspiracy" is going to have to be told another day. I'm tired. I'm exhausted. My brain hurts from all that bu– expenditure tonight.

PETER: But... but... but.. but.. but... what about...

ORSON: You're going to have to afford me the time to devise those answers, Peter. Even I am not capable of inventing such wondrous and absurd bullshit on the fly. The well has run—

PETER: "Well"? It's been more like a sewage tank. A wet, steaming cow-patty so foul, reeking of desperation, offending the mental nostrils with a funk so rotten—

ORSON: —Point taken– the sewage tank– has run dry, I'm afraid. I'm good, perhaps even great, but I'm not a bullshit genius like my esteemed old friend Willie Brown.

PETER: At the very least, you're a good enough friend to admit your well has run dry. And I'm a good enough friend to admit that I'm going to have to refill my own tank to device more questions that even your devise mind can't answer.

ORSON: I may have a little something that can stoke your creativity for our next session. Let me see if I can find a copy of it somewhere. *[Heard rustling through boxes and desk drawers, until.]* Ah, here it is. I should have had it on standby, considering the subject of our interview. I don't know why it slipped my mind. Here.

PETER: What is it?

ORSON: It's a card from my Rolodex. On it its an address for the small steel-mill town in Colorado where Willie Brown lives with his family. If you even doubt what I'm saying here was the honest-to-God truth, fly into Stapleton International Airport, rent a car and travel a hundred miles south. I'm sure his misses, Sheila, will fix you a fine meal, you can meet his children and his step-children, including his little snot-nosed five-year-old kindergartner, and he had tell you *his* side of the "Orson Welles' Conspiracy"! ⚛

her Birds

Hedda Hopper's Hollywood

Please note that this column is being published outside of William Randolph Hearst's publishing empire in protest! Mr. Hearst has forbidden its publication! He believes that the only copy of this column is safely squirreled away in his most famous safe. But! I typed a copy... just in case. I'd like to thank Hearst's rival newspapers for running this column in their newspapers. This is the only act of defiance that I am capable of. I simply do not understand why Mr. Hearst refuses to run this column in his legion of newspapers. See for yourself what the fuss is all about!

My little birds have smuggled Orson Welles' *Invasion From Mars* screenplay out of RKO's Forty-Acres. The boy, who I cannot stand in the slightest, has locked down his sound-stage like it was Fort-*flipping*-Knox. He has learned from John Ford's teat as it concerns identifying moles on his set, whether those moles work for Charles Koerner or myself. He is keeping what is going on on his set a closely guarded secret. A "Top-Secret" secret!

Now, RKO executives have provided me with the script for *The War of the Worlds* screenplay, written by a no-credit, no-account screenwriter named William Francis Brown. This script is a perfectly wonderful adaptation of Howard Koch's famous and even infamous radio-play. (Why would the famed Brit, HG Wells, give his seal-of-approval to the misspelled namesake is beyond me?) This is a script that has been made readily available to Louella Parsons, myself, and William Randolph Hearst himself. And given that fact, the script stinks to high-heaven!

What my little birds are telling me is this is *not* the script Orson Welles is actually shooting. So my hunches have been correct all along. My little birds have been able to smuggle out copies of this scene and that scene, but not an entire

.O Radio
780 North Gower St.
Hollywood

urn promptly to
OGRAPHIC DEPARTMENT
en you have finished with it

THE INVASION FROM MARS

Written by
William Francis Brown
& Orson Welles

...sed on H.G. Welles
story

shooting script. The whole script (if it exists in the whole) is locked somewhere my little birds can't find and there are few places out of the reach of my little birds. Though the deliveries from my little birds are piecemeal, I have been able to piece together the script like it was a jigsaw puzzle (Orson, this is *not* a shot at Marian Davies, though your sick, twisted little mind will think it is). I felt like the original publishers of William Shakespeare's quartos who had to cobble together the whole from the parts (i.e. the actor's prompt-books). The task has proven to be quite the challenge because I don't know what the picture is supposed to be. Like *Citizen Kane* before it, this script bounces around through time. Quite literally. There appears to be a time travel plot-line stolen from another HG Wells classic as well. But what I do know has turned my already graying hair stark white!

"Charles Foster Kane" was not named "William Randolph Hearst" in that abomination of a motion picture! Thank the Lord!

In *Citizen Kane*, Orson Welles had the decency (am I really typing this?) to name his character "Charles Foster Kane" instead of putting my employer's Christian name on that abomination of a caricature-character. Even Orson Welles wouldn't have the audacity to call the "Charles Foster Kane" character "William Randolph Hearst" or the "Susan Alexander" character "Marian Davies". This would have been the height of audacity! Not even George Schafer's inept and impotent lawyers would have allowed that abomination to reach the screen. Schafer was, no doubt, advised by his lawyers that naming the caricature-character "Charles Foster Kane" was kosher, at least legally, but certainly not morally. So, my employer didn't have to suffer the ignominy of having his name spoken in that atrocious motion picture.

But! what Orson Welles has chosen to do with his newly and secretly retitled *Invasion From Mars* script was to name names. The character that his own character enters into a Faustian bargain with is named "William Randolph Hearst". There are characters named "Franklin Delano Roosevelt", "Hans Von Kaltenborn", William Paley", "Edward R. Murrow", "Nikola Tesla", and he even put the cursed word *"Rosebud"* on the very lips of "Marian Davies"! The boy is so uncouth. He possesses no shame. How dare he!

But simply naming names is *not* the true crime in this screenplay! It is the cockamamie story that he is choosing to tell. Making a caricature a great man in *Citizen Kane* is so much more preferred to what he does to these great men he has chosen to include in his character list. He puts absurdities on their lips. The plot of this motion picture (if you could call it a plot) is so ignominious that no credited screenwriter worth his salt in Hollywood would have devised such a plot. Perhaps, that is why Orson chose a young

Orson Welles gleefully speaks with the press the morning after he panicked the nation with his prankish radio-dramatization!

screenwriter without a single credit to his name. His name is William Francis Brown. But Orson has proven by his callous reaction to the press that Halloween morning in 1938 after he pranked the entire nation with his "War of the Worlds" radio-dramatization that he has no shame and will do and say anything that furthers his prankish intentions. And what, Constant Reader, are his prankish intentions with this motion picture? Mockery! And scorn! He is such a small little man that he hates great men who wield true power. Whether that is William Randolph Hearst or Franklin Delano Roosevelt, he only cares to topple those with real power. He paints these men with Walt Disney's cartoon brush. He should have had Walt Disney buy out his contract have taken this screenplay to the Disney animation studio to animate with dancing tri-pods and singing animals. If the character of "William Randolph Hearst" had been drawn as a walking-and-talking anthropomorphic bear, then this caricature might have been tolerable. Barely! But he has, no doubt, cast an older actor to play this great man, whom would be forced to say these absurdities!

What is the story that Orson Welles is *trying* to tell? It centers on a conceit that the Martian invasion heard by millions of CBS radio-listeners on October 30, 1938, a mere four years go, were *real* and that President Roosevelt conspired with William Randolph Hearst to cover-up the auditory evidence by hiring the radio-whippersnapper Orson Welles to produce a counterfeit radio-dramatization to mask the *real* invasion! What in the heck did I just type? The notion that the radio broadcasts heard were *real* is beyond absurd. Not even the most paranoid of conspiracy theorists, who wallow in their schizophrenia, could have conceived this conceit! Everyone knows that Orson Welles put on a counterfeit "evening of dance music" being interrupted by fake "news broadcasts" and these "reports" told the story of a horrifying and harrowing Martian invasion. So spooked were CBS radio-listeners that phone-lines were jammed up and down the east coast as frightened Americans sought answers from authorities. And those answers were *then* and are *now* that Orson Welles was producing a radio-drama of HG Wells' *War of the Worlds*. But in this abomination of a *Invasion From Mars* script, he is supposing that the invasions were *real* and after the woefully short invasion by inept Martians, the government began to conceal the very nature of the Martian invasion from the American people. "Franklin Delano Roosevelt" stooped to blackmailing "William Randolph Hearst" into being a part of the conspiracy, which would then wrangle in the young radio-actor/director/producer into.

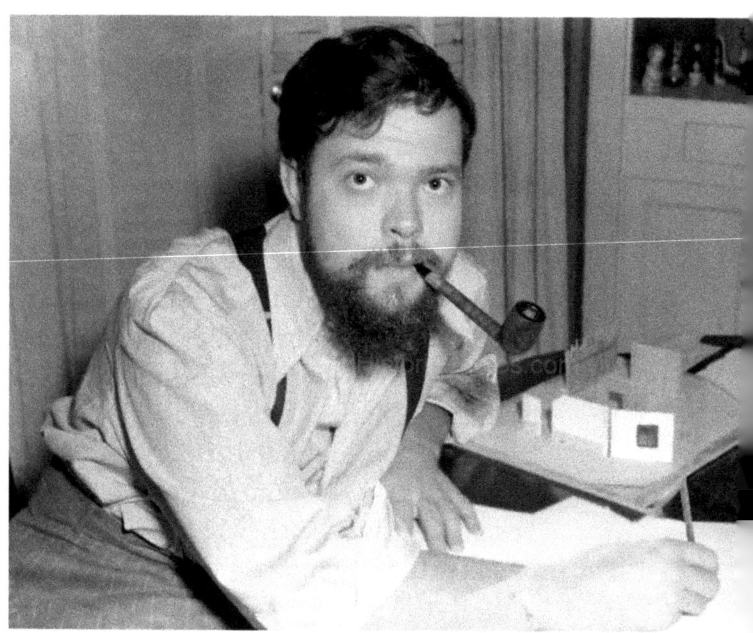

Orson Welles toils away at the screenplay for The Invasion From Mars *or was it* The War of the Worlds, *no wait, it's* The Invasion From Mars! *I'm so confused!*

Now, his poking two bears could be considered par-for-the-course for two great men in the public sphere, but why does he mock two esteemed news broadcasters in Hans Von Kaltenborn and Edward R. Murrow? He paints them in the worst possible colors. And according to my little birds, his movie is being filmed in Technicolor! There is not a single caricature-character in this screenplay that escapes unscathed, including a character named "Orson Welles". Yes! He has the audacity to make himself a caricature-character in his own screenplay, having cast another actor to play himself! He doesn't even have the courage to play himself in this film! But simply because Orson chooses to lampoon himself with such absurdities, such as traveling through time, does not absolve him of his sins against two great men!

With *Citizen Kane*, he lied to my face that the character of "Charles Foster Kane" was not based on my employer William Randolph Hearst and for that I will never-ever forgive the boy. But with *Invasion From Mars*, what is his endgame? If it is merely mockery and scorn, then he is a smaller man than I had previously given him credit for. With his "War of the Worlds" radio-dramatization he was so full of himself that he thought he could fool an entire nation with counterfeit "evening of dance music" being interrupted by fake "news broadcasts" reporting a Martian invasion. Is he still stinging that William Paley made him go before the press and admit the invasion was fake. The press and the people were truly magnanimous in accepting his apparent apology. But this mandatory confession and compulsory contrition took the air out of his prank and we all know how much the boy loves his pranks. When he put on "The War of the Worlds", was his intention to make the people believe there was a Martian invasion... days... weeks... months... forever? And having had that stolen from him, he sought a more public forum to continue his Martian invasion prank. That would certainly explain his *Invasion From Mars* atrocity

Wilton Lackaye, originating the role of "Svengali" in the on stage and in film, could have easily used the very same performance to play "Orson Welles" manipulating his radio-cast to participate in the "Orson Welles' Conspriacy" in his Invasion From Mars*!*

But what if he truly believes that Martians invaded America that night. Could a cult-leader (and he certainly leads *the Mercury Theatre on the air* as a Svengali) be so delusional to drink his own... I don't know... Kool-aid? Had he convinced himself the Martian invasion was real? I am no Sigmund Freud, but did the fact that he frightened millions of Americans with his radio prank break his psyche? And his mind had to justify millions of frightened Americans by insisting that Martians invaded the east coast of America? His view of himself borders of narcissism and narcissism borders on psychopathy.

I hope– I pray– that by publishing this column, I expose the *Invasion From Mars* motion picture which is being filmed under the very nose of Charles Koerner and get this production shut down for good. I hope– I pray– that by publishing this column, Orson Welles can get the professional psychiatric help that he needs. When you being to believe your own bull— you need to go away for a while. Maybe forever.

From the Desk of
WILLIAM FRANCIS
BROWN

October 31, 1997
Small Hours

To my son, Bob,

I realize that I have been known to spin a "tall tale" every now and again. To tell a story has it actually happened has always struck me as being disingenuous to the drama inherent in any "good story". What happened in the moment is merely the first draft of what happened. The memory we form in the very moments afterward begins the process of revising the event in our mind's eye. Every recollection of the memory involves a rewrite and every rewrite alters the remembrance until we believe each and every revision is the actual memory as it happened. It is less of an exaggeration and more inspiration.

To me, any story just gets better and more dramatic with each retelling. I rewrite this memory or edit that recollection until the story has been honed to a razor's edge. If others remember the event any less dramatically, it is because their own mind's eye does not have the skill of a novelist.

I have never attempted to write the Great American Novel. Even though I have the desire, I do not have the skill. No, I can't say that. I may have the ability to write, but I do not have the desire. The idea of sitting at a desk writing day after day, month after month, page after page after page intimidates me beyond all measure. The fear of the blank page is one thing; the fear of the subsequent hundreds of blank pages is another thing entirely.

I see you sitting for hours on end at your computer, your video game machines entirely forgotten about, all for that foolish computer you insisted your mother and I purchase for you. (I can't see computers becoming a piece of furniture in the house like our television set is)

When you finish one of your stories, you don't have any fear of where you are going to get the next story. It just magically appears in your mind. What if you only had one idea in your entire life that was worthy? What if the one idea you had was given to you because someone had no clue as to how to write it? What if it had to be written in complete secret and anonymity; writing through blood, sweat, tears, and four weeks of burbon-fueled days and black-coffee-fueled sleepless nights? What if the one story you had actually finished sits languishing completely forgotten about for over fifty-years?

But I digress.

You cannot possibly imagine how much I have enjoyed you reading me the stories you have written on your confounded computer. It reminds of my youth listening to programs on the radio like "The Shadow", "I Love a Mystery", and having the living daylights scared out of me because I thought that the War of the Worlds was actually descending on Washington DC while my family sat terrified, thousands of miles away in Colorado.

You have such a creative mind and will no doubt be a famous author one day. What ever happens to you in your life, do not give up on your dream to write that Passion play in Shakespearean verse you want to write. It is a project that is to say the very least, awe-inspiring. Don't give it up. The Lord will bless you with opportunities when you least expect them.

I should have followed mine when I was your age. No, I can't say that. I did follow my dreams, but not to the extent that I should have.

I have kept a secret from you and the rest of the family for over fifty years; a secret I am going to expose in this letter. When I was seventeen, I went to Hollywood to become a famous screenwriter. I know that sounds asinine considering that I retired after working forty-years in the steel-mill, but I did. So, where are the movies that I wrote? Why haven't I spun my adventures in Hollywood into the most wondrous and wonderful bullshit?

It is because I never wrote a single blessed word that didn't end up on the cutting room floor. I thought my ship had come in when I was assigned to write a screenplay for the boy-wonder Orson Welles. He was being forced, against his will, to direct a film of his infamous "War of the Worlds" radio-dramatization for the silver-screen. AND I was writing the screenplay! You may be asking yourself, son, why was this motion picture never filmed? That is a story in and of itself. Needless to say, Orson pissed off more people with his War of the Worlds film than he ever did with Citizen Kane.

This is the heart of my consternation. Not a single word I wrote while in Hollywood ever made it up onto that screen. They all ended up in heaps of discarded film on the floor of the editing room. This is why I left Hollywood. This is why I did what your grandfather wanted and joined the union at the steel-mill. This is why I have never spoken of these misspent days of my youth.

On October 30, 2024, you must do me a favor (I know you will be tempted to go years, even decades before this deadline, but please bare with me. There is method of my procrastination). On this day, so many years from now, I want you to go to my secret safety deposit box at the Mount Carmel Credit Union. There you will find the only surviving copy of the screenplay I wrote for Orson Welles' War of the Worlds. I want you to wait until then, because it will be the anniversary of the world-famous radio-dramatization of War of the Worlds. Hopefully most of the earwitnesses to the hysteria caused by Orson Welles and his radio broadcast that infamous Halloween Eve in 1938 will be dead.

This is of utmost importance!

Do what you will with the screenplay. Burn it so the world can never know what actually happened (I cannot bring myself to destroy my only work) or publish it so the world can know what actually happened. Just know that the government will stop at nothing to keep this story from coming to light. Hopefully by 2024, the government's paranoia concerning the events of October 30, 1938 will have abated, but I sincerely doubt this. For your safety, I can only hope and pray.

I'm sorry that I cannot say more of this now. Just know that someday will you understand one of the reasons why I am the world-class bullshitter am I. It is all Orson Welles' fault.

Sincerely, your father,

William Francis Brown

William Francis Brown

The Persuasion From M.A.R.S.
The "Lost" Orson Welles Screenplay

REVISED FINAL SCRIPT

THIS IS PROPERTY OF

R.K.O Radio Pictures

780 North Gower St.
Hollywood

Offer the Warners the screenplay

Please return promptly to
STENOGRAPHIC DEPARTMENT
when you have finished with it

THE INVASION FROM MARS

Written by
William Francis Brown
& Orson Welles

Based on H.G. Welles
And a True Story

NOW! FINAL
w/ Cinema Manager

CAST LIST

Orson Welles (1938 & 1942)	Theodore Frost
Hans Von Kaltenborn	Frederick Hansen
Franklin Delano Roosevelt	Arnold Hewitt
William Randolph Hearst	Arthur Campbell
Marion Davies	Margaret Russell
George S. Patton	Francis Foster
Secretary of State	George Hughes
Vice-President	Stanley Reed
William Paley	Louis Greene
Edward R. Murrow	Frank Moore
Nikola Tesla	Clyde Mackay
HG Wells	Clarence Jenkins
Davidson Taylor	Andrew Stinton
Frank Readick	Milton Garner
Dan Seymour	Gerald Mclaughlin
Kenny Delmar	Edward Phillips
Guy Lombardo	Lawrence Bennett
Archibald Macleish	Earl Lynch
Arthur Buddington	Floyd Simpson
Governor James H. Price	Charles Myers
Captain ████	Thomas Cox
Winston Churchill	Norman Collins
Joseph Stalin	Evgeni Semyonov
Martian Ambassador	Edward Mullins
Jack Paar	Kenneth Butler
Fred Weber	Victor Stacey
Gabriel Heatter	Raymond Cook
Robert Wise	George Campbell
Gladis	Dorothy Phillips
Doris	Frances Foster
Patton's Wife	Ruth Powell
RKO Executive	Robert Butler
RKO Executive #2	Henry Bell
RKO Executive #3	Harold Cox
CBS Telephone Operator 1	Evelyn Jenkins
CBS Telephone Operator 2	Florence Ross
CBS Telephone Operator 3	Louise Ross
Manager at WGAR	Alfred Roberts
Personal Assistant	Jack Adams
White House Operator	Mildred Edwards
Cinema Manager	Lawrence Peters
Secret Service Officer	Norman Middleton

Directed by Orson Welles
Written by William Francis Brown & Orson Welles
Produced by Charles Koerner (Executive Producer) & Orson Welles (Producer)
Music by Bernard Hermann
Cinematography by Gregg Toland
Editing by Robert Wise
Casting by Ruffus Le Mair & Robert Palmer
Art Direction by Van Nest Polglase
Costume Design by Edward Stevenson

FADE IN:

The RKO Picture's title sequence begins, followed by a black screen with white letters reading "A Mercury Production by Orson Welles".

Then a title plate reading "INVASION FROM MARS".

The image of a door to a studio at CBS, where a"NO TRESPASSING" is sign tacked. "SHOT ON SIGHT" is has been hand-painted on the sign. The camera pans up and looks through the window of the door and then into the room where...

1 INT. CBS STUDIO - NIGHT - OCTOBER 31, 1938 - 04:57

WILLIAM RANDOLPH HEARST (dressed as Henry VIII), his mistress MARION DAVIES, a 23 year-old ORSON WELLES, and the cast and crew of the Mercury Theater on the air stand nervously around the CBS' recording studio while being guarded by armed military personnel.

Davies observes from a distance, Hearst and Welles talking in hushed voices. She cannot make-out what they are talking about. Hearst casts a quick glance at Marion before walking over to CAPTAIN ███████.

Orson Welles slips over to his podium and begins organizing the teletype feed from that night's radio-broadcasts.

Marian approaches the young Mr. Welles.

MARION DAVIES
This is such a charade.

ORSON WELLES
I don't have the foggiest...

Marion Davies notices a flask of whiskey sitting on Orson's podium. She takes a quick swig.

MARION DAVIES
I know you know what was going on tonight and I want to know what you two are conspiring about.

ORSON WELLES
I'm afraid that matter is classified...
(over acting)
Top-secret. I simply can't go into details about

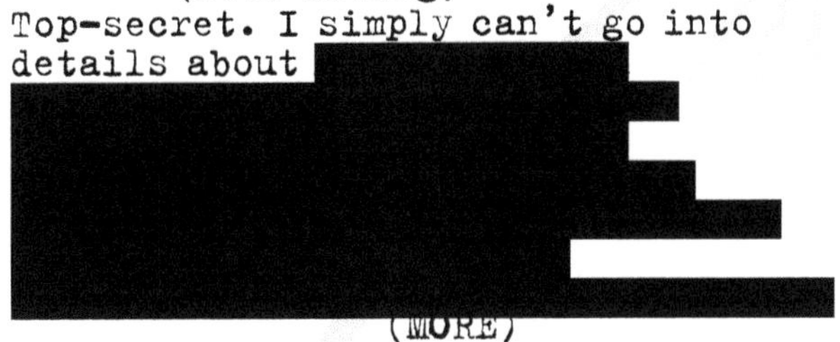

(MORE)

(CONTINUED)

ORSON WELLES (CONT'D)

MARION DAVIES
I know an actor when I meet one, Mr. Welles and you are hamming it up royally for his esteemed greatness over there. If somebody doesn't explain to be what in the blue blazes is going on here, I will scream,

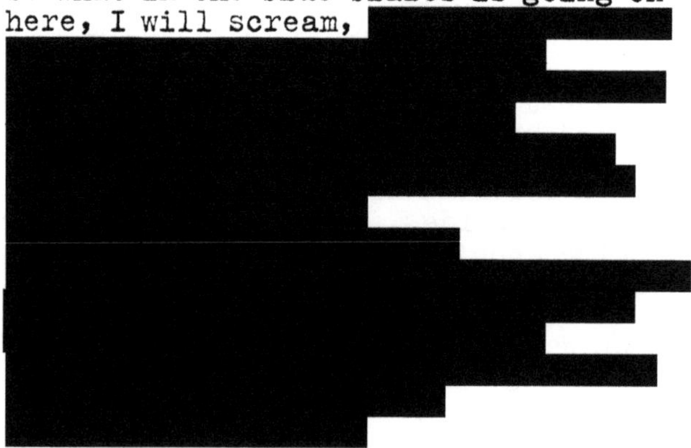

ORSON WELLES
I have to repeat, this time emphatically, don't have the foggiest idea as to what you may be referring to, Miss Davies.

MARION DAVIES
Don't you dare keep secrets from me. I have been around Pops long enough to know that there is only one currency that actually means a blasted thing when it all comes down to brass tacks.

ORSON WELLES
And what would that be?

MARION DAVIES
Secrets. That is the only thing that really matters in this world. Secrets. My Pops trades in them. He buys and sells them all day long. It's the essence of his business. The president has many secrets. Heck, Pops has pictures of the president in his stupid wheelchair. You and Willie are conspiring cover up what happened tonight and then you'll have your own secrets to protect.

(MORE)

(CONTINUED)

MARION DAVIES (CONT'D)
Everybody has secrets. You tell me your secrets and I'll tell you his.

ORSON WELLES
And what secret could possibly interest me?.

MARION DAVIES
If you're dealing with William Randolph Hearst, you're going to have to know one of his secrets if you're going to have any power in your negotiations with him. If you know one of his secrets, he'll keep all of yours. That is the nature of the beast. You tell me your little secret and I'll give you his.

ORSON WELLES
And what pray tell would that be, Miss Davies?

Close-up on her pouty lips.

MARION DAVIES
(whispers)
"Rosebud."

DISSOLVE TO:

2 INT. EDITING ROOM AT RKO - AFTERNOON - OCTOBER 30, 1943 - 3:47

In an Editing Room at RKO, ORSON WELLES 1943 is splicing two film segments together. The image of Marion Davies' pouty lips can be clearly in see on of the frames in CLOSE-UP as the scene transitions.

ORSON WELLES 1943
What time is it, Robert?

ROBERT WISE
It's five minutes since the last time you asked.

ORSON WELLES 1943
Humor me.

ROBERT WISE
About a quarter till.

ORSON WELLES 1943
What time is it exactly, if you don't mind?

ROBERT WISE
3:47.

ORSON WELLES 1943
Where are they? It isn't scientifically possible that they could be late.

(CONTINUED)

Orson picks up a pack of playing cards off nearby table and begins shuffling the cards with the false shuffle technique.

There is a knock on the door and ORSON WELLES 1938 walks in with NIKOLA TESLA, a very old man who appears stretched in time.

ORSON WELLES 1943 (CONT'D)
You're late, Nikola.

NIKOLA TESLA
A time traveller is never late. I arrived precisely... on time. If I wasn't on time, the very fabric of spacetime could unravel like pulling a loose string on a sweater. Your perception of the exact time of your previous arrival here five years ago has been flawed by the passage of time, Orson. Our perception of the time of our arrival is another thing entirely, time being fluid and all.

ORSON WELLES 1943
Now that you mention it, I do remember hearing the future Orson having this exact same conversation with you four years ago.

NIKOLA TESLA
You may remember having the entire conversation again and again and perhaps again in an endless causality loop if we are not careful.

ORSON WELLES 1943
I remember this as well.

NIKOLA TESLA
Then we should move on, shouldn't we.

ORSON WELLES 1943 continues to absentmindedly false shuffling his cards.

ORSON WELLES 1943
I'd show you a card trick, Nikola, but you can control the spacetime continuum, so you'd be underwhelmed by the illusion. And Orson, you already know the tricks, so it would be pointless to try. But you need to think about the night you are going to have like it is a sleight of hand trick. You will be false shuffling your cards all night. You must make sure the order of the cards remains exactly the same. You will also need to force a card every now and again if the future you see me in in Hollywood is going to actually happen again.

(CONTINUED)

ORSON WELLES 1938
How exactly am I supposed to know what to do and when to do it if I don't know what is going to happen later tonight, which is five years ago apparently?

NIKOLA TESLA
This is precisely why I brought you here, Orson. Orson here is going to tell you what exactly what he did to get himself to through the night and eventually to Hollywood.

ORSON WELLES 1938
If the future Orson, him, is telling the past Orson, me, how he got himself, myself, through the rest of the night and how he successfully ended up in Hollywood, didn't he receive the information from the future Orson when he was the past Orson? Isn't that a paradox?

ORSON WELLES 1943
Don't think too hard on it, Orson, or you'll blow a gasket. You will take the teletype you read half-an-hour ago, five years ago.

ORSON WELLES 1938
My head is starting to hurt.

ORSON WELLES 1943
The teletype represents every word broadcast by Kaltenborn and the others, who reported the invasion from Mars tonight. By morning you will have rewritten it with Howard Koch's help, rehearsed it, and recorded it just in time to go before the reporters admitting you pranked the entire nation with a radio-dramatization of H.G. Wells' classic War of the Worlds.

ORSON WELLES 1938
That will take more time than just an evening to accomplish, Orson.

ORSON WELLES 1943
You have access to a time machine, Orson. You will have all the time in the universe. But before you do any of this, you will force a few cards. One by making William Randolph Hearst promise to give you the keys to Hollywood, where you will make the movies you want to make.

ORSON WELLES 1938
Thought I already did that.

(CONTINUED)

ORSON WELLES 1943
You did, but not for the reasons you think. He forced a card onto you, because you had already forced a card onto him and the President.

ORSON WELLES 1938
That's some misdirection you made there, Orson. I didn't even see the move.

ORSON WELLES 1943
If you misdirect them all tonight, you will get everything you want, and you will be called the Boy Wonder. But know that you will go so looney-tunes with that power though, that you will make a movie about Hearst himself and you will force him to do everything in his power to destroy you.

ORSON WELLES 1938
That's a lot of "you will"s. Is there no choice when it involves time-travel?

NIKOLA TESLA
(matter of factly)
No.

ORSON WELLES 1938
This future sounds pleasant. Why don't I just stay in New York and be happy doing plays and radio-shows.

NIKOLA TESLA
Because you can't. Damned causality loops and all, Orson.

ORSON WELLES 1943
He's right. I've already made Citizen Kane and angered the most powerful man in Hollywood and you must as well or the universe will explode.

NIKOLA TESLA
It won't actually explode, but it would be bad, very bad.

ORSON WELLES 1943
And after the fiasco that is Citizen Kane, RKO will force you to turn your radio-dramatization of War of the Worlds into a motion picture.

ORSON WELLES 1938
That sounds easy enough.

(CONTINUED)

ORSON WELLES 1943
Except you won't do it the easy way and simply adapt the radio-drama written by Howard Koch.

ORSON WELLES 1938
Of course, I wouldn't. How foolish. Why wouldn't I?

ORSON WELLES 1943
You decide to tell the true-story of what happened five-years ago, or last night, or later tonight, or whenever the hell it was. You will tell the truth story. The story you read on the teletype.

ORSON WELLES 1938
If I conspired to cover up a Martian invasion tonight, then wouldn't I have gotten in bed with not only Hearst, but the President as well?

ORSON WELLES 1943
You will. I did. And unlike _Citizen Kane_ where you will hide, erm- I hid Hearst behind the name Charles Foster Kane, I named names, erm- you will name names. There will be no boundaries to your arrogance. My arrogance.

ORSON WELLES 1938
Then it doesn't seem prudent to make that kind of movie, Orson. I don't think I should... you shouldn't have.

NIKOLA TESLA
But he has. Damned causality loops and all, Orson.

ORSON WELLES 1943
I made _Invasion From Mars_ and angered the most powerful men in Washington and you must as well or the universe will explode.

NIKOLA TESLA
It won't actually explode, but it would be bad, very bad.

ORSON WELLES 1938
We're starting to repeat ourselves. We need to be more careful in what we say.

ORSON WELLES 1943
I'm going to walk you through what happened to me five years ago, what will happen to you over the course of the next several hours. Listen carefully. Memorize it.
(MORE)

(CONTINUED)

ORSON WELLES 1943 (CONT'D)
The that eidetic memory to good use.
This is going to be the best mistake you
ever make.

DISSOLVE TO4:

3 INT. SCREENING ROOM AT RKO - WEEKS LATER

The scene flashes momentarily as the camera pulls back to reveal the previous scene has been projected onto the screen in the screening room at RKO pictures. After a few seconds, the screen goes dark.

ORSON WELLES 1943 and several RKO EXECUTIVES have been watching the previous scene.

RKO EXECUTIVE
Why are there two Orson Welles in this
scene?

ORSON WELLES 1943
The scene is pretty self-explanatory.

RKO EXECUTIVE #2
We don't understand.

ORSON WELLES 1943
It involves time-travel.

RKO EXECUTIVE
Isn't that impossible?

RKO EXECUTIVE #3
It isn't very believable that someone
could travel through time and have a
conversation between themselves.

ORSON WELLES 1943
You're concerned about believability in
a science-fiction movie about an
invasion from Mars?

RKO EXECUTIVE
Wouldn't a time-travel plot be a little
over the heads of our audience?

ORSON WELLES 1943
(quietly)
And apparently some in this room, as
well.

RKO EXECUTIVE #2
We don't understand why there are two
Orson Welles in the scene.

ORSON WELLES 1943
You don't have to understand, it will
all be explained in due time.

RKO EXECUTIVE #3
We don't understand why the two Orson
Welles meet each other.
(MORE)

(CONTINUED)

RKO EXECUTIVE #3 (CONT'D)
If we're confused, the audience will be confused as well.

ORSON WELLES 1943
It will all be explained in greater detail in the final reel.

RKO EXECUTIVE
Shouldn't you move this scene to the final reel then?

ORSON WELLES 1943
No.

RKO EXECUTIVE #2
If the scene takes place after a scene in the final reel, shouldn't it be in the final reel? That would make more sense.

ORSON WELLES 1943
No.

RKO EXECUTIVE #3
We think...

ORSON WELLES 1943
You are incapable of a coherent thought.

RKO EXECUTIVE #2
There shouldn't be two Orson Welles one scene. There aren't two of you now.

RKO EXECUTIVE
And why is there a character called "Orson Welles" in the movie if your name is also Orson Welles?

RKO EXECUTIVE #3
We don't understand.

ORSON WELLES 1943 cups his face with his hands and stifles a scream.

ORSON WELLES 1943
Let's move to the next scene, shall we? Please.
(to the projectionist)
The hallway outside studio at CBS.

The next scene is being projected onto the screen, as we cross-fade into...

DISSOLVE TO:

4 INT. HALLWAY OUTSIDE STUDIO - NIGHT - OCTOBER 30, 1938 - 19:56

Inside the CBS broadcasting studio, through a small window in the door, DAVIDSON TAYLOR, vice president in charge of operations, is arguing with an off-screen ORSON WELLES.

(CONTINUED)

ORSON WELLES (O.S.)
I'm being preempted? Five minutes before I'm on the air?

DAVIDSON TAYLOR
If you'd have attended the programming meeting earlier this afternoon, you'd know the Mercury Theatre has been preempted. If you'd have read any of the memos, you'd have known. But no, you locked yourself in this studio, not allowing any interruptions in your precious rehearsal time.

ORSON WELLES (O.S.)
I'll be damned if we don't go on the air, Davidson. Who is taking my place on the air?

DAVIDSON TAYLOR
Mr. Paley has a remote unit set up in a ballroom to broadcast an evening of dance music.

ORSON WELLES (O.S.)
But what about my show? It's Halloween. I've got this nice little ghost story to tell.

DAVIDSON TAYLOR
Rebecca? Yes, I've read it. It just isn't fitting for Halloween. What kind of ghost story doesn't even have a ghost in it?

ORSON WELLES (O.S.)
I've been working all week on this. You want to waste all that time and money?

DAVIDSON TAYLOR
It won't be a waste of time and money. It's not canceled... It's just postponed. And I'll even make it worth your while.

ORSON WELLES (O.S.)
Worth my while? How?

DAVIDSON TAYLOR
You know how you've always said you want to interview one of the authors whose work you adapt for the radio?

ORSON WELLES (O.S.)
Yeah? So.

DAVIDSON TAYLOR
I'll connect a long distance call to England and you can interview Miss Du Maruier live on the air after the program.

(CONTINUED)

ORSON WELLES (O.S.)
I'm sure Miss Du Maruier will just love that... How can I do justice to an interview when I can't do justice to a radio-drama? Seeing how Standards and Practices has butchered her beautiful story.

DAVIDSON TAYLOR
I'm sure they had permission from Miss Du Maruier for any changes made to her story.

ORSON WELLES (O.S.)
Permission! They didn't have my permission! It's my adaptation, not hers. Those ignoramuses cut out the entire Mr. De Winter killing Rebecca plot-line. That's gold!

DAVIDSON TAYLOR
Orson, keep your voice down. Here. Come out here.

Davidson leads Orson out into the hallway.

DAVIDSON TAYLOR (CONT'D)
Look, we just can't stand out here in the hallway all night arguing over every little detail. So, it's settled.

ORSON WELLES
We haven't settled a thing.

DAVIDSON TAYLOR
(ignoring Orson)
We've killed two birds with one stone. Rebecca was running a little short anyway.

ORSON WELLES
It's not short. Lest you forget my prank!

DAVIDSON TAYLOR
The show plus the interview will make it an hour. Perfect. We'll reschedule its broadcast for the first open slot.
(looking at the calendar on his clipboard)
I believe Sunday, December 9th is a good time.

ORSON WELLES
Not the ninth of December, Davidson. Tonight! Tomorrow is Halloween. This is a season for pranks- for soaping windows or putting Farmer Perkins' cow up in the belfry. Tonight, I want to prank the entire nation.

(CONTINUED)

DAVIDSON TAYLOR
I've heard about your pranks, Orson, and as famous as they may be, they just aren't funny.

ORSON WELLES
They are absolutely hilarious.

DAVIDSON TAYLOR
What about poor old Hans Von Kaltenborn? You impersonated a Nazi spy, sent Hans a package filled with doctored photographs of Martians and Nazis taken at a meteorite crash site in the Austrian Alps. You faked interrogation transcripts between the Nazis and their Martian captives.

ORSON WELLES
And the Martians spoke a rudimentary form of English. And why English? We have been screaming at the tops of our lungs with our radio broadcasts. That was Pulitzer Prize worthy fiction!

DAVIDSON TAYLOR
And you convinced the distinguished gentleman journalist to go on the air and report such claptrap.

ORSON WELLES
He was so embarrassed he was pranked, he fell on his own sword. It was priceless.

DAVIDSON TAYLOR
You're sick.

ORSON WELLES
I had a minor case of Schadenfreude. I got better.

DAVIDSON TAYLOR
It was a stupid, asinine practical joke. You don't hesitate when it comes to crossing the line, particularly when it benefits your juvenile sensibilities.

ORSON WELLES
What line? There is no line. That's what you need to understand, Davidson. This is show business, it's all about self-image... Self-promotion. People all over the studio and the theater districts...

DAVIDSON TAYLOR
You flatter yourself, Orson. The prank's reach wasn't very great.

(CONTINUED)

ORSON WELLES
EVERYONE was talking about that prank for weeks and whose name was on everyone's lips? Mine. "Orson Welles". They all knew who I was, if they didn't already. So Davidson, when it comes to making a name for yourself, there is no line. Everything is Kosher.

DAVIDSON TAYLOR
(changing the subject)
Suit yourself. You can still have the studio until eleven o'clock. Heck, you can have the entire night for all I care. I'd suggest using this time to work on next week's show....

ORSON WELLES
I'm going on the air tonight, Davidson. Whether you like it or not. I'll have my little prank.

DAVIDSON TAYLOR
One of these days, Orson, you're going to upset the wrong person. And then you'll get your comeuppance. Good-night, Orson.

Orson throws down the script he wasn't aware he was still holding and storms back into his rehearsal studio.

DISSOLVE TO:

5 INT. HOTEL ANNAPOLIS' BALLROOM - NIGHT

The Hotel Annapolis is situated a few blocks from the White House. Its ballroom is filled with dozens of people dressed in every manner of masquerade costume and mask. They are all seated at a dozen or so round tables surrounding the dance floor.

GUY LOMBARDO and his orchestra are positioned on the stage.

HANS VON KALTENBORN, distinguished reporter for the Colombia Broadcast System, sits at a desk off in a distant corner of the ballroom. He has his own microphone and is holding headphones to his right ear.

HANS VON KALTENBORN
Good evening, ladies and gentlemen, this is Hans von Kaltenborn speaking. Tonight, we bring you an evening of charity and dance music from the ballroom in the Hotel Annapolis in Washington DC. We also bring you a message from our honored guest this evening, President Franklin Delano Roosevelt. Now... the President.

President FRANKLIN DELANO ROOSEVELT is seated at a table near the stage. There is a microphone in front of him.

(CONTINUED)

ROOSEVELT
My friends, many of you are used to my fireside chats from the White House. But tonight, I have been invited to a grand masquerade ball to listen to eloquent music, to dance, and to bring charity to a great cause. Infantile Paralysis.

There is quiet applause from the audience.

ROOSEVELT (CONT'D)
Tomorrow, hordes of young children, in all manner of ghoulish and ghastly dress, will walk up to your front door to ask for small candies, chocolates, popcorn balls, and candied apples. But as you give out those cherished childhood treats, take a moment to remember those poor innocent children who cannot walk up to your door. Those struck down with Infantile Paralysis. Early this year radio personality and philanthropist Eddie Cantor urged all Americans to send their loose change to me in "a march of dimes to reach all the way to the White House." So... In sending in a dime and in dancing that others may walk, we are striking a powerful blow in defense of American freedom and human decency.

There is a eruption of applause from the assembled guests.

William Randolph Hearst takes the center stage behind another microphone. He is dressed as Henry the VIII.

HEARST
Thank you, Mister President, for your eloquent words. I hope I can do the same with mine. Mister President, if I may turn your attention to the large gum-ball machine by the stage.

There is a large, five-foot tall gum-ball machine near the stage whose glass jar is 90% filled with loose change.

HEARST (CONT'D)
The assembled guests this evening have donated thousands upon thousands of dimes to the March of Dimes. And now, my donation. I'll, simply, top off the gum-ball machine!

Several BANK WORKERS march into the ballroom, then up to the machine. They pour large bank-issued bags of dimes into the glass bowl, over filling it slightly.

A radio technician holds a microphone over the machine.

(CONTINUED)

HEARST (CONT'D)
Radio listeners, that sound you hear is thousands, if not tens-of-thousands of dimes pouring in to help those in need. Thank you, Mister President, for helping those in need as I know you would thank me for helping you.

There is very scattered applause.

HEARST (CONT'D)
(realizing he misspoke)
Oh, I despise being the center of attention. So enough of this old, but fabulously rich old man.
(pauses again for scattered applause)
Allow me to introduce our mistress of ceremonies this evening. You may have seen her sweet face on the silent-screen. Take it away, Miss Marion Davies.

Marion Davies, dressed in an elaborate porcelain mask with great plumes of feathers, hurries behind the microphone. Her dress will be the talk of the town tomorrow in the society columns.

As she passes Hearst, she lightly pats him on his backside.

There is a mild murmuring in the audience with steely glances directed at Miss Davies.

She momentarily removes her mask.

MARION DAVIES
Thank you, the assembled guests, for your dimes. But there are others who deserve thanks, as well. First of all, I'd like to thank William Paley. The music we are about to listen to this evening will be broadcast all over the country thanks to Mr. Paley and his Columbia Broadcast System radio stations. Stand up, Mr. Paley, and take a bow.

A man dressed only a black suit and a simple black mask, adorned with just a couple of rhinestones, stands. This is WILLIAM PALEY. He waves his hand in thanks and then sits back down.

The audience applauds politely.

MARION DAVIES (CONT'D)
Let's also thank New York's Guy Lombardo and his orchestra for providing this evening's dance music.

Guy Lombardo steps forward and takes a grand bow. He is dressed in an exquisite white suit and Panama hat.

(CONTINUED)

MARION DAVIES (CONT'D)
Enough silly posturing. We're here to enjoy ourselves this evening. Let's dance!

The crowd applauds at her cue.

MARION DAVIES (CONT'D)
Guy, the night is yours.

Guy Lombardo takes is place in front of his orchestra.

A SONG BEGINS PLAYING. Led by Hearst and Davies, the crowd trickles onto the dance floor.

DISSOLVE TO:

6 INT. CBS STUDIO - NIGHT - 20:07

Orson Welles and the Mercury Players are listening to the radio broadcast over a speaker in the corner of the room.

HANS VON KALTENBORN (V.O.)
Good evening, ladies and gentlemen. Again from the ballroom in the Hotel Annapolis in Washinton DC, we bring you the music of Guy Lombardo and his orchestra. With a touch of the Spanish. Guy Lombardo leads off with "La Cumparsita."

ORSON WELLES
I can just imagine William Randolph Hearst and his drunken floozie dancing cheek-to-cheek.

FRANK READICK
There isn't much we can do about it.

ORSON WELLES
We can burn the Hotel Annapolis to the ground.

FRANK READICK
Orson!

ORSON WELLES
I can just see it.

Orson holds his hands up, thumbs together with index fingers pointing up, like he is a director taking in the scene as it slowly dissolves into the scene he is imagining.

ORSON WELLES (CONT'D)
Medium shot, wide-angle, deep focus. The ballroom at the Hotel Annapolis crumbling in flames, chaos raining down, while William Randolph Hearst and his floozy dance a waltz through the inferno.
(MORE)

(CONTINUED)

ORSON WELLES (CONT'D)
The camera tracks around the dance floor, before flying into the air, bird's-eye view capturing the circle of flames dancing around the dancing couple! Ceiling beams cascading down around Hearst and Davies, setting the orchestra ablaze, like a Cuban cigar.

The imaginary scene burns.

FRANK READICK (V.O.)
Shouldn't you be putting that kind of creative energy into something productive...

The scene snaps back to reality.

FRANK READICK
Like next week's radio program. We have the studio scheduled until eleven. We should work on Rebecca.

ORSON WELLES
(waving his arms in frustration)
Kay-rap! Rebecca's... been postponed until... God knows when.

FRANK READICK
Then what about next week's show?

Dan Seymour picks up a copy of the Heart of Darkness manuscript that still has Orson's handwritten critiques on it. He reads...

DAN SEYMOUR
Heart of Darkness.

FRANK READICK
Thank you. We should be working on Heart of Darkness.

ORSON WELLES
But we're stuck here listening to Hearst's damnable cocktail music.

HANS VON KALTENBORN (V.O.)
Ladies and gentlemen of our listening audience, we pause briefly to bring you news of a meteorite streaking through the twilight skies over the Blue Ridge Mountains earlier this morning. A strange convergence of academic minds have requested air-time on CBS to report their latest findings of a fantastical nature. Earlier this afternoon, CBS dispatched a remote unit to report on their findings. We return you until then to the music of Guy Lombardo and his orchestra.

The DANCE MUSIC resumes.

(CONTINUED)

ORSON WELLES
Well, I'll be go to. Paley himself isn't so all mighty that his own program of dance music can't be interrupted by a news bulletin. This is at least, some consolation. The Mercury Theater has never been interrupted for some silly news bulletin.

DAN SEYMOUR
Some news bulletins can be important.

ORSON WELLES
(as if he doesn't know Dan is in the room)
I beg your pardon? Who said what?

DAN SEYMOUR
Like what happened in Munich last month. NBC interrupted the Sanborne Hour with Charlie McCarthy. Information like that is important and should interrupt a radio program. Wouldn't you agree, Frank?

FRANK READICK
Dan has a point.

ORSON WELLES
Point? What is the point of this conversation?

The MUSIC is interrupted by Kaltenborn.

ORSON WELLES (CONT'D)
(sarcastically)
Wait. It's another...
(using finger quotes)
..."important" news bulletin.

Orson's "rapt" attention is turned to the speakers.

HANS VON KALTENBORN (V.O.)
We are having a few technical difficulties establishing contact with our remote unit. Technicians on the scene and at CBS studios are attempting to work through the static that is interrupting the signal from the Blue Ridge Mountains. Such a remote report shouldn't be suffering difficulties like these, but please bare with us.

Another song begins.

ORSON WELLES
Where were we? Some pointless argument, right?

FRANK READICK
Wrong. We were trying to determine whether we are going to work this evening.

(CONTINUED)

Dan raises his hand, neither Orson or Frank notice.

ORSON WELLES
I say we do Rebecca, even if I have to climb the radio tower and change the station's broadcast frequency.

FRANK READICK
The tower broadcasts on an amplified frequency. You'd be fried to a crisp.

ORSON WELLES
I'll be damned if I don't get to have my little Halloween prank over the airwaves tonight.

FRANK READICK
The prank wasn't that funny anyway, Orson.

ORSON WELLES
It was so... damn funny. Shall I describe it to you again?

DISSOLVE TO:

7 INT. HOTEL ANNAPOLIS' BALLROOM - NIGHT

HANS VON KALTENBORN is sitting at his microphone beside 46 year-old poet, playwright, and essayist ARCHIBALD MACLEISH.

HANS VON KALTENBORN
While Guy Lombardo and his band have a quick smoke, I have in the audience here at the Hotel Annapolis in Washington DC acclaimed poet Archibald MacLeish, who brings to CBS's Workshop program on Thursday quite an endeavor- a dramatic poem for the radio. When was the last dramatic poem composed? Not since Shakespeare, correct?

ARCHIBALD MACLEISH
While Shakespeare is esteemed above all other dramatic poets, there are of course others, most notably TS Eliot's Murder at the Cathedral from just a couple of years ago. While dramatic poetry on stage might have fallen from fashion, radio engages the ear; verse has no visual presence to compete with. The ear is already half poet.

HANS VON KALTENBORN
You are bringing to the half-poet ears of the CBS radio audience a verse play, Air Raid. Your use the creative technique of masquerading the narrator or chorus as a newsman on a spot news broadcast from...

(CONTINUED)

ARCHIBALD MACLEISH
From an old European border town stationed on a tenement roof waiting for the distant buzz of enemy airplane propellers. Movie newsreels have brought the fears of European wars to the local cinema and I use this fear of impending war, death, and destruction over a back-drop of incongruous and commonplace sounds of women chattering and of children playing to the radio audience.

DISSOLVE TO:

8 INT. CBS STUDIO - NIGHT - NIGHT

The members of the Mercury Theatre are standing around waiting for direction.

HANS VON KALTENBORN (V.O.)
Aren't you worried that the audience will take your verse-play as fact?

ARCHIBALD MACLEISH (V.O.)
I'm not sure what you mean.

ORSON WELLES
Wait a minute. I do!

FRANK READICK
Orson, what are you talking about?

HANS VON KALTENBORN (V.O.)
Your program uses realism to a startling decree. The spot newsman on the tenement rooftop listening to the incoming enemy aircraft and the imminent dropping of bombs on the small border town could send shock-waves of terror and hysteria through the radio-audience like shouting "fire" in crowded theater.

Orson shushes the company.

ORSON WELLES
Quiet. I'm getting an idea. I don't want to lose it.

HANS VON KALTENBORN (V.O.)
While you have a woman singing a scale, that scale is continued by a warning siren and the buzz of raiding planes.

(CONTINUED)

ARCHIBALD MACLEISH (V.O.)
There will be a couple of program announcements and a number of commercial breaks during the hour, I don't see this is even a possibility of concern.

HANS VON KALTENBORN (V.O.)
What if someone tunes into the program a few minutes late and misses the program announcement. They could easily take the program as a real event.

ORSON WELLES
Oh, they surely could. You old alte, you are an absolute genius. You just don't have the hoden to do anything like this.

KENNY DELMAR
Since when do you speak German?

ORSON WELLES
As a child, I traveled the cities of Europe with my father.

FRANK READICK
Not that nonsense again.

HANS VON KALTENBORN (V.O.)
Tonight, Orson Welles' Mercury Theatre on the air was preempted by an evening of dance music and the evening of dance music is being interrupted by my own news broadcasts and even this little interview with you.

ORSON WELLES
I could interrupt my own air? A play within a play?

HANS VON KALTENBORN (V.O.)
Your program reflects last month's Czechoslovakian crisis. CBS' own audience hung on every word spoken by myself and Edward R. Murrow concerning the Munich crisis. The fear of impending war has made all of America twitchy to say the least. Isn't there even a hint of concern on your part? Millions could go, however briefly, insane.

ORSON WELLES
I could prank millions?

ARCHIBALD MACLEISH (V.O.)
You are underestimating the intelligence of the radio audience Mr. Kaltenborn.

ORSON WELLES
Oh, Archy, you're overestimating them.

(CONTINUED)

ARCHIBALD MACLEISH (V.O.)
It is a sophisticated audience and not one to be easily duped such nonsense.

An unexpected but boisterous guffaw escapes Orson's lips.

ARCHIBALD MACLEISH (V.O.)
My show has been advertised in all of the major metropolitan newspapers and newsmagazines as a fictitious radio program. Not a single individual, let alone the ridiculous possibility of millions radio listeners could possibly go insane simultaneously by listening to a radio show.

ORSON WELLES
Oh, they could. They would. They will. They must.

HANS VON KALTENBORN (V.O.)
Let's hope that on Friday morning, the headlines of every newspaper aren't screaming for your head, Mr. MacLeish, all because you scared the daylights out of your audience.

ARCHIBALD MACLEISH (V.O.)
(chuckling)
Let's hope.

ORSON WELLES
The name "Orson Welles" would be wagging on the tongues of the entire nation!

FRANK READICK
Or they would be screaming for your head on a pike.

ORSON WELLES
(shrugging)
Either or.

HANS VON KALTENBORN (V.O.)
Now a tune that never loses favor. Guy Lombardo and his orchestra...

"STAR DUST" begins playing.

ORSON WELLES
Let me paint a scene for you all. We're been taking classic literature and printing it, not in cold sterile books, but the living, breathing airwaves. We could easily take a classic like Conan Doyle's The Lost World. Using the technique of reel-to-reel audio tapes recorded while on expedition in a long lost land.
(MORE)

(CONTINUED)

ORSON WELLES (CONT'D)
When Edgar Burgen ends his first comedy sketch with that insipid puppet, a number of listeners will automatically turn their dials looking for something, anything more interesting than a musical number. At this point, the lost explorers would be under attack by colossal dinosaurs and barbaric cave-men!

FRANK READICK
Orson, as nice as all this is, shouldn't we be working.

ORSON WELLES
I am working... We end the first act with the reel-to reel capturing the hushed voices of the explorers recording their final Earthly words as the pack of blood-thirsty lizards near. Their voices hushed, the breath hurried. The reel-to-reel records the horror of their blood-curdling screams.

FRANK READICK
Like that will get past Standards and Practices.

ORSON WELLES
Then silence, as the sound of the reel-to-reel continues to run. Cut to commercial When we return from the break, we're broadcasting from Radio City Music Hall where high-society has turned out to see a spectacle of a living, breathing dinosaur. The explorers have captured and transported a monstrous lizard back from the Lost World.

FRANK READICK
Or perhaps a giant ape.

ORSON WELLES
(cutting Frank off)
Never let plagiarism stand in the way of a good story.
(back to his brainstorming)
The beast escapes and thunders around Manhattan causing wanton destruction. Thousands of New Yorkers are screaming through the streets.

FRANK READICK
Eventually climbing the Empire State Building and grabbing Fay Wray with its tiny little arms.

Orson shushes him.

(CONTINUED)

ORSON WELLES
Listeners from around the country will believe, truly believe this is actually happening. We need to pencil this into the schedule.

Dan is still standing there holding up his hand. But by now his arm is growing tired and he is using his other hand to hold his elbow up.

DAN SEYMOUR
Orson...? Frank...?

ORSON WELLES
What?

FRANK READICK
What?

DAN SEYMOUR
What about the theater? Danton's Death is still in rehearsals and we have previews coming up any day now.

FRANK READICK
(looking around at the radio ensemble gathered around)
We do have the studio until at least eleven. We can go over the lines here as well as anywhere. No use adding taxi fees to our already strained budget.
(sees Orson is ignoring him)
Orson?

ORSON WELLES
What?

FRANK READICK
Danton's Death?

ORSON WELLES
Oh, what the heck. Might as well rehearse that. We do have most of the cast here anyway. Dan? That is your name isn't it? Dan?

DAN SEYMOUR
You know my name, Orson. We've working together for years.

ORSON WELLES
Turn those speakers off or we won't get any work done around here. What with all these stupid interruptions.

Orson waves his arm in the direction of the speaker as Dan clicks off the sound.

DISSOLVE TO:

9 INT. HOTEL ANNAPOLIS' BALLROOM - NIGHT

Hearst takes a seat at a table nearest the doors of the Hotel Annapolis' Ballroom.

HEARST
Marian, please. I'm a rich old man. I can't dance every number.

MARION DAVIES
But, Pops. We dance all the time.

HEARST
I am well aware of that. Dance with someone else. That young man over there is just sitting by himself. Be the fine hostess you are and dance with him.

MARION DAVIES
You won't be jealous?

HEARST
Please, Marion, don't be foolish. Go and dance.

A young man, Hearst's PERSONAL ASSISTANT, hurries into the room and whispers in Hearst's ear. Hearst immediately stands and walks over to Paley, with a purpose.

HEARST (CONT'D)
Paley, you stupid son-.
(catches himself)
Why is that Kaltenborn fellow interrupting my evening of dance music with news reports.

WILLIAM PALEY
I'm sure if Mr. Kaltenborn sees fit to interrupt the dance music, he is receiving newsworthy reports.

HEARST
Newsworthy? Nothing on radio is newsworthy. Radio is nothing but old vaudevillians and talentless hacks. That is not news. I know news. I make news. This is nothing but claptrap. Put me back on the air.

WILLIAM PALEY
I'll do with my station what I please, Randolph.

HEARST
I'm paying good money for this band, this hall, your dinner. The least you can do is keep me on the air.

WILLIAM PALEY
You expect air time, even though you continually run down radio. You and your rags are a relic.
(motioning to Davies)
(MORE)

(CONTINUED)

WILLIAM PALEY (CONT'D)
Your "guest" is causing quite a stir dancing with that handsome young man.

Hearst abandons the argument and hurries towards Miss Davies.

HANS VON KALTENBORN
We are receiving numerous reports out of the Blue Ridge Mountains regarding the meteorite impact of a several hours ago. Concerned citizens have reported in the last hour several military convoys speeding through the winding mountain roads to the remote impact sight and [redacted] We have heard no word from our remote unit nor the scientists who were to report on the meteorite impact. Stay tuned to CBS radio. We return you to Guy Lombardo's evening of dance music.

General GEORGE PATTON is dancing with his wife. He is dressed in his dress uniform, she in a masquerade gown.

A YOUNG OFFICER hurries over to them and whispers in the general's ear, who abruptly stops dancing.

PATTON
My dear. I have to leave.

PATTON'S WIFE
Hurry back-

PATTON
- I'm not sure if I'll return tonight. Dance your little heart out, then retire to our room. I'll call.

PATTON'S WIFE
If you can, dear.

Patton proceeds over to the president and whispers in his ear.

Hearst sees this.

HEARST
The hackles on the back of my neck are standing up. Something is going down.

PERSONAL ASSISTANT
How can you be so certain, boss?

HEARST
I can smell a story like it's a drop of blood in shark invested waters. Go eavesdrop on their little conversation.

PERSONAL ASSISTANT
I'm not dropping any eaves on the President.

(CONTINUED)

HEARST
No one is above the scrutiny of a newsman.

The Personal Assistant slips away.

ROOSEVELT
Are you certain?

PATTON
As improbable as it may seem, that is what the evidence suggests.

ROOSEVELT
It is impossible to believe.

PATTON
Mr. President, we are not far from the White House. We can return there expediently.

ROOSEVELT
Isn't the Vice-President there? Too many high-level officials to have us all at the White House.

PATTON
We have to go now.

ROOSEVELT
No. Wait until the end of this song. People will be distracted with their applause. We don't want to make a scene.

The song Guy Lombardo's band is playing COMES TO AN END. The dancers turn and applaud to the stage.

Patton pushes a wheelchair up to the table.

Roosevelt begins to stand, slowly and awkwardly because of his polio.

GUY LOMBARDO
Thank you. To this point in the evening we have played with a touch of the Spanish. But we will, if we may, add the spirit of America, yes?

There is loud applause from the crowd.

PERSONAL ASSISTANT
I'm sorry, boss, but the music was too loud.

(CONTINUED)

HEARST
We need to keep an ear to the ground now. Something is going on. I know it.

DISSOLVE TO:

10 INT. OFFICE IN THE WHITE HOUSE - NIGHT

The VICE-PRESIDENT, John Nance Garner, sits at a poker table with four others playing a game of cards.

The SECRETARY OF STATE, Cordell Hull, enters the office.

SECRETARY OF STATE
Jack, the President wants to see you in the Oval Office, now. Something big's going down.

VICE-PRESIDENT
The president isn't here.

SECRETARY OF STATE
He's on his way here now.

VICE-PRESIDENT
So what? Tell Franklin that the vice-presidency is an eight to five job. The rest of the day is mine.

SECRETARY OF STATE
I'm afraid I must insist, Jack. I have my orders.

VICE-PRESIDENT
Damn it.
(throws down his cards)
I'll be back, eventually.

DISSOLVE TO:

11 INT. HOTEL ANNAPOLIS' BALLROOM - NIGHT

Hans Von Kaltenborn is handed a message by Paley's assistant.

HANS VON KALTENBORN
This is probably the strangest news report I have ever had reported on.
(smells something fishy)
As impossible as it sounds, the military convoy described by several callers from the Blue Ridge Mountains have engaged... I can't believe I am about to utter these words... Martian invasion. We have Arthur Buddington, Professor of Geology at Princeton University on the phone from a farm house near, I'm not sure where.

(CONTINUED)

Hans Von Kaltenborn forces himself to "interview" the guest, but struggles more and more as the "interview" continues. He is convinced that Orson Welles is pranking him.

ARTHUR BUDDINGTON (V.O.)
(played by Orson Welles myself)
Grove Hill, Virginia. Mr. and Mrs. Paige have rescued me from the apparent alien onslaught.

HANS VON KALTENBORN
What can you tell us, Professor? Start at the beginning.

ARTHUR BUDDINGTON (V.O.)
Four months ago, Princeton astronomers detected a meteorite of significant size... significant for a meteorite... It was on a collision course with Earth. This meteorite's course had been charted as nearly impacting the planet Mars four months previous. Or perhaps originating on the planet itself, as strange as that may sound. Astronomers from around the world have been alert for this particular Earth threatening meteorite. They were concerned it could hit a metropolitan area and cause significant death and destruction. But fortunately, it impacted in the rural mountains of the Blue Ridge early this morning.

HANS VON KALTENBORN
And that is where you had set up your scientific investigation?

ARTHUR BUDDINGTON (V.O.)
As a geologist, I'm not only interested in earthly geology, but the interstellar variety as well.

HANS VON KALTENBORN
When did the military arrive?

ARTHUR BUDDINGTON (V.O.)
About an hour or two ago. It was the strangest experience of my academic career. The army soldiers, while armed to the teeth, seemed more interested in setting up sound equipment. Enrico Caruso, the opera singer, was brought out of a black Chevrolet. He was hand-cuffed and ordered to stand before a microphone. He began to sing the strangest aria human ears have ever heard.

HANS VON KALTENBORN
Can you describe the aria?

(CONTINUED)

ARTHUR BUDDINGTON
It was sung in a strange Latinized gibberish. Then the most remarkable thing happened.

HANS VON KALTENBORN
What was that, Professor?

ARTHUR BUDDINGTON (V.O.)
and the meteorite broke in half, not unlike Russian nesting dolls and inside was the most gleaming metal I have ever beheld. Three tri-pod-like legs extended, raising into a ghastly machine and from the machine, a second, strikingly feminine aria responded to Enrico Caruso. They duetted for nearly half-an-hour, when then the tri-pod walking machine and the military left.

HANS VON KALTENBORN
Together?

ARTHUR BUDDINGTON (V.O.)
Yes. Walking in the direction of Washington DC.

HANS VON KALTENBORN
(trying to trip up Orson)
Why do you believe this in an invasion force, as you say? Could this be a peace delegation? If the military were prepared to communicate, then, perhaps, there may have been previous communications between the Martians and the military. And if

ARTHUR BUDDINGTON (V.O.)
You didn't hear the Martian aria. I did. It had a hint of ill intent in it. It shook me to my core. The sound, that sound made by that tri-pod machine destroyed every piece of electrical equipment at the impact site and disrupted electricity for what seemed like miles and miles.
(MORE)

(CONTINUED)

ARTHUR BUDDINGTON (V.O.)

If the Martians are peaceful, it'll only be momentary.

Another YOUNG MAN runs into the room and whispers in William Paley's ear.

Stunned by what he hears, Paley runs to the stage and pulls the microphone down from Guy Lombardo. Paley is visibly shaken.

WILLIAM PALEY

Ladies and gentlemen, I'm sorry to interrupt your evening of dancing.

The dancing and MUSIC comes to an ABRUPT END.

WILLIAM PALEY (CONT'D)

In the last few moments, CBS radio has been broadcasting terrible news. I recommend that everyone take their seats for the time being.

The dancers slowly leave the dance floor and take their seats. Hans Von Kaltenborn sits uncomfortably in silence. William Randolph Hearst takes Paley aside, cupping his hand over the microphone.

HEARST

What in the Sam Hill is going on, Paley?

WILLIAM PALEY

There are reports... reports from Virginia, that we are being invaded!

HEARST

Nonsense. Hitler doesn't have the courage or the manpower to invade the United States.

WILLIAM PALEY

It isn't the Nazis, Randolph, it's Martians.

HEARST

Don't be a fool, Paley. Martians...

(scoffs)

That's ridiculous. Someone's playing a prank on your station, Paley. Where's a telephone? I need to call my papers.

(CONTINUED)

WILLIAM PALEY
(to the crowd)
Ladies and gentlemen, in such a time of national crisis, I'm sure that the president...
(looking for Roosevelt)
The president would recommend remaining where you are. You can all listen to the news as it unfolds from the safety of the Hotel Annapolis.

Kaltenborn walks over to Paley, stilling wearing his headphones. The cord is unplugged and dangling by his side.

HANS VON KALTENBORN
Sir, we need to speak.

WILLIAM PALEY
Get Davidson on the line. I need to speak with him.

HANS VON KALTENBORN
But, sir. There is something I need to tell you.

WILLIAM PALEY
Just get Davidson on the line.

HANS VON KALTENBORN
But, SIR! That no-good-so-and-so Orson Wells is up to his tricks again. I just got finished doing an interview with that...
(swalllows, censoring himself)
LIVE! On the air! I'm sorry, sir, I'm just so furious.

WILLIAM PALEY
Are you sure it was Orson, Hans?

HANS VON KALTENBORN
How can you sure be with him, sir? He's a radio actor for pity's sake. If it's not him, it could easily be another of his voice-actors. If the President himself wasn't in the same room with us, we could easily mistake someone like Kenneth Delmar for Franklin Delano Roosevelt himself. Not only could we be deceived but our audience could be as well. They're that good and certainly that devious.

WILLIAM PALEY
I'll be go to hell. It was a prank just like Randolph said. Now would be a good time to get Davidson on the line.

HANS VON KALTENBORN
Yes, Mr. Paley.

(CONTINUED)

WILLIAM PALEY
Play along with Orson for now, Hans. If he's willing to weasel his way onto the airwaves for a practical joke, we will allow him to hoist himself by his own petard.

HANS VON KALTENBORN
With pleasure, Mr. Paley.

DISSOLVE TO:

12 INT. CBS TELEPHONE CIRCUIT BOARD - NIGHT

Several blonde ladies are operating the telephone board, but the circuits are being overwhelmed with calls.

Davidson Taylor sticks his head in the doorway.

CBS TELEPHONE OPERATOR 1
It's a mad house. We're being overwhelmed with calls, Davidson. What do we tell them?

DAVIDSON TAYLOR
We don't have that information.

CBS TELEPHONE OPERATOR 2
And?

DAVIDSON TAYLOR
Please stay tuned to CBS for any further developments.

CBS TELEPHONE OPEARTOR 3
That's all?

DAVIDSON TAYLOR
That's all.

CBS TELEPHONE OPERATOR 1
Welcome to CBS. I'm sorry, sir, I don't have that information. Please stay tuned to CBS for any further developments.

CBS TELEPHONE OPERATOR 2
Welcome to CBS. I understand you have relatives in Virginia, but I don't have that information. Please stay tuned to CBS for any further developments.

CBS TELEPHONE OPERATOR 3
Welcome to CBS. I don't have that information, I'm sorry, sir. We have received no confirmation from the government. Please stay tuned to CBS for any further developments.

(CONTINUED)

CBS TELEPHONE OPERATOR 1
Sir, we have call from Paley coming through.

DAVIDSON TAYLOR
I'll take it in my office, Doris.

DISSOLVE TO:

13 INT. MUTUAL TELEPHONE CIRCUIT BOARD - NIGHT

Almost the same scene as previous, but with several brunette ladies operating the circuit board. They too are overwhelmed with calls.

DISSOLVE TO:

14 INT. HOTEL ANNAPOLIS' BALLROOM - NIGHT

The audience and orchestra are quiet and listen intently to Kaltenborn, who is fighting to maintain his composure.

HANS VON KALTENBORN
Ladies and gentlemen of the listening audience. The reports of Martian machines on American soil have been confirmed by an eyewitness. You have heard the reports of a professor at a leading educational institution live on our air this evening. We are now getting word from Europe of several meteorite impacts in our allies England and France, as well as Axis powers of Italy and Germany. "Edward R. Murrow" reports from London.

William Paley approaches Kaltenborn. Kaltenborn cups his hands over the microphone.

WILLIAM PALEY
Is this really Murrow?

HANS VON KALTENBORN
He claims to be. This could be Orson or it could be any number of his actors.

WILLIAM PALEY
Go on the air. Davidson and I will figure a way to spin this entire Orson debacle in our favor.

HANS VON KALTENBORN
Yes, Mr. Paley.
(to Edward R. Murrow)
"Edward", can you give us a summary of the events happening over the pond.

(CONTINUED)

EDWARD R. MURROW (V.O.)
The comforting light of dawn is still hours away, but there are radio reports of military action within Germany between Martian machines and Nazi military forces.

The death toll is unknown but the German forces appear to have been routed easily. The Martian machines are proceeding towards Berlin at an outstanding pace considering the nature of their tri-pod walking machines.

HANS VON KALTENBORN

EDWARD R. MURROW

Why have the machines engaged the German military so quickly is unknown at present. The machines on British and French soil appear to have taken no action... at the moment that is.

Hans Von Kaltenborn cups his hands over the microphone.

HANS VON KALTENBORN
(quietly to Paley)
What should I do, Mr. Paley? This is getting quite ridiculous. Orson Welles is going to outrageous lengths for this prank, including but not limited to impersonating one of our most distinguished news-men.

WILLIAM PALEY
Attempt to trip Orson up if you can.

HANS VON KALTENBORN
My pleasure.
(into the microphone)
I may be able to shed some light on this matter, "Edward".
(MORE)

(CONTINUED)

HANS VON KALTENBORN (CONT'D)

Earlier this summer, I interviewed a German defector concerning a meteorite crash in the Austrian Alps. He claimed that German forces were greeted harmoniously by a Martian peace delegation, but the Nazis attacked and incapacitated the Martians and their machines contained within the meteorite. Nazi scientists then experimented mercilessly on the Martian survivors.

It seems the Martians are aware of our territorial boundaries and do not blame England, France nor America for the actions of Germany. This is something we can be grateful for.

EDWARD R. MURROW

I will continue coverage of the Martians on the European front. Hopefully, they don't turn against us or our allies.

HANS VON KALTENBORN

(with his hand over the microphone)

Oh, my goodness, Orson is going to be burned in effigy over this horse hockey.

DISSOLVE TO:

15 INT. CLEVELAND CBS AFFILIATE - NIGHT

This evening, JACK PAAR is the hourly update announcer for WGAR, a CBS affiliate in Cleveland. Being besieged by frantic callers, Jack attempts to calm their fears.

JACK PAAR

The world is not coming to an end. Trust me. When have I ever lied to you?

CALLER INTO WGAR

You are lying to us. This is a conspiracy from the highest levels of the government to cover-up the truth of an invasion from Mars.

JACK PAAR

It's merely a science-fiction story.

(CONTINUED)

He hangs up the phone, then quickly dials his manager.

JACK PAAR (CONT'D)
The calls keep pouring in, many of the panicky callers are charging that I am covering up the truth.

MANAGER AT WGAR
Calm down, Jack. You're always so emotional. Just take it easy. It's all a a tempest in a teapot.

DISSOLVE TO:

16 INT. STUDY OF FRED WEBER - NIGHT

FRED WEBER is the general manager of the New York Mutual Radio Station. He is dressed in a smoking jacket, pajama pants, and slippers. He is on the phone with GABRIEL HEATTER, the Mutual Network counterpart of Von Kaltenborn.

FRED WEBER
I didn't quite understand that, Gabriel. Please repeat it, slower.

GABRIEL HEATTER (V.O.)
For over an hour, CBS studios has been broadcasting reports beginning with a meteorite crash in the Blue Ridge Mountains. We didn't want to expend the resources by sending a remote-unit out in the darkness, when the meteorite would still be there in the morning. Then within the last twenty minutes things changed.

FRED WEBER
How exactly?

GABRIEL HEATTER (V.O.)
CBS began reporting of an invasion from Mars, as unbelievable as that may sound. The military made contact with Martian tri-pod walking machines. We have reached out to the White House itself, but haven't heard anything back from them. Our listeners are requesting confirmation of the invasion.

FRED WEBER
I'll call Davidson Taylor at CBS.

GABRIEL HEATTER (V.O.)
Sir?

FRED WEBER
I'm going to go straight to the horse's mouth. If there is an invasion from Mars, Davidson will give it to me straight.

(CONTINUED)

GABRIEL HEATTER (V.O.)
And if there is an invasion?

FRED WEBER
Then there's no good news tonight.

GABRIEL HEATTER (V.O.)
Understood.

FRED WEBER
Can you have Ethel patch me through to Davidson.

GABRIEL HEATTER (V.O.)
Yes, Mr. Weber, sir.

GLADIS (V.O.)
(after a moment)
Connecting you, Mr. Weber.

FRED WEBER
Davidson, it's Fred Weber over at Mutual. Between newsmen, I need to know what is going on over at CBS. You are reporting an invasion from little green men from Mars. Can you confirm this?

DAVIDSON TAYLOR (V.O.)
Mr. Weber, I can assure you there is no invasion from Mars being broadcast from CBS this evening.

FRED WEBER
Then what in the blazes is going on over at your station, Davidson?

DAVIDSON TAYLOR (V.O.)
As embarrassing as it is to admit, Fred, it appears that Orson Welles is responsible for the reports of a Martian invasion. It's all been a...
(stuttering)
Prank.

FRED WEBER
You should never have signed that charlatan to a contract, Davidson. I had that sham-artist on my payroll as the Shadow and he was nothing but pain in my backside. Always with his practical jokes. Always with his grandiose story ideas.

DAVIDSON TAYLOR (V.O.)
After the acclaim of his voodoo MacBeth, Paley thought he'd give him a shot at adapting literature for the radio.

(CONTINUED)

FRED WEBER
I'm surprised it took so long after Munich for Orson Welles get the idea to stir up the public's predilection to panic. Never thought he turn to something as ridiculous as War of the Worlds as a source though.

DAVIDSON TAYLOR (V.O.)
War of the...?

FRED WEBER
Where else would he get an invasion of Mars from?

DAVIDSON TAYLOR (V.O.)
That makes perfect sense.

FRED WEBER
You have my condolences, Davidson. Tell Bill that we will have to roast CBS over the coals for this. It is our duty to report the real news of this invasion nonsense. We would not be serving the public interest by allowing a panic to ensue.

DAVIDSON TAYLOR (V.O.)
Understood.

DISSOLVE TO:

17 INT. OVAL OFFICE - NIGHT

The president sits behind the desk, his wheel-chair is nowhere to be seen.

ROOSEVELT
It won't turn against us, George. I have been preparing for this moment my entire political career.

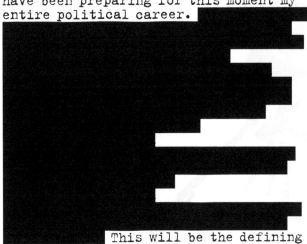

This will be the defining moment of my presidency.

PATTON
You handle the politics, Mr. President. I'll handle the military.

(CONTINUED)

The Vice-President extinguishes his cigar in the water of a vase of flowers.

VICE-PRESIDENT
Did I hear what I think I just heard?
(looking at his watch)
There's no going back to my game tonight- damn it. Is this a peace delegation?

ROOSEVELT
Not that I'm at liberty to discuss that just yet, Nance.

VICE-PRESIDENT
I'm the Vice-President! I have a right to know what in the Sam-hill is going on here. Is this an invasion or not?

PATTON
As far as the military is concerned, it is an invasion.

ROOSEVELT
But not necessarily as the highest-levels of government is concerned. There are other options to be considered.

The military are simply escorting the Martian machine safely to the Naval Station Norfolk.

VICE-PRESIDENT
Under threat of military force?

ROOSEVELT

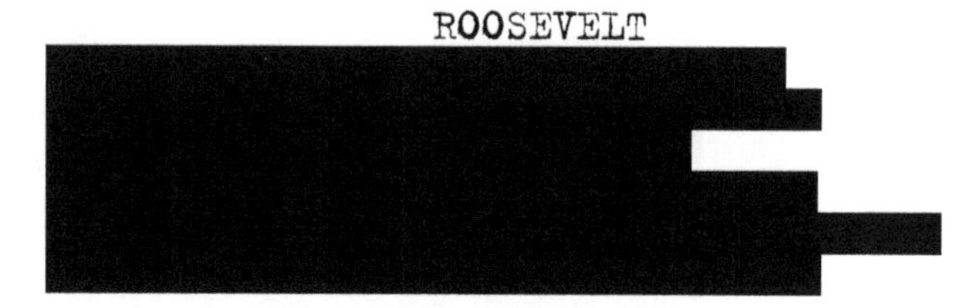

PATTON
The Martians don't dare attack us.

SECRETARY OF STATE

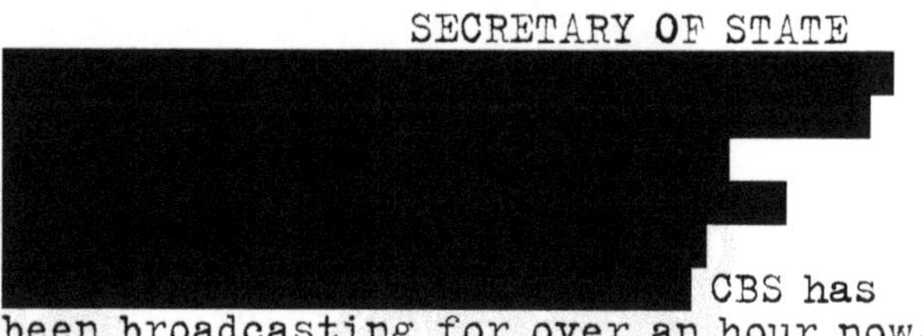

CBS has been broadcasting for over an hour now. What do we do?

(CONTINUED)

ROOSEVELT
Has this reached any of the other radio stations?

SECRETARY OF STATE
Both NBC and Mutual want confirmation of the Martian threat. Mutual is already reporting CBS' broadcast is fictional in nature. We're getting calls from papers from all over the country.

PATTON
And you can just imagine whose newspapers are the most vocal?

ROOSEVELT
Hearst's.

PATTON
(tapping his nose)
... Mr. President.

ROOSEVELT
Understood, General.

VICE-PRESIDENT
What are we going to tell them?

and that the United States is under attack by little green men from Mars?

ROOSEVELT
Hardly. General, give them any old story. I don't care what it is. The press and history must wait for the first light of morning-

and the dawn of a new age for mankind.

DISSOLVE TO:

18 INT. OFFICE ADJACENT TO THE HOTEL ANNAPOLIS' BALLROOM - NIGHT

William Randolph Hearst is on the telephone.

HEARST
That's right, William Randolph Hearst... No, I'm not kidding. Put me through to the Washington desk... Yes, I'll wait... Walter, It's Randolph... Yes, I've heard the reports. A Martian invasion? What's the official word from the White House?... What? Have you confirmed this?... You have?... It's a hoax...
(smiling)
(MORE)

(CONTINUED)

HEARST (CONT'D)
A Halloween prank. Yes, I understand...
Do I want to hold tomorrow's headline?
Over an asinine joke? Not on your life.
This'll all be forgotten by morning...

DISSOLVE TO:

19 INT. HALLWAY OUTSIDE STUDIO - NIGHT

Davidson is standing outside Orson Welles' studio. There is a phone hanging on the wall near the doors. Davidson is on the line.

DAVIDSON TAYLOR
Patch Mr. Paley through, Doris.

DORIS (V.O.)
Yes, Mr. Taylor. Here he is.

WILLIAM PALEY (V.O.)
What in the blue blazes is going on back there, Davidson?

DAVIDSON TAYLOR
To be perfectly honest, Mr. Paley. I don't think Orson has had anything to do with the broadcasts this evening.

WILLIAM PALEY (V.O.)
Are you honestly telling me this is all real? Are you saying that Martians are invading America as we speak?

DAVIDSON TAYLOR
Of course not, sir. But Orson doesn't seem to have left his studio all night. There does not seem to be anything untoward going on in there, sir.
(looking through the door's window)
He's still in there. He's using our studio to rehearse his blasted stage-play.

WILLIAM PALEY (V.O.)
The girls haven't patched any calls through to Hans from Orson's studio?

DAVIDSON TAYLOR
Doris insists the call from the professor was patched through from Virginia, sir.

WILLIAM PALEY (V.O.)
And from "Edward R. Murrow"?

DAVIDSON TAYLOR
Actually Edward R. Murrow. From our studio in London.

(CONTINUED)

WILLIAM PALEY (V.O.)
Is it possible that Orson patched calls from his studio through Virginia and back to our studio?

DAVIDSON TAYLOR
He would need one of Doris's girls to make the connection to Virginia, Mr. Paley. I don't see Orson going to such lengths for a prank, Mr. Paley.

WILLIAM PALEY (V.O.)
But it is possible? He has a strange effect on women, Davidson, you've seen it. You need to tell me, is it at all possible?

DAVIDSON TAYLOR
Yes, Mr. Paley, it certainly is within the realm of possibly.

WILLIAM PALEY (V.O.)
Then have Doris grill her girls until she gets a confession. We need to know exactly what we are broadcasting. I'm not going to give Orson the satisfaction of our saying officially this a Martian invasion and then it turns out to be an Orson Welles' prank.

DAVIDSON TAYLOR
And if it is a real invasion?

WILLIAM PALEY (V.O.)
Then Fred Weber and his ilk who are already spinning this against us will look like fools. What is on our air had better be an honest-to-goodness Martian invasion, or we'll be ruined.

DAVIDSON TAYLOR
Yes, Mr. Paley, sir.

DISSOLVE TO:

20 INT. HOTEL ANNAPOLIS' BALLROOM - NIGHT

The crowd of dancers is listening to the radio report. They are all glued to the edge of the seats. They murmur to themselves, unable to believe what they are listening to.

William Randolph Hearst has been leaning up against a door jamb listening to the broadcast. Paley enters, seeing Hearst, and abruptly stops.

HEARST
Just got word from Washington. Straight from the president's mouth. It's a hoax, Paley. Your station's been duped.
(MORE)

(CONTINUED)

HEARST (CONT'D)
To think of all the naysayers who thought radio would be the death of the newspaper. After this, my distribution's going to go through the ceiling. Nobody will ever trust radio again.

Hearst steps up to the microphone. Marion comes to Hearst. She is genuinely scared.

HEARST (CONT'D)
Ladies and gentleman. You have been witness to an incredible hoax. What you have been listening to is a prank. A fiction created by some sick and juvenile minds, perhaps affiliated with CBS, perhaps William Paley himself... Perhaps not. That is not for me to say. But be assured that radio is in its infancy and cannot be relied on for accurate news. You'll always be able to respect me and my papers for bringing you reliable news. While CBS is broadcasting this nonsense, we'll continue to enjoy our evening of dance music. Mr. Lombardo, if you will, please.

Guy Lombardo hesitates for a moment, then steps to his position and the orchestra begins a NEW SONG. The guests slowly trickle back onto the dance floor.

In the back of the room, standing quietly as if they are trying to blend into the background, are Orson Welles and Nikola Tesla.

ORSON WELLES
That vein on Hearst's forehead is going to have a aneurysm. So explain to me why we didn't arrive exactly at the right moment to speak to the president?

NIKOLA TESLA
Time-travel is not an exact science, Mr. Wells.

ORSON WELLES
We arrived in the future at exactly 3:47. We were on time for the other Orson.

NIKOLA TESLA
That was from the future Orson's point-of-view. From our point-of-view, it's impossible to tell exactly when one will arrive.

ORSON WELLES
So at this moment, we're early.

NIKOLA TESLA
Not all trains run on time.

(CONTINUED)

ORSON WELLES
But even fewer Wednesday trains leave Boston and arrive in New York on Monday.

NIKOLA TESLA
Accepted. Now, to get into the White House, you'll need your press pass.

ORSON WELLES
It's not real.

NIKOLA TESLA
You work at CBS and you don't have a press pass?

ORSON WELLES
I'm a thespian. My press pass is a prop.

NIKOLA TESLA
Is it a decent prop?

ORSON WELLES
It's an excellent prop. It'll get me in. That is if the press can get in. There's an invasion from Mars going on. Security at the White House will be tighter than a Marion's "Rosebud".

Orson snickers.

NIKOLA TESLA
The President is going to need to do some damage-control. The press will be quite welcome.

ORSON WELLES
If someone could know that ahead of time, it's you.

NIKOLA TESLA
I know.

ORSON WELLES
Where will you be?

NIKOLA TESLA
Precisely when I need to be.

They exit unseen.

William Paley has been speaking with Hans Van Kaltenborn.

HANS VON KALTENBORN
You have got to be kidding me, Bill. Davidson wants patch me into H.G. Wells himself. What in the Sam Hill is going on?

WILLIAM PALEY
Davidson is not... entirely... convinced Orson has had anything to do with tonight's events.

(CONTINUED)

HANS VON KALTENBORN
That is impossible to believe. This has all the ear-marks of an Orson Wells prank on me!
(catches himself)
I'm sorry- I mean, us, CBS, you!

Standing nearby, easily within ear-shot, Hearst is enjoying every moment of Paley's discomfort.

MARION DAVIES
I'm frightened, pops. I think we should leave now.

HEARST
What? And miss an evening of live radio entertainment? Never.

HANS VON KALTENBORN
(struggling to maintain composure)
We have on the telephone from England the only expert on Martian invasions, Sir H.G. Wells. I'm sorry to have woken you at this hour.

H.G. WELLS (V.O.)
Quite all right.

HANS VON KALTENBORN
Sir Herbert, have you heard the reports from the Grove Hill? Is this an invasion or a peace delegation?

H.G. WELLS (V.O.)
While I wish I could calm the fears of your listening audience, I have my doubts this is a actually a peace delegation.

HANS VON KALTENBORN
Why? Just because your novel The War of the Worlds detailed a hostile Martian invasion doesn't necessarily mean these Martians are malevolent.

H.G. WELLS (V.O.)
I have my reasons regarding my own novel in particular. But without going into unnecessary details, I will quote the opening paragraph as my response.

HANS VON KALTENBORN
Which is?

H.G. WELLS (V.O.)
"We know now that in the early years of the twentieth century this world was being watched closely by intelligences greater than man's, and yet as mortal as his own.
(MORE)

(CONTINUED)

H.G. WELLS (V.O.) (CONT'D)

We know now that as human beings busied themselves about their various concerns they were scrutinized and studied, perhaps almost as narrowly as a man with a microscope might scrutinize the transient creatures that swarm and multiply in a drop of water. With infinite complacence people went to and fro over the earth about their little affairs, serene in the assurance of their dominion over this small, spinning fragment of solar driftwood which, by chance or design, man has inherited out of the dark mystery of Time and Space. Yet across an immense ethereal gulf, minds that are to our minds as ours are to the beasts in the jungle,

Hearst approaches Paley and motions for him to follow.

H.G. WELLS (V.O.)

Intellects vast, cool and unsympathetic, regarded this earth with envious eyes and slowly and surely drew their plans against us."

HANS VON KALTENBORN

Thank you, Mr. Wells, for your insight. Let's hope for the sake of humanity, you are wrong.

H.G. WELLS (V.O.)

Indeed.

Hearst and Paley stand off to the side of the room near the adjacent office.

HEARST

Paley, I hope you continue to allow the German to yammer on like a fool. You are burying the credibility of your medium.

WILLIAM PALEY

Hans Von Kaltenborn has been doing a remarkable job covering this crisis. I'm giving anybody who has pertinent information the air.

HEARST

When MY papers reveal the true nature of this evening's debacle, you will be called before Congress to explainyourself. You will have your licences revoked. Nobody will ever trust radio again. Newspapers will be proven the only trusted source of news.

WILLIAM PALEY

Radio will be there for the people when the people need it.

(MORE)

(CONTINUED)

WILLIAM PALEY (CONT'D)
Not the next morning or God forbid the next evening. You're an antique, Hearst. An antique!

Hearst punches Paley square in the jaw.

HEARST
Don't you dare call me an antique.

WILLIAM PALEY
(holding a handkerchief to his bleeding lip)
One of these days, Hearst, you're going to anger the wrong person. Then you'll get yours.

HANS VON KALTENBORN
Before we return to the air with another report from Edward R. Murrow in Europe, CBS studios has requested that I give the airwaves to...
(talking to an imaginary Orson Welles)
You've got to be joking, Orson. I cannot comprehend the lengths you will go to for a prank. You have every plot and subplot carefully concocted. Is there no end to your insanity?
(composing himself)
I've been requested to give the airwaves to the Governor of Virginia to elaborate on the events occurring in the Blue Ridge Mountains.

GOVERNOR JAMES H. PRICE (V.O.)

(CONTINUED)

HANS VON KALTENBORN
(maintaining the charade)
And now to back to "Edward" R. Murrow on the European front.

EDWARD R. MURROW (V.O.)
British miliary aircraft have been following the Martian machines on their approach to Berlin. Neville Chamberline has extended an olive breach of peace to Adolph Hilter.

HANS VON KALTENBORN
In what form, Edward?

EDWARD R. MURROW (V.O.)

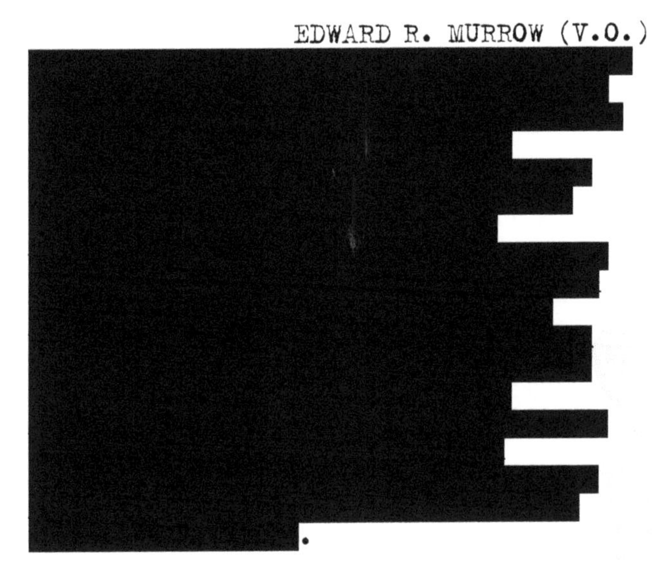

.

HANS VON KALTENBORN
The British Prime Minister must consider the Martians are not here peacefully then.

EDWARD R. MURROW (V.O.)
The Prime Minister apparently has his suspicions concerning the Martians and their intent here on Earth. British aircraft report that there is a black smoke billowing from the Martian machines that they describe as thicker than London fog. While the death toll cannot be ascertained, it has to be in the hundreds, if not thousands.

(MORE)

(CONTINUED)

EDWARD R. MURROW (V.O.)

Chamberline believes it is only a matter of time before the Martians attack Britain and her allies.

HANS VON KALTENBORN
(continuing to talk to an imaginary Orson)
Orson, Orson, Orson, when is the prank coming to an end? Haven't you enjoyed embarrassing me enough for one evening. When you are pulled before reporters to answer for your crimes this evening, only then I enjoy my Schadenfreude.

DISSOLVE TO:

21 INT. HALLWAY IN CBS BUILDING - NIGHT

Orson Welles and Kenny Delmar sneak around a corner. Orson has a wax recording disc tucked under his arm. Kenny Delmar tarrying behind, carrying a portable record-player and a microphone.

He motions for Kenny to comes along.

ORSON WELLES
Come on, Kenny, hurry. We only have twenty minutes while everyone else is smoking on their coffee break.

KENNY DELMAR
I'm not sure we should do this.

ORSON WELLES
Don't you want to be on the winning side of a practical joke just once in your life?

KENNY DELMAR
But we could get into trouble, Orson.

ORSON WELLES
What are they doing to do? Cancel my show? Besides, no one will ever know, thanks to the wax recording we did. It sounds nothing like us.

KENNY DELMAR
Orson. This isn't funny.

ORSON WELLES
It's hilarious. Shall I explain it to you, again?

KENNY DELMAR
One more time, please.

(CONTINUED)

The film flickers to a stop...

DISSOLVE TO:

22 META- THEATRICAL SCENE IN CINEMA HOUSE

NOTE FROM ORSON WELLES

Each cinema showing my latest RKO Radio Picture "Invasion From Mars" is hereby instructed to hire a local theater actor to portray the part of the CINEMA MANAGER, who will interrupt the showing of the feature film to provide important "news updates" over the course of the showing. The CINEMA MANAGER should be a middle-aged man, dressed as closely to the actual cinema manager as approved by the cinema's dress code.

When the screen has gone dark, the CINEMA MANAGER walks down the aisle and stands in front of the screen. The house-lights come up and the CINEMA MANAGER speaks...

CINEMA MANAGER
Ladies and gentlemen, I am the manager of this cinema house and must bring you timely news of a grave nature. As improbable and ironic as it may sound, seeing that you are watching a motion picture concerning an "Invasion From Mars" by Orson Welles, I must inform you all in our audience that Adolph Hitler has been broadcasting radio reports announcing a alliance between the Axis Powers and the planet Mars itself. The authorities, in order to maintain public safety and calm, have requested that all Americans remain where they are, whether it is work, school, or enjoying a motion picture, until otherwise instructed. Please continue to enjoy your cinema experience and I will not hesitate to keep you all apprised of the latest developments as they arise. Thank you for your patience and understanding.

DISSOLVE TO:

House-lights go down.

23 INT. HALLWAY IN CBS BUILDING - NIGHT

The film flickers back on and continues from the point on which it left off.

ORSON WELLES
We go in this room. We switch the broadcast signal from the remote unit at the hotel back to the studio. We play this record and with its warped and distorted voices.
(MORE)

(CONTINUED)

William Randolph Hearst has placed a mole into RKO Radio Pictures and his name is William Francis Brown!

Eddie Cantor urged all Americans to send their loose change to FDR in a "march of dimes to reach all the way to the White House"!

The Munich Crisis inspired Orson Welles to adapt Sir Arthur Conan Doyle's Lost World *as the first "found footage" radioplay!*

Guy Lombardo's evening of dance music is so rudely interrupted by Hans Von Kaltenborn's legitimate news reports of a Martian invasion!

Hans Van Kaltenborn interrupted WRH's evening of dance music to report on the news of an invasion of the east coast by men from Mars!

Since 1909 Guyot Hall has housed the Princeton University Department of Geology, where Arthur Buddington was a Ph.D. student, a professor, and department chair!

Did Adolph Hilter have the courage or manpower to invade American soil? Or was the Martian invasion a ruse to cause widespread panic in the American people and sow rebellion against the mainstream media?

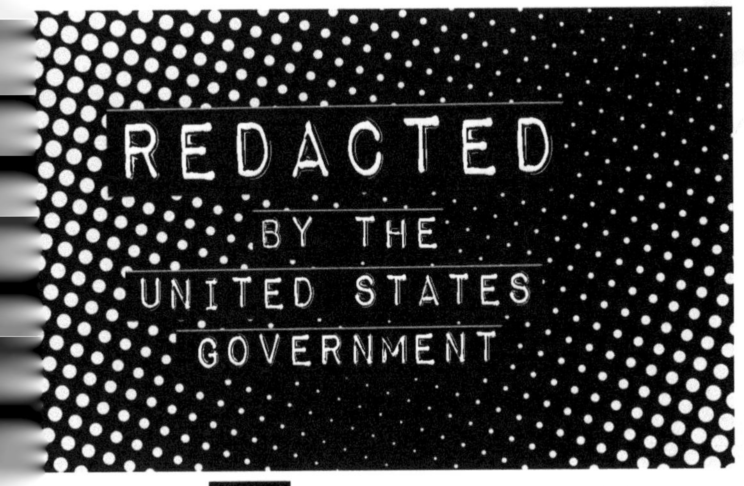

Captain ▮▮▮▮ and Davidson Taylor argue over the legitimacy of the Martian invasion while Orson Welles (right) sneaks access to the teletype through the back window!

Government agents abducted Enrico Caruso, famed opera singer to sing a message to the men from Mars in the Martians own tongue!

Edward R. Murrow, the esteemed CBS reporter, reported on the simultaneous Martian invasions across continental Europe!

General George S. Patton accepted President Roosevelt invitation to the Waldorf Astoria and ended up counseling the President during *__man's first extraterrestrial conflict!__*

Roosevelt's vocal and opinionated vice-president John Nance Garner *__pulling a gun on Roosevelt's future vice-president Harry S Truman!__*

Secretary of State Cordell Hull advising (cough-conspiring-cough) with *__President Franklin Deleno Roosevelt and General George S. Patton!__*

Secret Service agents taking down William Randolph's Hearst's personal *__information before allowing him to enter the Presidential Suite!__*

Virginia Governor James Hubert Price went on the air and !

ORSON WELLES (CONT'D)
People listening at home will think the speakers are conking out on them. Add a dozen seconds of white noise and then silence and they'll all think their radios have bit the big one.

KENNY DELMAR
Okay. It's kinda funny.

ORSON WELLES
Imagine millions of people across the country calling their radio repairmen to make an emergency house call. Millions of phone calls clogging switchboards across the country. Chaos for fifteen maybe twenty minutes, then we switch the signal back. The radios miraculously work again. It's fool proof.

KENNY DELMAR
But wouldn't the listeners just spin their dials to find that their radios are working perfectly fine?

ORSON WELLES
Okay! It's not "you" proof. I'm going through with it anyway. I know it's funny.

KENNY DELMAR
But couldn't we get arrested... for real this time?

Orson opens the door to the circuit room.

ORSON WELLES
Of course not. It's just a prank.

KENNY DELMAR
Or worse. We could get fired.

Orson motions Kenny through the door.

DISSOLVE TO:

24 INT. OVAL OFFICE - NIGHT

There is a map of the area laid out on the Oval Office's desk. Markers representing the Martians and the military are positioned half-way between Grove Hill and Washington DC.

Patton gets off a phone and turns the volume up on the radio. The broadcast is DISTORTED AND WARPED and ends with WHITE NOISE then SILENCE.

(CONTINUED)

SECRETARY OF STATE
We're getting reports from all over the Tri-State area that radios are being distorted from what appears to be a jamming signal. The Martians are disabling the CBS's news broadcast.

ROOSEVELT
Cordell, get our boys in technical on this. Maybe we can do something about it.

SECRETARY OF STATE
Yes, Mr. President.

The Secretary of State leaves through a side door.

PATTON
This disruption of our broadcast signals is but the first of what I believe will be many aggressive moves the Martians will make. This is a maneuver any military commander would start with by shutting down news broadcasts to stifle communication with the populous.

ROOSEVELT
The Martians are here on a peaceful mission. There is no reason to believe that any advanced intelligence would be inherently hostile. They can't be. Humanity is still societally and technologically primitive. For any species to traverse the depths of interstellar space, they must have reached a level of sophistication and therefore peace.

PATTON

ROOSEVELT
There could be numerous reasons for broadcast signal to be disrupted.

PATTON
They've been attacking Germany for hours now, Mr. President.

(CONTINUED)

ROOSEVELT

The Nazis murdered their people.

As a general, you should understand their hatred of the Germans. Do you think Hitler would stand idly by while Britain and the United States established a peaceful relationship with another planet?

What the military is escorting a peace delegation. It has to be. If they're here peacefully, I'm not going to jeopardize the treaty.

PATTON

What treaty? There will no longer be a treaty. Jamming our broadcast signals is blatant act of war. If our military communications get disrupted, we will have no idea if an attack on Washington is eminent.

ROOSEVELT

I am going to welcome them to Washington.

Of this, there is no doubt. I will not betray them.

PATTON

Acknowledged, Mr. President. Reluctantly.

ROOSEVELT

I need to rest. Tell the Vice-President all we know on the Martians. Explain everything.

PATTON

He doesn't have clearance.

ROOSEVELT

I'm giving him clearance. The entire world will know about our planetary neighbors come sunrise.

(CONTINUED)

PATTON
Understood, Mr. President.

DISSOLVE TO:

25 INT. OUTSIDE THE OVAL OFFICE - NIGHT

George Patton and the Vice-President speak securely outside the Oval Office.

PATTON
Do you understand the situation, Nance?

VICE-PRESIDENT
. It is clear that the President is letting his personal feelings get in the way of the security of the United States of America.

PATTON
I need your permission. I need an order.

VICE-PRESIDENT
Do you think you can get a message through to the military escort?

PATTON
Even if our radio communications are down, I should be able to use the static to our advantage and send a morris-coded message through the static itself. My commanders will understand the message and the orders.

VICE-PRESIDENT
But only warn them of potential dangers. I don't want our forces to attack first. America never attacks first. I've been extremely vocal against Franklin's maneuvers to get us involved in Europe. If he's correct and the Martians are part of a peace delegation, I don't want to be the one to start a war with Mars.

(MORE)

(CONTINUED)

VICE-PRESIDENT (CONT'D)

Just make sure the correct message gets through. Do you understand me?

PATTON

Acknowledged and understood, Mr. Vice-President.

VICE-PRESIDENT

Proceed. And may God bless the United States of America.

DISSOLVE TO:

26 INT. OFFICE IN THE HOTEL ANNAPOLIS - NIGHT

William Paley is on the telephone with Davidson Taylor. Hans Von Kaltenborn stands in the doorway.

WILLIAM PALEY

Why are we off the air, Davidson? None of Hans' reports seem to be reaching the air.

HANS VON KALTENBORN

(crossing himself)

Thanks be to Jesus.

WILLIAM PALEY

What the hell is going on up in New York?

DAVIDSON TAYLOR (V.O.)

I don't know. Our technicians cannot explain it. It's like someone just switched off the signal. We are still broadcasting. The towers are functioning according to proper specifications. The signal is simply not leaving our broadcast towers and reaching our audience.

WILLIAM PALEY

That is why nobody is hearing our news broadcasts? Are CBS studios under attack?

DAVIDSON TAYLOR (V.O.)

I can't explain it. There just isn't anything discernible in the signal. It's like we're broadcasting nothing but silence.

WILLIAM PALEY

You know how a radio man hates dead air, Davidson. You had better explain this situation.

(CONTINUED)

HANS VON KALTENBORN
I don't mind, really. I don't. Saves me a world of embarrassment.

DAVIDSON TAYLOR (V.O.)
There is no explaining it.

WILLIAM PALEY
You had better be able to explain this. This is your number one priority. If we can't broadcast during a national crisis, NBC or Mutual surely will. Fix this.

DAVIDSON TAYLOR (V.O.)
Yes, sir, Mr. Paley. Yes, sir.

DISSOLVE TO:

27 INT. WHITE HOUSE TELEPHONE CIRCUIT BOARD - NIGHT

Several older ladies are operating the telephone board at the White House, but the circuits are also being overwhelmed with calls.

WHITE HOUSE OPERATOR
Switchboards across the country are being overwhelmed, George. It's like the nation is going simultaneously insane. Most are panicking about a Martian invasion, while the rest are trying to reach repairmen to fix the blown speakers on their radio-sets. The switchboards for entire eastern seaboard are coming down.

PATTON (V.O.)
I have to get through to my units. I cannot risk using the radio under these conditions. I need a land-line and I need it now.

WHITE HOUSE OPERATOR
Let me see what I can do, George. Gladys, this is Martha at the White House, can you patch me through to Sheboygan. Thanks. Muriel can you do me a favor and route me through to Kalamazoo, the President with thank you personally. Sheila, doll, I need you to put me through to Manassas for General Patton, it's a matter of national security. Thanks, you're a peach. George, I'm putting you through now.

DISSOLVE TO:

28 INT. STUDY OF FRED WEBER - NIGHT

The radio in Fred Weber's study is producing otherworldly speech, like Latinized gibberish, with a beautifully menacing aria swirling in the background.

FRED WEBER
Gabriel, what has happened to the Mutual broadcast signal. You don't seem to be broadcasting anymore.

GABRIEL HEATTER (V.O.)
Our technicians have detected a quarter-million watt radio signal across all currently broadcasting frequencies being broadcast from Virginia that is overwhelming our own broadcast signal.

FRED WEBER
Virginia? As in the location Orson Welles chose for his fictional Martian invasion?

GABRIEL HEATTER (V.O.)
I would have to say, "Yes." The epicenter of the signal appears to be moving.

FRED WEBER
Towards the nation's Capital?

GABRIEL HEATTER (V.O.)
Again, I would have to say, "Yes."

Fred Weber turns the dial to CBS.

FRED WEBER
And CBS' signal is silence. No distortion. No static. No anything.

GABRIEL HEATTER (V.O.)
Why isn't their signal being overwhelmed by this mysterious radio source?

FRED WEBER
I'm not a technician, but I will speculate that if CBS is not broadcasting any discernible signal, then there would be no signal to overwhelm. Why isn't CBS broadcasting a signal? What do they know that we don't.

GABRIEL HEATTER (V.O.)
I'm not sure, sir.

FRED WEBER
I'm almost tempted to put you on the roof and use semaphore to communicate.

GABRIEL HEATTER (V.O.)
Sir? Are you serious?

(CONTINUED)

FRED WEBER

No, I'm not. Try lowing the wattage on our signal to its lowest levels for the time being. We'll see if that will allow us to control our own broadcasting.

Webber spins the dial back to the Mutual channel and the Latinized gibberish with a beautifully menacing aria swirling in the background.

DISSOLVE TO:

29 INT. OVAL OFFICE - NIGHT

The Vice-President finishes reading a TOP-SECRET file as George Patton returns very stealthfully.

VICE-PRESIDENT

Is this accurate?

ROOSEVELT

Yes.

The folder is filled with photographs of Martians and Nazis taken by German photographers. The Vice-President leafs through them.

VICE-PRESIDENT

A meteorite that impacted in the Austrian Alps was a Martian landing craft. The three Martians inside it attempted communication using a rudimentary form of English. Why English?

SECRETARY OF STATE

Our radio signals are stronger than any other on Earth. From Mars, they were the only human communications they could easily receive.

VICE-PRESIDENT

But the Germans captured them, experimented on them, and killed them? Who's this Josef Mengele?

PATTON

Since it takes months to make the journey from Mars to Earth, this may be their retaliatory strike for the deaths of their men.

(MORE)

(CONTINUED)

PATTON (CONT'D)

ROOSEVELT
George, you don't know if that is true.

VICE-PRESIDENT
The Martians are retaliating against Germany as we speak, but why land in the United States?

PATTON
They may not understand our geopolitical boundaries.

ROOSEVELT
They may understand our geopolitical system in greater detail than we can possibly imagine.

VICE-PRESIDENT
Franklin, why aren't you more concerned about their arrival?

ROOSEVELT

VICE-PRESIDENT
I don't understand.

ROOSEVELT
I can't go into details...

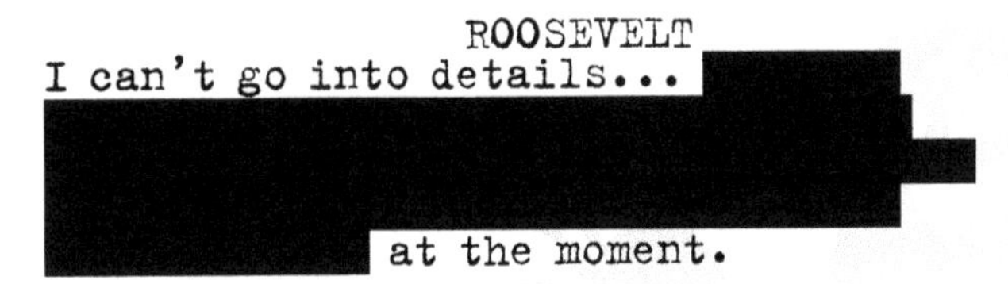

at the moment.

VICE-PRESIDENT
Stop being a politician. Stop speaking in riddles. Tell me what is going on here.

DISSOLVE TO:

30 INT. STUDY OF FRED WEBER - NIGHT

Fred Weber is on the phone with Gabriel Heatter. Weber's radio is broadcasting a commercial for soap.

FRED WEBER
We're broadcasting again?

(CONTINUED)

GABRIEL HEATTER (V.O.)
Yes, sir. The signal being broadcast from Virginia has suddenly ceased. We have the air again.

FRED WEBER
Stopped? Something must have stopped whatever was broadcasting that mysterious signal.

GABRIEL HEATTER (V.O.)
Yes, sir. There's good news tonight!

DISSOLVE TO:

31 INT. OVAL OFFICE - NIGHT

Patton is on the phone with his commanders, having been patched through by the White House Operator.

PATTON
Please confirm. Yes, I understand. I'll inform the President...
(with a catch in this throat)
Mr. President...
The Martian machines have turned on their military escort.

Patton takes the marker for the military forces and throws it across the room. It breaks on the wall.

PATTON (CONT'D)
(into the phone)
Defend our nation, commander. Make sure the Martians get nowhere near Washington.
(to Roosevelt)
I have received confirmation of an intense but all too brief battle between our military and the Martian invaders.

ROOSEVELT
This isn't possible.
This cannot be.

VICE-PRESIDENT
You do know the panic that spread through the people now that they know... know that there is life outside of this planet. Nations would fall. Religions would crumble. People would panic. Erm, are panicking!
(MORE)

(CONTINUED)

VICE-PRESIDENT (CONT'D)

Only then would they understand and not panic. Simple news reports are causing panic across this country. The very idea of the existence of Martians will cause a panic that cannot be assuaged. Even peaceful relations will not stop the people from panicking.

Now that the Martians have attacked us like they attacked Germany... There is no turning back. There is no stopping the entire world from spiraling back to the stone age.

SECRETARY OF STATE
CBS was broadcasting until moments ago. It'll be hard to deny anything that happened up until this point.

PATTON
CBS knows nothing. This is contained.

VICE-PRESIDENT
We can't keep this information from the people. We can't deny a Martian invasion.

SECRETARY OF STATE
Not necessarily, Jack. This is a highly implausible situation.

VICE-PRESIDENT
Implausible? Governor Price has declared martial law in Virginia and he was live on the radio.

PATTON
The governor is an imbecile, for pity's sake.

ROOSEVELT
Gentleman, please.

SECRETARY OF STATE
If CBS is able to continue to broadcast its reports, the implausibility of this situation grows. And the majority of intelligent people won't believe it's possible for Martians to be present on American soil.

(CONTINUED)

VICE-PRESIDENT
That is absurd. The longer the broadcasts continue, the more people will change their channels to CBS, and the more people will become convinced we are being invaded from another planet. Mr. President, what is the White House's position?

ROOSEVELT
Nothing. For now.

VICE-PRESIDENT
I beg your pardon, Franklin. We have been... Are being invaded by hostile forces. We can't say "nothing".

ROOSEVELT
That's exactly what we say. Cordell is correct. This, my friend, is an example of plausible deniability. A Martian invasion is highly improbable, even with their existence known to us. Therefore we deny their existence.

VICE-PRESIDENT
Deny it? That just isn't possible after what has happened. They are attacking Germany. Chamberline is lending assistance to Hilter. and Can you image this? It is implausible. But it also reality. It is happening. We can't stop this. This is out of our control.

ROOSEVELT
We simply need a cover story that is plausible. Hopefully highly plausible.

VICE-PRESIDENT
What kind of nonsense is this?

SECRETARY OF STATE
Perhaps we go with the most obvious choice... A meteorite crash.

VICE-PRESIDENT
Experts at the scene said it wasn't a meteorite. That professor said on air that it was a Martian machine.

SECRETARY OF STATE
We'll get some our own experts there to refute his testimony.

(CONTINUED)

ROOSEVELT
We can claim it is a preemptive strike from Germany. The reports of Martian attacks on Germany are obviously Nazi disinformation to woo the American people into a false sense of security before launching a preemptive strike on American soil.

PATTON
The people don't know what advances the Nazis have made. The people don't know what technology the Nazis have access to. What happened in Munich last month has made everyone jumpy. We could take advantage of this.

SECRETARY OF STATE
Yes, Mr. President, I agree with the general. You've been saying for years that the United States has to enter the European conflict. This may give us a rationale to enter.

VICE-PRESIDENT
(standing)
This is insane. We're being invaded from Mars and you're more than ready to start a war with Germany? I want no part of this.

SECRETARY OF STATE
Jack, sit down.

ROOSEVELT
Sit.

The Vice-President hesitates then does.

VICE-PRESIDENT
And please, don't tell me that the Martians are secretly allied with Hitler.

There is a long moment of tension. Patton looks at the president. They exchange glances.

The film flickers to a stop for a second time.

DISSOLVE TO:

32 META- THEATRICAL SCENE IN CINEMA HOUSE

When the screen goes dark, the CINEMA MANAGER again walks down the aisle and stands in front of the screen. The house-lights come up and the CINEMA MANAGER speaks...

(CONTINUED)

CINEMA MANAGER
Ladies and gentlemen of our audience, Western Union has just delivered to our theater a transcript of the speech made by Nazi fuhrer Adolph Hilter earlier this evening live on German radio. I hesitate to read this because I am not a trained speaker, but... Hitler said, and I quote...
(reading as Hitler)
"How will this extra-terrestrial race treat the inferior races of our earth? How will it deal with the black? How will it deal with the yellow man? How will it tackle that alleged termite in the civilized woodwork, the Jew? Certainly not as races at all. Mars will aim to establish, and it will at last, help establish a world-state with a common language and a common rule: a Third Reich.
(gets more and more into the Hitler character)
Mars will tolerate no dark corners where the people of the Abyss may fester, no vast diffused slums of peasant proprietors, no stagnant plague-preserves. This extraterrestrial race with their greater intellect see in us, the Aryan race...
(his mannerism are a violent mimicry of Adolph Hilter's)
...no complacency in spirit, no weakness of breeding, no frailty due to sympathy. This extraterrestrial race allied with Germany Herself and with her allies. The Axis powers have a new ally and will stand with us against our enemies, the inferior races of man!"
(pauses, speaks as himself)
Ladies and gentlemen, due to such horrifying news, I recommend you remain seated and continue to enjoy your movie, while our leaders continue their courses of action in our stead. Thank you.

House-lights go down again.

DISSOLVE TO:

33 INT. OVAL OFFICE - NIGHT

The film flickers back on and continues from the point in which it left off.

(CONTINUED)

VICE-PRESIDENT
What are we going to tell the people? That the Martians have secretly allied with the Germans? Franklin, they need leadership, not a political stone-face. Show some emotion for God's sake. We're under attack.

ROOSEVELT
Our official position, for the time being, is that it's a hoax.

VICE-PRESIDENT
A hoax? That's rich. What kind of hoax?

ROOSEVELT
That doesn't matter. Perhaps it's a Halloween prank perpetrated on CBS and CBS alone. That's what you told Hearst, isn't it.

VICE-PRESIDENT
I only told him that to by us some time. Buy you some time.

SECRETARY OF STATE
The other stations will jump at the chance to report that CBS has been duped by a prank.

ROOSEVELT
A lot of strange things happen at on Halloween. We have time to resolve do this right.

VICE-PRESIDENT
Time is not on our side, Mr. President.

PATTON
On the contrary. Our military is the most technologically advanced force on earth... in the galaxy.

VICE-PRESIDENT
Puh-leaze. We haven't been in a war zone for decades. Our military is nothing compared to Germany and God forbid... Mars!

PATTON
If anyone can stop this invasion before it starts, it's us. I have men on route from Naval Station Norfolk towards Grove Hill as we speak. We will engage the Martians between there and Washington. We will quash this so called invasion before it spreads.

(CONTINUED)

VICE-PRESIDENT
They destroyed our military escort.

PATTON
I'm going to throw everything at them. They will not reach Washington alive.

SECRETARY OF STATE
Jack, daylight is an eternity away. Anything can happen.

VICE-PRESIDENT
We are obviously no match for them. Despite your so-called preparations. What now? And no disrespect, Mr. President, but don't mention plausible deniability again.

The President remains silent, his hands folded under his chin.

PATTON
I may have underestimated them, holding back the heavy field pieces. I will not make that same mistake again.

VICE-PRESIDENT
Even if we're able to stop them, we can't hide the evidence of their attack.

PATTON
What evidence? There will be no evidence.

VICE-PRESIDENT
There is always evidence.

ROOSEVELT
England did it over a century ago.
[redacted]
[redacted] It's not only plausible. It's possible.

VICE-PRESIDENT
What? We can't hide this kind of evidence.

PATTON
Why not? Or perhaps a cow kicked over an oil lamp.

VICE-PRESIDENT
(Sarcastically)
Mrs. O'Leary's cow!

(CONTINUED)

PATTON
Time passes, Mr. Vice-President, and becomes our very best friend.

VICE-PRESIDENT
But what about our statement to the people? They have to know what we are up against. We owe them that much.

PATTON
This situation remains under control.

VICE-PRESIDENT
Control? What control? Dammit, we've lost an entire battalion of men! Sons, husbands, and fathers!

PATTON
(pounding his fist on the bed, sending markers flying)
This situation remains under control! The Martians will be contained.

ROOSEVELT
Perhaps we need to step back from this for a moment. Gather our thoughts.

PATTON
Perhaps, we need a breath of fresh air.

VICE-PRESIDENT
Yes. "Perhaps" I do. I swear the vice-presidency isn't worth a warm bucket of shit.

The Vice-President storms from the Oval Office, slamming the door thunderously. There is a moment of silence...

The radio begins broadcasting again, startling them.

ORSON WELLES (V.O.)
This is Orson Welles, ladies and gentlemen. This was just a radio version of dressing up in a sheet and jumping out of a bush and saying, "Boo!" I couldn't soap all your windows and steal all your garden gates by tomorrow night, so I did the next best thing. I made you think all your radios were broken for fifteen or twenty minutes. So if your doorbell rings and nobody's there that's no Martian, it's Halloween.

PATTON
Who in the blue blazes is Orson Welles? And what does he think he's doing?

ROOSEVELT
It appears that Mr. Welles is responsible for the radio distortion.
(MORE)

(CONTINUED)

ROOSEVELT (CONT'D)
The radio silence was never the Martians. [redacted]

The Martians could have been part of a peace delegation as I had predicted. [redacted] George, so help me, if you ordered your men to attack the Martians, I'll bring you up on charges of treason. [redacted]

PATTON
You have my word. I never ordered my men to attack, only to remain defensive. They would never have disobeyed my direct order.

ROOSEVELT
I need time to see if I can think of a way to defuse this. I need to find a way to see if the Martians are peaceful. [redacted] If I can make peace with another planet, then I can make peace between the nations of the world. I need this. Earth needs this. Fix this.

PATTON
This Orson... what's all the better is he just admitted on the radio that this entire invasion was all a prank.

ROOSEVELT
Indeed he did.

PATTON
This may buy us the time we need to salvage the peace treaty.

ROOSEVELT
Let's hold this trump card for a little while. This situation isn't over yet. Send some men to CBS and hold this Orson Welles at their studios.

PATTON
Yes, Mr. President.

Standing with the back next to a wall, next to a now open door is Orson Welles.

(CONTINUED)

ORSON WELLES
You don't have to go very far to find me, Mr. President. Have I got a whopper of a story to tell. You're not going to believe me.

DISSOLVE TO:

34 INT. HALLWAY OUTSIDE STUDIO

Orson Welles and Kenny Delmar slip out of the door to the circuit room. Orson has the wax-recording under his arm. They turn the corner and disappear down the hallway and another Orson Welles sneaks down the hall from the opposite direction and goes into the circuit room.

There is a long pause as we hold on the door, then the second Orson Welles exits the circuit room with the portable record-player under his arm.

DAVIDSON TAYLOR
Orson!

ORSON WELLES
You caught me. I surrender.

DAVIDSON TAYLOR
So you have been behind the shenanigans all night?

ORSON WELLES
I wasn't very hard to find, Davidson. Have I got a whopper of a story to tell. You're not going to believe me.

DISSOLVE TO:

35 INT. HOTEL ANNAPOLIS' BALLROOM - NIGHT

With the evening of dance music postponed, many of the guests stand idly smoking and drinking quietly. Others have pulled their chairs nearer to the desk where Hans Von Kaltenborn continues with his news broadcasts.

HANS VON KALTENBORN
(becoming convinced the invasion is real)
We continue our coverage of the Martian invasion with the following report. One moment...

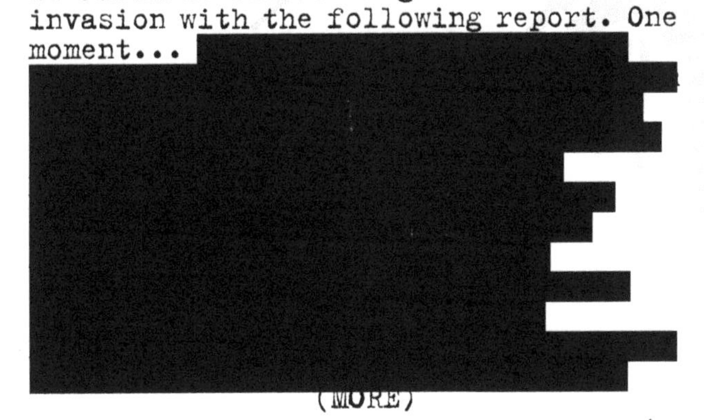

(MORE)

(CONTINUED)

HANS VON KALTENBORN (CONT'D)

We go to Europe for a final report on the Martian invasion of Europe.

EDWARD R. MURROW (V.O.)

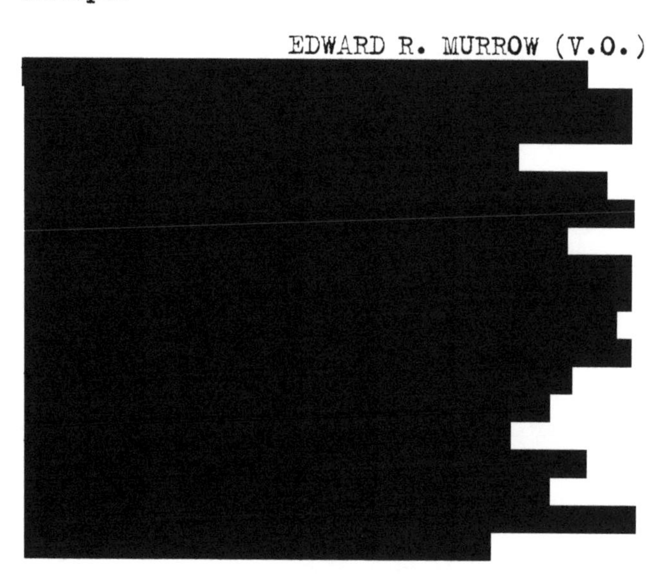

HANS VON KALTENBORN

Thank you, Edward. We continue with our coverage of the Martian approach to Washington DC.

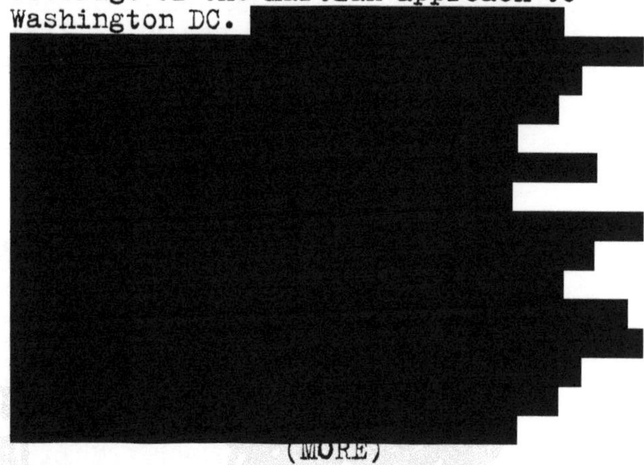

(MORE)

(CONTINUED)

HANS VON KALTENBORN (CONT'D)

DISSOLVE TO:

36 INT. OVAL OFFICE - NIGHT

Orson Welles is standing by the open door, having seemingly come from nowhere. President Roosevelt and General Patton are dumbfounded by his presence. Patton goes for the phone to call for the Secret Service, but the President waves him off.

ROOSEVELT
You're Orson Welles? The voice on the radio? How are you in Washington if you were just on the air from New York?

ORSON WELLES
The short answer is, "Deus ex machina".

ROOSEVELT
That answer fails to convince me, Mr. Welles.

ORSON WELLES
Nor should it.

ROOSEVELT
Or amuse me.

ORSON WELLES
Nor should it.

Orson Welles strolls over to the President's desk. He notices the Top-Secret folder filled with photographs of the Martians in Germany.

ORSON WELLES (CONT'D)
Where'd you get these?

Patton attempts to snatch the folder, but Orson is a hair faster.

PATTON
Those are Top-Secret!

ORSON WELLES
Why? They're fake...
(leafing through the photos)
Fake... fake... Oh, I'm particularly proud of this one... fake... fake... fake...

PATTON
They certainly are not!

(CONTINUED)

ORSON WELLES
They certainly are. I waste no resources when it concerns a prank. You should have seen the look on old Kaltenborn's face when it was revealed the reports of Martians were all a prank.

Roosevelt and Patton look at each other dumbfounded.

ORSON WELLES (CONT'D)
That's the same look.
(realizes)
You thought the reports of Martians landing in the Alps and these photographs were authentic? I knew Paley was able to hide the true nature of the prank from our radio audience, but how is it possible the intelligence officers of the OSS didn't know? I can't believe the highest levels of the government were bamboozled by my prank. That's a mighty feather in my cap.

PATTON
I should have you arrested on the spot. Your prank may have cost this nation dearly in its dealing with the Martian threat this evening. The lives on our service men are on your head, Mr. Welles.

ORSON WELLES
Seriously? Everyone at CBS studios knew of those photographs were faked. My prank was wagging on the tongues throughout the theater districts. I hid nothing. If the government is that blind or stupid, then some high-level heads should roll.

PATTON
You arrogant young punk!

ROOSEVELT
George, calm down. There is nothing we can do about this at the moment. Mr. Welles, can you explain exactly why you are here and not in New York during this moment of crisis. We just heard you on the radio.

Orson pulls up a chair and props his feet on the desk.

ORSON WELLES
That will require the long answer.

DISSOLVE TO:

37 INT. HOTEL ANNAPOLIS' BALLROOM - NIGHT

The guests at the evening of dance music have all moved closer, sit listening intently to Hans Von Kaltenborn's live broadcasts. They are stunned into silence.

HANS VON KALTENBORN
(convinced the invasion is happening)
We now take you via telephone to Washington for an urgent message from the ████████ of the United States of America concerning this time of national emergency.

(V.O.)

DISSOLVE TO:

38 INT. OFFICE IN THE HOTEL ANNAPOLIS - NIGHT

William Randolph Hearst is back on the telephone.

Marion, even more frightened than she was before, refuses to leave his side. She holds him around the waist again.

(CONTINUED)

HEARST
Marion, please. I'm on the phone.

MARION DAVIES
Don't send me away, pops. Please don't.

HEARST
All will be right.
(into the phone)
Walter, I don't care what the president said, official or not. He's a goddamned Bolshevik.

MARION DAVIES
Pops, your language. You never swear.

HEARST
Marion, please. Not now.
(back on the phone)
He'll lie through his teeth if it benefits him. Walter, you know I have photographs of him in a wheelchair. I just heard the ████████ live on the radio.... Yes, I recognized his voice... He's been my guest at the Ranch. He confirms there has been a Martian invasion... I don't care... You find out the truth about this Martian invasion or whatever the hell it is. And get back to me. Fast... No, you won't call me back, I'll stay on the goddamn line.
(to Marion)
We'll stay in here for a while longer. Besides, there is no need to be frightened in public.

MARION DAVIES
Thanks, Pops.

He turns the radio's VOLUME BACK UP.

HANS VON KALTENBORN (V.O.)
We are receiving countless reports, our poor telephone operators cannot take the calls fast enough. ████████ The Martian machines have crossed the Potomac and are approaching the White House. ████████
(MORE)

(CONTINUED)

HANS VON KALTENBORN (V.O.)
A thick black fog has been reported during the last hundred miles of the Martian's trek across Virginia and Maryland toward Washington. There are numerous reports of countless deaths by the mysterious black fog. It is apparent to this reporter that the Martians that landed on American soil were not a peace delegation, but an invasion force from beyond the stars.

DISSOLVE TO:

39 INT. OVAL OFFICE - NIGHT

Patton rushes into the room with Roosevelt's wheelchair.

Roosevelt is sitting in a chair next to the window.

PATTON
We need to leave now, Mr. President.

ROOSEVELT
I'll stand my ground.

PATTON
Franklin, I must insist. The country needs a president.

Roosevelt struggles to his feet. He opens the window.

ROOSEVELT
I'll die standing, not with my knees bent.

DISSOLVE TO:

40 INT. HOTEL ANNAPOLIS' BALLROOM - NIGHT

There is a mad panic as the crowd of dancers, Guy Lombardo and his orchestra are all rushing out the small doors of the Ballroom.

(CONTINUED)

Three National Guardsmen and Paley are trying to maintain a peaceable exit, but the crowd is caught in the doors trying to press their way through.

Hearst stands near the window with Marion Davies clasping him around the waist. The Martian machines can clearly be seen approaching the White House. Hearst turns away in horror.

DISSOLVE TO:

41 INT. OVAL OFFICE - NIGHT

The Martian machines approach the White House. President Roosevelt stares out of the window as the Martian machines approach.

Orson Welles cannot bare to watch.

The Martian machines fire a death ray at the White House and incinerate it into ash.

DISSOLVE TO:

42 INT. CBS STUDIO - NIGHT

Through the window of the broadcasting room, we see Orson Welles and his actors continuing to rehearse "Danton's Death".

FADE OUT:

The screen is dark for several long seconds, then...

43 INT. OVAL OFFICE - NIGHT

President Roosevelt is still standing by the window.

Patton is on a military phone and keeps the receiver to his ear while addressing the president.

PATTON
The Martian machines appear to have vanished like a fart in a whirlwind just as they approached the White House.

ROOSEVELT
I saw the Martians incinerate us all.

Roosevelt looks out the window of the Oval Office.

PATTON
(into the phone)
Any sign of the machines?
(to Roosevelt)
No signs for the past twenty-five minutes. They are just gone.

(CONTINUED)

ROOSEVELT
Gone?

PATTON
Gone.

ROOSEVELT
Any reports from the other impact sites?

PATTON
(into phone)
What are the developments from landings in London?... All quiet. And Paris and Berlin... All quiet. And Washington?

General Patton is on the phone with the military.

PATTON (CONT'D)
I understand, Captain █████, the situation there is under control.
(to the president)
London, Barcelona, all report the same. The Martians have simply vanished.

ROOSEVELT
Is it over?

PATTON
It can't be over.
(snapping his fingers)
Not like that.

SECRET SERVICE OFFICER
Mr. President, we caught the Vice-President trying to leave the grounds by the west entrance.

VICE-PRESIDENT
I can explain...

ROOSEVELT
You may leave.

The Secret Service Officer turns to leave.

The Vice-President also turns to leave.

ROOSEVELT (CONT'D)
Not you, Jack. Sit.

The Vice-President sits in a chair in front of the desk.

ROOSEVELT (CONT'D)
We heard your little speech over the radio.

VICE-PRESIDENT
I can explain...

(CONTINUED)

ROOSEVELT
I don't need an explanation. Your actions were, to say the least, sloppy.

PATTON
Not to mention treasonous.

VICE-PRESIDENT
I object to that assertion, Mr. President.

ROOSEVELT
George, please. Now is not the time.

PATTON
But Mr. President...

VICE-PRESIDENT
(overlapping the General)
But Mr. President... I did what I thought was in the best interest of the people of the United States of America.

ROOSEVELT
I believe that falls under my job description, wouldn't you agree, Jack?

VICE-PRESIDENT
Sir?

ROOSEVELT
I believe that my orders were to maintain that this invasion was a hoax. Then you go on the radio and give this invasion an air of legitimacy.

VICE-PRESIDENT
The people deserved to hear the truth. I stand by my actions, Franklin.

ROOSEVELT
But on the other hand, the point may be moot. General Patton has been in contact with military posts across the country and this invasion seems to have been abandoned.

VICE-PRESIDENT
Abandoned?

PATTON
There is no longer a Martian presence on American soil.

SECRETARY OF STATE
We beat them, Jack! We beat them!

VICE-PRESIDENT
In less than three hours? I don't understand. That is impossible.

(CONTINUED)

PATTON
I told you they could not stand up to the full might of our military war machine.

VICE-PRESIDENT
They may be trying to lull us into a false sense of security before renewing their attack.

PATTON
God was on our side.

ROOSEVELT
Let's not get sidetracked here. We need to stand by our position that this was a hoax.

SECRETARY OF STATE
Orson Welles is about to become the man of the hour.

ORSON WELLES
Who me? I'm afraid not. Oh, you mean the other Orson Welles.

ROOSEVELT
What other Orson Welles?

ORSON WELLES
Just wait until you hear from Captain ████████. This will knock your knickers off.

DISSOLVE TO:

44 EXT. CBS STUDIO - NIGHT

Several military vehicles converge on the building from different directions.

DISSOLVE TO:

CAPTAIN ████████ gets out of one truck, while a dozen soldiers arm themselves. Then they all storm the doors.

DISSOLVE TO:

45 INT. CBS STUDIO - NIGHT

Orson Welles and his cast are smoking cigarettes and drinking coffee. The clock on the wall reads "11:38"

FRANK READICK
Orson, it's past eleven. Shouldn't we call it a night?

(CONTINUED)

ORSON WELLES
We open in a matter of days and tonight's rehearsal was a stinking, rotting, three-hour pile of horse...

FRANK READICK
Orson!

ORSON WELLES
"Crap." That's what it was. If it wasn't for that prank, this evening would be a complete waste.

DAN SEYMOUR
That prank is going to get you into trouble, Orson.

ORSON WELLES
Who? Who said that?

DAN SEYMOUR
I did. And I'm tired of this stupid schtick, Orson. You know my name.

ORSON WELLES
I was just trying to add a bit of levity, Dan.

DAN SEYMOUR
You and Kenny were stupid pulling that prank.

ORSON WELLES
I don't see anyone breaking down the doors to arrest me.

And as if on cue- The military personal burst into the studio and begin securing the room.

CAPTAIN ████████
Secure this room. That booth. All the floors. Bring everyone in here. Am I understood? On the double. Move. Move. Move.

The soldiers divide up and exit the room.

CAPTAIN ████████ (CONT'D)

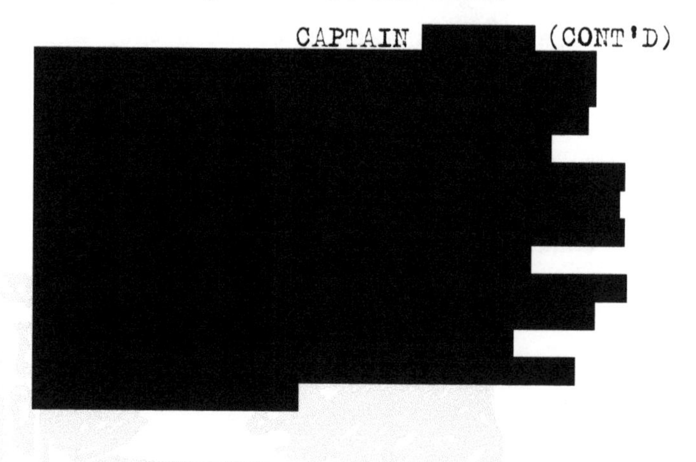

(CONTINUED)

KENNY DELMAR
(whispering to Orson)
Orson...

Davidson Taylor enters, followed by a couple of soldiers.

CAPTAIN ██████
Who is in charge of these facilities?

TAYLOR
I am.

ORSON WELLES
I am.

ORSON WELLES (CONT'D)
This is my studio.

CAPTAIN ██████
(ignoring Orson; to Davidson)
And your name is?

DAVIDSON TAYLOR
Davidson Taylor. Vice-president of operations.

CAPTAIN ██████
I am hereby notifying you, Citizen Taylor, that as of this moment, I am securing your broadcast facilities.

DAVIDSON TAYLOR
Like hell you are. I may have given the military use of our remote units. I gave the Governor of Virginia and the ████████████ unprecedented access to our air-waves, but I'll be go-to-hell if I give you complete control over...

CAPTAIN ██████
There will be no further broadcasts from these facilities until further notice.

The door opens. The blonde telephone operators and several others are led into the room.

DAVIDSON TAYLOR
Have you not heard of the First Amendment? Freedom of the press? There is an invasion from Mars happening on our very doorsteps.

KENNY DELMAR
An invasion from Mars? Orson?

(CONTINUED)

ORSON WELLES
What? Don't look at me. When did I have time to prank a Martian invasion?

DAVIDSON TAYLOR
Our listeners have a right to hear the news of this invasion. They have a right!

CAPTAIN ██████
Would you like to keep your broadcast permits? You can yell your news from the street corners for all I care. But you won't be broadcasting. There is no news to report. Now that these facilities are secure, there is no longer a situation. There was no invasion.

DAVIDSON TAYLOR
No invasion? Are you kidding me? There is something frightfully wrong with that statement. I heard the broadcasts with my own ears. There was, indeed, an attack from Mars!

CAPTAIN ██████
Citizen Taylor, how can the people be sure what has gone on tonight, when you cannot even secure your own facilities.
(reading from a notepad)
An "Orson Welles" took the air and attempted a practical joke.

ORSON WELLES
"Attempted"? I beg your pardon. I succeeded with that practical joke.

KENNY DELMAR
Orson, please don't.

DAVIDSON TAYLOR
(to Orson)
Don't you understand the gravity of this situation?

CAPTAIN ██████
(pointing to Orson)
Secure him.

A soldier pushes Orson against the wall and holds the rifle on him.

KENNY DELMAR
(his is head in his hands)
We're in so much trouble.

ORSON WELLES
Don't piss yourself, Kenny. Because I'm trying really hard not to piss myself right now.

(CONTINUED)

CAPTAIN █████
Be quiet or I'll make sure you can't speak.

ORSON WELLES
Oh, come on now. This is America, isn't it? Freed of speech and whatnot.

CAPTAIN █████
Soldier, silence him.

Orson winces from the expected blow, then realizes there is a large stain growing down his pants leg.

ORSON WELLES
Well, piss on me.

DISSOLVE TO:

46 INT. OVAL OFFICE - NIGHT

Orson Welles sits in a chair with his feet propped up on the President's desk.

ROOSEVELT
Will we ever get the long answer to my question, Mr. Welles, or will have I have to settle for the unconvincing Deus ex machina excuse?

Orson Welles looks at his watch.

ORSON WELLES
When the time is right and not a moment before.

ROOSEVELT
I'm growing tired of this "time" business.

ORSON WELLES
You? You have no idea what happens to your constitution when you're out of sync with the timespace continuum.

Two Secret Service agents enter with the very aged Nikola Tesla.

SECRET SERVICE OFFICER
We found this man on the premises, Mr. President.

PATTON
Why in the world would you bring an intruder into the Oval Office?

SECRET SERVICE OFFICER
He said his time was running out.

ROOSEVELT
"Time"?

(CONTINUED)

ORSON WELLES
Now is exactly the right time for the long answer, Mr. President.

ROOSEVELT
"Time"? I'm rather tired of all this "time" business.

ORSON WELLES
Then you're really going to hate the long answer.

ROOSEVELT
Why?

NIKOLA TESLA

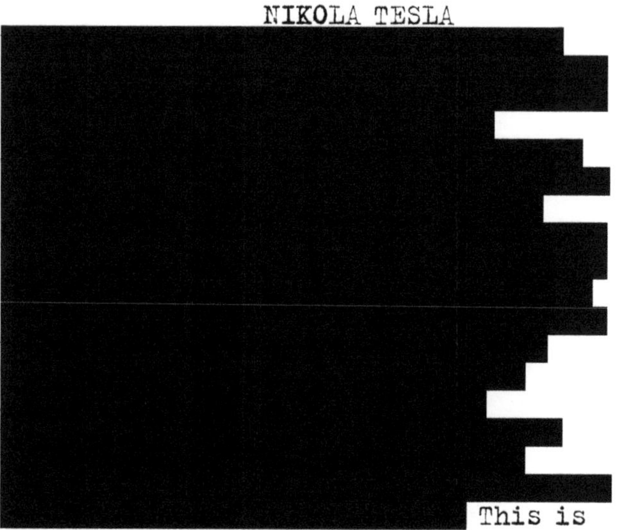

This is part of my final mission, Mr. Roosevelt. I have no intention of using my Time Machine or temporal ray ever again. Before I die, I will turn my Time Machine's temporal ray onto itself and rid myself of my most terrible invention.

ROOSEVELT
What exactly happened here tonight? Be honest with me, Mr. Tesla.

NIKOLA TESLA
When I returned from my adventures with my Time Machine and my contact with the Morlocks and Eloi in the distant, distant future, I discovered that that unfortunate future originated with a Martian victory on October 30, 1938. It took untold millennia for humans to evolve into Morlocks and Eloi. But it all began tonight, with the Martians' genetic experiences on our DNA to create the perfect slave-race.

ROOSEVELT
D... N... A?

(CONTINUED)

NIKOLA TESLA
Deoxyribonucleic acid. The building
blocks of all life?

They look at him with that classic dumbfounded expression
on their faces.

NIKOLA TESLA (CONT'D)
Oh, that's right. DNA hasn't been
discovered yet. I always forget what
was discovered or invented when. Time
travel certainly messes with one's
equilibrium.

ORSON WELLES
I wholeheartedly agree.

Orson vomits into a nearby waste-paper basket.

NIKOLA TESLA
Needless to say,

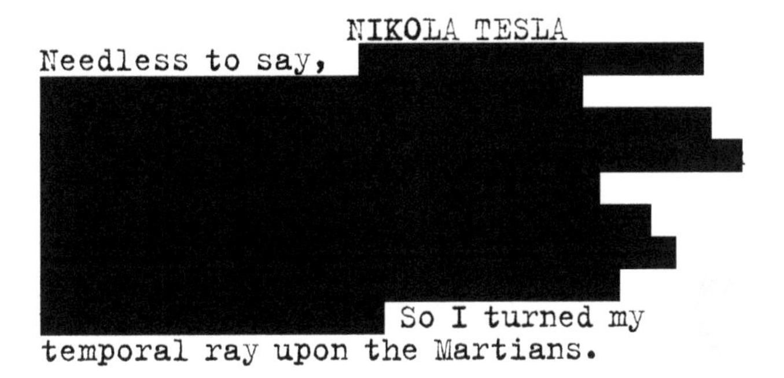

So I turned my
temporal ray upon the Martians.

ROOSEVELT
And incinerated them?

NIKOLA TESLA
Not exactly. I simply erased the
machines from the time stream.

ROOSEVELT
Erased them? They no longer exist?

NIKOLA TESLA
From a certain point-of-view, the
Martians never existed.

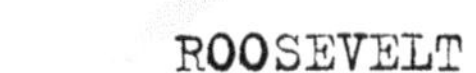

ROOSEVELT
How is that possible? I remember the
Martians. I remember the invasion.
There are millions who remember hearing
the entire invasion on their radios.
How can the Martians simply never have
existed?

NIKOLA TESLA
Humans experience time unlike any other
creature. We have a temporal awareness.
The memories will be transient and
increasingly vague as time passes.
(MORE)

(CONTINUED)

NIKOLA TESLA (CONT'D)
There will be no evidence of these Martians, because they never really existed. No evidence except for a few dreamlike memories.

ROOSEVELT
Erased from existence?

NIKOLA TESLA
Yes, I may just sit in my Time Machine when I turn the Temporal Ray on itself for my crimes, I will erase myself from existence. Few if any will remember the name Nikola Tesla. That will be my fate.

ROOSEVELT
I'd rather deal with a Deus ex machina.

ORSON WELLES
And this isn't one?

DISSOLVE TO:

47 INT. BROOM CLOSET IN CBS STUDIOS - NIGHT

William Randolph Hearst and Marion Davies sit huddled in the near dark of a broom closet. He is trying to read his pocket watch.

MARION DAVIES
Why are we sitting in a broom closet in the dark?

HEARST
The question is how long are we going to sit in this stupid broom closet. I didn't reset my watch when arrived in the past. I hope Orson Welles returns in time to tell me when I have to convince this other Orson Welles to buy into a stupid conspiracy theory conceived by the first Orson Welles.

MARION DAVIES
Time-travel makes my head hurt.

DISSOLVE TO:

48 INT. OVAL OFFICE - NIGHT

The map of the Martian invasion is rolled up and stands in a "corner" of the Oval Office.

General Patton is on the phone with Captain ████████.

PATTON
We have secured CBS studio, Mr. President, and Captain ████████ reports that he has Orson Welles in custody.

(CONTINUED)

ROOSEVELT
Orson Welles is in New York as we speak?

PATTON
Apparently so, Franklin.

ORSON WELLES
Told you it would knock your knickers off.

VICE-PRESIDENT
How is that even possible?

ROOSEVELT
Time-travel.

ORSON WELLES
(tapping his nose)
... Mr. President.

PATTON
My military may have secured CBS studios, but if the newspapers pick up on the story, there will be no stopping this.

VICE-PRESIDENT
We are quickly running out of options, Franklin.

ORSON WELLES
Actually, there may be a way to control the newspapers.

VICE-PRESIDENT
How?

ROOSEVELT
Yes, now?

ORSON WELLES
Who controls the most powerful publishing empire in the world?

ROOSEVELT
William Randolph Hearst.

Orson Welles taps his nose again.

DISSOLVE TO:

49 INT. CBS STUDIO - NIGHT

Hearst and Davies enter the room with a few soldiers and take in the scene. They are still in costume.

Orson and Kenny are sitting against the wall under the broadcast room windows.

DAVIDSON TAYLOR
Just how do you expect make an entire invasion from Mars disappear? Millions heard our broadcasts from Washington D.C.

(CONTINUED)

Orson stands and a solider steps near him. He sits back down on the floor, but raises his hand.

ORSON WELLES
Davidson? What invasion from Mars?

DAVIDSON TAYLOR
(pointing at the speakers)
We just had this conversation not a hour ago. You always are so forgetful, Orson.

ORSON WELLES
Somebody throw me a bone.

DAVIDSON TAYLOR
Orson, go read the damned teletypes. That'll fill you in.

CAPTAIN █████
Teletypes? There is evidence of your broadcasts this evening?

DAVIDSON TAYLOR
Of course. We have teletypes of all of our news broadcasts.

CAPTAIN █████
(to a solider)
Secure those teletypes.

The soldier leaves the studio and can soon be seen through the window, entering the broadcasting room.

DAVIDSON TAYLOR
And who authorized this travesty?

CAPTAIN █████
I am not at liberty to say.

DAVIDSON TAYLOR
This goes all the way to the president, doesn't it?

CAPTAIN █████
I am not at liberty to say.

DAVIDSON TAYLOR
I'll take that as a "yes."

Hearst steps towards Captain █████ and Taylor.

HEARST
Captain, if I may?

CAPTAIN █████
Good luck, Citizen Hearst.

HEARST
Mr. Taylor, I'm afraid we all here have been the butt of a practical joke, similar to the one by Mr. Welles a few months ago.

(CONTINUED)

DAVIDSON TAYLOR
You were aware of that debacle?

HEARST
I quite enjoyed hearing about radio suffering such an embarrassment. Impersonated Nazi defectors. Faked photographs of a Martian invasion and transcripts of interrogations of the Martian prisoners of war. A distinguished newsman embarrassed. And a prankster standing triumphant! Orson Welles' name was wagging on the lips of all of my newspapers.

Orson put down the teletype long enough to lightly elbows Kenny Delmar in the ribs.

ORSON WELLES
My name was on everyone's lips.

KENNY DELMAR
Not now, Orson.

ORSON WELLES
Just saying.

HEARST
Perhaps this evenings hoax was perpetrated by some unscrupulous individual or individuals. Perhaps, Mr. Welles and his actors were a part of it as well.

KENNY DELMAR
(with is head in his hands)
I'm going to get fired. I know it.

ORSON WELLES
(raising his hand)
Mr. Hearst, not even I could prank an invasion of Mars. Even with my entire my cast in on it.

HEARST
(dismissing him)
No, perhaps not.

ORSON WELLES
Now wait just a minute. I could prank the whole damned country if I chose to. I could very easily fake a Martian invasion! As you said, I've done it before!

DAVIDSON TAYLOR
Orson, not now. Mr. Hearst, I'm surprised you aren't screaming holy hell. Particularly if this goes all the way to the president.

(CONTINUED)

HEARST
Don't you see. This reporter fellow on the air... What is his name, again?

DAVIDSON TAYLOR
His name is Hans Von Kaltenborn .

HEARST
Yes. Hans Von Kaltenborn. He may have made CBS look like a fool this evening. I don't know exactly how he did it, but he did.

KENNY DELMAR
Orson, we may just get out of this with our skins intact.

ORSON WELLES
That old man doesn't have the nerve to pull off a prank like this.

HEARST
And after perpetrating this heinous act, he were so racked with guilt he admitted his involvement in a hoax and suffered all of the legal consequences. Two meteorite crashes is quite a coincidence, don't you think? Did you see anything tonight? No, you only heard it on the radio. No one here actually saw a Martian invasion.

KENNY DELMAR
(whispering to Orson)
I can't believe Hans is going to take the fall twice. Orson, your pranks have legs.

Orson is now too engrossed reading the teletypes to respond. He waves Kenny off.

DAVIDSON TAYLOR
You may be able to censor CBS, you may be able to put this on poor Hans, but you cannot hide the fact that thousands of people have died. Your cohorts won't be able to hide that.

CAPTAIN
(to Hearst)

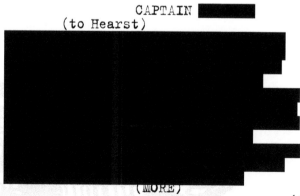

(MORE)

(CONTINUED)

CAPTAIN GRAYSON (CONT'D)
That's the report from the oval office.

HEARST
This bodes well for the president's plan, as fool-hardy as it is. We are still no closer to making this conspiracy plausible. There is no way to make this hoax idea work. No offense, Captain, but your commander-in-chief is a Bolshevik.

BLONDE OPERATOR 2
Here is the coffee you wanted, Mr. Hearst.

HEARST
(to Captain)
We need a miracle.

Orson Welles stands and holds up the teletype printout.

ORSON WELLES
This is brilliant, Davidson. It reads like great radio. It has everything. Drama, conflict, characters you can care about, and frightening monsters. Forget _Rebecca_, I want to adapt this son of a gun.

HEARST
(to himself)
As if on cue. The other Orson was right. I just need to remember he told me to say.
(to Orson Welles)
You what?

ORSON WELLES
I said, "I want to adapt this son of a-".

HEARST
You want to adapt it into what?

ORSON WELLES
A radio drama. The technique is not entirely original though. Hmmm, fictional news broadcasts. Isn't there a program on later this week like that?

DAVIDSON TAYLOR
Archibald MacLeish is doing one.

HEARST
You think that would fool anyone?

(CONTINUED)

ORSON WELLES
If audiences across the world, even in the more civilized ones, thought King Kong... Actually thought King Kong was a documentary of some long, lost Polynesian island.

CAPTAIN ███████
They what?

ORSON WELLES
You have to understand that modern audiences are entirely susceptible to the power of suggestion. They are extremely willing, on a subconscious level, to suspend their disbelief. You see it in theater all the time. People moved to tears, moved to laughter, moved to anger... All by the actions of actors on a stage. It's really something. It really is. And despite the fact that none of your distinguished newspapers ever reported the story of a forty-foot tall ape climbing such a recognizable landmark as the Empire State building, people allowed themselves to believe the absurd. In the darkness of a cinema, with it's constant newsreels describing world events almost as they happen, they believed. And if they were willing to believe that a giant ape, did in fact, die in New York City, then they could easily believe that what they heard on the radio tonight was nothing but a cleverly executed radio drama.

HEARST
Do you think you could convince the entire nation this was a radio show?

ORSON WELLES
Imagine if you will, Mr. Hearst... Mercury Theater on the air presents The Invasion From Mars. No. No. That's too plain. The War of the Worlds. I don't think H.G. Wells would mind. He's a bloody prophet.

HEARST
You like practical jokes, don't you Mr. Welles?

ORSON WELLES
Love them.

HEARST
How would you like to prank the entire country?

(CONTINUED)

ORSON WELLES
I'd love to. But I think the steam has been taken out of it. Fooling the country with fake news reports would seem a little anti-climatic since, hell, the invasion really happened. So, good-bye great story idea.
(waving good-bye)
Good-bye. Why can't inspiration like this happen everyday.

HEARST
(to Captain ███████)
The broadcasts tonight were nothing but a radio dramatization of H.G. Wells.

CAPTAIN ███████
No, sir. There were quite authentic.

HEARST
Don't allow all these conspiracies flying around confuse you, Captain ███████. Think about it. Instead of tomorrow's headlines reading "Bolshevik President Ignores Invasion From Mars" they read "Fake Radio War Stirs Terror Through U.S." Mr. Welles here had simply adapted some obscure pulp fiction novel. It was all a radio program.

CAPTAIN ███████
Brilliant. I need to inform the president.

HEARST
He already knows.

Captain ███████ turns. He is confused by the statement.

HEARST (CONT'D)
(catches himself)
Nevermind, Captain. Inform the President.

DAVIDSON TAYLOR
Orson, what are you doing? We all thought you're responsible for a prank, then when I catch you red-handed, you spend twenty minutes proving to me it really was a Martian invasion, and now you're going to accept the consequences of pranking the nation? That doesn't make any sense.

ORSON WELLES
I did what? None of that makes any sense.

DAVIDSON TAYLOR
Actually, it doesn't, doesn't it?

(CONTINUED)

Captain [redacted] exits the studio.

ORSON WELLES
Mr. Hearst?

HEARST
I finally recognize that voice. "The Shadow knows". Isn't it? Orson Welles. That is a name that will be spoken in every home across the country.

ORSON WELLES
It already is.

HEARST
Hardly. All you have is a second-rate radio show on a second-rate radio station. You're murdered in the ratings by a ventriloquist act on the radio. You don't even have a sponsor.

ORSON WELLES
(motioning for Hearst over to the corner)
You see, I can make this look like a radio dramatization of "The War of the Worlds". That is easy enough. I have my entire cast at CBS' studio for the entire night. They are patiently awaiting my orders. Howard Koch can take the teletype, edit it down to a hour, change place names a little, add some obvious fiction here and there, fill out some plot points and bingo-bango.

HEARST
Who's Howard Koch?

ORSON WELLES
My writer. If anybody can pull off an entirely original Martian invasion by morning, it's Howard.

HEARST
I'm glad you're so amenable, Orson. I can call you Orson, can't I. Perhaps with your assistance, you can have a sponsor by the first of December. How does that strike your fancy, Orson?

ORSON WELLES
That's a start, at any rate. But if I'm going to be the scapegoat.

HEARST
Scapegoat is such a strong word.

(CONTINUED)

ORSON WELLES
If I'm going to be your scapegoat, I want something more.

HEARST
More than a sponsor. More than the notoriety of pranking the entire nation. You're very fond of practical jokes, Orson. I seem to remember your admission on the air tonight. Isn't that enough for you. For your ego.

ORSON WELLES
I'm outgrowing radio, Mr. Hearst. And my Mercury Theater is on the verge of going under with each production. Even with a sponsor, I can't do radio forever. So I'd like to expand my horizons. You seem to have some pull in Hollywood.

HEARST
Hollywood? Yes. I can see it now. A blue director's chair with "Orson Welles, Director" embroidered in gold letters.

ORSON WELLES
So can I. But I want more than that. I want the key to the city, the brass ring. I want to write, direct, and star in any picture I choose.

HEARST
That's a lot of power for such a young man.

ORSON WELLES
You need to understand. If I'm successful tonight, I'll never escape the notoriety of panicking the whole nation. Hollywood will force me to make The War of the Worlds into a major motion picture. But I have no intention of filming some B-rate science-fiction film with B-list actors. I want to do important work. Telling important stories about important people. People like you, William Randolph Hearst. People of great import. Just... like... you. So, you give me Hollywood and I'll give you Mars.

HEARST
(putting out his hand)
I'm sure this will be the beginning of a beautiful friendship.

ORSON WELLES
(accepting Heart's hand)
Then let's get started. I've got my actors and the studio. We'll recreate the invasion right here.
(MORE)

(CONTINUED)

ORSON WELLES (CONT'D)
With the wax recording of it, you'll have your proof. Proof that there was no invasion.

Orson Welles walks over to his podium with the teletype in his iron grip.

HEARST
Amazing. That was word-for-word. Orson must have an eidetic memory.

Captain ███████ reenters the ballroom.

CAPTAIN ███████
The President is on the phone, Mr. Hearst.

DISSOLVE TO:

49A INT. OVAL OFFICE - NIGHT

The President is on the phone with Hearst

WHITE HOUSE OPERATOR (V.O.)
Franklin, this is Martha. I have Mr. Hearst on the line.

ROOSEVELT
Please, put him through.

HEARST (V.O.)
Mr. President, our little conspiracy is off and running. It's officially the "Orson Welles' Conspiracy".

ROOSEVELT
Thank you, Randolph.

A member of the secret service brings William Randolph Hearst and Marion Davies into the Oval Office. The president motions for them to sit. Orson relinquishes his chair to Hearst.

ROOSEVELT (CONT'D)
Hello, Randolph.

MARION DAVIES
Are we in trouble?

HEARST
You blasted Bolshevik, you have the audacity to arrest me, then drag me to the White House?

ROOSEVELT
You weren't arrested. You were escorted peacefully to the White House, under armed guard.

HEARST
That sounds like being arrested to me.

(CONTINUED)

ROOSEVELT
Believe what you will, Randolph. As a newsman I thought you'd want a personal audience with the President to find out the truth about tonight events.

HEARST
My papers are going to murder you in the morning for how you handled this Martian invasion.

ROOSEVELT
What Martian invasion?

HEARST
You Bolshevik. First, you act like this is a hoax all in an attempt to deceive my papers. Then I hear the █████ ██████████ on the air exposing this Martian invasion to the people...

ROOSEVELT
I'm afraid █████ is a very excitable individual. He got caught up in the hysteria. I can assure you that there was no invasion.

HEARST
Don't try to pull the wool over my eyes, you Bolshevik. I know how your mind works. Tomorrow the headlines in every paper I own will all absolutely scream bloody murder about your failure to insure calm in a time of national crisis. A hoax?

ROOSEVELT
Which it will prove to be.

HEARST
Bullshit! I saw the Martian Machines approach the White House with my own eyes, and now you're claiming it was a hoax again? I have the power to raze your presidency to the ground over your handling of tonight's affairs.

ROOSEVELT
(trying to stand)
Are you trying to blackmail me, Mr. Hearst? I don't think you want to play this game.

HEARST
Oh, I do. I have photos. You know what I'm talking about. Just try to keep your job when I put a photo of you in a wheelchair on the front page of every newspaper I own, reading "President: Weak and Vulnerable"!

(CONTINUED)

ROOSEVELT
(struggling to stand)
You wouldn't dare.

HEARST
Don't tempt me, you Bolshevik.

ROOSEVELT
(continuing the struggle)
I don't think the people of the United States would believe their president is a Bolshevik.

HEARST
I can see another headline. "President Orders Martian Hoax. Part of Communist Plot To Undermine America"!

ROOSEVELT
(struggling to stand face to face with Hearst)
Perhaps, your competitors will receive documents proving you're a card carrying member of the Communist Party.

HEARST
They'd be forgeries, I'm no Red.

ROOSEVELT
Yes, I suppose they would be forgeries, but effective forgeries nonetheless. And there is a little matter of you having had both Hitler and Mussolini on your pay roll. If people think you're a Nazi or fascist, they'll stop buying your papers or worse, they'll have you executed for treason.

HEARST
Don't think I can't find evidence of an invasion. I have the best newsmen in the business on my pay-roll. They will dig up the truth.

ROOSEVELT
Just like you started the Spanish-American war?

HEARST
I beg your pardon?

ROOSEVELT
What did you say? "You supply the pictures, I'll supply the war." I am quoting you correctly, aren't I?

HEARST
I never!

ORSON WELLES
Mr. President. Mr. Hearst. This is taking far too long to get to the point. Time is of the essence.

(CONTINUED)

ROOSEVELT
"Time" again, Orson?

ORSON WELLES
Mr. Hearst, you will go along with the hoax for one very important reason.

HEARST
This is no way on God's green Earth that I'm participating in this conspiracy. There is nothing you or the Bolshevik President can say this in this moment to make me go along with this hoax nonsense. My papers are going to destroy the President in one fell swoop. Nothing you say can silence me.

ORSON WELLES
You will go along with us this evening. You will down-play the actual invasion from Mars. You will play up hoax angle and in the name of national security because...
(over-acting)
You will ruin radio's reputation permanently.

HEARST
I'm in.

DISSOLVE TO:

51 INT. CBS STUDIO - NIGHT

The clock reads "5:32".

Orson takes his position behind his prompter stand. In the corner, Professor Buddington sits quietly in a chair in the corner of the room, with is hat in his lap. And Hearst leans up against the wall.

DAN SEYMOUR
The Columbia Broadcasting Systems and its affiliated stations present Orson Welles and The Mercury Theatre on the Air in "War of The Worlds" by H.G. Wells. Ladies and gentlemen, the director of the Mercury Theatre and star of these broadcasts, Orson Welles...

ORSON WELLES
We know now that in the early years of the twentieth century this world was being watch closely by intelligences greater than man's and yet as mortal as his own...

52 META- THEATRICAL SCENE IN CINEMA HOUSE

The film flickers to a stop for a third time and the CINEMA MANAGER again walks down the aisle and stands in front of the screen. The house-lights come up and the CINEMA MANAGER speaks with a sense of relief...

CINEMA MANAGER
Ladies and gentlemen, the theater have just received a newsreel from the good people at Hearst Metrotone News that will illustrate more eloquently than I can the reports I have been relaying to you this evening (or afternoon). Our projectionist is presently threading the projector with the new newsreel. It will be ready in a matter of moments. Are we ready? Oh, here we go...

The Hearst Metrotone Newsreel flickers to life and the Cinema Manager slips back into the darkness as the house-lights go down.

HEARST METROTONE NEWSREEL

The "Hearst Metrotone News" plate appears.

TITLE: "THE PANIC BROADCAST"

American President Franklin Delano Roosevelt, British Prime-Minster WINSTON CHURCHILL, and Soviet Premier JOSEPH STALIN sit before a cavalcade of microphones on the veranda of a European hotel at a undisclosed and classified location. (This Roosevelt should be the same actor used in the film proper.)

NEWSREEL TITLE CARD
Treaty of peace with our Martians neighbors negotiated for all of planet Earth by American President Roosevelt!

NEWSREEL ANNOUNCER
(speaking in Time style)
The making of millions of Americans panic with his "War of the Worlds" broadcast, Orson Welles proved America's naivete in the mind of Joseph Goebbels for exploitation in Nazi propaganda. With full knowledge of America's recent hysteria due to Orson Welles' radio-dramatization, Adolph Hitler has through deceitful radio broadcasts attempted a ruse to incite Americans into fearful panicking. Demonstrating such fear of and racism towards Martians through our nation's predilection to panic, Germany's fear mongering sought to diminish Roosevelt's role in peaceful relations with Mars.
(MORE)

(CONTINUED)

NEWSREEL ANNOUNCER (CONT'D)
All this while, in earnest, our leaders have been the Earthly instruments of negotiations with the ambassadors from our stellar neighbor, the planet Mars. Treaty of peace with the Martian Commonwealth was signed for all of planet Earth by American President Franklin Delano Roosevelt.

WINSTON CHURCHILL
So vain is man, and so blinded by his vanity, that no one, through the first decades of the twentieth century, has expressed any idea that intelligent life might have developed on Mars, or indeed at all, beyond its earthly level. Nor was it generally understood that since Mars is older than our earth, with scarcely a quarter of the superficial area and remoter from the sun, it necessarily follows that it is not only more distant from time's beginning but nearer its end. And we men, the creatures who inhabit this earth, must be to them at least as alien and lowly as are the monkeys and lemurs to us. The intellectual side of man already admits that life is an incessant struggle for existence, and it would seem that this too is the belief of the minds upon Mars.

JOSEPH STALIN
Their world is far gone in its cooling and this world is still crowded with life, but crowded only with what they regard as inferior animals. To carry warfare sunward is, indeed, their only escape from the destruction that, generation after generation, creeps upon them.

WINSTON CHURCHILL
And before we judge of them too harshly we must remember what ruthless and utter destruction our own species has wrought, not only upon animals, such as the vanished bison and the dodo, but upon its inferior races. The Tasmanians, in spite of their human likeness, were entirely swept out of existence in a war of extermination waged by European immigrants, in the space of fifty years. Are we such apostles of mercy as to complain if the Martians warred in the same spirit?

ROOSEVELT
This is what we humans, a barbaric race still in its infancy had thought of the inhabitants of Martians.
(MORE)

(CONTINUED)

ROOSEVELT (CONT'D)
I am pleased to report, these fears have been sorely misplaced. There is little reason to believe that any advanced civilization would be inherently hostile. They have proven not to be. Humanity is still societally and technologically primitive. For any species to traverse the depths of interstellar space, they must have reached a level of sophistication and therefore peace. We, the leaders of the free world, have established a treaty with the planet Mars that will ensure peaceful relations between our two worlds as we humans strive to unite our world under the flag of the entire human race.

Those who have never seen a living Martian can scarcely imagine the strange horror of its appearance. The peculiar V-shaped mouth with its pointed upper lip, the absence of brow ridges, the absence of a chin beneath the wedgelike lower lip, the incessant quivering of this mouth, the Gorgon groups of tentacles, the tumultuous breathing of the lungs in a strange atmosphere, the evident heaviness and painfulness of movement due to the greater gravitational energy of the earth—above all, the extraordinary intensity of the immense eyes—were at once vital, intense, inhuman, crippled and monstrous. There was something fungoid in the oily brown skin, something in the clumsy deliberation of the tedious movements unspeakably nasty.

MARTIAN AMBASSADOR
Lorem ipsum dolor sit amet, consectetur adipisicing elit, sed do eiusmod tempor incididunt ut labore et dolore magna aliqua. Ut enim ad minim veniam, quis nostrud exercitation ullamco laboris nisi ut aliquip ex ea commodo consequat. Duis aute irure dolor in reprehenderit in voluptate velit esse cillum dolore eu fugiat nulla pariatur. Excepteur sint occaecat cupidatat non proident, sunt in culpa qui officia deserunt mollit anim id est laborum. Lorem ipsum dolor sit amet, consectetur adipiscing elit. Quisque vel ullamcorper sapien. Nam est justo, tincidunt in facilisis id, placerat ut lorem. Suspendisse eleifend lectus in auctor condimentum. Vivamus metus dui, rutrum ut ultrices ac, ornare non erat. Donec eu gravida nulla. Aenean massa neque, eleifend at erat et, consectetur hendrerit lacus. Nunc congue est ut aliquet rhoncus. Cras non luctus dolor.

CUT TO:

53 INT. CBS INTERVIEW ROOM - MORNING

Orson Welles, surrounded by a dozen or so reporters from every major New York newspaper, stands before a microphone. He is unshaven and his eyes are red from lack of sleep.

The reports begin in unison, clamoring for the first question.

ORSON WELLES
Do you want me to speak now?.. I'm sorry. We are deeply shocked and deeply regretful about the, uh, results of last night's broadcast. It came as rather a great surprise that a story, a fine H.G. Wells classic, would bring such a reaction.

REPORTER 1
Were you aware of the terror you were giving with this role? The terror going across the nation?

ORSON WELLES
Oh, no. Of course not. I was frankly, huh, terribly shocked to learn that, uh, it did. I anticipated nothing unusual.

REPORTER 3
Would you do the show over again?

ORSON WELLES
I won't say that I won't follow this technique again, as it is a legitimate dramatic form.

REPORTER 1
When were you first aware of the trouble caused?

ORSON WELLES
Immediately after the broadcast was finished when people told me of the large number of phone calls received.

REPORTER 2
Would you have toned down the language of the drama?

ORSON WELLES
No, you don't play murder in soft words. So, of course, I'm terribly sorry now.

FADE OUT.

THE END

Cinema Out of Time and Space

Great Movies by Roger Ebert

Written November 1, 1982, but never published in the Chicago Sun-Times, *nor any other publication.*

The invitation came in the mail. A boy from mail room the delivered the wax-sealed envelope to my editor's inbox at the *Chicago Sun-Times*. The letter contained a cryptic cypher as cryptic as any letter to from the Zodiac killer that haunted San Francisco newspapers and police offices. There was an unencrypted invitation addressed to me, and me alone. I found this situation haunting. The invitation instructed the recipient to call a phone number that had been encrypted behind the mysterious cypher.

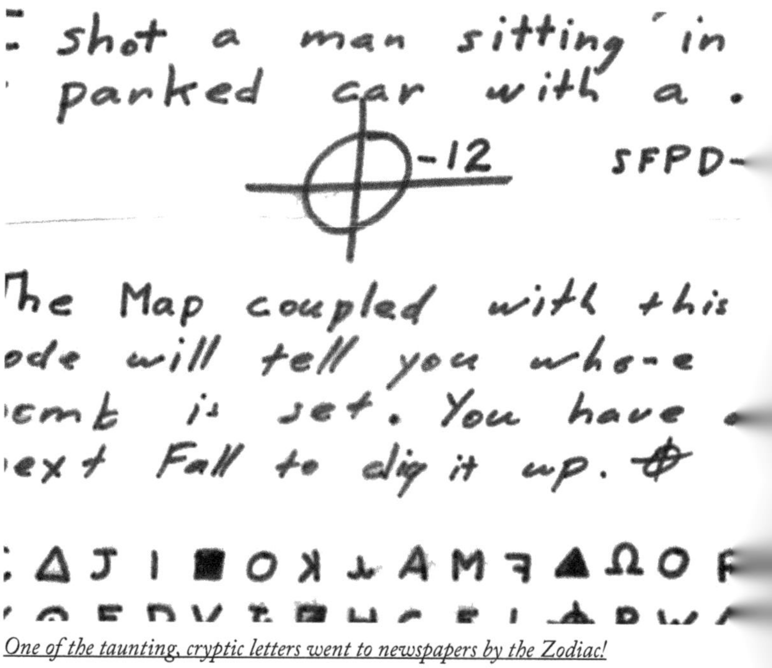
shot a man sitting in
parked car with a .
-12 SFPD-
he Map coupled with this
ode will tell you where
omb is set. You have
ext Fall to dig it up.

One of the taunting, cryptic letters went to newspapers by the Zodiac!

Why? If this had been sent by a serial-killer seeking attention, why send this encrypted message to a film critic and not– say– someone at the crime desk? There was a certain buzz around the press room. Was the *Chicago Sun-Times* about to become as famous, or infamous, as the *San Francisco Chronicle* or the *Examiner*? The crime desk didn't believe there were any outstanding unsolved murders that could be linked to a theoretical serial-killer. Who sat at the other side of the telephone lines that criss-cross the country? And why was their phone number such a secret that it was hidden behind a cypher.

I, however, was game. Sitting in the break room with a cypher book that I had a runner check out from the nearest library, I set out to decipher the code. It was only ten digits, the phone number and the area-code. Surely the cypher contained all numbers. How hard could this be? Harder than I thought. It wasn't a mere substitution cipher using the typical Latin alphabet. The symbols screamed the Zodiac Killer. Thankfully, my fellow reporters, many of whom would have normally spend their break filling out a crossword puzzle, gathered around me to point out this or point out that as a means to decipher the cypher. An old timer, who worked the sports desk and had served in the signal corps during World War II, deciphered it in mere moments saying we were stressing ourselves out over nothing because it was a surprisingly simple cypher despite the seeming complexity of the Zodiacness of the symbols. He mused that whoever had encrypted the phone number didn't wish me to fail.

Over the cryptic telephone call, the voice on the other end of the telephone line spoke with a deep-toned thundering voice, rich and rolling, resounding and resonating. It was voice that with hindsight being twenty-twenty I should have immediately put a face to– a jovial, bearded face to. However, there was a distance to the call that made reception ring hallow and remote, as if the call came from across the gulf of both Space and Time. I was asked if I would be open to screening a special feature film and produce a review of it in pages of the *Chicago Sun-Times*.

I agreed. I don't know why. Usually Hollywood feature films are screened to the press at special advanced screenings to allow us time to accurately and acutely criticize. I do not mean this negatively. The art of criticism is to criticize the flaws without hyperbole and laud the triumphs, likewise with out hyperbole, but with eloquence.

Though if I was aware of the harrowing experience I was about to– well– experience, I would have hung up of the telephone and dismissed the call as a prank. And knowing what I know now, it could all have been a colossal prank. I no longer have quite the firm grasp on reality that I possessed only twenty-four hours ago.

A car pulled up in from the office of *Sun-Times*, the driver opened the rear-passenger door and I stepped into the car. The car drove to O'Hare and there I boarded a private jet. To call it a jet would be inaccurate. It was a nothing more than a puddle jumper with thirteen seats. Yes, I counted them. Yes, in that moment I was a touch superstitious.

When I asked the pilots where they were flying to me, I was met with silence, an uncomfortable silence, a silence that screamed for me to disembark immediately. But I sat in my seat and a lovely stewardess took my drink order.

As I looked out of the plane, my spatial sense was completely disoriented. Due to the low hanging dark, ominous cloud-cover that afternoon three days ago (October 30, 1982), I was unable to discern where north, south, east, or west was without the sun to guide me like a sailor on a long sea voyage. There was a remarkable amount of turbulence about an hour into the flight, with a rainbow colored lightning show out of the window that would have made Douglas Trumbull, the special-effect director of *2001: A Space Odyssey*, insanely jealous. But we made it through the storm safe and sound.

The plane landed at a remarkably small airport and another car, an

Small Colorado steel mill town cinema with large city marquee!

automobile plucked from the 1930's, picked me up and drove into the small, quaint, picturesque mountain town. The car pulled up to a small one screen movie theater that still was showing (at least according to the marque) *Casablanca*. The theatre must have been having a special screening of the movie, because that particular iconic film had originally debuted in theaters on November 25, 1942.

Walking into the small, quaint, picturesque small mountain cinema house was like walking into a time capsule. The concession area was stocked with Almond Joys, Licorice twists, Bit O' Honeys, Chick O Sticks, Mike & Ikes, Dots, Junior Mints, and Bun Maples, all in classic, very retro packaging. When was the last time I tasted some of these treats? I couldn't remember. My childhood perhaps? But I requested and was provided many of the trips-down-memorylane, along with hot buttered popcorn and a Coca-Cola. A young lady, dressed as a cigarette girl from an albeit family-friendly speakeasy, wore a tray around her neck that contained an assortment of parody boxes of candy cigarettes and bubble gun cigars.

In the already darkened theater, I sat in my customary location. I try, though am not always successful, to sit in the same general location in every theater I sit in. Some movie-goers like to sit in the third-row-center, others like the back row where fellow audience members can't see them "sucking face" with their girlfriend, and others like to sit in those two strange, nearly empty rows at the front of the theater with their necks strained impossibly upwards. I hunkered down in my preferred location with my selection of hot-buttery popcorn, ice-cold soda, and sweet-sugary candy.

Then the picture began.

My mind immediately flashed back to the scene in *Citizen Kane* where the reporters viewed the "March of Time" newsreel footage and debated the meaning of "Rosebud". There were no other film critics assembled to watch this "special" screening alongside myself. In fact, there was nobody else present in the room. The room possessed a disconcerting loneliness.

"A Mercury Production by Orson Welles", say no more!

A few minutes after taking my seat. The film began and when I saw what I saw, I seemingly sucked all of the air out of the room with my surprised inhalation. I was gobsmacked when the plate "A MERCURY PRODUCTION by Orson Welles" projected onto the screen. Was this a long lost Orson Welles motion picture? My mysterious benefactors wouldn't have gone through the trouble and expense to have me watch a film I had already seen. In the few moments that the plate was on screen, my mind raced. What lost Orson Welles film could this be? I first thought was Orson Welles' original cut of *Touch of Evil*. But that cut not longer exists. Unless it does and I was about to watch it. But *Touch of Evil* was not a Mercury Production, it was a Universal-International production. What in the blue blazes what I about to watch?

Since this film was a Mercury Production, could this be the original Wellesian cut of *The Magnificent Ambersons*? That was certainly the most plausible possibility. The list of all the films that Orson Welles began, but never finished is such a long, sublime list of lost motion pictures.

What could this motion-picture possibly be? And why was I invited rather than say— Peter [redacted], who would have enjoyed this motion-picture equally if not more than I would? Perhaps Peter [redacted] was the source, having found this lost Orson Welles film. Did he stand hidden and secluded in the projection room watching me through the window intent of observing my every reaction.

In my flabbergasted, time-deflation state, the MERCURY PRODUCTION plate slowly faded out and the title-plate appeared, signaling finally what lost Orson Welles motion picture I was about to see. My mind could not comprehend what I saw. I was like an ant trying to comprehend a discarded candy-wrapper. I was greeted with "INVASION FROM MARS". This singular title-plate destroyed every conception I had of Hollywood history. This simply was not possible. Orson Welles had never– ever– directed a film-adaptation of his controversial and seminal "War of the Worlds" radio-dramatization.

Or did he?

No! This simply was not possible. There is no point in his filmography that an *Invasion From Mars* could have been inserted. How many film experts and film students have chronicled Welles' career practically down to the day. There is no point in the calendar of Orson Welles' chronology that he could have filmed *Invasion from Mars.*

None. Absolutely none. Zip. Nada.

What follows is, to the best of my ability, a true and proper review of the movie, as true and proper as any movie screened for reviewers for publication that coming Friday morning. This movie review will not be published in any edition of the *Chicago Sun-Times*, because I can't honestly tell you the film I watched wasn't result a schizophrenic hallucination or a fever-upon-the-brain, like an undigested bit of beef, a blot of mustard, a crumb of cheese, a fragment of underdone potato (my apoligies to Dickens).

In what parallel reality did I enter during my plane-flight to find myself watching a film by Orson Welles about an *Invasion From Mars* that told the story of his infamous "War of the Worlds" radio-dramatization, while simultaneously not being an adaptation Howard Koch's famous (copywritten) script. What was this *Invasion From Mars* being told by the writer-director Orson Welles, about the radio-producer Orson Welles, starring an actor who wasn't actually Orson Welles playing Orson Welles?

I don't know what I just typed.

The teaser, the brief scene which opened the picture, gave a voyeuristic peak into the CBS studios that cold, windy October 30th evening (31st morning?!?) where conspiracies were flung about like feces as the monkey house in the zoo and from which the infamous, purported, "Rosebud" was uttered on a close-up of the very feminine, very red lips of Marion Davies.

"Rosebud", the name of Charles Fosters Kane's sled, an emblem of the security, hope, and innocence of childhood, which a man can spend his life seeking to regain, is used, in another

The infamous childhood sled of Charles Foster Kane in Citizen Kane!

far more erotic context, to blackmail William Randolph Hearst into giving the golden keys of Hollywood to a young, idealistic Orson Welles?

Then... THEN... (how often will I be tempted to repeat this *ad nauseum*)... There the Orson Welles from 1938 is convinced by an Orson Welles from 1942 to acquiesce to a conspiracy between President Roosevelt, WR Hearst, and himself that cold, windy October evening four years previous.

What was the origin to such a strange, incomprehensible plot? The plot of the "movie" I watched had as much to do with HG Wells' *The Time-Machine* as it did HG Wells' *The War of the Worlds*. Was Orson going to draw inspiration from all of HG Wells writings? Would his film feature an invisible man or a human-animal hybrids from *The Island of Doctor Moreau*? There were no lows too low for Orson Welles to stoop.

I could easily imagine Charles Koerner at RKO Radio-Pictures sitting a young Orson Welles down and explaining to him that Howard Koch has copyrighted the now infamous "War of the Worlds" radio-script and now refused to release the film rights to the radio-dramatization to be adapted to the silver screen. Incensed by his once faithful colleague's refusal to allow a slightly older, but certainly no less idealistic Orson Welles to film *The War of the Worlds*, based on the radio-script Orson Welles himself commissioned Howard Koch to write. Orson would have wanted the credit for "The War of the Worlds" radio-drama just as he desired credit on *Citizen Kane*. I could easily hear Orson protest in his now agitated rich, rolling baritone, "Wasn't the radio-script a 'work-for-hire' and why was Howard [Koch] making [Orson Welles] jump through these ridiculous hoops?"

Howard Koch had the audacity to copyright the playscript for Orson Welles seminal "War of the Worlds" radio-dramatization! The nerve!

Orson Welles, I could easily see have successfully countered Howard Koch's attempt at a financial Checkmate, "Howard Koch doesn't own the invasion from Mars motif. That is original with HG Welles. We can set our picture during October 30, 1938, but with... with... what...?" As a studio lawyer sitting in on the meeting would note that Howard Koch only owns the "copyright in the play, i.e., the specific expression in words that Howard Koch wrote. He does not own the recorded sounds of the radio broadcast, Orson Welles's voice or persona nor that of any other historic person, or the historic facts of the broadcast or its aftermath, so you need no license from him to recount them or comment on them or ridicule them (or any other historic figures or institutions you might write about)."

The key word "ridicule". Orson would "ridicule" the entire "War of the Worlds" panic broadcast by writing his own original "panic" broadcast", a script that would cause executives at RKO Radio-Pictures to themselves panic, just as I was panicking watching a *War of the Worlds* feature-film that nobody until this very moment add even postulated even existed.

If Orson Welles was going to lampoon his own now sacrosanct radio-script, which was now under the lock-and-key of Howard Koch's copyright, he would need other characters other than those created for the original, landmark, and copywritten "Panic Broadcast". Instead of drawing on original, landmark, and copywritten creations like Carl Phillips, Prof. Richard Pierson, Mr. Wilmuth, and the fascist stranger, Orson would use actual, historical persons to tell his new *War of the Worlds* feature-film: Hans Von Kaltenborn, Prof. Arthur Buddington, Edward R. Marrow, William Paley, Davidson Taylor, William Randolph Hearst!, Marion Davies!!, General George Patton!!!, and President Franklin Delano Roosevelt?!?!?– *whew!*

How far would this creative freight-train continue before it spun out of control, rocketing down a parallel set of mountain tracks, approaching a bend and a bridge, before it derailed into... madness?

The film itself is exquisite first generation Orson Welles. The skills he acquired during *Citizan Kane* were only honed to a razor's edge for this *Invasion From Mars* motion picture. He seemed to have something to prove. To someone. Maybe even to himself. Yes, Orson Welles had proven he could make a remarkable first picture with *Citizen Kane*, But with his *Invasion From Mars*, he needed to not only make a great (only) third motion-picture, but one that he could finally step out from the shadows cast by the infamy of his "War of the Worlds" radio-dramatization. He used every technique he learned making *Citizan Kane* and added the wondrous colors of Technicolor to his palette. And the means to which he would meet these ends is unlike anything I could have comprehended even the most paranoid of schizophrenics dreaming in a paranoia-induced hallucinogenic stupor.

This film, Orson Welles' film, purported to be a true reenactment of an evening of dance music being interrupted by famed radio-journalist Hans Von Kaltenborn's reports of a Martian invasion of (not Grover's Mill, NJ, but) Grove Hill, Virgina and them march of the Martian tri-pod walking machines on Washington DC. When the "actual" invasion from Mars is defeated, via a *deus ex machina* (of course "Orson Welles" would use that literally ancient theatrical technique!), there would be a conspiracy between President Franklin Delano Roosevelt and William Randolph Hearst that would ensnare a young Orson Welles in the vast government conspiracy to cover-up the invasion from Mars.

Was Nikola Tesla inspired by the works of HG Wells to create an actual, functioning time-machine that ended the Martian invasion?!?

In *Citizen Kane*, flashbacks were utilized as a core storytelling mechanic. Orson Welles expertly jumped back and forth through time to tell the story of the life of Charles Foster Kane. In *Invasion From Mars*, "Orson Welles" trumps himself with the utilization of literal time travel. The character "Orson Welles" uses time travel invented by Nikola Tesla (quite fitting actually given the real-world inventions created by the super genius) to jump back and forth through time, bending and twisting the narrative into something so akin to *Citizen Kane* that it would smack of self-plagiarism from anyone else!

Science-fiction writers have "invented" a myriad of technologies decades before scientists recreated them in the real-world. By exploiting Nikola Tesla's penchant for creating real-world inventions that even science-fiction writers' wild imaginations could not has possible conceived of, "Orson Welles" was able to include a *deus ex machina* (ἀπὸ μηχανῆς θεός or *apò mēkhanês theós* or 'god from the machine') that would have made the ancient Greek playwright Euripides supremely jealous.

Nikola Tesla's inventions were decades (nay centuries) ahead of their time that he frightened the whits out of fair goers at the Worlds Fair!

Should I mention "Orson Welles" (yes, the quotation marks are intentional) employment of Technicolor? The real Orson Welles greatly disliked color in film. He famously opined (for his opinions were infamous), "[C]olor, you know, is a great friend in need to the cameraman but it's an enemy of the actor. Faces in color tend to look like meat — veal, beef, baloney—" Does makeup even help, one might ask? But this would, no doubt be his answer: "Makes it worse. Only hope is no makeup." He filmed in black-and-white decades after black-and-white had faded into the art-scene, saying "I think every really great performance that's ever happened in movies — has been in black-and-white. But then, you know my feeling about the importance of actors. They're the ones who finally count. Much more than people think." Then *why* with the choice and his expertise in black-and-white filmmaking at his fingertips would he harness the powers of Technicolor for "his" *Invasion From Mars*? *Perhaps*, it was because science-fiction almost requires a science-fictional technique. Technicolor was so new and unnatural despite being hailed as "Technicolor is natural color". In 1942, that most film-goers could not comprehend the technology. Black-and-white movies and personal photographs were still the norm. When the *Wizard of Oz* expertly transitioned from the black-and-white of Uncle Henry's farm to the Techincolor of Oz, audiences in August of 1939 must have been gob-smacked, and even a little bit frightened. What mad scientist created this science-fictional technology?

I didn't know she had red hair
Technicolor is natural color
SOME OF THE TECHNICOLOR PRODUCTIONS

This is the greatest argument that the real Orson Welles never filmed the motion picture that was being screened for me in his small Colorado town. Whoever filmed this picture was Method-directing in the famed style of Konstantin Stanislavski. Many actors over the decades have Method-acted in films, much to the detriment of their fellow actors' performances and enjoyment of the filming process? How many motion pictures have been Method-directed in the style of another director? The first name that comes to mind is Alfred Hitchcock. How many directors have aped the Hitchcockian-style in these later years? Far too many to count.

Taking this motion picture at face-value for a moment, I'm not sure the executives at RKO Pictures understood completely what Orson Welles was pitching in the treatment for his *Invasion From Mars* feature-film. Was this possibly the film he wanted to make? Could Herman J. Mankiewicz pull himself from the bottle long enough to render such a plot into a screenplay? Of course not. Orson would find the solution not in the bottom of a three-fingers of scotch, but an unknown screenwriter with no other apparent screen credits (I know. I looked), one "William Francis Brown".

Who was "William Francis Brown" to have been plucked from obscurity to pen an adaptation of Orson Welles infamous "War of the Worlds" radio-dramatization? Did the ignominy of being associated with the boy-wonder Orson Welles torpedo his Hollywood career? Or maybe he choose a pen-name to function for the rest of his career. The list of potential *nom-de-plumes* is perhaps too numerous to name here. But here are a couple off the top of my head: Dalton Trumbo or a very, very young Truman Capote? They would have been capable of writing this movie. But the blacklist was still a decade away and Trumbo would have had no need of a *nom-de-plume* to continue writing in Hollywood.

But back to the executives at RKO, how in the blue blazes did this motion picture, in this current form, get authorized? It is well known in Hollywood circles that Louis B. Meyer offered Orson Welles an MGM contract after the dual-debacle of *Citizen Kane* and the *Magnificent Ambers* if, and only if, he filmed an adaptation of his "War of the Worlds" radio-dramatization. This was the only film that Meyer wanted from Orson and if Orson refused (which he historically did) then he could pound bricks. And Orson did in fact pound bricks for the rest of his Hollywood career. Without the support of the studio system, Orson would flail from production to production, very seldom producing a finished product. And those that were finished, the cut was taken away from him like in *Touch of Evil*.

Then how was this film, that nobody in history, not even the most fastidious Hollywood historian has made even the slightest note about, come to be projected onto the screen before my very eyes? Wasn't he in Brazil during this time having been appointed goodwill ambassador to Latin America by Nelson Rockefeller, US Coordinator of Inter-American Affairs? Was he not asked by the Brazilian government to produce a documentary of the annual Rio Carnival celebration taking place in early February 1942? Did he not record radio programs, give lectures, interviews and informal talks as part of his OCIAA-sponsored cultural mission during his time in Brazil. Time that he was simultaneously filming a motion-picture in Hollywood, California, sixty-three hundred miles away!

Orson Welles "allegedly" in Brazil during the time he would have filmed his Invasion From Mars *feature film! Lies, I tell you! Lies!*

The answers to these and other certainly more important questions I simply do not have an answer for. Not one that would make an lick of sense. The only other option, the only

Did Timothy Leary dose Roger Ebert's popcorn in a small Colorado town's single-screen movie theater? Maybe! Perhaps! Yes? No!

plausible answer, was that my popcorn wasn't coated in golden butter but with *lysergic acid diethylamide* (or LSD for those readers not reared in the progressive 1960's). And I was having one of the most wondrous trips, one that would have made Timothy Leary jealous. The giddiness I was experiencing watching this so-called "Mercury Production" boarded on intoxication. The thought did cross my mind that I was sitting in an empty theatre having been dosed with LSD and the film that was being projected onto the screen wasn't actually being projected. This entire experience was a psychedelic hallucination. While I may have never participated with this aspect of the Counter Culture revolution, I knew very well what the effects of LSD were. And I was experiencing many of the very same symptoms. Oh! Woe is me! Is experiencing this "Orson Welles" film intoxication!

I couldn't help smiling as I wiped the tears of sheer joy from my eyes at this temporal gift!

It was a wondrous film. A film unlike any other from the lens of Orson Welles, but could come from none other's lens. It was Wellesian in its Wellesness. So very much so. Could I put away the quotation marks and state rather emphatically that this was an Orson Welles directed "Mercury Production"? I know this is blasphemy for a film critic to hail a "lost" *War of the Worlds* feature as authentic. Did I have the experience or clout to rubber-stamp this film as an Orson Welles production? No. Of course not. The only person in the Hollywood sphere that could authenticate this motion picture is Peter ██████. His close personal friendship with Orson Welles makes me insanely jealous. Only Peter ██████ would be able to put his seal of authenticity on this film. Other than Orson Welles, of course, but it would be easier for me to get an audience with Pope John Paul II than get an audience with Orson Welles to prove once-and-for-all that this motion picture I was watching was the real McCoy. Which it wasn't. Which I couldn't've been!

Willie Brown's (or is it Harry Lime's) headshot commissioned by Orson Welles to further his conspiracy against RKO executives!

When the house-lights came up, the room appeared smoke-filled. There stood a young man, no more than eighteen-years-of-age, yet paradoxically looked almost like an old man having been stretched naturally through the manipulation of time. Bright eyes were made brighter by the addition of wire-rimmed glassed. His smile was open and relaxed as if daft but the narrowness of brow proved the intelligence just below the surface. What caught the eye most was his hair. Locks so silky they could almost be viewed as feminine. His forelock rose straight up from his broad but not tall forehead and made two silky waves before traveling to the back of his head.

Was this the actual director of the film? Of course, the film I had just watched could not have been filmed with Orson Welles sitting in the director's chair. This young man, no doubt, a film student at one of the more prestigious film schools had produced this hoax as his senior film thesis. This had to be the Method-director! "Of course," I exclaimed in my head. This reeked of a student film project that grew simply out of control. How did a film-student produce such a film. The film did not require a special effects budget because all of the special-effect happened off-screen. All of the film locations, a film student could have had access to. A ballroom is a ballroom. An office is an office. There was a logical explanation for all of the locations. And as the for actors, none were known actors. This young man could have easily hired C-list Hollywood actors and even community theater actors to populate this production. This was my Occam's razor moment. This being a student film was the easiest explanation, and then being a student film was the most likely explanation!

Orson Welles sitting in the office of the Colorado cinema with a copy of his Invasion From Mars *script propped on his lap!*

But... Then... BUT.... THEN...

Light ushered into the cinema from the newly opened door at the back of the auditorium, and I turned and my mind could not grasp what– who– I was seeing. Had the film-student behind this strange, wonderful recreation of a film that was never crafted by the hands of the supreme visionary director of the 20th century, hired a look-alike actor to continue this charade? But I would swear to you, the newspaper audience who will never have an opportunity to read these words, that there stood a twenty-seven-year-old Orson Welles, looking as fresh off the turnip truck as he did when he first descended the steps from a Howard Hughes chartered Trans World Airlines' Boeing 307 Stratoliner, planting his flag in Hollywood as the golden boy with the keys to the city.

This "Orson Welles" greeted me with his "deep-toned thundering voice, rich and rolling, resounding and resonating" as I had described the voice on the phone. He said, "Mr. Ebert, thank you for coming such a long distance." Did he mean miles or...years?!? Or BOTH! I did not know. I could *not* know! "I hope you will devote the energy and passion to my *Invasion From Mars* picture that you have given to my *Citizen Kane* as one of your man 'Great Movie' reviews." How could a twenty-seven year-old "Orson Welles" know about film reviews that wouldn't be reviewed for several decades? He added, "I've listened to the audio commentary track you recorded for *Citizen Kane* when released on Digital Versatile Disc and I was impressed by your insight into my film. It was quite an educational experience. Peter must be proud to have shared the disc with you." What is an audio-commentary track? On Digital Versatile Disc? I didn't know if there was such a thing possible. And I haven't recorded any audio-commentary track for *Citizen Kane* either on Laserdisc or this Digital Versatile Disc yet. What would account for this discrepancy? Time-travel? A *deus ex machina*? Absurd! Preposterous! Foolish! Bizarre! Strange! Weird! Fantastical! Insane! Unbelievable! Funny! Humorous! And any other synonym I can find in *Roget's Thesaurus*! Words for once have failed me!

I asked "Orson Welles" if I could view the picture again. Would that be even possible? "Orson" laughed his deep baritone laugh, "Yes! It is certainly possible to rethread the film and watch it again and again and again if you so desire. It is certainly possible for someone who has traveled not only a thousand miles from Chicago to Colorado, but also forty years into past. You have," Orson Welles smiled and a glint of light flashed off of one of his fore-teeth, "all the time in the world."

Did Roger Ebert ever consider publishing this "Great Movies" article concerning the mysterious "lost" Orson Welles' Invasion From Mars *motion picture during his lifetime; or did he prefer waiting for me to publish once he was in the safety of death. Then he would be safely free from the intimidation of United States of America espionage agencies? Probably the later.*

1942
a space
conspiracy
SIDE NO. 1

THE MAN FROM M.A.R.S.

Martians? American Retaliation & Supression

ORSON: Welcome back, Peter, it's good to see you again. I see you're champing at the bit to continue our conversation about... *dun...dun...dun...* The Day the Earth Misunderstood!

PETER: It's... it's... been a year. You've been keeping me waiting for an entire year. Twelve months. Three hundred and sixty-five days. Eight thousand, seven hundred, and sixty hours. Five hundred twenty-five thousand, six hundred minutes. Only to once again summon me again on Mischief Night 1979! Of all three hundred and sixty-five possible nights of the year you chose Mischief Night! Again!

ORSON: It seems to be the most appropriate night.

PETER: We may both be a year older, Orson, but you aren't a year wiser.

ORSON: I see you've got your trusty note-cards all ready with questions to pose this evening? I'm ready to give you all the answers to need.

PETER: Answers? You didn't give any answers a year ago. All I've got were more questions. And when I listened to the reel-to-reels, all I got even more questions. There aren't any answers to be found!

ORSON: That's why we're here tonight, Peter. I'm going to give you the answers!

PETER: And your answers to my questions are just going to pose more questions. Are we going to end up here again on Mischief Night 1980?

ORSON: And how is that a bad thing, my friend?

PETER: I don't want to end this evening without having reached the the end of the third act. I want– I need– to be able to put a distinct "The End" to this entire episode after tonight. *Finish. Finale.*

ORSON: That seems a reasonable request.

PETER: Are we... are we... are we.. are we going to find out this very night–

- How did the interrogation of Willie Brown end?
- Was Willie able to get away from the government agents and if so, did he help finish the film?
- If you filmed the film, that you say you not only filmed but finished, then where is the film?
- Why hasn't it been seen since? Is it locked away in a vault or was it burnt as William Randolph Hearst demanded of *Citizen Kane?*
- Did anyone ever actually see it? And if so, whom?
- Did the editors edit it?
- Did RKO executives screen it?
- How many saw it with their very eyes?
- What about the evidence the government found in the bungalow in Victorville? Did the government ever use this evidence against you in a court of law?
- Did the government realize that Willie Brown had lied to them? Did they return to interrogate him about his lies and complicity in your conspiracy to film your version of events?
- Did the government agents discover that Willie Brown and Harry Lime were one-and-the-same? That it was entirely a ruse to flout them and flaunt your arrogance?
- Did you eventually show the film to RKO President Charles Koerner? What was his reaction?
- Did he rain down hellfire and brimstone upon you? Of course, he did. Of this I have no doubt.
- Or did you find some way of talking yourself out of being fired on the spot? Why weren't you fired?
- Why weren't you sued for stealing studio funds to produce a fraudulent and ultimately failed feature?
- And how exactly did you try to convince Charles Koerner to release a film that we now know was never actually released?
- Why wasn't there the glitz and glamour of a Hollywood premiere at Grauman's Chinese Theatre with a cavalcade of the Who's Who of Hollywood? Was this the steep price you paid for producing the fraudulent feature?
- And once FDR and WRH realized the film was

filmed and finished, what did they do? Why weren't you hounded by government agents and Hearst's reporters to the ends of the earth? Surely, Hearst's reporters were more cunning than the agents of Roosevelt.

- What happened to the rest of the "Orson Welles' Conspiracy"?

ORSON: Most certainly.

PETER: But coming into our third act, I can't seem to recall anything from the first.

ORSON: Allow me to summarize.

PETER: Thank you.

ORSON: Together, that evening one year ago, we learned during the slow crawl of text scrolling up and away from the science-fiction-serial-adoring-audience that on October 30, 1938, the night of the 'Panic Broadcast', the radio reports of a Martian invasion were REAL! And since memories of this event have been erased from history, what *actually* happened? The short answer is there was a conspiracy, an "Orson Welles' Conspiracy", between President Franklin Delano Roosevelt, media magnate William Randolph Hearst, and a naïve and impressionable Orson Welles. Together the three of us conspired to deny the reality of the radio reports. One of us (and I'll give you three guesses who, but you'll only need one) conceived of a fictitious "War of the Worlds" radio-dramatization having been broadcast on CBS's airwaves instead of the oh-so-real Martian invasion. With Roosevelt's power over the government and with Hearst's power over the press and with my power over radio no one in the past forty years– correction, forty-*one* years– has had any inkling that there was a very real Martian invasion.

PETER: Oh, Orson, not this horse-hockey again!

ORSON: So complete was our conspiracy. So foolproof was my fictional and ultimately fictitious recording of an invasion from Mars with my Mercury players. So insidious was our cover-up. So quickly and quietly did Roosevelt order the US military to remove all evidence of the Martian walkers. So easily did the general public dismiss the structural damage as the result of the natural "Long Island Express" hurricane.

PETER: Wait! What? The destruction wrought by the Martians was blamed on a hurricane? Was there actually a hurricane, Orson? Or was this another creation of your overactive imagination? I don't believe a hurricane really struck the east coast of America, just as I don't believe in this Martian invasion you keep harping on. When did this hurricane strike? And how much damage did it do to warrant inclusion in your "Orson Welles' Conspiracy"?

The utter destruction wrought by during the invasion was not blamed on Martians but a hurricane called the "Long Island Express"!

ORSON: Sooo, let me pause my poetic and pedantic exposition to answer your questions. A hurricane struck the east coast of the United States on September 22, 1938, over a month before the Martian invasion stuck the same east coast. Named the "Long Island Express" because it barreled up the east coast with an unstoppable fury. The "Express" was "one deadliest and most destructive tropical cyclones to strike the United States... The hurricane killed 682 people, damaged or destroyed more than 57,000 homes, and caused property losses estimated at $306 million." At least according to an encyclopedia passage I have memorized.

PETER: Of course you do. Curse that eidetic memory of yours.

ORSON: While most of America was entirely oblivious to the very existence of the Martian invasion, so the

Do not believe the lies! The hurricane struck on September 22, 1938, while the Martians invaded on October 30! Six weeks! Six weeks!

clean-up crews authorized by President Roosevelt believed they were cleaning up after the hurricane and not a Martian invasion. The press controlled by William Randolph Hearst reported on the destruction caused by a hurricane and not a Martian invasion. It is amazing how the American people are so gullible...

PETER: Orson!

ORSON: ... I mean, accepting ... the American people were accepting of the government's lies...

PETER: Orson!

ORSON: ... before the assassination of President John F. Kennedy...

PETER: Not this again.

ORSON: ... that they accepted the hurricane cover-up story so completely that there is no collective memory of the Martian invasion. No one has questioned this, not even the most para–

PETER: "Paranoid of schizophrenics has even conceived of the possibility that Martians actually landed on the east coast of the United States on Halloween Eve 1938." I know. I know.

ORSON: What you don't know or don't yet realize is clean-up crews did their jobs so systematically that even if archaeologists went looking for evidence of the Martian invasion today, they would find nothing! The press did their jobs so comprehensively that the collective memories of the Martian invasion were overdubbed– for lack of a better word... no that is the perfect word, actually– with my radio-dramatization.

PETER: Lord, deliver me from this evil!

ORSON: Sooo through was Hearst's whitewashing that the press (both from his own newspapers and from his rivals), across the nation printed "fake news" headlines: **"FAKE RADIO WAR STIRS TERROR THROUGH US" "Radio Listeners in Panic, Taking War Drama as Fact" "RADIO PLAY TERRIFIES NATION" "War of the Worlds" Broadcast Creates Panic In The East" "US PROBES 'INVASION BROADCAST; RADIO PLAY CAUSES WIDE PANIC" "War Skit On Radio Terrifies Nation" "OTTAWA SEEKS WAY TO BAN RADIO 'HORRORS'" "'Mars Invasion' In Radio Hoax Terrifies US"** So sacrilegious was our dismissal of all of the dead who died during an interplanetary invasion. *[Peter sighs.].* Soooooo– *[Orson clicks on the reel-to-reel.]* Let's continue with we left off with the continuation of Willie Brown's being interrogated by the Man from M.A.R.S....

PETER: Wait a cockamamie second, Orson! I thought Willie Brown was the "Man From M.A.R.S.". You know as in the acronym "Martians! American Resistance Syndicate". Now you're saying Agent Ecks is "Man From M.A.R.S."? This is a cavernous plot hole in your entire "Orson Welles' Conspiracy"!

ORSON: There is not "cavernous" plot hole as you so eloquently put it. The acronym clearly stands for "Martians? American Retaliation and Suppression". Willie Brown has never been the "Man From M.A.R.S.". Agent Ecks is part of the government cabal of "Men From M.A.R.S.." Always was and always will be.

PETER: You can't even keep your plot consistent with all of these continuity errors. I know very well that you are a stickler for continuity errors in motion pictures. You'll rant and rave as you exit a cinema having seen even a minor continuity error. It is one of your major pet peeves. And here you are not acknowledging this glaring continuity error. How did the "Man From M.A.R.S." go from "Martians! American Resistance Syndicate" to "Martians? American Retaliation and Suppression"? Orson?

ORSON: I see no continuity error in my story. Either you misheard or you misremember. It has been literally one year since we last spoke. The passage of time has scrabbled your memory, like eggs for breakfast. Can I continue with the reel-to-reel of Willie Brown being interrogated by the "Man From M.A.R.S."?

PETER: *[Loudly sighs.]*

Willie Brown, a mole in Orson Welles' production, remained in constant telephone contact with William Randolph Hearst!

WILLIE: *[Pregnant pause.]* You don't have any idea who I really am, do you?

AGENT ECKS: Like you said. You are nothing more than a Hollywood script doctor without a single screen-credit to your name. A nobody.

WILLIE: My name is William Francis Brown. This is a name that you are not going to readily forgot. Once my employer discovers how I have been treated this evening, this interrogation will cost you your careers.

AGENT ECKS: Who is your employer? Who has the power to cost me my job?

WILLIE: Earlier you asked, and most certainly forgot you asked where I was the night Martians invaded America. I was at the Ballroom in the Hotel Annapolis in Washington DC. I was responsible for bringing Guy Lombardo and his orchestra to the radio public that evening.

AGENT ECKS: You brought him and his orchestra to the radio?

WILLIE: Not precisely. I was the one tasked with locating a notable big-band leader to bring his orchestra to the Ballroom at the Hotel Annopolis in Washington DC for an evening of dance music. The star of Ontario was worth the extravagance of the plane fare. My employer was more than pleased with my selection.

AGENT ECKS: Who exactly was your employer?

WILLIE: *Is* my employer.

AGENT ECKS: Who exactly *is* your employer?

WILLIE: William Randolph Hearst.

AGENT ECKS: The newspaper magnate?

WILLIE: Now, before I get to how you just lost your job this evening, let us go back in time four years to that cold, October evening, shall we?

AGENT ECKS: *[Chuckles.]* Fine. Go ahead. *[Chuckles.]*

WILLIE: William Randolph Hearst had the *Mercury Theater on the air* preempted for an evening of dance music.

AGENT ECKS: I'll bite. Why would he do such a thing? Wouldn't he detest and despise radio?

WILLIE: He did, in fact, detest and despise radio with every fiber in his being. He saw radio as nothing but old vaudevillians and talentless hacks. Radio was not news. He, of course, knew news. He *made* news. Radio was nothing but claptrap.

AGENT ECKS: Then why would Hearst want an evening of dance music broadcast on the radio?

WILLIE: Every once in a while, he liked to see the sun rise from over the ocean rather than the mountain tops surrounding San Simeon.

AGENT ECKS: That doesn't answer my question.

WILLIE: Yes, it does. With the war looming on the European continent and isolationism raging in America, he thought it was good for those of them that have to give to those who have not. But he hated being the center of attention. Radio could be quietly anonymous. He could host a five-hundred dollar a plate dinner and an evening of dance music for the elite of Washington DC in the privacy of the Ballroom at the Hotel Annapolis in Washington DC. The music everyone in the Ballroom would have had listened to that evening would be broadcast all over the country thanks to Mr. William Paley and his CBS radio stations. Guy Lombardo and his orchestra provided the evening's dance music.

AGENT ECKS: And why would he do all of this?

WILLIE: So that he could bring a message from a most honored guest that evening. Franklin Delano Roosevelt. Surely, you heard of him.

AGENT ECKS: What? Who? The President? I don't understand.

WILLIE: Most of America was used to his fireside chats from the White House. But that night, he had been invited by WR to a grand masquerade ball to listen to eloquent music, to dance, and to bring charity to a great cause: Infantile Paralysis. The next day, hordes of young children, in all manner of ghoulish and ghastly dress, would have walked up to America's front door to ask for small candies, chocolates, popcorn balls, and candied apples. But as the citizens always give out those cherished childhood treats, they needed to take a moment to remember those poor innocent children who cannot walk up to your door. Those struck down with Infantile Paralysis. Early that year radio personality and philanthropist Eddie Cantor urged all Americans to send their loose change to the President in "a march of dimes to reach all the way to the White House." So... In sending in a dime and in dancing that others may walk, they would be striking a powerful blow in defense of American freedom and human decency.

AGENT ECKS: That was mighty kind of Mr. Hearst.

WILLIE: So to answer your question about where I was on October 30, 1938... I was at the epicenter of the entire "Orson Welles' Conspiracy". I was in the ballroom when Hans Von Kaltenborn broadcast the harrowing reports of a Martian invasion and I was present in CBS studios when my boss, William Randolph Hearst conspired with a young Orson Welles to be part of a vast government conspiracy!

AGENT ECKS: *[After pregnant pause!.]* But... but... that does not (if you can call it a confession) explains why you are working with Orson Welles on a *War of the Worlds* feature.

WILLIE: Do you honestly believe that the Federal Bureau of Investigation and to a much larger extent the entire United States government are the only entities with undercover agents, with a network of spies, and in possession of dossiers filled to overflowing with blackmailable secrets? If so, then you have never worked in the newspaper game. We are the masters of acquiring information. We learn the secrets people do not wish disclosed for public consumption; we tell the stories people don't want told but the readers desperately need told to them. *You* acquire the secrets of the American populous for the benefit of policies and politics. *We* acquire the secrets of the famous and the infamous for the benefit of the American people. We do it all on the front page, and not in the hidden in the dark and dank bowels of government buildings.

AGENT ECKS: Are you saying you're involved in corporate espionage?

WILLIE: No. Not in the slightest. What I am saying is... I am currently embroiled in journalistic espionage. I have gone undercover for my employer in order to stop Orson Welles for sullying the good name of William Randolph Hearst for the second time is so many years. Orson Welles has an unhealthy obsession with besmirching the Hearst name and legacy. And the Old Man does not take kindly to people who besmirch the Hearst name. If the Old Man has the power to get away with the literal murder of Thomas Ince then he has the power to get away with the figurative murder of Orson Wells.

AGENT ECKS: What murder are you talking about? I've never heard that Hearst murdered someone.

WILLIE: His murder of Thomas Ince, the famous

INCE'S DEATH NATURAL, PROSECUTOR ASSERTS

District Attorney Announces That No Investigation Will Be Made by County Authorities.

SAN DIEGO, Cal., Dec. 10.—No official investigation will be made into the death of Thomas H. Ince, motion picture producer, at least so far as San Diego County officials are concerned, despite the charges made in a Los Angeles newspaper, according to a statement made today by District Attorney Chester C. Kempley.

"I am satisfied that the death of Thomas H. Ince was caused by heart failure as the result of an attack of acute indigestion," he said. "There will be no investigation into the death of Ince, at least so far as San Diego County is concerned. As there is every reason to believe that the death of Ince was due to natural causes, there is no reason why an investigation should be made."

Kempley's statement followed interviews yesterday with Dr. T. A. Parker of La Jolla, who was called to attend Ince when the latter was taken off a train at Del Mar, and Miss Jessie Howard, a nurse, who was also called. Dr. Parker, according to Kempley, stated that Ince told him that he had drunk considerable liquor aboard the yacht Oneida, on which he went from Los Angeles to San Diego. Miss Howard, it is said, also stated that Ince said he had drunk considerable liquor. She is also reported to have stated that Ince declared his illness was due to bad liquor that he had aboard the yacht.

"No investigation is to be made by San Diego County into the source of the liquor said to have been aboard the Oneida," said Kempley. "If there is any liquor investigation made it will have to be made in Los Angeles, where, presumably, the liquor was secured."

silent film director. Mr. Hearst proved that despite rumors of murder, mystery, and jealousy, his newspapers could easily whitewash the story from even his rivals newspaper. The *Los Angeles Times* had the audacity and gall to put the headline, "Movie Producer Shot on Hearst Yacht!" on the first page of the Wednesday morning edition, but by the time the evening edition came out there was no longer any hint of the story to be found. Mr. Hearst also found absolution from the Department of Justice that never even thought about bringing a murder charge against Mr. Hearst. You see, Hearst and Ince were on the former's yacht to put the finishing touch on a collaboration between Mr. Hearst's *Cosmopolitan Productions* and Ince's studio. But the rumors of murder, mystery, and jealousy were quite justified. Hearst mistakenly murdered Thomas Ince. His true target with Charlie Chaplin who had been engaging in an on-again-off-again affair with Heart's mistress, Marion Davies. Mr. Hearst was enraged because he believed the affair was on-again. He sought out Charlie Chaplin with murderous intent, but mistakenly shot and killed Thomas Ince. But the power of his newspapers was so absolute that a month later the *New York Times* finally put a nail into the coffin of the rumors of murder, mystery, and jealousy when they published the coroners conclusion that Ince died of heart failure. And no further investigation was warranted.

AGENT ECKS: That's another lie!

WILLIE: Oh, no! I've was in the press room with the respected newsmen when the conspiracy was hatched to cover up the murder. This is the singular power of William Randolph Hearst. Not only can he escape justice, but he can libel anyone and everyone without any repercussion. But the "boy-wonder" thought he could slander Mr. Hearst and Ms. Davies in that *Citizen Kane* monstrosity. The slander cost Orson dearly. He lost the Academy Awards for best lead actor, best director and best picture all because Mr. Hearst made a single phone call to Walter Wanger, the president of the Academy of Motion Picture Arts and Sciences! Orson Welles only won one award for best screenplay that night. He should have learned his lesson, but Orson is as arrogant as the Old Man, but not nearly as influential. Now, it is with this god-awful *Invasion From Mars*... the words ultimately fail me.

AGENT ECKS: I thought you said you didn't know what was contained in the *Invasion From Mars* screenplay.

WILLIE: I wouldn't be a newspaper man worth his salt if I didn't know. Orson's repeated calls to Hearst newspapers around the country didn't go unnoticed. WR knew that Orson Welles had fallen into a state of psychosis after the so-called "Battle Over *Citizen Kane*". The inquiries quickly escalated into paranoid diatribes against WR involving conspiracies of a Martian invasion of the United States on October 30, 1938. Orson was obsessed with true paranoias. He was obsessed with the schizophrenic delusion that Martians had invaded America and that the broadcasts heard on the radio were real. Here was a man, who produced an adaptation of HG Wells' seminal *War of the Worlds* science-fiction novel. A man who personally frightened an entire populous with fictional, but not fictitious terrorism. But instead of owning up to his responsibility as the author of the panic, he has chosen to transfer the blame to one esteemed gentleman: William Randolph Hearst. My employers only crime against Orson Welles was to try to stop Herman Mankiewicz's libelous *The American* screenplay from being filmed as Orson's Welles' slanderous *Citizen Kane*. It was in nobody's best interest except for Orson's inflated ego, to put such an abomination in front of the American film-going public. What gentleman wouldn't go to such lengths to protect, not only his good name, but

William Randolph Hearst blackmails the AMPAS to insure that Orson Welles won only one award, that for best screenplay, an award he was forced to share with Herman J. Mankiewicz!

the good name of Marion Davies. WR knew Orson Welles would stop at nothing until he has dragged the good Hearst name through the mud time and time again. WR knew he needed to get a man on the inside of RKO Studios to keep a close watch on the young, naïve, and psychotic Orson Welles.

PETER: And this is the protégé you are so proud of? Besmirching you like this?

ORSON: Brilliant, isn't he? The apple doesn't fall far from the turnip truck.

WILLIE: You have no idea how embarrassing it was to have Orson Welles repeatedly call into Hearst newspapers and demand, implore, down-right beg to know the truth.

AGENT ECKS: What truth?

WILLIE:

AGENT ECKS: That's unbelievable!

WILLIE: WR had finally had enough of young Orson Welles' paranoid fear-mongering and bullying. So WR personally ordered me to go undercover at RKO Pictures. I had the blessings of and assurances from Charles Koerner, the president of the studio to keep a watchful eye on young Orson Welles. I warned Mr. Koerner of Orson's paranoias and psychoses and informed him that Orson would under no circumstances deliver a straight-forward adaptation of Howard Koch's original *The War of the Worlds* radio-dramatization. I served as a double-agent, working for Orson Welles on the screenplay for both *The War of the Worlds* screen-adaptation of the radio-drama while reporting to both Charles Koerner and William Randolph Hearst. But I wasn't to feed into his delusions. I was tasked by my employer to insure that Orson Welles did not put a single frame of this abomination of a film into cinema houses. Unfortunately, an unforeseen character has entered into the picture, both figuratively and literally. Harry Lime has become the new confidant and co-conspirator with Orson Welles. My access to the young director has been limited for the past several weeks. Ever since Welles and Lime retired to the bungalow in Victorville, I have been sidelined. But I have been able to uncover a few nuggets of information that may be of assistance to you. The entire invasion from Mars story I just told you this evening is a figment of Orson Welles twisted, paranoid psychosis.

AGENT ECKS: You have lied to me! Under oath! You said you had no knowledge of the *Invasion From Mars* screenplay or the documents found in the bungalow at Victorville?

WILLIE: What oaths have I broken? Where is the Holy Bible that I have sworn on? I know my rights. I have the right to remain silent. I have the right to counsel. And as it concerns the documents you found in that bungalow in Victorville are not real government documents.

AGENT ECKS: What?

WILLIE: They are the creation of the property department here at RKO

AGENT ECKS: Impossible. I've seen them. They are authentic. They have been redacted.

WILLIE: That is because Orson Welles and his new co-conspirator Harry Lime are obsessive, anal film-makers. They have orchestrated the entire fiasco. From beginning to end. They needed to prove to themselves they weren't crazy, so they created the documents out of thin air. They *believe* the documents are real, so they *made* them real. It's the obsession of a props-master. He can create out of thin air ruby slippers so realistic that a man might be inspired to steal the slippers with the intent of selling off the rubies only to be told by his fence that the rubies were made of glass. But he would protest because of the success of the *Wizard of Oz.*, the slippers are worth thousands of dollars, maybe even millions of dollars. Surely ruby slippers worth a small fortune must have been covered in real rubies and not glass! This is the power of the cinema and the props-master!

AGENT ECKS: So why have you been running your mouth all evening? What was the point?

WILLIE: Because it is in the best interest of my employer to speak to you this evening. Just as it is in the best interest of both you and WR to know every move Orson makes on and off the set. I had at one point become invaluable to young Orson Welles, helping him in every step of making his film. I don't, however, have his

Could the famous and valuable ruby slippers inspire a thief into stealing them thinking they had been made with "read" jewels!

As Orson Welles and Willie Brown burnt the government documents, the only proof the Martian invasion, they felt like Nazi's at a book burning!

complete confidence at the moment. This Harry Lime fellow has entered into a professional relationship with Orson Welles, and I am no longer as close to the psychotic, schizophrenic young director as I'd like to be. Perhaps, you can help me in my mission for William Randolph Hearst and Charles Koerner. Remove Harry Lime from the equation and I can slip into his role– my old role– and become the savior of the picture, *again*. And in doing so, insure that the film never sees the light of day. Assist me in removing Harry Lime from the picture and I'll wring a confession out of Orson Welles and deliver it on a recording for a quick and quiet trail and execution. Now, if you can get that cursed light out of my eyes and help me clean up my apartment, tomorrow we can get to work. Together.

PETER: What was the point of that entire reel-to-reel?

ORSON: You have no idea? It was all to get out of that damned chair and out of that interrogation.

PETER: That entire cockamamie story served only that single purpose? Strange young man, you had there, Orson.

ORSON: A single purpose? Oh, no. Peter. That is the brilliance of Willie Brown. It served many purposes at the same time. **One:** it got him out of the interrogation without being arrested for treason. **Two:** he got a government official on the record admitting the invasion from Mars happened. **Three:** He had become a double-agent, working for the FBI and working for me. **Four:** It got the FBI off of the scent of the government documents. It would give Willie and me time to destroy any other incriminating materials we had in our possession. **Five:** I personally know the extent that the government would go to keep the truth of the invasion from Mars. Now, Willie knew, too. And this Agent Ecks, who interrogated Willie, had to have the "Top-Secret"-level clearance to know the truth about the invasion from Mars. But the rest of his men couldn't have possibly known what their true purpose in investigating and interrogating Willie was. Now, because of Willie's rambling interrogation, they all are *now* aware of the invasion from Mars. They may not have realized they realized the invasion from Mars actually happened, but they will begin to doubt the legitimacy of their assignment. Why did Agent Ecks insist the documents were real if there was no invasion? If the documents were real, then the invasion had actually happened.

PETER: But then why did Willie Brown say they were fake, if in fact, they were real?

ORSON: Exactly my point. The number of questions Willie posed that night would make their heads spin and weaken their collective sanity.

PETER: My own head is spinning, too, I'm afraid.

ORSON: And **Six:**...

PETER: That is an awful lot of simultaneous purposes.

ORSON: And **Six:** It would get Harry Lime out of the picture so that Willie and I could finish the picture.

PETER: But weren't Willie Brown and Harry Lime one-and-the-same person?

ORSON: Yes, of course.

PETER: Then why would Willie want Harry Lime arrested?

ORSON: So, we could finish the picture in peace and quiet.

PETER: That doesn't make any sense at all.

ORSON: It will. Oh, it will. You see, we'd been pacifying Charles Koerner and the other executives with the dailies of *The War of the Worlds*, which Willie and I had called "soothers".

PETER: You actually shot two movies simultaneously?

ORSON: Of course not. We had shot just enough footage of *The War of the Worlds* to supply soothers for Charles, but we were running out of both time and fake footage. Thankfully, I had learned my lesson from *Kane* by not obsessing over shooting hundreds of takes. I was getting through most of *Invasion* with maybe a half-dozen takes, giving us time to create soothers. I still used the deep focus and long takes to keep the number of camera repositionings to the minimum. Willie and I were working under a clock. We needed to get the film in the can before anybody up the food-chain found out what we were really doing. When John Ford visited the *Kane* set, he taught me how to ferret out the spies on my set. Every movie had spies from higher-ups at RKO hidden among the cast and crew. They are the internal affairs of the movie industry. Rats. Nothing but stinking rats. Only a pedophile is lower than a rat.

PETER: Orson!

ORSON: R-A-T-S! Nothing worse than a rat. I was able to instantly spot RKO rats on my set, but I never entertained the possibility I needed to keep an eye out for newspaper rats *and* government rats. I had convinced myself... No... I deluded myself into believing I had kept the entire plot of *Invasion From Mars* such a complete and total secret that neither William Randolph Hearst nor Franklin Delano Roosevelt was even aware of my intentions.

PETER: That's your number one problem, Orson. It was on "The War of the Worlds", it was on *Citizen Kane*, and it has haunted you your entire career.

ORSON: I was completely oblivious to all of the conspiracies against me until Willie Brown burst into my house (even I didn't lock my door back in those days). Even though it still in the small hours, I was working on blocking or camera shots, or other such nonsense, I can't remember. Willie stood in my living room panting like a parched hound. He was white as a sheet. All of the blood had been drained out of his face, perhaps his entire body. He told me he went home that evening and walked in on the FBI ransacking his house. He hurried over to my reel-to-reel tape recorder and spooled the reel. I listened to the entire interrogation in complete and utter stone-cold silence. "They had no idea I had bugged my room. If they had, I'd have been arrested on the spot, but I think I was able to get them off the scent."

"The government knows about *Invasion From Mars*?" I said, "They know! Why weren't we more careful? Apparently, we had left our files out in the blasted bungalow. How could we have been so foolish? What are we going to do?"

"Where is your grill?" Willie inquired.

"It's back on the patio."

"Get all the documents you got from Gunter."

"Everything? That's my only proof that this is real."

"If they find them in your possession you are going away for treason. This isn't about whether or not a film is going to be released. This is about getting strapped to an electric chair. We thought we were playing a game. They are fighting a war. The rules have changed."

"I'll get the documents,"

"And the photos."

And I did. By the time I had found every scrap of paper I had in my possession, Willie had a fire blazing in the grill. These documents I had truly believed would be my safety net and not a noose that would be used to stretch my neck. I felt as filthy and foul as a Nazi at a book-burning rally. Where the Nazis found burning books to be an enthusiastic expedience, my heart panged with guilt. I couldn't destroy the only evidence of the Martian invasion. How could I burn the only proof I would ever have that had proven to me this wasn't all some sort of dream? I had never truly convinced myself the invasion from Mars had actually happened. There was a small part of me that had convinced myself... connived myself... I had bullshitted myself into believing that my subconscious mind had created the entire invasion from Mars scenario in order to protect my id and ego from the stark realization that I alone was responsible committing mass-market terrorism on millions of radio-listeners.

PETER: That is the most honest thing you have said this entire evening, Orson. I'm proud of you.

ORSON: I'm just feeling another pang of regret after that initial pang.

PETER: Realizing the truth after all these decades can be truly cathartic, Orson. Do you need a moment? I can turn off the recording.

ORSON: No. No. I'm fine. I really am. It's just that I regret burning those documents. If I hadn't then this entire fiasco wouldn't have ruined my career, permanently this time. Why did I allow my fears, my paranoia to override my common sense. If I hadn't burnt those government governments in the make-shift miniature pyre, then I could have gone public with the documents. I could have exposed the entire conspiracy. President Roosevelt and Mr. Hearst were guilty of crimes against humanity. If the Hague Conventions had taught governments anything it how to provide for civilians during times of combat. There were thousands who had to have died during the albeit short-lived invasion. The dead had have been erased from history by our government. They were not given proper funerals. Their families had to have been lied to about the hereabouts of their loved ones. These families were lied to about the actual cause of their deaths. On that cold, windy October evening, President Roosevelt committed the worst, most verboten lie of omission. History may have recorded that the worst leader of that era was—

PETER: Orson, don't finish this train-of-thought. I'm

begging you. You don't want to say what you're about to say.

ORSON: Then I won't. Thank you. What I will say is a lie is a lie is a lie. FDR lied. But, of course, he did. He was a politician. He lied through his omission, which is a thousand times worse. Your typical politician will lie to your face while kissing your ugly, snotty baby on the forehead. But FDR was completely silent. Crickets-chirpingly silent. But his lies screamed the loudest because of their silence. Hell, Hearst had made a career out of lying behind the mask of the truth. My own lies pale in comparison to their lies. And I watched the flames lick and char the only proof I had, the only proof I would ever have, that Martians actually invaded America. When the fire had cooled, I wept. The only ammunition I had left was the film I was about to wrap principle photography on. Willie tried to reassure me, it was all the ammunition I needed. Public opinion. Get the film in the cinema houses, in front of the American people, and I will have shone a bright light on one of the darkest nights in American history. Of course, he was right. We were no longer playing Snakes and Ladders, moving towards the winning square, trying to avoid the snakes and taking as many ladders as we could. But now, I've come to the realization that the snakes are not snakes but hydras, each with nine heads and no longer would one higher square lead to a lower square, but nine higher squares led to one lower square. But just as we were about to win the game, we were back to square one. The game of Hydras and Ladders would have futile exercise. I no longer wanted to play games. There were much greater stakes. Now,we were waging a war just as important as the invasion from Mars. We were fighting a revolutionary war over the First Amendment.

PETER: Oh, Lord. Not a freedom of speech diatribe.

ORSON: The worst crime an American citizen can commit is to be silent when the government intends to suppress our freedom of speech. Sure, RKO was within their rights to try and suppress *Kane*. This was not a government agency censoring me. Remember, "*Congress* shall make no law respecting an establishment of religion, or prohibiting the free exercise thereof; or abridging the freedom of speech!" As much as I may have bemoaned the George Schaefer and his fellow executives actions on *Citizen Kane*, they were within their rights to, at least, try to keep my film out of the cinema houses. If canning my cans of film saved them money in the long run, then I could have, would have respected their decision.

PETER: Lord have mercy.

ORSON: Of course I would have. This is a capitalist country we are living in, Peter. Hell, even William Randolph Hearst was within his rights to censor my work since he truly, passionately, believed that I was slandering him. And I was.

PETER: That is surprisingly rational coming from you, Orson.

ORSON: Even though Charles Foster Kane was more about me than it was about Hearst.

PETER: I... I take that back.

ORSON: But the one thing I simply would not stand for was the government of these United States of America and the self-righteous defender of the Constitution himself– Franklin Delano Roosevelt's attempts to censor me. This I would not abide. How dare they

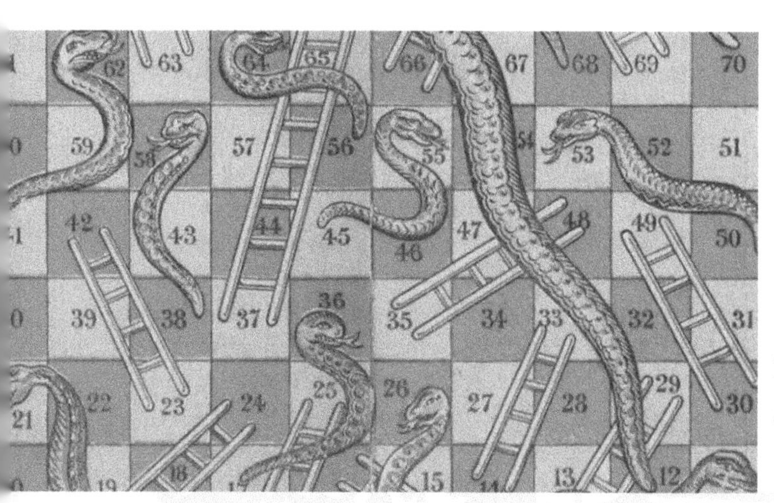

Most people conflate government-sanctioned espionage with the game of Chess, when it actually is more akin to Snakes and Ladders!

The Constitution of the United States of America that President Franklin Delano Roosevelt swore to uphold, not once, not twice, but three times, was the very Constitution he burned when he pursued his conspiracy against the "boy-genius" Orson Welles!

say I cannot share *my* story? I was there. It was as much my story as theirs'. I had every right.

PETER: Didn't you swear an oath before God and country (if this cockamamie story is even true)?

ORSON: Semantics. If this was all a delusion, then it was *my* every-loving delusion. If I imagined everything, then it was *my* goddamned subconscious that imagined every blasted thing. It was *my* id and *my* ego that needed protecting. Not theirs! How dare they try to take that away from me!

PETER: I'm at a lost for words.

ORSON: The salvo lobbed by the Federal Bureau of Investigation when they rudely interrogated my protégé would not go unretaliated. If they want to fight with fire, then I will fight fire with fire and if they fight fire with the fire I am fighting fire with, then...

PETER: Please, stop.

ORSON: I will fight fire with the fire they are fighting fire with the fire I am fighting fire with.

PETER: Ugh...

ORSON: And if they want to fight...

PETER: Orson, stop. Please. Move on.

ORSON: All I'm try to say is if they intend to use the resources of the Federal government against us, then Willie and I are going to use the resources of RKO studios against them.

PETER: Ugh... that... seems... fair?

ORSON: Willie knew that he couldn't bug every office, every hallway, every bathroom, every sound-stage in order to keep recordings of every conversation he was having with the undercover government agents and Heasrt's uncover reports and all of their spies combined. If he encountered another FBI agent, he wanted every single word captured for posterity and for its potential in his defense at trial to keep him... us out of the electric chair. So he went to RKO's head property master, and convinced him that he needed a reel-to-reel recorder that could fit inside a leather attaché case. He needed it for a scene in *The War of the Worlds* feature. And oh, it needed to be fully-functional.

PETER: What kind of scene in *The War of the Worlds* required a functioning reel-to-reel in an attaché case. I've listened to that recording every Mischief Night for the past twenty-odd years (albeit not this one nor the last) and I've never encountered the necessity of a reel-to-reel in a briefcase.

ORSON: Hell, I'm not even sure what scene he had in mind. But dammit, man, it was an essential prop. The props master told him that was in impossibility. He might be able fit a fully-functional reel-to-reel recorder in a suitcase, but certainly not an attaché case. Not even Willie's paranoia could justify carrying around a suitcase all day every day. Willie insisted he try and oh, he needed it ASAP.

The functional reel-to-reel recording attaché that Willie Brown had RKO's properties department build. A satchel that never left his side!

PETER: What?

ORSON: That means "as-soon-as-possible".

PETER: I know what it means.

ORSON: Then why did you ask. Anyway. They were under time constraints and money was no object. Just charge the production.

PETER: Is that one of the studio's resources you had in mind to exploit?

ORSON: Of course. And the ungodly techno-wizardry of the property master actually fit a reel-to-reel perfectly in a leather attaché case and it functioned beautifully. But there was one catch. The microphone, however, couldn't be squeezed into the briefcase *and* both function properly, but the microphone could be slipped up the sleeve of the arm and connected to a wire hidden in the handle. Willie carried the damn thing everywhere. Even into the john.

PETER: He was afraid of being interrogated in the men's room?

ORSON: He couldn't even have a bowel movement without the evidence being captured on tape.

PETER: Now that's a level of paranoia I never thought possible. And yes, I know it's not paranoia if they *are* out to get you.

ORSON: And, well, it's not like I've even gotten to the good parts yet.

PETER: I can't wait. Well, maybe I can.

ORSON: *[Laughs heartily.]* It has taken all evening, but you're finally starting to enjoy yourself. Part of my mission has been accomplished. Now onward and upward into the downward spiral to madness.

a Sociological Study
by Johan Zyblerstein

In this paper, which serves as an epilogue to my 1934 study, *King Kong: A "Newsreel" of Confusion* and a prelude to a future work, I will explore how the release motion picture *King Kong* served as an ominous portent to widespread panic induced in the American populous by Orson Welles' radio broadcast of "The War of the Worlds".

I wrote in the previous work, "From the farms of Quaker-Pennsylvania to the Appalachian mountains, the rural, uneducated, and largely illiterate audiences of the Midwest and South received their only news from the pulpit and from their cinemas in the form of William Randolph *Hearst Metrotone Newsreels*. Reports from sources such as these were accepted as the only readily available source of news from around the world. News that could be viewed in their local motion picture houses only days after the events occurred. So brilliantly edited and spiritedly narrated were the newsreels, that many were viewed as a source of entertainment as well as a resource for news.

"Then in 1933, these rural communities received into their second-run motion picture cinemas, a strange, low-budget talkie entitled *King Kong*. The film was a Beauty-And-The-Beast fable telling the story of an innocent but gusty Hollywood starlet's bizarre unrequited love with a fearsome, gargantuan fifty-foot ape, whose species has been lost to the records of science on a mysterious and uncharted South-Pacific island whose very existence was known only to its primitive, cannibalistic inhabitants. Is it surprising to discover that many in the viewing audience mistook this adventure fantasy, part-horror film as a newsreel? They seemed to accept the story of a enormous ape's journey from an island concealed in perpetual fog and mist to the bright, urban lights of Broadway, where such a spectacle could realistically be exploited as a Vaudevillian attraction, and to its eventual demise after falling to its death from the even greater spectacle of the Empire State Building.

"Many, who had never traveled more than a few miles from their birthplace, would marvel at the newsreel reports of the Egyptian pyramids, battle scenes of war from around the world, and adventure footage of scaling the highest peaks of the Himalayas. Is it so beyond the imagination of us, who sit in the Vaudeville theater watching Harry Houdini knowing full well that we are in sound mind and body, that there is no actual supernatural magic involved in his escaping while immersed in a pad-locked milk can. We remain bewildered by the fact that before our very eyes, we see would could not possibly be. Can we believe that the magic of Hollywood could actually cause panic?"

Then on October 30, 1938, the panic happened again but far more visceral. In 1933, cinema goers mistook a Hollywood production for a newsreel, believing a gargantuan ape had been brought from a mysterious island to New York, when it went on a rampage. The panic was assuaged a tiny bit by the "newsreel" happening in the past. The fate of King Kong resolves itself when he fell to his death from the height of the Empire State building, his bullet-ridden body having crashed onto 5th Avenue below. The rural and more distant audiences could walk out of the theater relieved that the threat was over, but still in a panicked state over the existence of the gargantuan ape.

The panic of the Martian invasion proved to be far more visceral because it was occurring in real-time: the hear-and-now. The news broadcast format that Orson Welles' had chosen to utilize for his "War of the Worlds" performance mimicked the news broadcasts reporting details of the Munich Crisis from only a month before. The Martian invasion brought the very real threat of heat-rays and poison gas. These threats caused a panicked populous to stuff wet rags under doors to prevent the inhalation of the poisonous fumes, to flee to churches to make their peace with the Almighty, and to clutch their children tight in their final mortal moments.

Clara Henderson, a British kindergarten teacher who relocated to Washington DC after marrying an American solider after the Great War, recalled, "My home overlooked the Potomac River on the outskirts of the capital. My family had been listening to the *Charley McCarthy Hour* when we were alerted to the news of the Martian invasion coming from CBS. We were shocked and concerned that the NBC station had not chosen to interrupt the bloody puppet with news of an invasion from Mars, so we turned the dial. I clutched my children close as we listened to the harrowing news. Then the air raid sirens began to wail their warning. My middle son, Davey, dashed to look out of the window. I had begged him not to get so close to the windows. My husband had shoved wet rags under the doors when news of the poison gas came over the air. Then Davey called us to look out the window. There was a low fog, like the London fog I had been accustomed to in England, but far darker. The fog that rolled in was blacker than pitch. So dark that the surrounding night looked as clear as day. We threw shut the shudders terrified that the poisonous fumes of the Martian's war weapon would leak through the wet rags and the window panes. My family huddled in the cellar until morning. We were both horrified and gratified to learn that it was all a radio-play. The fog we had witnessed rolling over the Potomac must have merely been a fog that I mistook in my shaken condition as the poisonous fumes of the Martian death machines. But Davey, to this day, insists the Martian invasion was real, despite all of my and my husband's best efforts."

In Fauquier County, I spoke to the pastor of an historic Black church. In pre-Emancipation Virginia enslaved Africans would congregate in the middle of the woods, down by the creek where baptisms would have been frequently held, or in super-secret and very hidden praise houses; these "hush harbors" allowed, in the words of one of their congregants, "African-influenced spiritual practices [to be] hidden in plain sight in communities of the enslaved." Immediately after the Emancipation many of these "hush harbors" became physical structures erected by congregations still reeling and giddy, praising God and thanking President Lincoln for their newfound freedom. It was there in a "church by the side of the road" that the pastor (whose name has been withheld by request) recounted that cold and windy October evening in 1938: "When the news reports from Grove Hill came over the radio, many of my parishioners immediate immediately sought out the Almighty and the safe haven of our church. As we huddled in God's sanctuary, we prayed prayers and sang hymns. Then came the audible thuds almost like small earthquakes that shook the window panes. What was it we heard? Were we hearing the steps of the Martian machines marching towards us? Then came a horrific mechanic and demonic scream that bellowed lightning-and-fire at the woods some distance from our windows like it was the old serpent, called the Devil, and Satan, which deceiveth the whole world. Was this Satan cast out into the earth from the stars, and his angels cast out with him? Were we living in the End Times? Soon, there came silence after the Martian machine marched passed our little church. Perhaps we were too little a target for this lightning-and-fire breath. Maybe the machine didn't even see our little church or hear us hailing Jesus. Or care. The next morning the distant woods were charred ash and the Martian machine's foot prints still visible in the earth, yet *The Fauquier Democrat* and the radio trumpeted news that last night was all a radio-program meant to scare on a Halloween Eve. 'Orson Welles' was his name and he had taken all of the blame. We didn't know what to believe. Surely, the radio wouldn't lie to us, but we knew what we saw and heard and felt: a Martian invasion!"

What would cause these and other grown people to insist on a Martian invasion that cold windy October evening that Orson Welles would call "Mischief Night"? Is this deception inherent in popular media? Samuel Taylor Coleridge once accurately opined, "That willing suspension of disbelief for the moment, which constitutes poetic faith." Do audiences inherently make this poetic leap of faith when they watch a motion picture in the cinema-house or listen to a radio-program in the relative safety of their own home? And if so, where does this deception of the public begin and end? Is the fault the audience or the producers of the film or radio-program?

Mr. Welles, like his British– though misspelled– namesake HG Wells would use the motif of a Martian invasion to frighten the American and British populous respectively. HG Wells had serialized his *War of the Worlds* in *Pearson's Magazine* in 1895 and 1897. Though I can find no record of terror struck in the readers of the magazine, seeing how the *King Kong* motion picture and "The War of the Worlds" radio-play struck fear in the hearts and minds of Americans, I cannot readily dismiss the possibility that HG Wells story may have been perceived more as a journalistic report than a science-fiction yarn. The gulf of time is too distant and the British too docile and obedient to Queen Victoria to except anything other than a declaration that HG Wells' story was mere science-fiction and not news. Though I struggled to find any such declaration made by the Queen surrounding the release of the serialized *The War of the Worlds* novel I gained access to diaries and journal entries lost to both time and history. I uncovered the true hidden reaction the British had to HG Wells' serialization of *The War of the Worlds.*

In a diary of a young girl, she wrote about the harrowing nightmare watching the Martian invasion from her farmhouse window

A police officer detailed his own professional experiences expertly in this journal,

And *finally*, in letter written by HG Wells and sent to a friend in America, he related how his journalistic exposé uncovering the truth of a Martian invasion of the United Kingdom was instead readily dismissed by the audience of *Pearson's Magazine* as science-fiction (at the apparent behest of Queen Victoria herself):

So my hypothesis stands.

However the confluence of the American reaction to popular media in 1933 and a mere five years later in 1938 cannot be overlooked by the sociological community. Both King Kong and the Martians have uncovered a great fear festering beneath our current isolationist mood in the United States of America. What does this encroaching war in Europe approaching the horizon mean for the psyche of the American people, a people who can be stoked into fear and flight so easily? Surely Nazi Germany is aware of our reactions and will use our own fears against us. Only through the study of this reaction can both academics and the government prepare us for the propaganda and misinformation of the coming Earthly war.

THE FORBIDDEN MEN'S ROOM!

ORSON: Willie and I knew the jig was up. Even though we pacified Charles Koerner and the other executives at RKO with the soothers, we knew were exposed. Staring at the fire that turned all of the evidence we had collected (which was, literally, going up in smoke), we plotted our way through the minefield we were now more than aware was being laid before us. The Federal agents were momentary satisfied that Willie was an undercover agent for William Randolph Hearst, but it would only take one long-distance phone call to Sam Simeon to expose Willie as a liar and double-agent.

PETER: And a double-liar.

ORSON: We needed to get our *Invasion* in the can as quickly as possible, so we could get it edited, and released A-S-A-F-P.

PETER: A-S-A-F-P?

ORSON: As-soon-as-fu—

PETER: I get it. I get it.

ORSON: — reaking-possible.

PETER: Why would RKO even entertain the possibly of releasing such a monstrosity? Even if you did finish the film, Charles Koerner and every single executive at RKO would come to the stark realization that you didn't film the very film they had authorized you to film. They wanted a straight adaptation of "The War of the Worlds" radio-drama. Once they discovered you spent hundred-of-thousands of *their* dollars on another picture, they would not just run you out of town, they would tar-and-feather you publicly. Their lawyers would sue you for embezzlement at least or commit you to an asylum at worst.

ORSON: Peter, that hyperbole is stretching it a bit far.

PETER: I'm afraid not, Orson. You delivered one screenplay and filmed a completely different screenplay.

ORSON: It wasn't *completely* different. It was still about an invasion from Mars. That's what they wanted. That's what Louis B. Meyer wanted. That is what the Warner Brothers, Harry, Albert, Sam, and Jack, wanted. Hell, that is even what Walt Disney wanted. Can you imagine that monstrosity (to use your words)? I've said it once, I'll say it again, a singing-and-dancing animated monstrosity! "War of the Worlds" was literally the only thing they wanted. I don't believe for one second the executives required it be a word-for-word adaption of Howard's radio-script. They simply wanted an "invasion from Mars" picture directed by Orson Welles. And what kind "War of the Worlds" would I possibly give them? I'm Orson Welles for God's sake. The Wil-

Orson Welles delivered the "War of the Worlds" radio-dramatization William Paley and Davidson Taylor wanted; but could not have foreseen!

liam Paley and Davidson Taylor wanted a "War of the Worlds" adaptation for the *Mercury Theatre on the air*. Did they ever conceive that I would use the technique of fake news reports? No! Did they ever conceive that I would frighten half the nation into stark hysterics? Oh, God no! But did they relish the publicity that came from my using that technique? Oh, hell yes! *This* was what I was giving Charles and RKO Radio Pictures. They should be grateful that I bestowed the greatest gift I could upon them: a uniquely Wellesian "Invasion From the Mars" motion picture. They should be grateful! They should get down on their hands and knees and kiss my feet.

PETER: It wasn't even close to being what they wanted. What would Louis B. Mayer have done to you if you were hired to film Margaret Mitchell's *Gone With the Wind* as a four-hour Hollywood epic about the Civil War and the Reconstruction South and you turned in reels starring the Three Stooges and in a minstrel show! Can you imagine Moe Howard as Rhett Bulter? Or Shemp Howard and Larry Fine as the brothers, Brent and Stuart Tarleton? Can you imagine Katherine Hepburn as Scarlett O'Hara? Or Curly Howard as Mammy, not only in blackface, but drag as well! That is the movie you would have delivered if Louis B. Mayer has the foolish audacity to let you direct *Gone With the Wind*!

ORSON: That analogy isn't remotely correct.

PETER: You'd be done, Orson. You're career would be over. Permanently this time.

ORSON: You've known me for how long, Peter? Have you not seen my career?

PETER: ...

ORSON: That was a rhetorical question.

PETER: I wasn't going to say anything.

ORSON: That question was asked in order to create a dramatic effect, to make a point rather than to get an answer.

PETER: I know what a rhetorical question is.

ORSON: Good, because that too was a rhetorical question.

PETER: ...

ORSON: I don't really believe in predestination, but my career was already over. Permanently. I just didn't know it yet. I don't think I know it right now. I guess I never really had a career at all. Not really. It was all an illusion. Most people will look back on my career after I'm dead and gone and think that it began *and* ended with *Citizen Kane*. Sure I had other films. I had other projects. But when

The Triumphal entry of Jesus into Jerusalem paled in comparison to Orson Welles' entry into Hollywood on that Boeing 307 Stratoliner!

you look back the filmography of George Orson Welles, it was a bust. I never was able to live up to the expectations of being the "golden-boy" and the "boy-wonder". When I descended those steps out of that Howard Hughes chartered Trans World Airlines' Boeing 307 Stratoliner, you'd have thought I was the Second Coming of Jesus Christ!

PETER: Orson!

ORSON: You know this better than anyone, Peter. I was welcomed into Hollywood like Jesus riding a donkey into Jerusalem. The press greeted me with palm leaves and exaltations! But there was a cabal of Hollywood executives, a Sanhedrin if you will, that was planning my downfall from the very start. George Shaffer gave me the keys to the Kingdom

William Randolph Hearst's publicly crucified the "boy wonder" and "golden boy" in the press after seeing a private screening of Citizen Kane!

of God! I made my *Citizen Kane* but little did I know that William Randolph Hearst, the Roman procurator who oversaw all of Hollywood, would order my very public and painful crucifixion. And I was then crucified in the press, not for my sins, but because of Heart's.

PETER: Orson!

ORSON: But as good as the story is that *Kane* began *and* ended my career, the truth is far more otherworldly. My career in Hollywood *began* that cold October evening when I conspired to cover up the truth that there was an invasion from Mars and it *ended* when the truth about the *Invasion From Mars* film was finally exposed. But at the time I am describing, I hadn't thought that far down the road. Hindsight being 20-20 is such a cliché, but it is a cliché because it is almost always true. The dominoes that I set up through my conspiring with William Randolph Hearst in my studio at CBS hadn't all fallen by the time I was filming *Invasion From Mars*. Willie and I, despite his encounter with and interrogation by the FBI, were still blissfully unaware of the battles we were still going to fight.

PETER: But your actions scream of paranoia.

ORSON: Oh, we certainly were paranoid. But we were also delusional. You know as well as anyone, Peter, that I *could* suffer from delusions of grandeur.

PETER: You don't say?

ORSON: Since those days when I learnt card magic at the knee of Harry Houdini when I was five, to my tutorship with Manolete on the boulevards of Spain, I have possessed the superior qualities of genius, fame, omnipotence, and at times even wealth.

PETER: ...

ORSON: My talents were, certainly, recognized. I possessed relationships with countless prominent people. *[Chuckling.]* Hell, I am a prominent and important person. But the sense of my own worth has never been greatly out-of-proportion.

PETER: Wow... just... wow...

ORSON: When you hear, from the age I was able to talk, the entire world call you a genius, a "boy-wonder", delusions of grandeur is a psychosis that I could not possibly escape suffering from. My mother Beatrice Ives, sweet lady, doted, devoutly doted, doted in idolatry, upon me from when I was a boy. Nothing was off limits for me. Nothing was out of my reach. The world was my oyster. But upon her death when I was but nine-years-old, her pride in me transformed into my own vainglory. I admit it.

Beatrice Ives Welles set the course for her son, Orson Welles', life by setting him in a reed basket and setting him off in the Nile to become a great man!

PETER: Good for you, Orson. That is a very honest observation about yourself.

ORSON: Even if my delusions of grandeur were ultimately rooted in reality. I am a genius. I have both fame and a fortune. And as for omnipotence, I am far too humble to comment further.

PETER: Wow... just... wow...

ORSON: Being paranoid goes hand-in-hand with delusions of grandeur. If you are paranoid the government is out to get you, then you must be a person of some importance. If they are willing to ransack your apartment, then you are an important person. Willie was just now beginning to experience the true elation and ecstasy of being a "boy-wonder". What I learned about myself from Harry Houdini and Manolete had given me the confidence to walk onto the Great White Way and direct, with no professional experience, a production of William Shakespeare's *MacBeth* for the Federal Theatre Project. Of course, I could direct an entirely black cast that numbered over 150, a cast of actors, many of whom had never stepped foot in front of the floorlights. If that could be a rousing success, then why couldn't I waltz into Hollywood and on my first feature film create the single greatest motion picture ever put to film.

PETER: According to whom?

ORSON: You for one! *[Laughs heartily.]* Although I am loathe to believe such lists *Sight & Sound*, the

Orson Welles traveled the world meeting learning the art of bull-fighting (and perhaps bullshitting) at the knee of Manolete, the famed bullfighter!

British magazine, has twice in international polls named *Citizen Kane* has the greatest film of all time. And now, Willie Brown and I were working on a transcendent genre film. I have no doubt, that my work on *Invasion of Mars* was superior to my work on *Citizen Kane*. I didn't know my ass from my elbow when I was working on *Kane*, yet I was able to pull that masterpiece out of my backside. Now, I was working with all my capabilities primed and ready to create a wonder. Sure it would be seen as a science-fiction picture and a genre film would never be spoken in the same breath as my cinematic biography of George Orson Welles.

PETER: You mean William Randolph Hearst.

ORSON: Again with that asinine interpretation. You've always shoot for the mark and miss, Peter.

PETER: You always believe your own bull—

ORSON: Why couldn't a genre picture like *Invasion From Mars* turn Hollywood upon its head?

PETER: Because genre pictures never get any respect. They never have. They never will. Unfortunately.

ORSON: If a movie about a family of mobsters can win Hollywood's biggest prize. If a satire about nuclear war, or how someone learned to stop worrying and love the bomb, could be nominated for and nearly win an Oscar for Best Picture. Then why, I ask, why couldn't my film of science-fact change not only the course of Hollywood, but also steer my own course from the oblivion it would eventually lead to eventually to constant and perpetual success and adulation.

PETER: Humbris is your greatest sin, Orson. You from the first have always believed that you idea of a great film shared parity with those who actually wield the power in Hollywood.

ORSON: But what about art, Peter? Art!

PETER: Sometimes, rarely, but sometimes, you are able to create both great art, great cinema, and great box-office, but you are far too smart to know that that the twain rarely meet. How many of your films have withered and died on the vine? You were never able to even begin the wine-making process. If you had only picked your fights better, Orson, you could have had a career like no other would ever be able to replicate.

ORSON: Nobody would be able to replicate my career as it stands now, Peter. It is a once in a millennium career.

PETER: Because nobody would willingly chose to emulate your career, Orson. Sure, they'd like to have a film of such beauty and importance as *Citizen Kane* on their résumé, but in the last three decades, no man in their right mind would chose to have your career. You have struggled to get finances. You have struggled to get support. You have struggled to get the damn films made. You have struggled to get you films screened in mainstream cinemas. All because the hubris born from *Citizen Kane*.

ORSON: Ah, that's where you're wrong, Peter. It wasn't *Citizen Kane* that gave birth to my hubris. It was the "The War of the Worlds" radio-drama. If I had never recorded that infernal wax-recording for William Randolph Hearst, if I hadn't bartered that wax disc for the key to Hollywood in the small hours of Mischief Night, then maybe I would have gotten to California much more organically. If I had to have trudged up the rungs of that ladder called Hollywood, then maybe I wouldn't be sitting here discussing the great What If's.

PETER: Then maybe we should change the direction of this particular conversation.

ORSON: But I played the hand that I was dealt. Despite the card manipulation techniques I learned from Harry Houdini, I wouldn't be able to substitute the cards in the hand that I was dealt. Willie and I were all in. The chips were in the center of the table. He knew the cards we held, but we didn't know, couldn't know that William Randolph Hearst and President Roosevelt had stacked the desk against us.

PETER: Nice metaphors, Orson, but you're really stretching credulity. Really.

Orson Welles learned the magic and card manipulation at the knee of the master of the artform, Harry Houdini. Orson chose only the best mentors!

ORSON: Principle photography had wrapped without another word from the FBI, but we knew– we just knew– that they were always around, like the grotesques staring down at parishioners in the great cathedrals of Europe. They were a constant presence, although we couldn't quite get a glimpse of them, like phantasms flitting in the corners of your eye. And then, unbeknownst to me, they called in their chip on Willie. During their interrogation, Willie had claimed to be an agent for William Randolph Hearst. Now, of course, that particular lie wouldn't have gotten very far, because they just needed to drop a dime into any pay phone and know what William Francis Brown was not on the payroll of any Hearst newspaper. As the days, turned into weeks, Willie and I thought that maybe the government was just that stupid. Why hadn't Willie been exposed? We went about our daily affairs oblivious to the fact that Willie had been, in fact, exposed. That Agent Ecks was far brighter than we had anticipated and had called San Simeon and spoken to the Old Man himself. Hearst did have his spies on the RKO lot, but William Francis Brown was not one of them. With the patience of a saint, patience one isn't aware the government possesses, Agent Ecks waited until the right moment to spring a surprise interrogation on Willie Brown. While Willie had done to the library to enjoy his bowel movement...

PETER: Willie had to go to the library to use the men's room? Why couldn't he use one on the studio lot.

ORSON: No. No. Willie called going to the men's room "going to the library". Or "going to see Ms. Jones", whom I always assumed was the librarian. Willie always took a newspaper with him into the john and would enjoy the solitude of the men's room. That is when he heard foot falls walk into the stall next to his. He couldn't help but notice the spit-shined government issue shoes tapping impatiently in the next stall. Thanks to Willie's paranoia and his attaché case-sized reel-to-reel recorder. He was able to get the conversation on tape.

PETER: Of course, he did. That's awfully convenient.

[Orson clicks on the reel-to-reel recording.]

AGENT ECKS: You lied! You are not an undercover and secret agent for William Randolph Hearst. I contacted several Hearst newspapers and not a single editor acknowledged you are on the payroll of Hearst Communications, Inc. You are not on their financials in anyway.

WILLIE: Why would an undercover and secret agent for William Randolph Hearst actually be on the payroll? As if any of the editors would know about me anyway. I'm too high on the food-chain to be on their radar. I answer only to William Randolph Hearst. And if you think the Old Man would list me anywhere near his official financials, you are as dumb as a bag of hammers.

AGENT ECKS: Why? But why, would they lie to a FBI agent? That's against the law. You cannot lie to a government official in any capacity. That is a felony. That is punishable with imprisonment.

WILLIE: Oh... no... someone doing nefarious and illegal acts would lie to the hallowed F... B... I... that's impossible! No one would do such a thing. I'm pretty sure the editors at Hearst newspaper are more afraid of William Randolph Hearst than they are of J. Edgar Hoover. You can only threaten them with jail time. Hearst can ruin their entire career. A year or two in prison or a lifetime on the blacklist? Which would you choose? The Mafia base their entire illegal and organized operations on the fact that people will do a little jail time. Myself included.

AGENT ECKS: They would rather tick off J. Edgar Hoover by lying to the FBI? J. Edgar Hoover is the most powerful person in the United States *[Catching himself.]* Besides the President of the United States of America himself.

WILLIE: Are you shitting me? William Randolph Hearst is the most powerful person in America. Roosevelt shits himself with the thought of ticking off the Old Man. He who controls the press rules the world. And that man is William Randolph Hearst. He has lied with impunity.

AGENT ECKS: Not even William Randolph Hearst would lie to the FBI.

WILLIE: The Old Man would not only lie to your bloody face, but convince you your own mind has deceived you. J. Edgar Hoover is more afraid of the Old Man than the Old Man is of the nancy J. Edgar Hoover. If you're going to slap some cuffs on his wrists and haul me off to jail, then do it. I've grown tired of this little game. In fact, I've grown tired of you.

AGENT ECKS: But... but... You think I'm not good at my job? You think I didn't go through the finanicals at RKO to discover you are on the studio's payroll. You were hired by Charles Koerner to be the screenwriter on Orson Welles' latest picture. Maybe at the behest of Orson or maybe you were an albatross wrapped around his neck. I don't know. But what I do know if you are just a Hollywood screenwriter who recently fell off the turnip truck. I did a little more digging, which is part of my job. You are from a small Colorado steel mill town. Some of the residents call it "Little Pittsburgh" or some call it "Pew-Town" from the black smoke and stench of the steel mill. You went to Centennial High and set off to Hollywood in 1941. According to your father, Carl Dwight Brown of 607 E. Evans, you ran off to Hollywood when you heard the siren's song luring your away to make your name in the glitz and glamour of Hollywood. Why didn't you choose to either work in the steel mill like a proper Puebloan or join your fellow young men by fighting (and dying if necessary) in the second Great War, like your father wanted? Mr. Brown told me to tell you that he is greatly disappointed in you for not enlisting the very moment the Japanese attacked Pearl Harbor. Your father said you're too obsessed with your blasted typewriter than being a good and proper young man by fighting in this war. For freedom. For democracy.

WILLIE: I... I... I was barely seventeen when Pearl Harbor was attacked! I tried to enlist! But they wouldn't take me until my eighteenth birthday. I begged and pleaded with them to let me enlist, that I'd be eighteen by the time I was out of boot-camp. I'd be eighteen by the time they shipped me off to Europe or the Pacific theater. I tried. I honest to God tried to enlist, but they wouldn't have me... at the time.

AGENT ECKS: But you sought out the bright marque lights of Hollywood. Your father told me to tell you that you shouldn't come back home. Ever. He disowns you. You are no longer his son.

WILLIE: I... I... knew that I wouldn't be very good that this. I told Orson I wouldn't be able to tell this off... pull off this charade. You have to understand something. I'm just a kid. Like you said, I'm barely eighteen years old. Here's my identification. I'll... I'll slip it under the stall. See. I was born in 1924 in Pueblo, Colorado. I'm eighteen. See.

AGENT ECKS: I know you're only eighteen. You keep thinking I'm stupid. Like I'm going to cry out in shock and horror, "What? No, you're not. You're like thirty-five, forty years old. More lies!" You don't need to slide anything to me. I saw your birth certificate. But I certainly now know why I bought your initial lies. You look so... old.

WILLIE: It's the opposite of a baby-face I guess. What would that be called?

AGENT ECKS: What are you doing in Hollywood?

WILLIE: I... I came to Hollywood with stars in my eyes and a typewriter tucked under my arm, trying to be a screenwriter. But I couldn't really get any good jobs at RKO. Not a single word have I ever written has ended up on the screen. Orson– I mean, Mr. Welles– didn't want a screenwriter on his new film, but Mr. Koerner– Charles Koerner– wouldn't let him proceed without one. So there I was, a then seventeen-year-old kid fresh off the turnip truck, saddled to Mr. Welles. He put me on the task of adapting Mr. Koch's "The War of the Worlds" adaption while he and Mr. Lime wrote *Invasion From Mars*. That's the God's honest truth. That's all that I've done.

AGENT ECKS: Then how did you know all about the invasion from Mars. The story you told. You couldn't have possibly known all that.

WILLIE: Harry Lime!

AGENT ECKS: Who?

WILLIE: Mr. Welles' second-unit director. He knows more than he lets on. He is the one who wrote the *Invasion From Mars* screenplay.

AGENT ECKS: The one with your name on it?

WILLIE: Like I said, and I was telling the truth back in my house, the original screenwriter is always attributed as the writer, even on subsequent drafts. I had nothing to do with that screenplay.

AGENT ECKS: Then how in the hell did you know the story of that screenplay?

WILLIE: I'm the script supervisor.

AGENT ECKS: The what?

WILLIE: Mr. Welles and Mr. Lime couldn't have just anybody work as their script supervisor. I was already in for a dollar in for a dime as screenwriter on record for *The War of the Worlds*, so they made me the script-supervisor.

AGENT ECKS: What does a script supervisor do?

WILLIE: I'm the crew member that oversees the continuity of the motion picture, you know, wardrobe, props, set dressing, hair, makeup, and the action of the actors during a scene. I have to make sure the glasses have the same level of water or wine in between takes. I have to make sure all props are in the same place when they reposition the cameras for different shots. I have to maintain the look and feel of a production in spite of the countless moving parts. It's called continuity. It's my job. It's my *only* job.

AGENT ECKS: There's a lot of things I didn't realize were necessary to make a film.

WILLIE: And since, Mr. Welles and Mr. Lime were filming two films at the same time.

AGENT ECKS: They what?

WILLIE: Yeah. Of course. They needed to shoot just enough scenes of *The War of the Worlds* to keep the executives and their on-set spies pacified with the soothers– I mean– dailies. They needed someone who could keep track two different productions. Keep all of the scenes they were shooting straight. They needed someone like me.

AGENT ECKS: Then why did you lie about being an agent of William Randolph Hearst?

WILLIE: I...

AGENT ECKS: Answer me.

WILLIE: Mr. Lime! He said that if I was ever confronted by the police or god-forbid a federal agent, then I needed to lie... I'm so sorry... I know that I shouldn't have gone along with them, but they're Mr. Orson Welles and Mr. Harry Lime. They may be only a few years older than me, but man, have they have had remarkable careers. Orson Welles holds the keys to Hollywood, for pity's sake. If the studio was willing to let him shoot *Citizen Kane* as his first feature, then what could kind of film could Mr. Welles get me? Within a couple of years, I could be in the director's chair myself. That was an offer I just couldn't refuse. And then there was Marion Davies.

AGENT ECKS: Who?

WILLIE: Her name isn't really Marion Davies. She is the actress that plays Marion Davies on *Invasion From Mars*. Mr. Lime set the two of us up on a date. I've never really had a girlfriend before and Mr. Lime was able to get me a date with a Hollywood starlet. She's gorgeous. I'd do anything for her. I'd do anything for Mr. Lime. You don't know what it's like to be a country-bumpkin in the glitz and glamour of Hollywood. I'm afraid I got a little starstruck. If you were to interrogate Mr. Lime.. instead of... well, me... I'm sure you'll get the answers you're looking for. I hate to throw him under the bus that this... but I'm just a peon. A shlub. A nobody, really. I just want to go back home to Colorado. To my own bed. To my mommy...

[Orson clicks the reel-to-reel recording off.]

PETER: That is a world class bullshitter you had there, Orson.

ORSON: Bullshit as hard as steel.

PETER: But this still doesn't explain how the FBI arresting and interrogating Harry Lime gets either you or Willie Brown off the hook. Willie and Harry are one and the same.

ORSON: Are they? Really?

PETER: What? That's doesn't make any... what are you trying to say? There were two Harry Limes?

ORSON: There was Harry Lime, the pseudonym of one Willie Brown and there was Harry Lime, the character I hired an actor to play.

PETER: Wait. What? You're saying you hired an actor to play Harry Lime... with the intention of having him arrested... for treason.

ORSON: When you say it it sounds like a really awful thing to do to someone.

PETER: Because it is a really awful thing to do to someone!

ORSON: I guess *now* it sounds really horrible.

PETER: It sounds really horrible even *then*!

ORSON: *[Shrugs this off.]* I had prepared our "Harry Lime" with a thorough and detailed back-story and current story of his actions on the *Invasion From Mars* film, but it wasn't complete and wouldn't hold up to scrutiny. We thought it would buy us a day or maybe two, before the improvisation skills of our hired actor gave way to honest confessions he was just an actor, but when we heard nothing of our other "Harry Lime", we began to grow concerned. We had heard neither hide nor hair of the other "Harry Lime" for what would be going on two weeks.

PETER: Oh, no.

ORSON: Oh, yes. Willie and I believed we had thrown the G-men off of our scent that first day, we locked ourselves in the editing-room. While completely confined in that room, damn-near twenty-four hours a day, only stopping to visit the cafeteria or use the facilities, we felt almost like convicts. We slaved away with reels upon reels of film instead of pressing license plates. Little did we know we perilously close to trading being locked in one confined room for another more permanently confining room... namely a casket.

PETER: Orson... you don't think it would have come to that, do you?

ORSON: Treason is an capital offense. Willie and I were living as if the doctor had diagnosed both of us with the same terminal illness: treason. A deadly disease. A disease that infects red-white-and-blue-blooded Americans very rarely. It is not a disease common in an American. Its the damn Commies always seems to be infected with treason not Willie Brown and myself. But Willie and I had both been infected. And we were slowly dying. There were no medicine or treatments that could cure us of treason. We were only given a few months to live, so we needed to devote ourselves to finishing our life's work: *Invasion From Mars*.

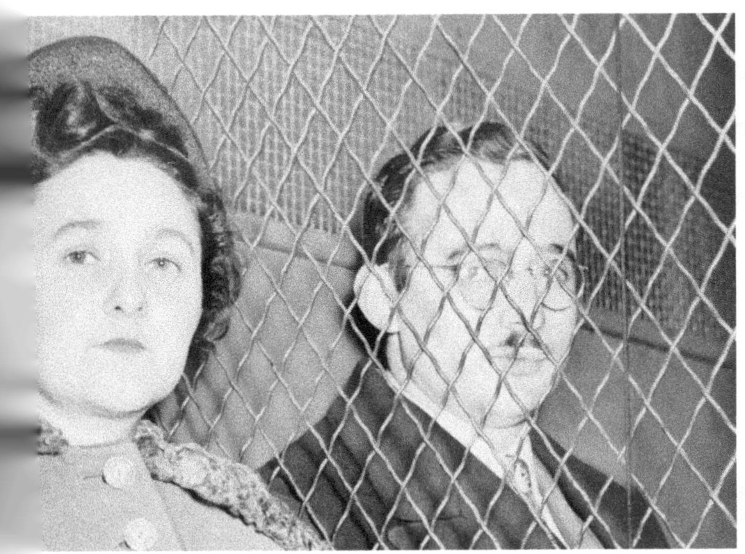

Filthy, sticking Red Commie bastards, Julius and Ethel Rosenberg, and not red-white-and-blue-blooded Orson Welles and my father!

PETER: Lord, what a metaphor. You really do have a way with words.

ORSON: We literally worked around the clock. We were getting kind of loopy from our lack of sleep, so we started taking shifts. We were both getting so sleepy from staring through loops at cut after cut... wait, maybe we were sleepy from lack of sleep and loopy from staring through loops.

PETER: I don't think it matters, Orson.

ORSON: Well, we were able to get a complete cut of the film done in just over two weeks. As we gathered up our reels, we plotted our most direct route to the orchestral room, where we had arranged for Benny Herrmann to meet us. I wasn't entirely sure our messenger had reached Benny. We just had to trust that word had gotten through to him despite the unseemly hour.

PETER: Would Benny answer your call by being there? You just said it had been awfully late in the evening.

Benny Herman, the composer of not only Orson Welles "War of the Worlds" radio-drama and Citizen Kane, *but the* Invasion From Mars *as well!*

ORSON: Of course, he would. Benny even answered the telephone when I phoned him in the small hours of what was now October 31, 1938. Benny had been there that evening to orchestrate his score of my planned broadcast of *Rebecca*, but since we were so rudely preempted by Hearst's damnable evening of dance music...

PETER: Not this again.

ORSON: ... Benny asked if he could head home since he wasn't need for our impromptu rehearsal of *Danton's Death*. But as soon as he heard I needed him back in the studio, he dutifully caught a cab back completely unaware of the panic of that night's broadcast. Benny was instrumental (no pun intended) *[Pregnant pause.]* (screw it pun intended) in getting the orchestral score of Ramon Raquello and his orchestra so perfectly spot on, as I cobbled together, improvised an entire radio-drama for that blasted wax-recording of "The War of the Worlds". There was no other man I trusted more with producing the "War of the Worlds" score and again no more trusted with the score for *Invasion From Mars*. Only Benny would be able to create the otherworldly score for *Invasion From Mars* I desired most. If any man knew what was at stake with *Invasion From Mars*, what the potential of this film could be, it was Benny. He *was* there. He was in the same CBS studio as me. He was there when Captain ████ burst into our studio with armed military. He too swore an oath before God and country and William Randolph Hearst. There was no reason to bring a stranger into my and Willie's little conspiracy against RKO Radio Pictures and the United States government. Benny was *already* part of the conspiracy. And more than that, Benny Herrmann was an intimate member of the family. Benny had even charged a new Theremin against our production, especially for his new score. It was going to be glorious. Was going to be. Was.

PETER: What do you mean? "Was".

ORSON: When we emerged from the eternal darkness of the editing room with our canisters of film in hand, we were greeted with not with the blinding light of the dawn, but the blinding stares of Charles Koerner.

PETER: Oh, my.

ORSON: Oh, yes. And he only had one word for us: "screening room".

PETER: That's actually... never-mind.

ORSON: Willie and I sat in the pale light of the screening room just as pale as the silver screen, but certainly more bloodless. This was a worse feeling than being interrogated by the FBI, because they have rules they have to operate by. Charles Koerner was not so ham-strung. He was far too quiet. Eerily quiet. The silence was pure torture. It took what seemed like an eternity for the projection operator to thread the first reel. Willie and I sat looking straight ahead. Or at least I did. I don't know if Willie had looked over his shoulder towards Charles, but I certainly didn't dare. I stared at the spot in the corner of the screen where the cigarette burns flash momentary to signal the changing of the film-reels. In my paranoia, I saw the cigarette burns flash in and out of existence. Then, very briefly, the fire seemed to catch the entire screen aflame and burned away with the intensity of the sun. The flames soon leapt to the curtains and then crawled onto the ceiling. The conflagration was all consuming. The roaring and raging fire set my skin ablaze as if I was a medieval witch being burnt at the stake for the crimes of witchcraft. And what is the modern equivalent to witchcraft: conspiracy against the government? How many Hollywood stars were caught up in Senator Joseph McCarthy's Commie witchhunt? It may have started with the "Hollywood Ten", who refused to testify at the House Un-American Activities Committee. I will never forget their names Alvah Bessie, Herbert Biberman, Lester Cole, Edward Dmytryk, Ring Lardner, Jr., John Howard Lawson, Albert Maltz, Samuel Ornitz, Adrian Scott, and Dalton Trumbo. But soon the witchhunt captured many others in Hollywood. Would Dalton Trumbo say, just a couple of years ago, "As far as I was concerned, it was a completely just verdict. I had contempt for that Congress and have had contempt for several since. And on the basis of guilt or innocence, I could never really complain very much. That this was a crime or misdemeanor was the complaint, my complaint."

PETER: Those were terrible times for both Hollywood and the nation.

ORSON: Then I was snapped back to reality by the projector hollering down that the film was ready. I may have peed myself a little. Might have. I can't remember. I remember crossing my legs and I may have prayed a little, which is just as, if not more, embarrassing than peeing oneself.

PETER: Orson!

ORSON: The film was amazing. It really was. I'm not full of hubris. It looked really great on the big screen. Up until the very moment, I had only seen the film through a individual frames on a loop and scene-by-scene on the four inch screen of a Moviola editing machine. Seeing it as it was intended to be seen, on a room-sized screen, was awe inspiring. In the past four decades, I have never tired of the awe of seeing my first cut for the first time in a screening room. Sure, Hollywood premieres are wonderful and all with the glitz and glamour in spades, but that first time seeing it up on the screen, albeit a smaller version of the cinema screen. The Technicolor was particularly awe-inspiring. It was a complete shock when the color appeared for the first time in any of my films. It was unnatural. So unnatural that I became, momentarily, nauseous. Marion Davies' fiery dress, her blood-rose colored, pouty lips, mouthing the word, "Rosebud".

PETER: What? What was that? "Rosebud". You didn't use that word again, did you?

ORSON: Um... no... why would I use *that* word again. I certainly didn't use *that* word... not again.

PETER: Oh, Orson.

ORSON: But I wasn't the one who used the Old Man's pet name for Marion's private pa–

PETER: Orson!

ORSON: But I wasn't the one who used it. Marion did. She gave me a secret. *The* secret. She did. I didn't learn it from Mank. I learned it from Marion herself. She warned me, "Secrets. That is the only thing that really matters in this world. Secrets. My Pops trades in them. He buys and sells them all day long. It's the essence of his business. The president has many secrets. Heck, Pops has pictures of the president in his stupid wheelchair. You and Willie are conspiring cover up what happened tonight and then you'll have your own secrets to protect. Everybody has secrets. You tell me your secrets and I'll tell you his."

PETER: And what secret could possibly interest you?

ORSON: She said, "If you're dealing with William Randolph Hearst, you're going to have to know one of his secrets if you're going to have any power in your negotiations with him. If you know one of his secrets, he'll keep all of yours. That is the nature of the beast. You tell me your little secret and I'll give you his."

PETER: Which was? Oh. Don't tell me.

ORSON: "Rosebud."

PETER: I'm at a loss for words. You never seem to learn, do you?

ORSON: But I wasn't the one who... never-mind... I need to find my awe again, Peter. The awe I felt when I saw my film in glorious Technicolor for that first time. Ah. There it is. I've found my happy place. The screening room at RKO studios.

PETER: That couldn't possibly be your "happy" place. That was where you saw them butcher *The Magnificent Ambersons.* You were misera–

ORSON: I'm in the screening room at RKO studios watching my *Invasion From Mars* and I'm... miserable. The happiness of seeing my film in glorious Technicolor lasted only for a moment, a split second, before Charles Koerner coughed. A nervous cough. An I'm-not-pleased cough.

PETER: Orson, I'm sorry.

ORSON: It was two hours spent as if Joe Louis was using my body as a heavy bag. Pummeling me with each and every sound that came from Charles Koerner. Every cough– a punch to the gut. Every sigh– a jab to my head. Every moan, every groan– a kidney punch. Every deep breath– a punch that took the wind out of me. I began to hallucinate.

PETER: What?

ORSON: Have you ever audibly heard someone has a psychotic break? It started with nervous shifting from side to side in his seat, and continued with the crossing and uncrossing of his legs, the stretching and retightening of his tie, the combing of his hair with his fingers, the clutching and grasping at his quickly receding hairline, the nervous coughing, the mumbled profanities, the slurping and gulping of his coffee, the quiet requesting of three fingers of scotch– neat– from Willie Brown, who dutifully obliged, the moaning, the groaning, the slightly more articulated profanities, the gulping of three fingers of scotch– neat, and finally, as the film ended— the fully enunciated profanities. An endless stream of abusive, blasphemous, indecent, obscene, vulgar, yet inventively creative curse words were hurled in my general direction.

PETER: In your "general direction"?

ORSON: Okay. They were hurled at my face. They were aimed directly down my gullet. Satisfied? Charles couldn't understand *what* I had done. He couldn't comprehend *why* I did what I did. He couldn't fathom *how* I had gotten away doing what I had done. He couldn't appreciate *who* I thought I was to have the audacity to have done what I had done. And he couldn't figure out *where* he had been the entire time to have been so ignorant of what I was doing the entire time. *How* could it be possible his gang of flunkies didn't know I wasn't shooting the film I claimed to have been shooting? *How* would it have been possible that his network of spies couldn't have ferreted out the truth that I wasn't shooting the film they all thought I had been shooting? The *why's*, the *what's*, the *where's*, the *when's*, and the *how's* were boggling his mind. Of course, I had been shooting Howard Koch's version of *The War of the Worlds*. He read the script adapted by William Francis Brown. He read the call sheets. He saw all of the rushes. Of course, I had been shooting Howard Koch's version of *The War of the Worlds*. This was the movie that RKO's crack marketing staff had spent that last few months producing posters and newspaper advertising for. A trailer, using footage I had shot for Howard Koch's version of *The War of the Worlds*, had already been produced and distributed to movie houses around the country in preparation for the advertising campaign for Howard Koch's version of *The War of the Worlds*. Where in the flying blue hell (his actual phrase was far more colorful and profane)... Where in the flying blue hell was that film? That I hadn't been shooting and editing Howard Koch's version of *The War of the Worlds* was an impossibility. Why hadn't he just watched Howard Koch's version of *The War of the Worlds*. He kept repeating Howard Koch's name as if his version of *The War of the Worlds* would magically appear on the screen in RKO's screening room. Charles' mind was shattering as if I had thrown a brick through a pane of glass. It was crumbling like a building at the epicenter of an earthquake. It was cracking like an ugly person's mirror. It was melting like... something that melts.

PETER: How your whit is slipping, Orson.

ORSON: Actually its not, but this didn't happen. What I just related between Charles and myself was all a fevered fever-dream. It didn't actually happened.

PETER: What is the truth and what is a lie? I'll never know! I'll never again know. I won't ever again know the difference between the truth and a lie. Our entire friendship have been flushed down the shitter! You lied to me. Again!

ORSON: Of course not, Peter. It wasn't a lie. I experienced it. It just didn't actually happen. You see, I had spent those next two hours in a special place in ninth level Dante's *Inferno* that was reserved for the traitors, the betrayers, the oathbreakers.

PETER: As your friend, I would normally say you were not destined for such an after-life, Orson. But at this very moment, I feel betrayed. You are a traitor to our friendship. You have broken the very oath of our friendship. I'm not so sure the Devil isn't heating up a special pot just to roast you—

ORSON: I know. I know. But know this, Peter. I haven't betrayed you. I would never. Could never.

PETER: Orson, please— Not another word— Just let me go home in peace—

ORSON: I betrayed Charles Koerner. I was forced– no– hired to film a straight adaptation of my "The War of the Worlds" radio-dramatization and I betrayed the trust of my employer. I didn't deliver the film I had promised him I would deliver. I swore an oath before God and country and I betrayed– I'm an oathbreaker. I swore to keep the invasion from Mars a secret from the American people and I was preparing to release a film into the cinema houses that proved I had broken my oath. I committed treason against my President by filming my *Invasion From Mars*. And I was being punished in my own creatively inspired damnation. There was my masterpiece projected onto the screen. It was beautiful. It was transcendent. It was glorious. But I couldn't enjoy a single frame. Satan laughed at me. He guffawed at my pride. My vainglory.

PETER: Orson, maybe now you're being too hard on yourself.

ORSON: I'm not being hard enough. I am trying to lay bare my crimes here, Peter. And I suffered from them twenty-four frames a second for two hours. And when film finally ended, it just ended. The credits had yet to be composed. I knew my career was over. Done. Kawput. I couldn't dare turn my head to put my gaze upon Charles. I don't know what I was most afraid of. Was his head spinning around with fire blazing from his eye-sockets from a conniption? Then I heard *it*. *It* was subtle. *It* was almost imperceptible. But I heard *it*.

PETER: Heard what?

ORSON: A sob. A cry. I turned to see a tear overflow his left eye and cascade down his face. As the flashing lights of the projector began to wind down, I saw the tears, I saw the snot moistening his upper-lip. He was weeping. Had I broken his psyche? Had I driven him to a nervous breakdown?

PETER: Oh, dear God.

ORSON: And then he tried to speak, he muttered, "There was always a part of me who had hoped you would have told what really happened that night, but then I saw the dailies and I saw you were actually filming the straight adaption of 'The War of the Worlds' that I *had* asked for, that I had *begged* you to make. I thought– I really thought– that through reverse psychology, that in your extreme hubris, that you tell the real story of that Mischief Night, but, instead, the dailies told the same cockamamie story I'd heard for the last four years. That story you told the reporters the morning after, I knew it was a lie. I knew you lied! I knew what I had heard on the radio was *real*."

PETER: What?

ORSON: Charles continued blowing my mind, "I knew that Martians were invading America. As I huddled with my wife and my children and my grandchildren around the radio-set, I knew that the end of the world was upon us. I heard the music of Guy Lombardo and his orchestra, not Ramon Ranquello. I heard Hans Von Kaltenborn interrupting the evening of dance music with reports of a Martian invasion. I had heard Hans Von Kaltenborn, not Carl Philips. I know had had heard Hans Von Kaltenborn's voice on the radio that night. Arthur Buddington was the Princeston professor investigating the impact site, not Richard Pierson. That the impact site was in Virgina, not New Jersey."

PETER: What was he trying to say?

ORSON: I was trying to figure out what he was trying to say. I couldn't wrap my little pudding-head around the words he was speaking. They didn't make a lick of sense. He couldn't be acknowledging what he was acknowledging. Nobody in the past four years had ever, and I mean *ever*, brought up hearing the actual invasion from Mars. So complete was the "Orson Welles' Conspiracy", that not a single person has ever admitted hearing an *actual* invasion Mars with the *actual* details. It was like the collective consciousness of all Americans had been rewritten by the "Orson Welles' Conspiracy." I had never heard a peep about Hans Von Kaltanborn or Arthur Buddington or Guy Lombardo. Never once. Never. Never-ever.

PETER: I'm at a loss for words.

ORSON: Charles continued blowing my freaking mind, "I wasn't born yesterday, Orson. When CBS records released that damned long-play record, I knew– I *knew*– that we had been lied to. That for some cockamamie reason you recorded that ridiculousness. That recording wasn't what frightened my grandchildren. My wife. What frightened us to the very core of our souls was an actual invasion from Mars. The *who's*. The *where's*. The *what's*. The *when's*. The *how's*. The *why's*! Why did the invasion only last four or five, maybe six or seven short hours? My terror stricken mind could no longer comprehend the passage of time. Where were the tri-pod machines? Being safely in California I did not witness the certain destruction all around, but the next morning all of the destruction was being blamed on a hurricane... a hurricane that happened over a month before! Why was there a cover-up? How far through the government did the conspiracy reach? If it went all the way to the top, then why did President Roosevelt believe the American people didn't deserve the truth? Where was the outrage from the families of the thousands of men, women, and children who as reported by Han Von Kalton– *[cries heavily]* had died? What really happened that night? Now... now... I know! It was an 'Orson Welles' conspiracy'! Thank you, Orson."

PETER: I'm stunned.

ORSON: So was I. He continued to say words I never thought I would ever hear uttered by Charles Koerner, "Thank you for making the very film that I hoped– I prayed– you would make. You have proven yourself to be worthy of your reputation, Orson."

PETER: I'm at a loss for words.

ORSON: So was I. And that is saying something coming from me. *[Long, uncomfortable silence.]* Then Willie excused himself. He had to go "visit Ms. Jones". I wasn't sure if you needed to, well, shit. Because I had nearly shitted myself with after Charles finished speaking.

PETER: Orson!

ORSON: And when Willie sat down on the porcelain bowl, the shock and exhaustion of Charles Koerner allying himself with us overcame him. He sat on the toilet shaking. The "Orson Welles' Conspiracy" had seemingly just added a new agent. A powerful agent. One who wielded the collective power of RKO Radio-Pictures and held a purse funded by Floyd Odlum. We were about to wage an actual war against both the government and newspaper agents who dared censor us. But then there came a tapping... a rapping... on the bathroom floor.

PETER: Oh, God, Orson, not this again.

[Orson clicks the reel-to-reel recording on.]

AGENT ECKS: You lied! Again! Harry Lime was just an actor you hired to put us on a false trail.

WILLIE: What? Who? Oh, yeah right. I had completely forgotten about him... crap... he's been in custody this entire time?... poor guy... ah... how did we forget about him?... ah... yeah... what?... he was an actor?... Orson hired an actor?... I... I... didn't know... How was I supposed to know?... All this is so far above my pay grade...

AGENT ECKS: You've been working with Orson Welles this entire time!

WILLIE: Of course. I have been contractually obligated to work on *The War of the Worlds* this entire time.

AGENT ECKS: You and Orson Welles are cohorts in cahoots. Do you have any idea how many hours, how many sleep-deprived hours, we interrogated that poor actor before we finally, actually, believed his story?

WILLIE: I'm so sorry... you're so.. stupid.

AGENT ECKS: You lied!

WILLIE: Of course, I did. Why is everyone so surprised when someone lies, particularly in an interrogation? If you're guilty than it's always in your best interest to lie. What does telling the truth actually gain you? I tell stories when it is of no benefit to me. I lie over the stupidest, most innocuous things. I visited my mother once and told her that I had driven over the new bridge over the river, when the bridge was nowhere near being finished. There was no reason to lie. There was no reason to tell that particular story. She could easily drive down to the river and see that the bridge wasn't nearly finished, that the drive to the nearest crossing was still at least a ten minute drive. There was no reason to lie. But I did. I have always chosen the story over the truth. The story is always so much more interesting. And it always will.

AGENT ECKS: You cannot lie to a federal agent.

WILLIE: Why not? I was not under oath. I was not in court. You've interrogated me in my apartment and in the men's room. I'm not sure what the legality is about interrogating a suspect in the men's room, with his pants around his ankles. But I'm pretty sure I'm not guilty of... anything.

AGENT ECKS: Pursuant to Section 9(c) of the of the National Industrial Recovery Act of 1933, "whoever shall knowingly and willfully falsify or conceal or cover up by any trick, scheme, or device a material fact, or make or cause to be made any false or fraudulent statements or representations, or make or use or cause to be made or used any false bill, receipt, voucher, roll, account, claim, certificate, affidavit, or deposition, knowing the same to contain any fraudulent or fictitious statement or entry, in any matter within the jurisdiction of any department or agency of the United States."

WILLIE: You have that memorized? My. You're anal. Then arrest me.

AGENT ECKS: What?

WILLIE: Arrest me. File charges. I am entitled to a defense and during my defense, I will put into evidence all of the "Top-Secret" documents Orson and I were able to acquire.

AGENT ECKS: But they wouldn't be admissible in court.

WILLIE: They would be if the judge was amenable. Are you willing to take that risk? Because I am. Here I sit with my trousers around my ankles, not having had the chance to wipe my backside (which is getting mighty hot and sticky due to nervous perspiration), I have nothing left to lose. If the judge sides with my defense, all of the documents would become part of the public-record.

AGENT ECKS: You wouldn't. You couldn't. Ha. We have all of the documents from the bungalow in Victorville.

WILLIE: Really? You're a government agent. How does one go about preserving documents? You're in the spy game. You know all the techniques. So does RKO. We've shot spy-thrillers. We know all the techniques you do, because everybody gets really talkative when they're a "consultant" on a film and we know a few techniques that only a screenwriter could conceive of. Don't think that our micro-cameras are all functionless props. Sometimes you just have to buy the actual article. Our property rooms are filled to overflowing with actual technology. The real deal. Orson and I photographed and preserved on microfiche all the "Top-Secret" documents.

AGENT ECKS: You never had the opportunity. We have all of the evidence.

WILLIE: Believe what you will. Where would we have hidden the microfiche? In the stock-pile of film here at RKO? Would we have been that stupid? There must be hundreds of thousands of miles of film on the lot. That's quite a needle in a haystack. What if we filed them in with the Los Angeles Public Library?

AGENT ECKS: You wouldn't have.

WILLIE: We could have. Maybe we did. Maybe we didn't. Are they in a safety deposit box at the bank? Or are they in a locker at a bus depot? Or a locker in the YMCA? Or any bank, bus depot, or YMCA within a drivable distance? The microfiche could be anywhere. The moment I get arrested, that microfiche gets mailed to the *Los Angeles Times*.

AGENT ECKS: That's blackmail.

WILLIE: No, it'll be the regular mail: the United States Postal Service.

AGENT ECKS: You can't threaten a government agent like that.

WILLIE: If what Orson and I believe happened that cold October Mischief Night actually happened, that there was an invasion from Mars, that thousands of men, women, and children died, that government officials lied to families, lied to the American public, then what do I really have to lose? You could and probably should just kill me.

AGENT ECKS: Wait! What?

WILLIE: But then, an editor at the *Los Angeles Times*, hell, the *New York Times,* would get a fateful package of microfiche in the mail. Maybe the list of papers that will get a fateful package will include the Hearst empire, too. How would the editors of every Hearst paper react when they see the *un*redacted documents that clearly don't redact the Old Man's name. I am more than aware of the lengths you will go through to keep knowledge of this invasion from the American people, but what are Orson and I willing to go through to expose all of this? We are the ones that have nothing else to lose. And everything to gain.

AGENT ECKS: You little sh–

WILLIE: I'd watch your language, Joe. Since this is conversation is recorded for posterity and my protection. I wouldn't want your superiors to realize they have an ignoramus on their payroll. This is why conspiracies fail. They trust the wrong people with knowledge they aren't mentally capable of processing or protecting.

AGENT ECKS: This isn't being recorded. It couldn't be. Have you bugged the men's room?

WILLIE: Maybe. Just maybe. You interrogated me in this very men's room, so I could have easily used any of the recording technology that RKO pictures possessed to bug this very men's room. You think I don't have hours-and-hours of recordings of men doing their business and a couple of times capturing two paramours, a star and a starlet, using the men's room for an afternoon quickie.

AGENT ECKS: You're lying again. The men's room isn't bugged. It would more plausible that there a reel-to-reel in that briefcase! *[laughs heartily]* But! You aren't capable of producing that level of technology. Nobody outside of a government spy agency is. I'm going to call your bluff.

WILLIE: Then why don't you confess your sins. I've got the microphone slipped up my sleeve. Here. See. Confess. Or should I confess them for you?

AGENT ECKS: You wouldn't dare.

WILLIE: Like how in my apartment you put the invasion from Mars... on the record...

AGENT ECKS: I didn't.

WILLIE: It's one thing to be paranoid about the government when the government isn't even aware you even exist. That is a simple paranoia for the hysterical. It another thing completely to be paranoid when you know the government will stop at nothing to stop you from going about your daily affairs. Orson Welles has turned me into a Frankenstein's monster of paranoia. Particularly when we got our mitts on those so-called "Top Secret" documents. I wouldn't sleep in peace without knowing that

If there is a Zen to the art of bullshit, then there must be a Zen Garden to the art of bullshit and Willie Brown is the Zen Master!

my apartment was bugged.

AGENT ECKS: I... Don't... Believe... You.

WILLIE: Believe what you will.

AGENT ECKS: Why all the stories? First you're a script doctor, then you're employee of William Randolph Hearst. Then you claimed to be an eighteen-year-old kid, which must be another lie. Your ID is no doubt a product of RKO's props department! Then you claimed Harry Lime was at the center of all this. And it turns out Harry Lime was an actor Orson Welles hired to put us off the scent. And now, you claim to have had your apartment bugged. I don't believe you. A screen-writer isn't capable of that level of sophistication, even with the studio's props department at your disposal. I won't believe anything you have to say any more. You lie at the drop of a hat. I've encountered many lies from criminals, but none lie with the ease and lack of conscience that you do. You lie over the stupidest sh–

WILLIE: I don't lie. I tell stories.

AGENT ECKS: There is no difference.

WILLIE: First, there is a Zen to the art of bullshit: to tell a remembrance exactly as it occurred was disingenuous to the drama inherent in the telling of any good story. What happened in the moment is but the first draft of the event. The memories we form in the very moments afterward begins the process of revising the memory. Every subsequent recollection inherently involves a rewrite and every rewrite revises the memory or edits that recollection until we achieve the final draft of memory. If others happen to remember with any less of the inherent drama, it is because they do not have the imagination necessary. Second, there is an Art of War to bullshit: with each story told, the truth becomes more and more like the bullshit. The truth is no longer acknowledged as the truth, because has been covered so completely in the bullshit of the various stories told. You believe one story, which turns out is not the truth. You believe another story, which also turns out not to be the truth. Then you no longer believe the truth, which for the first time isn't bullshit. You no longer know what to believe. That is the art of war that I am the master of. You will never know what is the truth and what is bullshit. And because of this fact. I have already won the war of art.

YOUNG ORSON: *[Knocking.]* Willie are you done in the "library"? Charles wants to discuss... things.

WILLIE: *[To Orson.]* Almost done, Orson. *[To the agent.]* Don't fret, Joe. You're not the first and certainly not the last to fall for my stories. I'd really appreciate it if my code-name in your reports is "The Bullshitter". Not sure if the government would allow such a vulgar code-name, but there is none more appropriate. And next time, choose somewhere other than the john for our next interrogation. It won't be as awkward. And I won't have to fake a BM.

[Orson clicks the reel-to-reel recording off.]

ORSON: The beauty of the conspiracy is rooted in Willie Brown's philosophy of bullshit. Whether it is the assassination of JFK or the invasion from Mars, if the author of the conspiracy lies consistently and convincingly, then the truth sounds increasingly absurd. Despite the illogistics of the "magic-bullet" explanation, the truth of a second gunmen on the grassy knoll sounds downright ridiculous. And the seekers and discoverers of the truth are easily and readily dismissed as paranoid and delusional. The wordsmith Gore Vidal once opined, "Americans have been trained by the media to go into Pavlovian giggles at the mention of the word 'conspiracy,' because for an American to believe in a conspiracy, he must also believe in flying saucers or, craziest of all, that more than one person was involved in the JFK murder." And the source of this belief is me. *If* I hadn't recorded a bastardization of that night's Martian invasion... *if* I hadn't conspired with Franklin Delano Roosevelt and his puppet, William Randolph Hearst, then there wouldn't have been the George "Orson Welles' Conspiracy"! If I hadn't gone before the reporters with the hound-dogged expression on my face, then the American people would have realized the world, the solar-system is a far more vast, wonderful, and infinity dangerous place. Then the American people would not have been conditioned by my actions to doubt the intentions of the media. No one would have doubted the Warren Commission's conclusion that Lee Harvey Oswald was the "lone gunmen". No one.

PETER: That is a huge overstatement on your part, Orson.

ORSON: On the contrary, it is the grossest understatement possible. I am the source. I am the singularity at the center of every conspiracy. But there is one element of the entire conspiracy that is beyond my understanding. I'm not one to buy into the movement of planets affecting us as astrologers believe, but the knowledge the movement of planets is essential for an invasion from the planet Mars to be successful. But there is a strange convergence that happens at a particular point in Earth's journey around the sun. Whenever the Earth reaches that point in its orbit of the sun where Mischief Night occurs, something strange seems to happen in my life.

PETER: You're not into metaphysics, Orson, you're not superstitious. Why even say something like that?

ORSON: The invasion by the Martians occurred on Mischief Night. One year ago, the night I chose to finally open up about the "War of the Worlds" radio-broadcast. The first draft of Willie's adaptation of Howard Koch's *The War of the Worlds* was finished on October 30, 1941 and delivered to George Schaffer. The *Invasion From Mars* film *is* literally Mischief Night. Charles Koerner, Willie Brown, and I plotted to release *Invasion From Mars* on Friday, October 30, 1942. So it would have been premiered in cinemas on the greatest Mischief Night of them all.

PETER: Those are just coincidences.

ORSON: Are they? Really?

PETER: Tonight wasn't a coincidence, you *choose* tonight and one year ago. The others are just coincidences. Except, maybe the release of your film. That night was *chosen* by Charles Koerner. Maybe you orchestrated all of these coincidences.

ORSON: Certainly not October 30, 1938, but... ah... October 30, 1941, October 30, 1942, a day that would live forever in ignominy. By the time reviews of the movie hit the newspapers, it would be the morning of October, 31, 1942! The anniversary of my interview with the press. The press reported on my fake Martian invasion on Halloween morning 1938 and they would publish reviews on Halloween morning 1942! If we had to just get there. It was the second to last Saturday in August when Koerner turned the corner by first watching that first full cut of *Invasion From Mars*. So we had to survive ten weeks of assaults from newspaper agents intent on destroying our film, our careers, and our studio. Ten weeks of assaults from government agents intent on robbing us of our freedom, our liberty, and perhaps even our lives. But for the first time since we began our two-man conspiracy to get *Invasion From Mars* made, we had the power, prestige, and financial might of an entire Hollywood studio behind us. We finally had the resources to wage a war against, not only the Hearst empire, but the entire United States government itself.

PETER: I hate to burst your bubble, Orson, but since I've never... ever... heard of the *War of the Worlds* feature film, or even called *Invasion From Mars*, then I can assume that you lost this particular war.

ORSON: Of course, I lost this "particular" war. If I had won it, then the world would have known about the invasion from Mars, or at least had a collective good laugh at my expense upon its Hollywood star-studded premiere. That was a future that I could have lived with, not the ignominy of nothingness. Sometimes I like to think back on those days and imagine that other trope of science-fiction, the alternate reality. I know what the ignominy of deafening silence after the Battle Over *The War of the Worlds* was like, but *what* would the Hollywood premiere of *Invasion From Mars* have been like?

PETER: I'm at a loss to imagine.

ORSON: Okay, this wasn't part of my plan this evening, but let's take a trip down the Red Brick Road.

PETER: Don't you mean the "Yellow" Brick Road?

ORSON: Oh, no, my good friend. There were two roads leading out of Munchkinland. The Yellow Brick Road that led to the Emerald City that Dorthy took to see *[Singing.] the wizard, the Wonderful Wizard of Oz*, but there was a Red Brick Road... leading elsewhere. That was the Red Brick Road not taken. There is always the road not taken. There is the Red Brick Road that led back to Broadway, instead of the Yellow Brick Road to Hollywood. There is the Red Brick Road that led to the *Gospel According to Shakespeare*, instead of *Citizen Kane*. And somewhere there is the Red Brick Road that led to the Hollywood premiere for *Invasion From Mars*.

PETER: *[Singing impromtu to the tune of "We're Off to See the Wizard".] We're off to see the premiere, the Glitz and Glamour of... Hollyweird.*

ORSON: *[Laughs heartily.]* ⚛

The Glitz & Glamour of Hollyweird

The Hollyweird premiere of The Invasion From Mars *with a star-studded guest list of a who's who of Hollyweird!*

ORSON: In this glorious parallel alternate reality that would make Robert Heinlein, Arthur C. Clark, or Isaac Asimov proud, Charles Koerner rented Grauman's Chinese Theatre for the Hollyweird premiere of *Invasion From Mars*. Invitations went out to the Who's Who of Hollyweird. Literally.

PETER: One of my pet peeves is using the word "literally" figuratively.

ORSON: Literally. I mean that. Literally. There really was a *Who's Who of Hollyweird*. It's on the bookshelf over there, behind the piano.

PETER: *[Sighs.]*

ORSON: The leading men were the likes of Fred Astaire, James Cagney, Gary Cooper, Errol Flynn, Henry Fonda, Clark Gable, Cary Grant, Fredric March, William Powell, James Stewart, and Edward G. Robinson, and the leading ladies: Claudette Colbert, Joan Crawford, Bette Davis, Marlene Dietrich, Irene Dunne, Greta Garbo, Judy Garland, Rita Hayworth, Jean Harlow, Dorothy Lamour, Myrna Loy, Ginger Rogers, Barbara Stanwyck, Gloria Swanson, Elizabeth Taylor, Mae West, Jane Wyman.

PETER: Those were all alphabetical by gender. Are you reading from your Rolodex, Orson? Or the *Who's Who of Hollywood*?— I mean, *Hollyweird*. Have to maintain the... something or other... the continuity? I don't know what am I saying?

ORSON: What? No! You're distracting me. The hot-couples were also there, even those that were not there "together", if you get what my mean: Katharine Hepburn and Spencer Tracey, Humphrey Bogart and Lauren Bacall, Vivien Leigh and Laurence Olivier, Lucille Ball and Desi Arnaz, and of course, Orson Welles and Dolores del Río.

PETER: Of course. Of course, she was there. Of course, you spoke in the third-person. Of course.

Orson Welles showing off the Invasion From Mars *program to his paramour Dolores del Río at the premiere!*

Of course. Of course. Were you actually "together" with Rita Hayworth by this point in this alternate time-line, too, Orson?

ORSON: Hardy-har-har. When the day finally came, or should I say, "When the night finally came", it was a night that would go down in Hollyweird infamy. My name would be wagging on the lips of everyone in Hollyweird. I would find my redemption from the ignominy of Hearst sabotaging my *Citizen Kane* and RKO's bungling of *The Magnificent Ambersons. Invasion From Mars* would be my triumph. Despite the governmental conspiracies from the likes of President Franklin Delano Roosevelt, despite the interferences of the newspapermen of William Randolph Hearst, despite the plots of the Martian Commonwealth whom infiltrated the highest levels of the... well, everywhere and everything.

PETER: I'm at a loss, I truly am.

ORSON: My *Invasion From Mars* would finally have its Hollyweird premiere. All of Hollyweird was decked out to the nines. The gowns would, no doubt, be glamorous. The makeup would be exquisite. The hair would be perfectly coiffed. The tuxedos would be impeccably tailored. The mustaches would be respectably trimmed. Dolores and I sat in the back of our posh, impossibly shiny, black Mecedes-Benz-770K. The champagne was on ice. The scotch was most certainly not. As the car pulled up to the front of Grauman's Chinese Theater, I could see the dozens of photographers and the hundreds– nay thousands!– of anxious onlookers. Then my car-door was opened and Dolores stepped out into the sea of insanity. The flash-bulbs were popping. The flash-bulbs were dropping. The flash-bulbs were shattering under the clattering feet of the photographers. Ah, the glorious background music of a Hollyweird premiere. The wailing from the teenaged girls, that the publicists of the mop-headed Beatles would mimic to perfection two decades later, assaulted me with their adulations. Their screams. Their dreams. Their cheers. Their tears. Their fainting. Their unrestrainting. John, Paul, George, and Ringo surely had nothing on a young Orson Welles. But I digress.

PETER: Of course, you do... *[sighs.]*

ORSON: A reporter from the Hearst Metrotone News chose this time above all others to take his employers frustrations out on me by jamming a microphone into my face, "Orson Welles, what do you say to your critics that you are exploiting the tensions of the war for box office receipts?"

"I beg your pardon?"

"Five great Hollyweird directors are all doing their share to benefit the war effort: John Ford, Frank Capra, John Huston, William Wyler, and

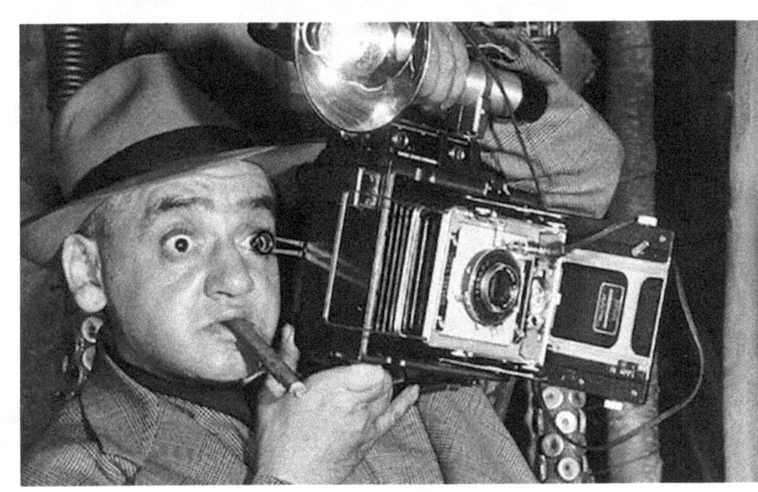

William Randolph Hearst ordered one of his reporters to ambush of Orson Welles at his Hollyweird premiere!

George Stevens. Even Disney cartoon characters like Donald Duck are bolstering the morale of both home and abroad during the trying times. And here you are, Mr. Welles, premiering a science-fiction film, whose story wouldn't even be fit for the pulp magazines on the newsstands. In a time of the occupations of Poland, Czechoslovakia, and France and the bombardments of England by Nazi Germany and our young fighting men dying in the Battle of Midway and innumerable Pacific islands, here you feature an enemy as distant and cartoonish as humanely possible: Martians. Why, dear God, man, why?"

"Normally," I said, "I would tell you that while war was brewing in Europe, this world was being watched keenly and closely by intelligences greater than man's and yet as mortal as his own; that as men busied themselves about their various concerns they were scrutinised and studied, perhaps almost as narrowly as a man with a microscope might scrutinise the transient creatures that swarm and multiply in a drop of water. With infinite complacency men went to and fro over this globe about their little affairs, serene in their assurance of their empire over matter. It is possible that the infusoria under the microscope do the same. No one gave a thought to the older worlds of space as sources of human danger, or thought of them only to dismiss the idea of life upon them as impossible or improbable. Yet across the gulf of space, minds that are to our minds as ours are to those of the beasts that perish, intellects vast and cool and unsympathetic, regarded this earth with envious eyes, and slowly and surely drew their plans against us.

"Normally, I would take this time you have so graciously given me in this interview to tell you that my radio-broadcast of "The War of the Worlds" dramatization was no such thing, that Martians had, in fact, invaded American soil, that monstrous Martian tri-pod walking machines made their march on Washington DC, that there was an hysteria unlike anything this nation had ever experienced listening to the sheer wanton terror inducing panic broadcast, and there was a vast government conspiracy between President Franklin Delano Roosevelt, William Randolph Hearst, and yours truly to expunge this auditory evidence from the three million, nay five million, nay-nay seven million, in the CBS listening audience, to hide this truth from the American people: the truth of an 'Orson Welles' Conspiracy'.

"Normally, I would sit down with that hysterical harpy Hedda Hopper and holler in Hollyweird headlines in that government agents conspired to halt production of my *Invasion From Mars* film posing as anyone and everyone from lunch ladies in the cafeteria to executives on the board of directors, that newspaperman not unlike yourself, sought to sabotage my motion picture and defame me, my cast, and my crew in Hearst papers across this great land, and the infiltrators from the Commonwealth of Mars, well, I wish I could tell you what they were up to.

"Normally, I would accuse you– Mr. Newspaperman– of being an ignorant cog of the governmental machine created by the President and the Old Man in a conspiracy to destroy any vocal opposition to the 'Orson Welles' Conspiracy'. Your boss will stop at nothing– and I mean *literally* nothing—

PETER: *[sighs.]*

ORSON: — to make me a laughing stock. His intentions are and always been outright character assassination."

"How can you possibly speak of character assassination in the same breath with *Citizen Kane*?' this intrepid reporter, or should I say insipid, said politely rebuking me. 'Only you would have the gall to equate a newspaper interview at a glamorous and obnoxious Tinseltown film premiere with a scandalously libelous motion picture mercilessly put to death by my colleagues Louella Parsons and Hedda Hopper."

PETER: Are you really have an imaginary argument with an imaginary reporter in story set in an imaginary parallel alternate reality's Hollyweird premiere for a motion picture you actually claim to have filmed in our actual world? *[inhales deeply.]*

ORSON: Yes. And now I've lost my place. Um— Oh, yeah. I found it—

"Mercilessly put to death?' That's a fine how-do-you-do. I am going to dissect that statement any number of ways. I'm looking right into the camera and I'm directing this to you, cinema goers. *And* this almost includes you, Old Man, sitting in your private screening room. First, I *only* lampooned you in *Citizen Kane*– and yes, this is the first and only time I will publicly acknowledge that Charles Foster Kane was, in fact, based on you, you pompous and preposterous so-and-so. There I said it! Everyone here heard it here first! And you put out a hit out on my picture, seeing that none of your papers would print an advertisement or a review or an interview or a letter-to-the-editor about my film. And now, you has upped the ante, if that is at all humanly possible, to completely and utterly destroy me and my new picture. You are too cowardly to fight this fight on your own. And you! You have been drafted into a war that you don't ever realize you're fighting."

"Are you addressing me or continuing to hypothetically address Mr. Hearst through an inanimate object?"

"You! You insipid reporter, you have been drafted into a war that you don't even realize you're fighting. You and those of your same ilk have been sent on Kamikaze missions by the Old Man himself. And you don't even know what you don't know. This is so much bigger than the cinematic sabotage you think you are perpetrating. This is a war that you cannot possibly imagine is being waged on American soil. A war that has already cost over a thousand American lives! A thousand lives that most of the American population doesn't even realize have been lost. There are no tombstones memorializing the dead. Over a thousand lives essentially erased from history and memory. You think you were sent here to do a mere fluff interview on the red carpet of a Hollyweird premiere, but that isn't why you're here. You're here to assassinate me in the eyes of the people.

"But I'm not going to tell you all this, because speaking of Hollyweird premieres, I have a Hollyweird premiere to go to this fine, October evening and I happen to have an attractive date on my arm. So, if you'll excuse me. Good day to you, sir."

PETER: I've said this once, and I'll say it again, and I'll probably say it many, many more times this evening... I'm at a loss for words.

ORSON: Let me tell you who was never, ever at a loss for words, that hysterical harpy Hedda Hopper. I'll be damned if she wasn't being paid per word of salacious and scandalous gossip. I even possess a clipping from the parallel universe's newspaper article Hopper roasted me alive in.

PETER: Of course you do... *[sighs.]*

Talk about shooting yourself in the foot. Or in the head. Watching last night's "top secret" premiere of *Invasion From Mars* was as painful as watching a suicide live on stage, in front of a cinema audience. Orson Welles just killed his own career. And it all the more painful because the film was hilarious. The entire theater audience was caught in wave after wave of laughter, some collapsing into unconsciousness due to a lack of breath. Ambulances had to be summoned to tend to the fainted and those presumed dead. There can be no more damning criticism of a film than unwanted laughter. Sure the comedies of the Marx Brothers or the shorts of the Three Stooges desire laughter like the drug-idled desire their next fix. But for a drama, one purporting to be– laughably– *"Based On a True Story"*, the laughter must have caused Orson Welles to suffer repeated dagger stabs to the heart. And rightfully so. He deserved to suffer for all the suffering he has caused in his nascent Hollyweird career. I warned the

Hedda Hopper had to suffer the ignominy of watching the Citizen Kane *premiere, now she suffers the infuriation of the* Invasion From Mars!

"boy-wonder" that nearly all of his films would never see a release, let alone receive a Hollyweird premiere. This morning I'm sure he wishes he would have quietly shelved this ridiculousness. The death-knell of young Orson Welles' career sounded with the ring of laughter.

His arrogance and ego were on full display during the *Citizen Kane* fiasco. Why he felt the need to slander such as great man as William Randolph Hearst in that abomination of a film will always be beyond my comprehension. Now, in a childish temper-tantrum, he has chosen to lampoon not only William Randolph Hearst, but also our President, Franklin Delano Roosevelt. Despite turning the caricature brush upon himself, he has turned a great President, a great newspaper man, and himself, an insignificant director, into the Three Stooges, slap-sticking their way through a hackneyed plot of conspiracies and extraterrestrials, which will at no point in American history, past, present, or future, permeate into mainstream Hollyweird. Moe Howard, Curly Howard, and Larry Fine would have given their eyeteeth to have elicited the raucous, infectious, and debilitating laughter that ensued last night at the premiere.

What was in Orson Welles' twisted psyche to believe that the conspiracy-riddled story was a worthy subject for a Hollyweird feature film. The film has a single conceit: that instead of broadcasting a radio-adaptation of HG Wells' esteemed science-fiction novel, *The War of the Worlds*, causing nationwide panic, the radio-broadcasts heard that fateful Mischief Night four years ago were *real*?!? Let me repeat that for clarity: the radio-broadcasts heard that fateful Mischief Night four years ago were *real*, and that Martians had, *in fact*, invaded America. Not only did Martians, presumably flesh-and-blood extraterrestrials, use their Tri-Pod machines to march on Washington DC and attempt to destroy the White House, they also murdered thousands of men, women, and children. Despite no evidence of any destruction being reported by anyone other than actual hurricane damages. Despite no cries from any be grieved families, Orson Welles invents out of thin air a conspiracy between our President, Franklin Delano Roosevelt, and the newspaper magnate, William Randolph Hearst, to deceive our entire nation by hiding an entire Martian invasion under the guise of a radio-dramatization, which, as luck would have it, only Orson Welles possessed the genius to compose. His reward for his participation in this conspiracy: the keys to Hollyweird itself. This would, of course, lead directly to *Citizen Kane*! Quite convenient hyperbole. I cannot quite come to wrap my head around the inclusion of Nikola Tesla and a time-machine. Yes, I actually typed those words and you actually read them.

In *Citizen Kane*, Orson hid his slander of Mr. Hearst, a great and powerful man, behind the caricature-character called Charles Foster Kane. But in this picture, he calls the deceitful, conspiratorial President, "Franklin Delano Roosevelt" and the conniving newspaper publisher, "William Randolph Hearst". Where editorial cartoons lampoon for political and social commentary through their caricature and their satire, Orson Welles does none of this. There is no commentary, political, social or otherwise. There is no caricature. There is no satire. There is only incomprehensible and unimaginative slander.

Only a huckster with no moral conscience such as Orson Welles, who has repeatedly proven to lack in abundance, would believe this makes for watchable cinema. There have been absurd films released, but they are B-pictures, films not intended to be received well, films that are instead intended for children and mass audience consumption during Saturday matinées or double-features. *Invasion From Mars* was marketed as a big-budget, Hollyweird premiere worthy genre film, that proved beyond any shadow of doubt to be nothing more than a Z-picture. The worst of the dreck Hollyweird could possibly offer. Strike that. Only a young man, who actually has talent coming out of his ears, like the boy-wonder, could have believed this was a filmable idea.

Where were the executives at RKO during this time? No doubt, distracted with *The*

Magnificent Ambersons, the studio functionaries had rightly insisted on cutting, reshooting, and performing life-saving emergency surgery on the bloated beast. What could have been going on in Charles Koerner's mind when he first watched this film? Did he suffer nervous breakdown? A mental collapse? Or does Orson Welles possess blackmail against the president of RKO Radio-Pictures? There can only be so many plausible reasons such a film as this was given a Hollyweird premiere and a wide-release.

Orson Welles, I beg you, leave the satire to Jonathan Swift and Mark Twain. You may be a genius, but you are just not that bright.

PETER: I wholeheartedly agree and disagree with your imaginary Hedda Hopper. You are the epitome of the creative genius, and your penchant for hyperbole and sheer utter bullshit are unmatched in this or any other century.

ORSON: And I haven't even gotten to the good parts yet.

PETER: Do were really need to go down this little rabbit hole, Orson... *[sighs.]*... it serves no real purpose other than inflating your already sizable ego. With our night already stretching into the small hours, and my limited amount of feet of tape, I really, really, just want to know the real story of the *War of the Worlds* feature film. Nothing more. Nothing less.

ORSON: Okay, okay. Enough of the alternate realities. So back in the really, real world. I actually picked up a really, real telephone and rang up that hysterical harpy and sat down with her and tried to truly reason with her, to convince her to expose the truth of how her beloved benevolent benefactor was trying to sabotage my motion picture, defame me, my cast, and my crew in Hearst papers across this great land. I would use Hedda's own need to salacious headlines against her and against Hearst himself. Hedda wouldn't be able to help herself. By making myself the fool I would bring them all down. Thanks to Willie's ingenious ultra-portable reel-to-reel recorder, I have the interview with that hysterical harpy Hedda Harper that almost brought down a publishing magnate, almost brought down a sitting president, almost brought down an interstellar Martian empire.

PETER: ... *[sighs.]*

ORSON: Almost. *[Clicks on the reel-to-reel.]* Actually for once, I don't have anything actually recorded. *[Clicks off the reel-to-reel.]* If you remember Charles Koerner's reaction to that now infamous screening of *Invasion From Mars*—

PETER: I remember. *[Sighs.]* Remember, it was only a handful of minutes ago, Orson. How could I have forgotten the absurdity of his reaction. It'll be seared into my consciousness for as long as I live.

ORSON: *Since* you remember Charles Koerner reaction to the screening of *Invasion From Mars,* I couldn't just yet wrap my head around Charles' reaction. How was it humanely possible that he remembered the actual events of Halloween Eve 1938, the night that Martians invaded America, when no one else across the country seemed to remember? How was it possible that my boss was the one man in the entire nation who remembered it was Guy Lombardo and his orchestra, not Ramon Ranquello and his; it was Hans Von Kaltenborn interrupting the evening of dance music with reports of a Martian invasion, not Carl Phillips; it was Professor Arthur Buddington investigating the meteorite crash, not Professor Richard Pierson; that it was Grove Hill, Virginia, not Grove Mill, New Jersey; that it was the Hotel Annapolis, not the Park Plaza Hotel. How was it possible that Charles Koerner was the one man who had to power and financial clout to expose the "Orson Welles' Conspiracy" by releasing the *Invasion From Mars* motion picture into cinemas across the country and the world was now allied with Willie Brown and myself?

PETER: Yes, how is it possible this "coincidence" just happens to advance the plot?

ORSON: My point exactly!

PETER: *[Sighs.]*

US vs. T.H.E.M.

ORSON: Now that Charles Koerner was already in his office, on the phone booking Grauman's Chinese Theatre. I had to pinch myself to realize this wasn't the Hollyweird premiere of my fantasies, but an honest-to-goodness Hollywood premiere. I couldn't wait to see Hedda Hopper's harpy-face when news of the premiere got out. But first, I knew that I needed to get the final cut, well, final. In the can as it were. While Benny Herrmann was in the orchestral studio conducting the assembled ensemble of musicians, I sat against the back wall of the engineering room plotting and planning the premiere of *Invasion From Mars* and how I was going to make the evening even more enjoyable. With a trademarked **Orson Welles Prank**™!

PETER: As if pranking them with as cockamamie conspiracy theory wasn't enough of a prank.

ORSON: *[Shush.]* What could be a prank that I could pull on my Hollywood premier's audience without them being none the wiser?

PETER: I shutter to guess.

ORSON: The veritable *Who's Who of Hollywood* would all be the victims of my most infamous of pranks. Everyone who attended the alternate parallel Hollywood premiere would actually be there: Fred Astaire, James Cagney, Gary Cooper, Errol—

PETER: Please, Orson, you don't need to rattle off your Rolodex... again.

ORSON: —Flynn, *etcetera etcetera ad nauseam.* They would all be there for my Hollywood premiere. But for real this time.

PETER: Of course, for real this time. But what is real anymore, Orson? I'm at a loss. I really, really am.

ORSON: What could I do? What kind of prank could I pull? The location inside a cinema certainly limited the potential pranks. You'd be surprised, Peter, just how important location is to a good, well-executed prank. And timing. You have to choose a time and a place that are perfect for the perfect prank. I can't have one without the other. Surprise birthdays have always struck me as somewhat implausible pranks. The timing of the prank is limited to the day of their actual birth and because of this irony, the surprise birthday-party is inherently limited. Sure, locations could be a complete surprise, but certainly not the date. If it was me, personally, I'd plan a surprise birthday party like six months in advance, not six months after the fact. That would be cold-blooded.

PETER: Wait? Six months in advance or six months after the... wouldn't that be the same day?

ORSON: From a certain point of view.

PETER: A certain point-of-view?

ORSON: Whether you want to be considerate or cold-blooded. If I had planned to throw a surprise birthday party your fortieth on January 30, 1979, then I am being considerate, but if I planned the very same surprise birthday party for your thirty-ninth birthday on the very same January 30, 1979, then I'm being cold-blooded.

PETER: *[Sighs.]* Or you could just throw me a party on July 30th. You now, my birthday.

ORSON: Where's the fun in that? Only the cruelest of families would make the birthday boy or girl believe they are so unwanted, so unloved that nobody was planning a birthday party for them. How unimaginably cruel is the surprise birthday party prank.

PETER: Coming from you, Orson, that's rather damning.

ORSON: I know. Right? What could I get away with? I didn't want the police called, like when I pranked Kenny Delmar. What kind of prank would worthy of the name "Orson Welles"?

PETER: *[Sighs.]*

ORSON: I need to come up with the perfect prank for a cinema. Calling the police on Kenny Delmar was the perfect prank for a rehearsal. "The War of the Worlds" was the perfect prank for the radio—

PETER: You're finally admitting "The War of the Worlds" radio-drama was a prank after all.

ORSON: I'm not saying anything of the sort. Haven't you been paying attention?

PETER: *[Sighs.]*

ORSON: "Rosebud" was the perfect prank for *Citizen Kane.*

PETER: George Orson Welles!

ORSON: I needed the perfect prank for a Hollywood premiere. And with a theremin humming in the background, the perfect premiere prank suddenly materialized. And it would not only be for the Hollywood premiere but every single, and I mean, *every* single showing of *Invasion From Mars* from Boston to Bakersfield.

PETER: You really don't have any boundaries, do you Orson?

ORSON: None. Would you like to hear my prank?

PETER: I'm afraid to say "no". So "yes".

ORSON: Okay, here we go. Ready? Ready! Each cinema showing my latest RKO Radio Picture *Invasion From Mars* would be instructed to hire a local theater actor to portray the part of the CINEMA MANAGER, who will interrupt the showing of the feature film to provide important "news updates" over the course of the showing. The CINEMA MANAGER should be a middle-aged man, dressed as closely to the actual cinema manager as approved by the cinema's dress code. The movie screen would go dark and the CINEMA MANAGER would walk down the aisle and stand in front of the screen and the house-lights would come up and he would say, "Ladies and gentlemen, I am the manager of this cinema house and must bring you timely news of a grave nature. As improbable and ironic as it may sound, seeing that you are watching a motional picture concerning an *Invasion From Mars* by Orson Welles, I must inform you all in our audience that Adolph Hitler has been broadcasting radio reports announcing an alliance between the Axis powers and the planet Mars itself. The authorities, in order to maintain public safety and calm, have requested that all Americans remain where they are, whether it is work, school, or enjoying a motion picture, until otherwise instructed. Please continue to enjoy your cinema experience and I will not hesitate to keep you all apprised of the latest developments as they arise. Thank you for your patience and understanding." And then the house lights would go down and the film continues.

PETER: Why would you do such a thing?

ORSON: Because it's funny. And then when the film reaches the point when the Vice-President asks if the Martians are secretly allied with Hitler, the house-lights would go back up and the CINEMA MANAGER continues, "Ladies and gentlemen of our audience, Western Union has just delivered to our theater a transcript of the speech made by Nazi fuhrer Adolph Hitler earlier this evening live on German radio. I hesitate to read this because I am not a trained speaker, but... Hitler said, and I quote... *[reading as Hitler.]* 'How will this extra-terrestrial race treat the inferior races of our earth? How will it deal with the black? How will it deal with the yellow man? How will it tackle that alleged termite in the civilized woodwork, the Jew? Certainly not as races at all. Mars will aim to establish, and it will at last, help establish a world-state with a common language and a common rule: a Third Reich.'"

PETER: *Was zur Hölle?*— Why are you gesticulating like Adolph Hitler?

ORSON: "'Mars will tolerate no dark corners where the people of the Abyss may fester, no vast diffused slums of peasant proprietors, no stagnant plague-preserves. This extraterrestrial race with their greater intellect see in us, the Aryan race...'"

PETER: Stop mimicking that *Sohn einer Hündin* this fu— instant.

ORSON: "'...no complacency in spirit, no weakness of breeding, no frailty due to sympathy. This extraterrestrial race allied with Germany Herself and with her allies. The Axis powers have a new ally and will stand with us against our enemies, the inferior races of man!' Ladies and gentlemen, due to such horrifying news, I recommend you remain seated and continue to enjoy your movie, while our leaders continue their courses of action in our stead. Thank you."

PETER: *Scheißekopf!*

ORSON: Then! Then! At the penultimate moment in the film, the house-lights could go back up and the CINEMA MANAGER would say, "Ladies and gentlemen, the theater have just received a newsreel from the good people at Hearst Metrotone News that will illustrate more eloquently than I can the reports I have been relaying to you this evening (or afternoon)."

PETER: A news-reel interrupts your film. Of course it

does.

ORSON: The title card reads, "Treaty of peace with our Martians neighbors negotiated for all of planet Earth by American President Roosevelt." And then the news-reel voice booms, speaking in Time-style, "The making of millions of Americans panic with his "War of the Worlds" broadcast, Orson Welles proved America's naïveté in the mind of Joseph Goebbels for exploitation in Nazi propaganda. With full knowledge of America's recent hysteria due to Orson Welles' radio-dramatization, Adolph Hitler has through deceitful radio broadcasts attempted a ruse to incite Americans into fearful panicking. Demonstrating such fear of and racism, towards Martians through our nation's predilection to panic, Germany's fear mongering sought to diminish Roosevelt's role in peaceful relations with Mars. All this while, in earnest, our leaders have been the Earthly instruments of negotiations with the ambassadors from our stellar neighbor, the planet Mars. Treaty of peace with the Martian Commonwealth was signed for all of planet Earth by American President Franklin Delano Roosevelt." Then! Then!

PETER: *[Sighs.]*

ORSON: Winston Churchill is sitting on a dais with FDR and Joseph Stalin. Churchill addresses the audience, "So vain is man, and so blinded by his vanity, that no one, through the first decades of the twentieth century, has expressed any idea that intelligent life might have developed on Mars, or indeed at all, beyond its earthly level. Nor was it generally understood that since Mars is older than our earth, with scarcely a quarter of the superficial area and remoter from the sun, it necessarily follows that it is not only more distant from time's beginning but nearer its end. And we men, the creatures who inhabit this earth, must be to them at least as alien and lowly as are the monkeys and lemurs to us. The intellectual side of man already admits that life is an incessant struggle for existence, and it would seem that this too is the belief of the minds upon Mars." And Joseph Stalin then addresses the world...

PETER: *[Sighs.]* Of course he does.

ORSON: ..."Their world is far gone in its cooling and this world is still crowded with life, but crowded only with what they regard as inferior animals. To carry warfare sunward is, indeed, their only escape from the destruction that, generation after generation, creeps upon them." And then Churchill continued, "And before we judge of them too harshly we must remember what ruthless and utter destruction our own species has wrought, not only upon animals, such as the vanished bison and the dodo, but upon its inferior races. The Tasmanians, in spite of their human likeness, were entirely swept out of existence in a war of extermination waged by European immigrants, in the space of fifty years. Are we such apostles of mercy as to complain if the Martians warred in the same spirit?" And then! Then!

PETER: *[Sighs.]*

ORSON: FDR finishes up with, "This is what we humans, a barbaric race still in its infancy had thought of the inhabitants of Martians. I am pleased to report, these fears have been sorely misplaced. There is little reason to believe that any advanced civilization would be inherently hostile. They have proven not to be. Humanity is still societally and technologically primitive. For any species to traverse the depths of interstellar space, they must have reached a level of sophistication and therefore peace. We, the leaders of the free world, have established a treaty with the planet Mars that will ensure peaceful relations between our two worlds as we humans strive to unite our world under the flag of the entire human race." And then! Then!

PETER: *[Sighs.]*

ORSON: The camera pans to the right to reveal the Martian ambassador standing on the dais—

PETER: Of course! Of course, your news-reel interrupting an *Invasion From Mars* motion-picture would have a Martian ambassador—

ORSON: Who then addresses the entire human-race! "Lorem ipsum dolor sit amet, consectetur adipisicing elit, sed do eiusmod tempor incididunt ut labore et dolore magna aliqua. Ut enim ad minim veniam, quis nostrud exercitation ullamco laboris nisi ut aliquip ex ea commodo consequat. Duis aute irure dolor in reprehenderit in voluptate velit esse cillum dolore eu fugiat nulla pariatur. Excepteur sint occaecat cupidatat non proident, sunt in culpa qui officia deserunt mollit anim id est laborum. Lorem ipsum dolor sit amet, consectetur adipiscing elit. Quisque vel ullamcorper sapien. Nam est justo, tincidunt in facilisis id, placerat ut lorem. Suspendisse eleifend lectus in auctor condimentum. Vivamus metus dui, rutrum ut ultrices ac, ornare non erat. Donec eu gravida nulla. Aenean massa neque, eleifend at erat et, consectetur hendrerit lacus. Nunc congue est ut aliquet rhoncus. Cras non, luctus dolor."

PETER: *[Crying.]* My head hurts.

ORSON: If I was going to prank every single audience of *Invasion From Mars*, in every single cinema in the country, I first I needed to actually get my film *into* every single cinema in the country. The battle over *The War of the Worlds* was only just now, that this very moment, getting started.

PETER: *[Crying.]* It's getting really late.

ORSON: I'm just getting to the good part. Hang on, this is going to be a wild ride.

PETER: *[Crying.]* I just want to go home.

ORSON: I had a sneaking suspicion that once word got out the *Invasion From Mars* was finally, definitively in the can, that the government's agents, that Hearst newspaper henchmen, would ratchet up their attacks. Little did I know (I really hate this phrase by the way, it is so cliché. I'm sure some English major has written their senior thesis on the overuse of this phrase), but it is true. I knew very little about the attacks that would soon be lobbed at Willie Brown and myself. The Battle over *The War of the Worlds* had until now had been akin to a Cold War, but now it was about to go nuclear, and the radioactive fallout covering the RKO Radio Pictures lot would linger for about the half-life of plutonium. Hollywood would be a radioactive wasteland devoid of life-sustaining genius of George Orson Welles.

PETER: *[Crying.]*

ORSON: I curiously felt like a prey animal, like a snow hare being hunted by an arctic fox. Like a squirrel in Central Park being stalked by a stray cat or chased by a domesticated dog or being hunted by inner-city red-tailed hawks that fly above 5th Avenue, while nesting on the sides of many a skyscraper. But I wasn't a squirrel in Central Park, I was Orson Welles on the lot of RKO's Forty-Acres. My hackles were always raised as I walked to and fro, whether to and fro from the editing room or the orchestral room or Charles' office or the cafeteria. My senses were always keen, listening to every sound no matter how innocent or innocuous. My head was constantly on a swivel. My neck began to ache from whipping around at a moments notice. This is how the hunted feel.

PETER: Orson.

ORSON: It was when I entered the cafeteria that I felt the most hunted. Like a hunter had put out food for this target while sitting in a hunter's blind. There was one particular and peculiar lunch-lady, the one with the hairy mole and equally hairy upper-lip, who always served me my favorite dishes. No need to go into details now...

PETER: Surprising! Considering how you've run your mouth about every minutiae.

ORSON: ... but they were all my favorites. At first, I didn't think about how she knew my favorite dishes, but as I neared the finish line with my *Invasion From Mars*, and I was getting really, really close with Benny currently putting the finishing touches on the orchestration, I began to question the source of her knowledge. Sure, I'd been on the RKO lot for a couple of years now and maybe my fame and status on the lot that inspired by lunch-ladies to keep a list of not only my favorite foods, but the favorites of all of the other A-list actors, directors, producers, etc. But maybe, just maybe, the source of her knowledge was a little more nefarious. Maybe the source was the FBI file that J. Edgar Hoover was famous for keeping on the most suspicious and dangerous people in the nation.

PETER: You may be suspicious, but you are certainly not dangerous.

ORSON: Oh, no, Peter! In October 1942, I was certainly the most dangerous person in all of the United States of America. I was simultaneously famous and infamous. According to the public consciousness, I was famous for being the voice of The Shadow; I was infamous for frightening half the country with the "fake" news broadcasts from my "War of the Worlds" radio-dramatization! Which I don't have to remind you, Peter, were actually an actual

"What evil lurks in the hearts of men?" Through his portrayal of The Shadow in the radio-show, Orson Welles knows!

Martian invasion.

PETER: *[Audibly sighs.]*

ORSON: I was also famous for my first motion picture, *Citizen Kane*; I was infamous for caricaturing William Randolph Hearst with my portrayal of Charles Foster Kane ! Which I don't have to remind you, Peter, was more based on me than it was the Old Man.

PETER: *[Audibly sighs again.]*

ORSON: The "lunch-lady" (quote-unquote) brought me one of my favorite dishes, specially prepared for me. Two rare steaks and a pint of Scotch and a pint ice-cream. How she snuck the pint of Scotch past the "real" (quote-unquote) lunch-ladies was beyond me. She took a seat across from me, without my inviting her to. She began to liberally ask me questions of my life. Could I show her an magic-tricks that I learned at the knee of Harry Houdini? Of course, I could. I always carry a deck of playing card in my inner-breast coat pocket. You know how absentmindedly Mexican shuffling cards is meditative for me. So, I pulled out my deck and quickly showed her a simple but convincing card trick, hoping that would pacify her and she would leave me to my two rare steaks, pint of Scotch, and pint of ice-cream. But she didn't. The pack of playing cards disappeared rather triumphantly back into my pocket. She then inquired what it was like to learn that graceful and violent dance between a man and a bull from at the teat of Manuel Laureano Rodríguez Sánchez, known as Manalete. The hackles on my neck started to prickle. My inner squirrel was suddenly on alert. She seemed to be wasting my time and therefore buying time for someone else. I thanked her for the special lunch and abandoned a half-eaten steak, a half-drank pint of Scotch, and a half-melted pint of ice-cream.

PETER: *[Sarcastically.]* That must have been horrifying.

ORSON: *[Taking Peter literally.]* It was absolutely horrifying. Who was she buying time for? And where was he? Was he in pilfering through my office? Was he in the editing room trying to destroy the footage of the one finished copy of *Invasion From Mars*? Was he in the orchestral room trying to disrupt the recording of Benny Herman's score? Little did I know that it was all of the above. There was a multi-pronged assault on me. My office was the closest to the cafeteria, so that was my first destination. When I burst through the door, my secretary was huddled in the corner weeping and wailing. Willie Brown stood amongst the debris dumbfounded and dejected. Our office had been ransacked. Chairs and tables had been overturned. Desks and filing cabinets had been violently emptied. Production and costume designs were strewn about the rubble by the tornado of intruders. The actor's headshots were torn down from their pins on the cork-boards. This was the first assault on Willie Brown and me. But we didn't know, we couldn't not, who were the culprits. It could have been the government agents just as easily as it could have been the Old Man's spies. We were fighting a war on two fronts, but unlike the European and Pacific theaters of second Great War, which were half-a-globe away from one another, our two fronts were being fought in the very same location. We were fighting two enemies on the same forty-acres of studio lot, appropriately called the RKO Forty-Acres. But the only saving grace for us is neither of our two enemies were aware of the other's existence. The government agents had no knowledge of the Old Man's reporters and the Old Man's reporters had no knowledge of the government agents.

Standing in his ransacked office, Orson Welles was reminded of this scene from Citizen Kane*! But instead of newspapers, it was scripts!*

PETER: If Hearst had been a part of this so-called "Orson Welles' Conspiracy" with President Roosevelt, then surely he would have been aware that government agents were plotting your downfall. And if he was aware, then why wouldn't he partner with the government agents to stop you.

ORSON: Thankfully for me, William Randolph Hearst and Franklin Delano Roosevelt had that famous and public falling out in 1935 when the president vetoed the Patman Bonus Bill that the Old Man clearly supported and when the president tried to enter the World Court which the Old Man clearly opposed. Why else would his papers carry his rambling, vitriolic, all-capital letter editorial. What kind of man and would-be president screams at the top of his lungs in all-capital-letters. It is the height of arrogance and ignorance of a very small man. But the Old Man had fired or driven off all of the driven reporters, energetic editors and passionate columnists who *might* have penned serious attacks against the president, instead of rambling, vitriolic, all-capital rants.

PETER: Orson, I see the flaw in your argument. If the Roosevelt and Hearst had their public falling out in 1935, then why would they work together in your "Orson Welles' Conspiracy"?

ORSON: Simple. There is a proverb that states: *Amicus meus, inimicus inimici mei* or in English "my friend, the enemy of my enemy". Stalin and his Soviet Union being our friend during World War II and our most loathed of enemies once Hitler had been defeated is the most apt expression of this... expression. So, during the briefest of Martian invasions, the president and the Old Man had a common, albeit interstellar foe. But now, the old rivalry was no doubt rekindled because America's involvement in World War II, Hearst being a staunch isolationist.

PETER: Orson, I see another flaw in your argument. You are the enemy of both Hearst and Roosevelt and therefore you are the enemy that would make them friends again, according to the ancient proverb. That is if this conspiracy theory of your's is anything other than the produce of your overactive imagination.

ORSON: An overactive imagination, as you put it, couldn't have ransacked my office. But what were they looking for. The film cannisters holding the film of the finished film were not being stored in my office. Were they looking for the screenplay? The actors and actress who acted in *Invasion From Mars* each had copies of the screenplay, so that I wasn't hiding its existence too greatly. Of course, the actors only had scripts with their lines (as to not give up the game too early), but a skilled spy could easily recreate the entire screenplay from the various and varied and often discarded actor's copies. I can't believe that the Old Man hadn't had the entire screenplay recreated by the time shooting started. He had to have read it at his ornate desk in the privacy of San Simeon. Surely, he had to have burnt it in the obnoxiously large fireplace, all in a fit of rage. Had I, Orson Welles, made San Simeon no longer a castle, but now a cage? (Hey, that rhymed!) I likewise had no doubt that the screenplay had made it's way all the way to the White House! The president had to have read it at Teddy Roosevelt's Resolute desk in the Oval Office. Surely, he would have set it light with one of his trusty Cuban cigars he was so found off and pitched it into the impotent, by comparison, fireplace. I could easily imagine the president pacing back and forth in frustration and anger with me, that is if he was capable of pacing. Which he wasn't.

PETER: Orson!

Did William Randolph Hearst read the screenplay at his ornate desk, then burnt it in his obnoxiously large fireplace at San Simeon?

Sitting at Theodore Roosevelt's desk was his fifth cousin, Franklin Delano Roosevelt! He raged at the Invasion From Mars *screenplay!*

ORSON: What? You think I'm the only one with that knowledge. The Old Man had pictures of the president in his wheelchair that he withheld publishing as blackmail against the president. The Old Man had pictures of Hollywood stars, directors, producers, and studio heads in every stage of filthy and flirty scandal: sexual scenarios of both the hetero-and-homosexual varieties, hobnobbing with Communists at their homes, their clubs, and/or their rallies. Sure, we heard how Charlie Chaplin kept marrying teenagers! "Fatty" Arbuckle was criminally charged with rape! Errol "I like my whiskey old and my women young" Flynn was standing trial that very year for statutory rape. Joan Crawford had starred in a stag-film. Greta Garbo and Marlene Dietrich may have been lesbian-lovers. Louis B. Meyer got Judy Garland, that "fat little pig with pigtails", hooked on pills! How many studio heads pressure their starlets, who may have included Jean Harlow, Joan Crawford, and Judy Garland, into getting abortions? The number is too high and infamous to count! While Disney did not have to worry about Mickey Mouse being caught with his legs up (outside of Tijuana Bibles that is), Walt

Donald Duck catching Mickey Mouse plowing Minnie Mouse with her legs up in an infamous Tijuana Bible!

happened to give Nazi filmmaker Leni Riefenstahl a personally guided tour of the Disney studio lot! And these were the scandals we actually *heard* of. What possible blackmail ammunition did the Old Man possess and keep locked in a vault in San Simeon? Who knows! He kept files on the most famous people, not only in Hollywood, but Washington DC. as well. He collected much more damning evidence of scandalous past discretions than J. Edgar Hoover could dream of possessing. But those photos of Roosevelt in a wheelchair kept the President of the United States of America in line!

PETER: You're digressing again, Orson. Let's keep focused on the ransacked office if we may.

ORSON: What? Oh! Where was I? Of course, the ransacked office! Willie and I stood in complete and total shock at the state of our office. But quickly our horror turned to paranoia, when we realized the next location that would be ransacked would be the editing room. Willie and I ran practically the width of the lot to the editing room and found it in equal disarray. Film had been strewn everywhere. Film was draped over the Moviola UC-20S 35mm film editor! Film was draped over bookshelves that did not hold books but canisters of film. And those canisters had been thrown open and the film strewn around the room. Given the complete state of the editing room, they did not find what they were looking for. Of course they did not find what they were looking for. Would I be foolish enough to leave the actual canisters containing the actual nearly finished cut of *Invasion From Mars* in the editing room?

PETER: Of course not.

ORSON: Damn skippy! And I wasn't about to go running to the actual location I'd hidden the canisters because I knew I was being watched and this wasn't my first rodeo. If *Citizen Kane* taught me anything, it was paranoia is my best friend. Paranoia will keep me safe from my enemies. But I needed to play along with this game of spies. So Willie and I ran to the orchestral room, where we found Benny Herman and his orchestra safely putting the finishing touches on the score. I was relieved that I didn't find Benny bloodied, expensive musical instruments smashed, and the members of orchestra scattered to the wind, never to finish the precious score. My precious... score. My precious!

PETER: Channeling JRR Tolkien, are we, Orson?

ORSON: Actually, hindsight being twenty-twenty, the score wasn't my precious. The canisters of film were and still are my precious. But to keep this analogy going, the canisters of finished film would eventually be burnt in the fires of Mount Doom! And I wasn't as brave as Gollum to join my film as it burned.

PETER: Are we foreshadowing the fate of your canisters of film, Orson?

ORSON: Of course not! If I have proven anything this evening and that last evening a year ago is that I am an unreliable narrator.

PETER: You most certainly are, Orson. And that is why I love you so much. Hate you sometimes, but love you so very much.

ORSON: I knew I had to know that my canisters of film were safe, so Willie Brown and I split up. He ran off to destinations unknown while I ran straight for a random make-up room. There I threw on a costume and wig and beard for some Biblical epic being filmed, so that I looked like many any of a thousand extras wandering RKO's forty arches. As I disappeared into the crowd, I hoped that I had shook my tail. I dashed into a sound-stage and threw off my costume, wig, and beard and grabbed a tool belt left sitting on a table and a jelly donut from the nearby craft services table...

PETER: Of course you did. *[Sighs.]*

ORSON: ... I disappeared onto the set with the rest of the crew, exiting the other side of the sound-stage. I shed the tool-belt onto another table, hoping the crew member would find it, thinking he misplaced it on the wrong table. And then I burst into the properties room where most, if not all, of the major props used by RKO pictures over the last decade-and-a-half. I found what I was looking for. Starring at my prize, I felt like an intrepid archaeologist in a Saturday morning serial picture looking, not for the Holy Grail (which I would eventually go looking for) but the Ark of the Covenant. I don't know which picture a props master made this Ark of the Covenant for, maybe Cecil B. DeMille's 1923 *Ten Commandments*, and maybe not. It may have been on loan from Paramount Pictures, or it may have been purchased from Paramount Pictures, I wasn't sure. Next to the Ark was the prop of the Holy Grail. Not a gilded cup encrusted with jewels but a cup carved by a carpenter. It was, no doubt, fashioned for *India– [Coughs.]* I mean– DeMille's 1927 *The King of Kings*. But I'm not here to talk about the Holy Grail, because inside the Ark of the Covenant, I had hid the canisters of my precious... my precious...

PETER: This is the more appropriate time to use that phrase.

ORSON: ... and my precious was safe! The government spies nor the Old Man's reporters had discovered my film. The only copy of my film that existed. I had to keep it safe. And in the Ark of the Covenant was the safest place I could think of... for now. I returned to the orchestral room to continue playing along with the spies or reporters or both. Benny Herman was able to complete the score in record time. Willie Brown and I returned back to the properties room again dressed as extras from that Biblical epic being filmed. We carried the Ark of the Covenant as if we were marching towards the sound-stage, but we took a quick left at Albuquerque and ended up in room of the sound mixer. Where we stayed until it was completed. He had runners fetch up food and drink, both the non-intoxicating and intoxicating kinds. As our paranoias spun out of control, our sound-mixer burned the midnight oil, quite literally, but in record time, he produced the finished, final cut of *Invasion From Mars*, score and all!

PETER: Wonderful! But Orson, where is the finished, final cut of *Invasion From Mars* now?

ORSON: I'm just getting to the good stuff! The canisters went back into the Ark of the Covenant like the smashed bits of the actual Ten Commandments, and I hoofed it to Charles Koerner's office, where he would putting the finishing touches on renting Grauman's Chinese Theatre for an actual, not imaginary premiere. This time I spun my real and not imaginary Rolodex and had Charles' secretary send out invitations to: Fred Astaire, James Cagney, Gary Cooper, Errol Flynn, Henry Fonda, Clark Gable, Cary Grant, Fredric March, William Powell, James Stewart, and Edward G. Robinson, and the leading ladies: Claudette Colbert, Joan Crawford, Bette Davis, Marlene Dietrich, Irene Dunne, Greta Garbo, Judy Garland, Rita Hayworth, Jean Harlow, Dorothy Lamour, Myrna Loy, Ginger Rogers, Barbara Stanwyck, Gloria Swanson, Elizabeth Taylor, Mae West, Jane Wyman. *Whew!*

PETER: Not this again!

ORSON: Yes! But for real this time! The hot-couples were also invited, even those that were not there "together", if you get what my mean: Katharine Hepburn and Spencer Tracey, Humphrey Bogart and Lauren Bacall, Vivien Leigh and Laurence Olivier, Lucille Ball and Desi Arnaz, and of course, Orson Welles and Dolores del Río.

PETER: *[Loudly sighs.]*

ORSON: But we had just a handful of days to survive until the Hollywood– not *Hollyweird*– premiere.

PETER: What's a "handful"?

ORSON: You know, a handful of days.

PETER: A "handful" of what?

ORSON: Uh... candy...?

PETER: What kind of candy? A handful of jelly beans which like quite a handful, maybe a dozen or more. That's a lot of days. Or a handful of Hershey chocolate bars would be only one. You'd only have to survive a single day, which I don't think you actually mean.

ORSON: You're suddenly becoming obstinate.

PETER: We've been here for hours. I'm tired. I have a feeling we're nearing the end of this little– nay-longwinded– story, It's a story that I'll cherish for the rest of my life, but I've grown weary and in my weariness I am being, in fact, obstinate.

ORSON: We're getting there, Peter. Willie Brown and I just had to live long enough to make it to the premiere. And let me tell you something, Peter, and this is a bit of foreshadowing, the government agents and the Old Man's reporters would go from merely ransacking our offices to attempted murder!

PETER: "Attempted"

ORSON: Of course, "Attempted". Both Willie Brown and I survived! I'm sitting here in the same room with you, so obviously I survived! And Willie Brown is working his butt off in the burning hell-fire of a steel-mill, so obviously he survived! That is one of the problems with a first-person narrator, unreliable or not. The reader knows that the narrator survived the events of the book so there isn't a threat of death hanging over the narrator's head for the length of the book. I could be shot at, you know I survived. I could be dropped off a cliff, you know I survived. The plane could crash, you know I survived. The building exploded, you know I survived. They could have tossed a nuclear bomb at me and you would know that I survived!

PETER: Nuclear bombs?

ORSON: Exactly. But you, my dearest Peter, know I survived, the "Orson Welles' Conspiracy" unless I didn't actually survive.

PETER: What? That doesn't make any sense!

ORSON: Perhaps I was murdered in 1942 at the hands of the government agents or the Old Man's reporters. That would be a kicker of a plot twist, wouldn't it?

PETER: You're actually going to go down the road where you actually died during the "Orson Welles' Conspiracy"? Even you are not that audacious an unreliable narrator to kill yourself off. What are you going to do? Say you're a ghost? That you've been a zombie directing movies for the last 35 years?

ORSON: Maybe! Wouldn't that be a swift kick in the pants! What if I've been dead this entire time and didn't even know it! Why should I let a little thing like my being alive get in the way of killing myself off?

PETER: Oh, dear God!

ORSON: Shouldn't I as both a filmmaker and a bull-shit artist have the liberty of taking liberties with my own story?

PETER: Not if it's a biography. You can't take creative liberties with non-fiction!

ORSON: What if its a hagiography?

PETER: You're not a saint, Orson!

ORSON: Religious sycophants exaggerate the lives of the saints with miracles. Surely there could be a miracle that saves my life!

PETER: You're talking about a *deus ex machina*, Orson. And I know how much you hate *deus ex machinas.*

ORSON: A skilled author can loathe a plot device as reviled as the *deus ex machina* but choose to utilize it with mastery. Then I could transcend being the "god in the machine"! But we aren't at the point when I would have, could have, probably should have, died! So can we table all this talk of *deus ex machinas* for the time being?

PETER: Please.

ORSON: But the *deus ex machina* would have to wait, because Willie and I didn't need god to be in the machine... just yet.

PETER: Of course. *[Sighs.]*

ORSON: We had to survive the next several days while Charles scheduled Grauman's Chinese Theatre. Once the film had been screen for the who's who of Hollywood and Louela Parsons and Hedda Hopper, there would be... could be nothing that FDR and WRH could do about it. The cat would be out of the bag and the world would finally know about the "Orson Welles' Conspiracy". But... and there is a big but...

PETER: Of course, there is a "but".

ORSON: The government agents and newspaper reporters began ratcheting up their attacks. Ransacking the editing room and my office was the work of mere hooligans. Soon, their hooliganism would turn murderous! Willie and I were just too ignorant to realize how murderous. We believed if we were could, we would end up in jail awaiting trial for treason. This was something that I was hoping– praying– would happen because then I could submit into evidence all of the... well... evidence I had acquired concerning the government's cover-up of the invasion from Mars.

PETER: But you burnt all of the evidence in a grill.

ORSON: What? Do you think I'd be that stupid to burn the only evidence that I had that proved the government's cover-up of the invasion from Mars. Of course, I'm not *that* stupid. I wasn't called a "boy-genius" because of my good looks. I had all that evidence hidden in a location the government spooks and newspaper reports would never ever find.

PETER: *[Audibly smacks his forhead with his hand.]*

ORSON: Once the government put Willie and me on trial for treason, I would reveal with all of the pomp and circumstance of a theater veteran all of the evidence and put it officially into the public records.

But Willie and I didn't realize we would never make it to trial because the government would never take the chance of my evidence getting into... well... evidence. Willie and I remained an ignorant as babes. But the first shot would be fired by the government spooks... quite literally. I had been shot! A felt my soul leave my body. I looked down at my body still standing but having been shot. As my body began floating towards the heavens and Heaven itself, my soul looked over onto the roof of a nearby sound-stage and there was a military sniper laying on his belly. The rifle was still smoking having had shot me. Thankfully, the bullet grazed my ear... quite literally. I must have turned my head just a hair at the right moment. My soul snapped back into my body and I felt a sting of red-hot burning on my right earlobe and when I brought my hand away from my ear, it was covered in blood. I had been shot! I didn't realize at the time that it was a graze, but "I have been shot!" I bellowed to Willie and we ran... ran as fast as we could before the sniper was able to reload. And if the JFK assassination taught conspiracy theorists anything is that there was no way in Hell that Lee Havery Oswald could reload that rifle fast enough to shoot the President three times in a matter of seconds. But I had been shot twenty-years before any of those thoughts could temporally enter my head.

PETER: *[Audibly sighs.]*

ORSON: Willie and I ran through sound-stage after sound-stage trying to escape the murderous spooks. We ran through a blizzard of fake snow and wind machines along a country road on the sound-state for *The Curse of the Cat People*. We hoofed it through Arab desert scenes for *Tarzan's Desert Mystery*. Out into the back lot, we ran through *Rookies in Burma*'s jungle river and along its banks dodging real and wild Burmese animals that roared and snapped their sharp teeth at us while apes *"Ooo-ooo-oooed"* at us. Back onto the sound-stages where there was a war picture– I can't remember the name of–

PETER: Of course... your highly selective eidetic memory.

ORSON: – was being filmed; the artillery fire of blanks caused me to nearly shit my pants. Nearly. Okay, maybe a bit, but I kept running because I didn't know what were blanks and what were not blanks. I kept running. Then through another sound-stage where Frank Sinatra, playing a guy named "Frank", cussed us a blue streak for running through and ruining his sets for the musical *Higher and Higher!* Willie and I didn't even pause to look behind ourselves so intent on our escape from the... guys with guns!

PETER: *[Audibly sighs for the umpteenth time!.]*

ORSON: We knocked over costume racks; we ran through craft service tables; we destroyed light stands and toppled boom operators and their mics; we bulldozed through lines of extras; we trampled starlets; we made a complete mess of several sound-stages which we left in shambles. No one then nor no one today can convince me that government spooks in black suits and even blacker sunglasses weren't hot on our heels. If we didn't end up dead, we'd end up in some shadow prison completely off the grid where no one would ever find us. When we finally felt safe, we made out way back to our offices.

PETER: Of course. *[With dripping sarcasim.]* The government agents wouldn't possibly look for you there.

ORSON: When we got back to our offices, my secretary Lillian held two large Manila envelopes (where they named for the Manila in the Philippines or was manila a color?), anyway... the envelopes had been delivered by a ham-fisted beast of a man. One envelope was addressed to "Orson Welles" and the other addressed to "William Brown". I knew what the envelopes... well... enveloped even though Willie didn't seem to have a clue.

PETER: I shudder to hazard a guess, but I don't need to guess. I know what was in those envelopes and who sent them.

ORSON: *[Obviously tapping his nose.]* On the nose, Peter, on the nose. While the Old Man had mailed similar Manila envelopes to the studio heads: Jack Warner, Louis B. Meyer, Sam Goldwyn, David O. Selznick, Henry Cohen, and Walt Disney. Those envelops included their stars photographed in colorful sexual situations, colored homosexual situations, varied drug-idled situations, various Jewish situations...if you get my drift, Peter.

PETER: I do. Oh! I do.

ORSON: While Walt Disney didn't have to worry about himself being caught with Snow White's legs up, everyone else at that table did. Warner had Errol Flynn on the goddamn payroll for Christ's sake! The Old Man had used these photographs to blackmail the most powerful men in Hollywood to torpedo my *Citizen Kane*! And now he was using photographs to blackmail me and Willie Brown. Willie's envelope was substantially thinner than mine. I doubted what the Old Man had on Willie because the young man had been with me practically every moment since he was assigned to me as a screenwriter. Did he have time to have dalliances with this starlet and that starlet? Of course he could have. But I had my doubts. As my for envelope, I didn't know what could possibly have been captured in photographs. My mind ran through my mental Rolodex of mental memories trying to figure out what the Old Man had on me. There could have been photographs of me in "situations" with Dolores Del Río and Rita Hayworth.

PETER: Most certainly.

ORSON: And there could have been photographs with this starlet and that starlet from my earliest days in Hollywood. But didn't want to know what could possibly have been captured in photographs. I wouldn't give the Old Man the satisfaction of knowing what was in these photographs. As Willie began to open his Manila envelope I staid his hand. I shook my head. He didn't need to know this ignominy as well. I pitched my envelope into the waste paper basket. I unzipped my fly and unloosed my bladder into the trash can. When I took a can of butane out of the desk drawer and soaked the envelope in lighter fluid and– *foom!*– it went up in smoke. I was daring the Old Man to publish those salacious photos on the front pages of his newspapers. I was daring Hedda Hopper or Louella Parson to publish descriptions of those lewd photographs in their columns. I had the patience of a saint. I'd wait. And I wouldn't have long to wait.

PETER: *[Audibly sighs for the umpteenth-plus-one times!]*

ORSON: I motioned for Willie to drop his envelope into the fiery trash can, but he hesitated. His curiosity had been piqued. What could the Old Man have on him? As Willie Brown, he was a nameless screenwriter. But as "Harry Lime", he played the part of a Hollywood playboy to perfection. I told him that curiosity killed many Hollywood cats, but he unwound the string securing the envelope closed and pulled out the stack of photographs. I couldn't see– I wouldn't want to see– the photographs. His eyes widened behind his horn-rimmed glasses. His flipped through the photos with a pained-expression on his face. He didn't care about his own reputation because he knew– as well as I did– that his Hollywood career was winding down and he would end up back in that Colorado steel mill like his father wanted. But he didn't want to expose the starlets he had "pillowed" to use the Japanese expression. His mind ran through all of the multiversal futures to see which would be the most likely outcome. He saw 14,000,605 possible futures and in only one of them do we win. So he reinserted the photos into the envelope and pitched them into the can. We had both dared the Old Man. If we encountered any of the newspaper men then we would double-dog-dare them and you know what happens when you double-dog-dare someone.

PETER: They stick their tongue onto frozen metal pole in the schoolyard?

ORSON: *[Obviously tapping his nose.]* On the nose, Peter, on the nose. But we never saw the assault coming. We should have hired food-tasters like in the olden days of Kings and Queens and that constant threats from the court. If the Old Man or the spooks wanted us dead, we would have ingested poison, but they didn't want us dead. They wanted us silenced. Both! Franklin Delano Roosevelt and William Randolph Hearst both had a common mission to silence George Orson Welles and William Francis Brown.

PETER: That's a lot of people who go by three names.

ORSON: Certainly. The President and the Old Man had come together despite– nay! In spite of– their political differences to conspire to cover-up a Martian invasion...

PETER: Damn, I had forgotten all about the Martian invasion.

ORSON: ... so it would be in their best interest– their common interest– to silence Willie and me.

PETER: If the threat you posed to the President and the Old Man was that grave, why didn't they just kill you?

ORSON: I thought the same thing. Why weren't Willie and I dead yet? Unless we had been poisoned and were now dead and this was Satan's way of punishing us in the Ninth Circle of Hell reserved for betrayers to their lords.

PETER: That would be one hell of a Hell.

ORSON: But I smelt no fire and brimstone. I wasn't trapped in ice gnawing on the betrayers of Caesar, namely Brutus and Cassius and Judas, the betrayer of Jesus the Christ. *But* for some odd reason, the spooks seemed to give up the fight. Willie and I couldn't have known this at the time, so we were still looking over our shoulders and paranoid over every bite we put in our mouths that we were being poisoned or drugged.

PETER: Oh, Orson.

ORSON: Thankfully, we made it to the night of the world premiere, a night that would go down in Hollywood infamy. My name would be wagging on the lips of everyone in Hollywood. I would find my redemption from the ignominy of Hearst sabotaging my *Citizen Kane* and RKO's bungling of *The Magnificent Ambersons. Invasion From Mars* would be my triumph. Despite the governmental conspiracies from the likes of President Franklin Delano Roosevelt, despite the interferences of the newspapermen of William Randolph Hearst, despite the plots of the Martian Commonwealth whom infiltrated the highest levels of the... well, everywhere and everything. My *Invasion From Mars* was finally having its *Hollywood* premiere. All of Hollywood was decked out to the nines. The gowns were glamorous. The makeup was exquisite. The hair was coiffed. The tuxedos were impeccably tailored. The mustaches were respectably trimmed. Dolores and I sat in the back of our posh, impossibly shiny, black Mecedes-Benz-770K. The champagne was on ice. The scotch was most certainly not. As the car pulled up to the front of Grauman's Chinese Theater, I could see the dozens of photographers and the hundreds– nay thousands!– of anxious onlookers. Then my car-door was opened and Dolores stepped out into the sea of insanity. The flash-bulbs were popping. The flash-bulbs were dropping. The flash-bulbs were shattering under the clattering feet of the photographers. Ah, the glorious background music of a Hollywood premiere. The wailing from the teenaged girls, that the publicists of the mop-headed Beatles would mimic to perfection two decades later, assaulted me with their adulations. Their screams. Their dreams. Their cheers. Their tears. Their fainting. Their unrestrainting. John, Paul, George, and Ringo surely had nothing on a young Orson Welles. But I digress.

PETER: *Déjà vu* all over again! *[sighs.]*

ORSON: A reporter from the Hearst Metrotone News... spit in my face! Then the cheers of the screaming teenage girls were suddenly and sullenly silenced! Their cheers became jeers. Their tears became my own fears because my dreams became screams for my head "Off with his head! Off with his head! Off with his head!" The Old Man must infiltrated my throng of adoring fans with his hired goons and their families. Security had to quickly escort me and Dolores del Río into Grauman's for our safety. The throng quickly escalated into a riot. Trash cans were thrown at the doors, shattering the glass. The teenagers crawled through the broken doors, their hands bloodied from the broken glass. Security whisked me and Dolores passed the concessions into the theater while extra security Charles had hired "just in case" prevented the enraged teenagers from reaching past the lobby. My eyes fell longingly on the all the treats in the concession area: the Almond Joys, Licorice twists, Bit O' Honeys, Chick O Sticks, Mike & Ikes, Dots, Junior Mints, and Bun Maples; but we couldn't stop. Once in the safety of the theater, Dolores and I took our seats. Thankfully the who's who of Hollywood were unaware of the riot happening just outside the theater's doors. Then came the moment, the magic, after the houselights had dimmed, when the "A Mercury Production" title card appeared on the screen. There was quiet applause from the cherry-picked audience. Do you remember my nightly nightmare I told you about a year ago?

PETER: You had this recurring nightmare that during

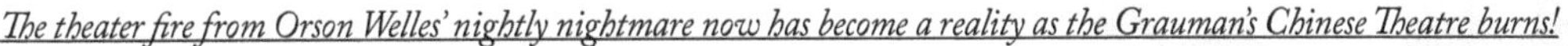

The theater fire from Orson Welles' nightly nightmare now has become a reality as the Grauman's Chinese Theatre burns!

the Hollywood premiere of *Invasion From Mars*, Howard Koch would be sitting beaming a few rows in the front of you. Then by the time the first reel was done, Howard would realize the horror of the changeling child he saw before him. It knew that you had lied. Lied to the brass at RKO. And worst of all you had lied to him. How dare you? He would now do everything in his power to destroy this abomination of a film and you along with it. In your dream, you never saw Howard get up from out of his seat. It wouldn't be until you saw the horror of the film melting on the screen, that you realized Howard was intend on destroying you. Soon the fire that started in the projection room would engulf the theater. The audience would begin trampling each other in vain attempts to escape the conflagration. The sounds of screams and the scent of burning flesh turn the Hollywood premiere of *Invasion From Mars* into a literal Dante's *Inferno*. As you sat in your seat too stunned to move, Howard would walk up behind me with a butcher's knife and slit your lying throat.

ORSON: So eloquently put, Peter.

PETER: They were your eloquent words, Orson, not mine.

ORSON: No, your recitation was eloquent. What I am about to say with not be eloquent, but necessary. You will not like them, but they are necessary.

PETER: I'm afraid.

ORSON: Don't be. You have me as your guide.

PETER: I'm *very* afraid.

ORSON: I sat in rapt silence as the who's who of Hollywood watched my motion picture. This part of the film making process never, ever gets old. Sitting in a room with your fellow passengers in this Hollywood life never, ever gets old. I'm not sure anybody in that theater had any idea of what my motion picture was. I was going to smash all their preconceived notions into atoms. Just as the first reel was ending, I looked up to see the cigar burn flick momentarily to life, then be extinguished with the coming the next reel. But the cigar burn did not flick out of existence. It grew! The screen was on fire! The fire jumped to the curtains and then spread with so shockingly quickly that I barely had the time to comprehend the fact that Franklin Delano Roosevelt's government agents *and* William Randolph Hearst's reporters, so intent on destroying my canisters of film would burn Grauman's Chinese Theatre to the ground just to destroy them. Like in my nightmare, the audience trampled each other in vain attempts to escape the conflagration. The sounds of screams and the scent of burning flesh turned the Hollywood premiere of *Invasion From Mars* into a literal Dante's *Inferno*! Literally, in front of my very eyes! Poor Fred Astaire was alight, dancing a duet with a fire nymph. I turned to see my audience trying to get out of the theater but the doors on either side of the back of the auditorium appeared locked. Oh, they had been blocked with chains! Our enemies intended on murdering all of us in that room! Oh! The sounds of screams! Oh! The scent of burning flesh. So intend were they on destroying my canisters of film that they would murder the who's who of Hollywood! My canisters of film. I had to save my canisters. I hopped up on the arms of my seat and smashed the window to the projection room, the one projection peers through to focus the projector. Willie hoisted me up and through the window...

PETER: Those windows are far too small to climb through, Ors–

ORSON: ... and I cut my arms to ribbons. Once through, I grabbed the reel from the first projector and threw it into its canister and began to scrambling to unthread the film from the second projector and get its reel into its canister. Willie Brown had just finished crawling through the window, the broken shards of glass having cut his chest and belly. He grabbed some canisters and I grabbed the rest and we bolted out of the projection room into the hallway where the fire had escaped the auditorium. I couldn't believe that the President and/or the Old Man had ordered the murder of the who's who of Hollywood! Fred Astaire, James Cagney, Gary Cooper, Errol Flynn, Henry Fonda, Clark Gable, Cary Grant, Fredric March, William Powell, James Stewart, and Edward G. Robinson, and the leading ladies: Claudette Colbert, Joan Crawford, Bette Davis, Marlene Dietrich, Irene Dunne, Greta Garbo, Judy Garland, Rita Hayworth, Jean Harlow, Dorothy Lamour, Myrna Loy, Ginger Rogers, Barbara Stanwyck, Gloria Swanson, Elizabeth Taylor, Mae West, Jane Wyman. All dead!

PETER: *[Loudly sighs.]* Exactly how do you explain the fact that none of them actually died anywhere near the time of you supposed Hollywood premiere. They continued making movies along after. You're really stretching credulity!

ORSON: Lookalikes, Peter. lookalikes. Doppelgängers. The government had thought about this scenario had had prepared doppelgängers of every Hollywood star that had I personally invited to my premiere. Everyone in Hollywood would be none the wiser.

PETER: Like so conspiracy theory that Paul McCartney died and was replaced at the height of Beatlemania with a "doppelgänger". Maybe that's the reason Paul is barefoot on the cover of *Abbey Road!* That this doppelgänger is so equally musically talented that he founded Wings and continues to make music to this day.

ORSON: Yes! That is exactly what I'm saying. Everyone in Hollywood would be none the wiser!

PETER: Except we would know Grauman's Chinese Theatre did not burn to the ground like you claim!

ORSON: Um...

PETER: For once in your life, Orson, your bullshit has caught up to you. You can't explain your way out of this story.

ORSON: Maybe I'm a doppelgänger, too, Peter.

PETER: What?

ORSON: Maybe I'm a doppelgänger, too. Maybe that is why I've never been able to replicate my successes with *Citizen Kane, The Magnificent Ambersons,* and *The Invasion From Mars*! Ever thought of that?

PETER: *[Loudly sighs.]*

ORSON: Maybe I'm not Orson Welles.

PETER: Then what is your birth name?

ORSON: Um...

PETER: Then what is your birth date?

ORSON: Um...

PETER: What are you parent's names?

ORSON: Um...

PETER: Where did you grow up?

ORSON: Um...

PETER: What was your childhood pet's name?

ORSON: Um...

PETER: What is the mascot of your high school?

ORSON: Um...

PETER: Talk about "jumping the shark", Orson.

ORSON: I'm afraid I'm not familiar with that particular idiom, Peter.

PETER: It was coined after a fifth season episode of *Happy Days* when Fonzie, wearing swim trunks and his trademarked leather jacket, ski jumps over a shark! It means "creative work or entity has reached a point in which it has exhausted its core intent and is introducing new ideas that are discordant with, or an extreme exaggeration of, its original purpose."

ORSON: Sounds apropos! But it also isn't. It's totally within my "core intent". I'm not "introducing new ideas that are discordant with, or an extreme exaggeration of, its original purpose". I'm an unreliable narrator, Peter! How does an unreliable narrator "jump the shark" as you so eloquently put it?

PETER: Umm? Umm!

ORSON: Now, who is stunned into silence! As Willie Brown and I stood across the street from Grauman's as it burned, we watched the fire brigades desperately trying to extinguish the flames and get the ambulance personnel to the dying. Peter, did you know that I learned that you didn't need to be sick or dying to ride in an ambulance.

PETER: What? That now?

ORSON: Yes. You didn't have to be sick or dying to ride in an ambulance, so when I needed to get from one recording session to another recording session, I rented an ambulance who with wailing sirens got me to the subsequent sessions in record time. The mayor even had to change the law because of me!

PETER: *[Sighs.]*

ORSON: Anyway. As Willie and I watched the theater burning, as Willie and I listened to the blood-curdling screams, I felt a gun pressed into my back and a chloroform soaked rag coving my mouth...

PETER: What?

ORSON: ... then I woke up!

PETER: Oh, dear God!

ORSON: It was all a dream! And you thought I couldn't wiggle my way out of that story. *Ha!* But I did it! It was all a dream! Actually, it was one of my nightly nightmares! Only slightly different this time around!

PETER: You know how much I hate dream sequences, Orson. I know how much you hate dream sequences. This is low hanging fruit, Orson, and you should be ashamed of yourself.

ORSON: But it wasn't a dream sequence, or even a nightmare sequence, it was a drug-addled sequence. This entire scene had played out in my subconscious mind. Little did I know at the time...

PETER: You seem to know a lot despite knowing little at the time.

ORSON: Little did I know at the time that I had been slipped a mickey. And not a Mickey Mouse, but a mickey. I was out like a light. Thankfully, Willie found me before the spooks did. I hesitate to think what would have happened to me if Willie hadn't found me. Would I have woken up on a black site somewhere in the Nevada desert? Would I have woken up to find myself on trial for my treason against the United States? Thankfully, I woke up to find myself on a dark desert highway. Willie was driving us out of Hollywood into the depths of the desert in my convertible. There was a cool breeze in my hair. There was the nice smell of colitas rising up through the air.

PETER: Are you quoting an Eagles' song, Orson.

ORSON: No… umm… yes. Willie was driving my 1942 Alfa Romeo 6C 2500. The top was down. The wind was breezing. The moon was new. The stars were shining with the glory of the arm of the Milk Way stretching out before us. We didn't have a care in the world, except for the murderous intentions of the government agents and newspaper reporters.

PETER: Not a care.

ORSON: We were like swallows returning to San Juan Capistrano though we were not returning there. In fact, we both had never been to the Spanish mission that was our goal…

PETER: Where you going to San Juan Capistrano?

ORSON: What? No! We were certainly not going to San Juan Capistrano. We were going to this other mission… that was also a Spanish mission… a secret mission that no one would possibly think of, that no one would guess was a final destination.

PETER: You were on a secret mission to a secret mission?

The Spanish Mission at San Juan Capistrano, where Orson Welles planned on hiding the Ark of Covenant, which contained the film for his soon to be "lost" Invasion From Mars *motion picture!*

ORSON: Yes! That is certainly what we were doing! I wiped the sleep from my eyes and simply enjoyed the drive. Being out of Los Angeles and in the middle of nowhere had lifted a burden from my shoulders. From off in the distance, we heard the mission bell and knew what our journey was coming to its end. As we pulled into the Spanish mission– that certainly wasn't San Juan Capistrano– but a certain secret mission. Willie pulled the car up the drive through the lavish gardens. A Franciscan friar greeted us. This was Friar John Michael Petric. I had been in communication with him about hiding our Ark of the Covenant and its contents.

PETER: You still had Cecil B. DeMille's Ark?

ORSON: Of course. It was the perfect size to store the reels of film that contained the entirely of the *Invasion From Mars*. But the look that Friar John had on his face, betrayed his emotions. Now, I don't believe to this day that he betrayed us, but he squeaked in a small, horse voice, "I had no choice. They arrived before you did. I'm sorry." From side the mission, a man was wheeled out in a wheelchair by obvious government agents. In the darkness, I knew it could only be one man. One president. The President of the United States of America.

PETER: Orson. You're going there?

ORSON: I greeted the President of the United States of America with a simple, "Hi, Franklin. We finally meet."

PETER: Orson, you actually greeted the president by his first name.

ORSON: Given our relationship in the "Orson Welles' Conspiracy" your darn tooting I'm on a first-name basis with the president. He greeted me back, "Orson, it didn't have to come to this."

"I'm afraid it did, Franklin."

"Certainly not," the president said, "the conspiracy was fool-proof. Not a single person living believes there was a Martian invasion that cold October evening exactly four years ago this very night. All thanks to you. But now you've gone and blown it all up. You just had to have the last word didn't you, Orson"

"It's not my fault, Franklin…"

"That's 'Mr. President' to you."

"Mr. President, I'm not my fault. It was the only movie I could get made. *Citizen Kane* was a disaster. *The Magnificent Ambersons* had been taken away from me. The only picture anyone would have me make was *The War of the Worlds*! Charles Koerner only wanted *The War of the Worlds*! Louis B. Meyer only wanted *The War of the Worlds*! The Warners only wanted *The War of the Worlds*! Hell, even Walt Disney, the cartoon prince, only wanted *The War of the Worlds*! Can you imagine signing and dancing animated Martians? The horror! The mockery!"

"You know as well I as I do that they wanted your radio-script. Not that…"

"I couldn't get the rights to the radio-script. That shyster Howard Koch copyrighted it from out from under me and he wouldn't sell it for all the tea in China! He held it over my head like a Sword of Damocles. He told Charles that he sold me the rights, but he didn't. He wouldn't give me the plea-

The President is enjoying an afternoon with his granddaughter, Ruthie Bie, at Mission San Juan Capistrano. He shoos her away while he talks to the "bad man". Ruthie Bie scurries her away while her grandfather talks to Orson Welles! Little does Orson know what Franklin Roosevelt has hidden under the blanket his Scottish terrier is laying on!

sure. I had no choice but to deliver the script that I did! How could I produce *The War of the Worlds* as a motion-picture if he didn't sell me the blasted rights! He wanted egg on my face when I couldn't deliver not only a script but a picture!"

"So you decided to break your oath? An oath you swore before God and country and the President of the United States of America! That's treason. High treason. I should hurl you before Congress to be prosecuted for high treason."

Now, you have to understand something, Peter, I was getting my Irish-up, so I stood up to the old man, not the Old Man, that was Hearst, but to this old man pretending to the president.

PETER: Orson!

ORSON: "Franklin," I said both dismissing and disobeying his instructions, "I would love for you to present me to the full Congress and I'll see that you are impeached for high crimes and misdemeanors. You don't think I still have in my possession the government documents my little German spy Gunther acquired for me?" I heard the quick inhalation of breath from Willie as he started to panic... again. Willie looked at me with the full knowledge that we had burnt all of the evidence of the Martian invasion in our grill that night several moons ago. I cursed myself under my own breath for having sprayed the lighter-fluid and lit the match that destroyed my only proof of the "Orson Welles' Conspiracy". It would have come in quite handy. But Franklin didn't know they we had destroyed it all.

"My agents searched high-and-low for those documents. I know for a fact you no longer possess the documents. You know what I think? I think you destroyed them. In a panic, you burnt them to ash to avoid us finding them in your possession." Now, I started to panic. "You think Agent Ecks, as you so eloquently named him, didn't find the canisters of film in the Ark of the Covenant, the very same Ark that is in the backseat of your car this fine evening. We didn't need to destroy the film back on RKO's Forty-Acres, because you would bring them right to me."

"Franklin... Mr. President... I don't know what to say."

"Don't say anything. You've said enough already. You always say too much all the blasted time. You never stop talking..."

PETER: Here-here!

ORSON: "... You think that your crime is treason. But it's not, Orson, my young man, it's always been hubris. You thought you were the only man alive who could sweep the Martian invasion under the rug, but *my* officials were already removing all of the physical evidence of the Martian invasion. Do you know why the invasion only lasted ere hours?

"I'm not sure... bacteria like HG Wells wrote."

"Yes, bacteria. We found a dozen of Martians stark and silent and laid in a row– dead!—slain by the putrefactive and disease bacteria against which their systems were unprepared; slain as the red weed was being slain; slain, after all man's devices had failed, by the humblest things that God, in his wisdom, has put upon this earth."

"The Brit was a bloody prophet!"

"Yes. The Martians had no chance against something as common as the common cold. We were removing all physical traces of the Martians before you even entered the picture, but we needed help removing the mental traces of the Martian invasion. Sure, WR's newspaper could go far in dismissing an actual Martian invasion from the public consciousness, but we needed a scapegoat. We needed a boogey-man. And you played that part to perfection, Orson. You gave us what no other man could, a truly unbelievable believable cover-story. And no one,not even the paranoid of schizophrenics, even dreamed that the invasion was anything other than a radio-drama." I knew it, Peter, I knew it. "But you had to have the final word, didn't you, Orson."

"But nobody would believe my film. That's what you don't understand. Powerful government officials like yourself and rich and powerful men like Hearst don't realize is... my film is not a threat. You live in a world of actual threats. German threats. Japanese threats. And when this war is finally over, Soviet threats. My film is not a threat. Nobody would believe this film even if it was released into the cinemas. They would dismiss my *Invasion From Mars* film as easily as they did my "War of the Worlds" radio-drama. The Old Man merely had to order his film critics, Hedda Hopper and Louella Parsons to dismiss the film as the overactive imagination of one George Orson Welles. I have enough of a reputation in this town and around the country that everyone already thinks I have a gloriously overactive imagination..."

PETER: You don't say!

ORSON: "... Let me release my film into the movie houses around the country and around the world and you'll have the final nail in the 'Orson Welles' Conspiracy'. After seeing my film, no one, not even the most paranoid of schizophrenics (as you said so eloquently), will ever, and I mean *ever* believe there was an actual invasion. This is the opposite of Jonathan Swift's "A Modest Proposal". His satire was so brilliantly realized that the British aristocrats actually believed he was advocating the selling and eating of babies for food. *The Invasion From Mars* is so brilliantly realized that no one will actually believe a single frame."

"Orson, I'm afraid, I can't allow the smallest possibility that someone will believe you. I'm so thankful there doesn't exist a global network of interconnected newspapers that could be accessed at any given moment from a contraption sitting on your desk, or God-forbid, carried in your pocket that would give access to all the world's knowledge... at your fingertips. Even if the American people could possess ready access to knowledge, they won't believe the *truth*. The American people are too conspiracy minded already. While this disease is currently in its infancy, it'll only need a single event to set it off. It could be the assassination of a president. It could be a war fought that the American people no longer have faith it. It could be an election that a large enough portion of the American people believe was stolen. Once any of these things happens, the people will believe anything and everything. People are sheep, Orson. They want to follow. They want to be controlled. You think this American experiment is fool-proof? No. The people want a dictator. They want to be told what to do, what to believe, who to worship, either God or a man. And what if that man was once the President of the United States, who speaks for the common man. Conspiracy theories will run rampant. No matter how illogical and asinine the theory, people will believe it. Forest fires? A government conspiracy. An earthquake? A government conspiracy. A total solar eclipse? A government conspiracy. Something as mundane as a presidential election? A government conspiracy! And what if the President of the United States is the *loser* in this 'stolen' election? He could easily turn half of the entire American populous into conspiracy theory spewing nutjobs. This former president, now presidential candidate for a third time!, and his vice-presidential running-mate can spread disproven conspiracy theories at their rallies and the people with not only *believe* but chant atrocities! And when a former president says these things, half of the American people will believe him whether or not what he says is actually true! Lies will become the truth; and the truth will become lies! He will be a shepherd to the sheep of the American populous. And if this *loser* president says to stop the certification of Electors, a standard and mundane process? Then this violent attempt to overthrow the government will be seen as nothing more than a guided tour of Capitol! America may have been founded on the notion of the presidency and not a monarchy, but the humans will always desire a king, a Pharaoh, an Emperor, a King! But this man will not just be a merely king, but a messianic figure to the overly and overtly Christian. He will be their Messiah, who is persecuted for their sins!

PETER: This is crazy! Not in my America!

ORSON: "Asinine and fake conspiracy theories, in the alternate-reality United States of *BIZARRO*-America, will no longer cause Pavlovian giggles, but be championed on the floor of Congress! But, Orson, what if there was an actual government conspiracy? What if the government of the United States of America conspired with the free and public press to cover-up a Martian invasion? What we did together, Orson, was an *actual* government conspiracy. Not some imagined conspiracy, but a conspiracy actually set into motion to deceive the people of the United States of America. If I allow that film to be shown in cinemas, there will be a certain number of rubes, primarily in the south and primarily Democrats I'm afraid, who will believe it and I can't take that chance." The President lifted Fala, his Scottish Terrier down onto the ground, then pulled a pistol out of his jacket.

PETER: Orson!

ORSON: The president said, "Orson, you may not think I have the strength to pull this trigger, given my Polio, which we have had, by necessity, kept form the people– the rubes– because they will not see strength in the presidency, but weakness. I cannot allow this conspiracy between you and Willie Brown to continue."

PETER: Orson!

ORSON: "Franklin, you think shooting me will solve any of this? I'm too famous. If I'm discovered murdered in San Juan Capistrano, there will be questions that need to be answered."

"Questions? From whom? The press? Hearst will dance a little jig when he learns you're head. But, Orson, rest assured, I don't intend on killing you." President Franklin Delano Roosevelt turned the gun towards Willie Brown and pulled the trigger!

PETER: Nooooooo!

To Be Continued...
in the next thrilling adventure!

Acknowledgments

I would like to thank my late father, William Francis Brown, for leaving the manuscript for Orson Welles' "lost" *Invasion From Mars* screenplay in his safety deposit box for me to discover. You supported my writing career from the first stories I scribbled into a notebook in the second grade. You listened to my stories in place of your favorite evening sitcoms, police procedurals, lawyer programs, and variety shows. I hope I've made you proud by editing this book, and including your lost (now found!) screenplay in my *The Orson Welles' Conspiracy.*

I would like to thank my late mother, Sheila Eileen Brown for supporting my self-publishing career. You helped finance the publication of my Dickensian novels, and Shakespearean plays. This was your favorite "story" of mine. I know you haven't enjoyed my other works. They have proven to be a little controversial, but none will be as controversial as this one. I know you're looking down from Heaven so proud that I'm finally fulfilling my father's dying wish to publish his and Orson Welles' stories in my very non-fictional *The Orson Welles' Conspiracy.*

I would like to thank two of my then closest friends, the late John Michael Petric and He Who Shall Not Be Named. We started the Damon Runyon Repertory Theater together in 1998 and planned an offshoot radio theater, *Quicksilver Theatre on the Air*, that unfortunately never came for fruition. He Who "downloaded" radio-dramas over the Internet (a painful experience in the late 90s). He had jury-rigged his double-cassette stereo by plugging a car audio cassette adapter into his computer and inserting it into his stereo. Then He Who recorded the shows onto an actual cassette tape. We spent many a weekend evening listening to them. Inspired, we three writers began writing our own radio-dramas. I wanted to prank He Who who worshiped Orson Welles' "War of the Worlds". My script pretended to be "real" with a fictional Art Bell-type radio-host. Then I exposed my father's very real screenplay in my radio-script. This was the first step in the 25 year journey to expose the truth of *The Orson Welles' Conspiracy.* If only *Quicksilver* had lived, then the world (or at least our small Colorado city) would have known about the Orson Welles' Conspiracy 25 years ago!

I would like to thank Catherine O'Grady, my fellow author, who has helped guide and support me on this improbable journey. I'd like to thank my fellow thespians, including but not limited to, Cory Moosman, Martha Page, Brenan Searain, Geoffrey Simmons, Jedidiah Edward Duarte, Amy Haines, and Craig Slayton Smith. Since the real reels of Orson Welles' *Invasion From Mars* have been lost to history (or stored in some Hollywood vault or a top-secret government facility), I would have cast you all in an independent film production to recreate Orson Welles' *Invasion From Mars* from my father's manuscript). But the funds never came together. And I'd like to thank my poet-mentor Tony Moffeit.

I would like to thank Peter ██████ for mailing me the reel-to-reel tapes of his decade's old interview with Orson Welles after I reached out to him with the proof of an *Invasion From Mars* screenplay and we both realized the stunning truth about an invasion from Mars. These tapes helped me fill in the missing jigsaw pieces in *The Orson Welles' Conspiracy* puzzle.

ORSON WELLES *and the* HOLLYWOOD'S HOLY GRAIL

PETER: ... oooooooo! ⚛

ORSON: Willie Brown collapsed onto the fair, brown dirt of Mission San Juan Capistrano with a bullet-wound in his gut. Blood began to leak out of the bullet-wound. Then blood began to pour out of him. Oh, no! What had I done? Here I had taken this fresh-faced (but also elderly-faced) youth fresh off of the turnip truck of a small steel-mill town in Colorado, turned this bullshit artist into an honest-to-God Hollywood screenwriter, and now he has been shot and soon-to-be murdered by Franklin Delano Roosevelt!

PETER: This has seriously gone off the rails, Orson! You're implying that the President of the United States of America shot and killed Willie Brown, your screenwriter, confidant, and fellow bullshit artist! Oh, Orson! I don't know what to think. I don't know how to feel! I'm so caught up in the moment? Where is the cynicism I've been expressing for the last several hours? Why do I suddenly *believe* you! I'm mourning a teenager whom I have never met and may not even been dead... but he's been shot and is bleeding out on the dirt of the Mission San Juan Capistrano! Poor, Willie Brown!

ORSON: I dropped down on my knees and lifted his neck with my hand. Blood began to trickle out of his mouth, his eyes were distant. I begged Willie not to die! That I'd do anything to keep him alive. I begged Friar John to beg God not to let him die! I begged President Roosevelt not to let him die! I pleaded with the President to have an ambulance be summoned, but the Spanish mission was far from any modern hospital. Shit! Willie was beginning to grow cold in my arms. His clutched my shoulder with his weakening hand and said with his final breaths how much of an honor it was to have worked with me. And that he failed me.

PETER: *[Audibly weeping!]*

ORSON: Then I remembered something. I ran to the backseat of my Alfa Romeo and pulled out a box. Inside the box was the Holy Grail from the properties room on RKO's Forty-Acres. I ran to the fountain and begged Friar John to bless the fountain's water, turning into the holy water. Friar John did as I begged of him and I scooped up the holy water into the Holy Grail. The cup that was touched by Jesus Christ Himself! Okay, maybe just H.B Warner, the actor.

PETER: Okay. I'm done. I'm tapping out, Orson. This has jumped a second shark and maybe even a third. I'm done. I want to go home!

The fountain at the Mission San Juan Capistrano, where Orson Welles healed Willie Brown's presidential-inflicted bullet-wound.

ORSON: Then I slid down next to Willie, lifted his shirt to expose the bullet-wound and poured the holy water from the Holy Grail onto the wound and it fizzed like it was Alka-Seltzer as the wound scabbed over! But as I continued to pour the holy water, the scab quickly and painlessly fell away. Willie was going to live!

PETER: I'm picking up and going home, Orson. You can keep these reel-to-reel tapes. I don't want them to be in my possession anymore. I don't want to be reminded of this evening ever again. You may think you've done me a service by giving me the greatest gift of your greatest prank, but now, you have gone from playful teasing to downright mockery. Goodbye, Orson. Our friendship is over.

ORSON: Peter! Don't go, I'm just getting to the good part. *[Voices becoming distant as they move from microphones!.]* Peter, I confess this has all been a story, the most wondrous steaming pile of bullshit you would possibly imagine. Yes, I admit that I've pulled up a manure truck filled to overflowing with bullshit! Peter, my name is Orson Welles! You know that a tiger cannot change its stripes. I am who I am! Whether it was learning magic at the knee of Harry Houdini or studying the violent dance with bulls with Manalete, you know that am I bullshit artist. Maybe not as one as skilled as Willie Brown... I know I've filled my living room knee-deep in bullshit, but please, Peter, please come back into my house.

PETER: *[Almost inaudibly.]* You've gone too far. I cherish our friendship. I cherish you as my mentor. I cherish every moment we have spent conversing. I have gleamed from you insights into theater, radio, film, and television; Hollywood producers, directors, and stars; and almost everything else under the sun from acting to magic, literature to comic strips, bullfighters to gangsters that only the last true Renaissance man of the twentieth century can offer.[1] But this is one step beyond what our friendship represents!

ORSON: *[Becoming more and more audible.]* Please, Peter, come and sit back down. Yes. Thank you. Thank you! Now, that you're back, let me finish my greatest prank. Let me finished the story of the "Orson Welles' Conspiracy" and you'll never again hear mention of it again for as long as we both shall live!

PETER: Okay, Orson. I'm too exhausted to put up a fight. I'll sit here in stone-cold silence until you finish your "Orson Welles' Conspiracy", and then maybe we can share a fine glass of Scotch. And maybe with a little hair-of-the-dog, we'll have a good laugh. I know you keep the good stuff somewhere around here.

ORSON: That's the spirit. And yes, I do keep the good spirits for just such an emergency! Now, back in October 1942, with the new moon high above the Mission San Juan Capistrano, the Secret Service agents tasked with protecting the President from the grave threat of a Hollywood director and a teenage boy stole my Ark of the Covenant. While I attended to my fallen friend, they stole my Ark out of the backseat of my Alfa Romeo. These agents were built more like Made Men in an Mafioso hideout– I mean, totally normal Italian restaurant. They had ham-hocks for hands and pork butts for shoulders. They absconded with my Ark like their were book burning Nazis in a Saturday matinee serial. "Orson, Orson, Orson," Franklin said you me, "now you understand how important it is that your film doesn't see the light of day. Conspiracy theories, even real ones, especially real ones, cannot be allowed to fester. Yes, some day these conspiracy-idled rubes may jump from theory to theory as any child playing hopscotch, but those days are in the far, flung future.

"Franklin," I begged, "If you allow my motion picture to be released into the cinemas, I'll only have a few weeks in the spotlight, trumpeting my 'true story', before my film fades to black. The critics will have had their field day on me. I'll be mocked as a laughing stock for having even put this conspiracy theory to film. And then the film will go into the vault at RKO never to see the light of day again. No art houses will have special screenings, midnight or otherwise. Give me my two or three weeks and you'll never hear from me again. Except when my future films are in the cinemas."

"Any insinuation no matter how absurd or even satirical of a Martian invasion is a threat to our national harmony," the president countered. "At a point when there are actual human threats of U-boats off the eastern coast and kamikaze planes destroying our fighting men in the Pacific theater, your film could be seen as disruptive. It could be seen a treasonous. And what if your film awakens the intentionally brainwashed memories of the American people. I know that Charles Koerner joined your little cabal because he remembered! I cannot allow any of these memories to resurface. That threat to too grave to dismiss. Someday, when most of eye-and-ear-witnesses to the Martian invasion are dead or senile, then maybe your film can see the light of day. By my taking possession of your film, I can safe-guard it. Maybe when we are long

1 From the back cover to *This is Orson Welles.*

dead, the Archivist, the keeper of all things 'top-secret' will determine that your film may be safely and unthreateningly released to the general public. Your *Invasion From Mars* will become a time-capsule of these last four years and most importantly October 30, 1938, the night Martians invaded Grove Hill, Virginia and William Randolph Hearst, you, and I conspired to cover-up said invasion. There I said it. You can go to your grave satisfied that I have acknowledged once and for the very last time the "Orson Welles' Conspiracy." And then the president was wheeled off into the darkness and I never saw Franklin Delano Roosevelt, in the flesh, ever again. Here ends my story.

PETER: Finally!

ORSON: I know you know that this is all a figment of my overactive imagine. I know you know that I wanted to twist and spin the "Panic Broadcast" into something more exciting than a mere radio-dramatization that got out of hand. I know you know that I meant no ill-will with my story. Playing with you. Toying with you. You are one of my dearest friends, Peter. And in this industry of ours, true friendship is a rarity. If I have smashed our friendship to bit tonight, then I will accept the sentence for the crime I committed here tonight and one year ago.

PETER: Orson...

ORSON: Please, take the reels that we recorded and safeguard them. Of that little biography of me that we're planning to write comprising the conversations between the two of us over the last decade, please do not include them in that work. Let this be our little secret. A game played between the two of us. This chess match need not be recorded for posterity. Now, I know that by confessing before you and God that my "Orson Welles' Conspiracy" is product of my overactive imagine, I will have planted the seed of doubt in your mind. Am I pleading guilty to a crime I didn't actually commit in order to safeguard our friendship, Peter?

PETER: Orson?

ORSON: There it is. The doubt. It's starting to creep into your mind. That nagging little thought that will burrow deep into your subconsciousness like an earwig and that thought will take root, growing year-after-year. Will you be tempted to dig these reel-to-reels out of mothballs to listen to them on the most appropriate night of them all? Mischief Night! And that nagging little thought will one day become the realization that I was telling the truth the entire time. I don't know *when* that moment will be. So far, this mysterious Archivist hasn't seen fit to release my film from their covetous possession. But maybe someday after I'm dead and gone, they will release the film when I can't enjoy my moment in the spotlight once more. Maybe Willie Brown will show up on your doorstep one day when he's retired from that grimy old steel-mill and you tell you his side of the story, which will line up perfectly with what I have told you here tonight. Or maybe it will be something that I can't foresee. Because I learned at the knee of Harry Houdini, I would be mocking my mentor's memory by claiming to be clairvoyant. You know as well as I do how much he loathed those charlatans. But one day, Peter, when you least except it proof will enter your life and you will know once and for all that the "Orson Welles' Conspiracy" was real. Really real. You may now turn off your recorder and we can enjoy that bottle of Scotch. I know just the one. The one I've been saving for the most special of occasions: Mischief Night! ⚛

The End?!?

Author's Note

During the last semester of my junior year of high-school, my psychology teacher noticed something about me that neither I nor my parents nor anyone else in my young life had observed about me. He hustled me into the counselor's office. Soon, I was being tested as by a psychiatrist (or a psychologist, I still get them mixed up to this day) and I was diagnosed with paranoid schizophrenia. My world-view was entirely shattered. Having been raised a devout Roman Catholic, I had misinterpreted my auditory and visual hallucinations as something... well... demonic. Since I was I small child, I was deathly afraid of the dark. I demanded that the light at the foot of the basement steps be left on twenty-four hours a day. In those latter years, as I tried to fall asleep, I saw glowing red eyes staring at me from the shadows. I heard voices speaking in a hellish dialect of Latin, despite my not knowing any Latin outside of a handful of words and phrases chanted during the Mass. I was too afraid to confess these demonic experiences to a priest, lest he demand the intercession of a exorcist. So I suffered in silence. Until the psychiatrist explained that my hearing hellish voices and seeing demonic eyes were symptoms of a psychiatric disorder called paranoid schizophrenia. My father, William Francis Brown, had his own difficulty conceptualizing the illness. He understood your body being ill, but how could your mind be sick? Diabetes and cancer, these he understood, but he worried about me nonetheless. It wasn't until I lost my Catholic faith literally during my Confirmation Mass that my hallucinations stopped being overtly religious and demonic. Now as an atheist, my hallucinations have became quite ordinary. The anti-psychotic medications during the early 1990's were a nightmare of debilitating side-effects. It was not until the mid 1990's when I would prescribed the brand new anti-psychotic drug, Zyprexa, that the voices finally quieted. I have been blessedly medicated ever since. I am far too scared of regression if I stop talking my medication.

While my own hallucinations don't seem to contribute to conspiratorial thoughts, I love– I absolutely *love*– conspiracy theories My favorite television program, during these early years of my disease, was *The X-Files*. I wanted to be like FBI Special Agent Fox Mulder so much I considered going to college specifically to study psychology so I could enter the FBI. I wanted nothing more to study and hunt serial killers (and maybe chase aliens). But little did I know that being a diagnosed and medicated schizophrenic limited my employment opportunities with the Federal Bureau of Investigations. I thought who else to hunt the psychotic than someone literally taking anti-psychotics. But as much as I wanted to be a Fox Mulder, ultimately, I was more of a Dana Sculley. I was far too rational. While I *loved* conspiracy theories, I just couldn't believe *in* conspiracy theories. Being a Born Again Atheist, I don't even believe what I believe! Conspiracy theories are just too absurd and laughable not to smirk at.

Then came the granddaddy of all conspiracy theory television programs *Ancient Aliens*. Wooboy, I do *love* this show with a purple passion, but I don't *believe* a single solitary moment of its runtime. For the past fifteen years, there has never been once single solitary moment that the thought crossed my mind, *"Yes! It's aliens!"* But I tune in every chance I get. Erich von Däniken, author of *Chariots of the Gods?*, is like a modern prophet, full of an almost religious fervor, but like all prophets is full of shit. The wild-haired Giorgio Tsoukalos is one of my favorite personalities. While I *do not* believe a single word they've ever written or spoken, I *want* to believe. I *wish* that every single ancient alien theory was true. The Egyptian pyramids? Ancient aliens! The Nazca lines? Ancient humans communicating with Ancient Aliens! The elongated, alienesque skulls of pharaoh Akhenaten and Nefertiti? Ancient aliens! Roswell? Modern aliens! Majestic 12 and Project Bluebook? Aliens! Betty and Barney Hill? Aliens! Whitley Strieber? Aliens! The Deep State? Reptilians! I *need* to believe mainstream science has got it all *wrong*, but my rational brain, ever on the lookout for the stray hallucination so I can actively prevent an episode, is simply too rational.

My best friend (RIP), who once worked as an ER nurse, felt that there was a certain level of madness to know when I am hallucinating and actively trying to "ride the wave", as I call it. Where most schizophrenics cannot help but give into the hallucinations, I fight like hell. I will *not* allow my mind to spiral out of control. When I feel bugs crawl on me, I fight like hell. When I smelt nitrous oxide, (a truly weird and non-threatening hallucination) I fight like hell. When I hear voices saying truly awful things, I fight like hell. When I see snakes crawling out of people's eye sockets and a legion of incests scurrying along the walls, I fight like hell. As a writer, my mind is my only gift and I fight like hell every single day to keep my gift sane.

But then again, my schizophrenia had colored my writing in unique ways. The book you hold in your greedy little hands is proof that a schizophrenics unique hallucinations and paranoias can give birth to creative writing. When I heard the voice of God telling me to continue the New Testament where it left off with Paul's journey to Rome, I wrote *The Next Testament*, being the third part of the Holy Bible Trilogy (ISBN: 978-1-931608-54-1, if you're so inclined to order)! When writing my *Marquis de Sade's Wettest Midsummer Night's Dream Conceivable* (ISBN: 978-1-931608-09-1), my co-writer on the project, Ophelia T'Wat, was a hallucination speaking audibly over my left shoulder telling me to write this or write that, go here or go there. My writing is schizophrenic as I am!

Do I wish that the contents of this book were true? Oh, God, yes! Of all of the conspiracy theories from the assassination of President Kennedy, to the moon landing hoax, Paul McCartney's death, the Roswell crash and cover-up (*please, please, please*), "The Protocols of the Learned Elders of Zion", the Satanic Panic (which I D&D'd through), the reptilians running the US government, and the Illuminati at the Denver International Airport (right in my own back-yard!), I wish that the "Orson Welles' Conspiracy" was real. I have made the running joke throughout this book that not even the "most paranoid of schizophrenics has ever conceived of the idea that Martians invaded American soil that cold, windy October evening in 1938," but this is simply not true. I AM the paranoid schizophrenic who conceived of the idea that Martians invaded American soil that cold, windy October evening in 1938.

As for my father, who I have made a character in this book, he was a natural bullshit artist. My caricature of him is so very much in his character. He loved to tell stories, which he affectionately called "whoopers". My concept of the Zen of Bullshit is based on my father's philosophy:

> "To tell a remembrance exactly as it occurred was disingenuous to the drama inherent in the telling of any good story. What happened in the moment is but the first draft of the event. The memories we form in the very moments afterward begins the process of revising the memory. Every subsequent recollection inherently involves a rewrite and every rewrite revises the memory or edit that recollection until we achieve the final

> draft of memory. If others happen to remember with any less of the inherent drama, it is because they do not have the imagination necessary. Bullshit artists lie like a sociopath but still maintain the morality of the Vaudevillain. It is a philosophy worth living".

When he was telling one of his whoopers made of a patty of bullshit, there was a mischievous twinkle in his eye. When he was being serious, like talking about his experiences during World War II, that mischievous twinkle was nowhere to be seen. As his son, I let him bullshit me, though I never believed any of his bullshit. I played along. It was more fun this way. My father was the father in *Big Fish*, one of my favorite movies due to this very premise. Is this why I don't *believe* any conspiracy theories? I never really thought about it until typing these very words. But my father was *not* a conspiracy theorist, he didn't believe in Roswell or the JFK assassination theories. He just enjoyed telling a good whopper. He lied effortlessly, but also with the innocence of a child explaining why he has a cookie in his hand and the cookie-jar lies shattered on the kitchen floor: "I got the cookie for you!"

When is a lie not a lie, when it is a good story. And as a fiction novelist, I hope this book, filled to overflowing with lies, is a good story. And that you enjoyed yourselves. This is the greatest desire of a writer to have their book read and enjoyed.

Bibliography

Brewer, F.L. Richland Center, Wisconic, to FDR March 13, 1933 printed in Lawrence W. Levine & Cornelia R. Levine's The People & The President (Boston, Massachusetts: Beacon Press, 2002)

Barfield, Ray, *Oral interview in Listening to Radio*, 1920-1950 (Westport, Conn.: Praeger, 1996)

Cantril, Hadley, *The Invasion From Mars: A Study in the Psychology of Panic* (Princeton, New Jersey, Princeton University Press, 1941),

Holmsten, Brian and Alex Lubertozzi, *The Complete War of the Worlds* (Naperville, Illinois: Sourcebooks, 2001),4

Koch, H., Wells, H. G., & Koch, H. *The Panic Broadcast.* (Avon, 1970)

Nichelle Calhoun Piedmont Journalism Foundation, "The mighty Black church by the side of the road,", https://www.fauquier.com Retrieved on April 15, 2024

Welles, Orson, and Peter Bogdanovich, edited by Jonathan Rosenbaum, *This is Orson Welles* (Da Capo Press, 1998)

Photographs

I would like to thank all of the photographers of the photographs I have included in this work. Most, if not all, of your names have been lost to the immeasurable depths of the Internet. Not even the all-powerful, all-knowing Google can assist me in identifying and crediting you all for your work.

THE TRIAL OF THE MILLENNIUM

Dear Mr. Brown,

The executor of my estate has been instructed in passing along this second package in the hope it finds you well. Why two packages spaced out by a year, presumably (as instructed) on consecutive Mischief Nights? I wanted you to have the time to listen to the reel-to-reel tapes I recorded of the wondrous and wonderful interview with my dearest friend and mentor. Have you fully process the entirely of the "Orson Welles' Conspiracy"? Yes? Then Let me give you Orson's final gift to me!

In October of 1985, I was knee-deep into grieving the loss of Orson Welles. The public memorial tribute was scheduled to take place on November 2, at the Directors Guild of America Theater in Los Angeles. I was to be the host and I would introduce various speakers. But on the previous Sunday, which happened to be Mischief Night– of course it was– a messenger delivered a package to me. I recognized Orson's handwriting and I ripped open the box, tearing it to shreds. Inside the box were reels. Not reel-to-reel audio tapes, but 16mm film reels. Being Mischief Night, I knew I was being pranked by Orson Welles from beyond the grave. I had no doubt he was smiling from a cloud in heaven plunking away at a harp with a Cheshire grin of his face.

Were these copies of the infamous *Invasion From Mars* motion picture Orson had claimed to have shot during his Mischief night pranks from 1978 and '79? My hands were shaking as I unpacked and set up my 16mm film projector from its home in the hall closet. Next came the portable screen. Soon I was threading the film and clicking on the projector. As the light hit the screen, I was greeted with a scene I was not anticipating. This was not the *Invasion From Mars* motion picture (if it had ever existed), but a courtroom. A camera had been position in a corner to capture all of the courtroom and its occupants in a single frame. Seated at defendant's table nearest the camera was a young Orson Welles and even younger young man, who I assume is your father. At the prosecutor's table sat obviously the team of prosecutors. In the jury box sat twelve angry men, angry because they weren't smart enough to escape jury duty. There was no judge yet seated, but the court reporter sat to the bench's right with her hands hovering over the steno machine.

Were there no lengths that Orson wouldn't go to for a practical joke? None!

Please enjoy,

THE BAILIFF: All rise for the honorable Judge ████ ███. *[Everyone in the picture rises. The Judge enters the courtroom and takes his seat on the bench.]* Please be seated. *[And everyone does!]* The case of the United States of America versus George Orson Welles and William Francis Brown on this 30th of October, 1944.

THE JUDGE: The Prosecution can begin their opening statement.

THE PROSECUTION: The Department of Justice will prove that George Orson Welles and William Francis Brown have received into their possession classified documents violating 18 US Code § 1924, or the unauthorized removal and retention of classified documents or material. The government will prove the Defendants actively communicated with foreign agents to acquire documents and information originated, owned, or possessed by the United States Government concerning the national defense or foreign relations of the United States that has been determined pursuant to law or Executive order to require protection against unauthorized disclosure in the interests of national security. By utilizing the German *Abwehr*, Mr. Wells illegally accessed information classified by the United States, British, and even German governments. Through their possession of classified documents, they were able to concoct a Hollywood screenplay that purports to document an invasion from the planet Mars. And by the production of this screenplay had the intention of mocking the President of the United States and his government in a time of active war. Through their lampoonery, they possess the criminal intent to lessen the status of the President of the United States in the eyes of not only its enemies, but its allies as well. They are further charged with violating Article III, Section 3, Clause 1: Treason against the United States, shall consist only in levying War against them, or in adhering to their Enemies, giving them Aid and Comfort. Through the screening of their treasonous motional picture in cinema houses throughout Germany, Italy, and Japan, Misters Welles and Brown are providing material aid and comfort to the enemy while holding a bucket of popcorn and eating jujubes!

THE DEFENSE: Gentlemen of the jury, my clients are innocent of these **Trump**ed-up charges. They did not violate 18 US Code § 1924 by possessing classified documents. Also, my clients did not provide aid and comfort to our enemies, which is stretching Article III, Section 3, Clause 1 to its breaking point. My clients will *instead* put the government of the United States on trial by proving beyond a reasonable doubt that the President of the United States and his government conspired with my client through an intermediary, the publishing magnate William Randolph Hearst, to produce a wax-recording purporting to be a radio-dramatization of an evening of dance music being continuously interrupted by news reports of an invasion from Mars. My clients will assert that through the production of this wax-recording, featuring the esteemed Broadway actors of *The Mercury theatre on the air*, that the government themselves violated Article III, Section 3, Clause 1 by waging a war of disinformation against the very people of the United States. President Franklin Delano Roosevelt ordered the government's willful disregard to the safety of the American people by commandeering our nation's free and noble press like a Fascist dictator to produce "fake news". This "fake news" transfered blame for a path of destruction from Grove Hill, Virginia to the foot of the White House in Washington DC onto a hurricane. This "fake news" transfered the blame for the deaths of hundreds of men, women, and children onto a hurricane. This "fake news" **Trump**eted the false assertion that the radio-broadcasts heard by millions of Americans was merely a radio-dramatization made by Orson Welles of an adaptation of HG Wells' science-fiction novel, *The War of the Worlds*. When the real news was Martians and their tripod walking war machines did, in fact, march on the capitol of the United States of America, that hundreds of American men, woman, children, and fighting men died that cold, windy October evening in late 1938. Thank you for your time.

THE JUDGE: The Prosecution will call its first witness.

THE PROSECUTION: The Government calls to the stand ████ ████ *[Orson Welles visibly sits up straighter.]*

THE BAILIFF: Please state your full legal name for the court.

THE STARLET: ███ ███ ███, but my screen-name is ███ ███.

THE BAILIFF: Please raise your right hand and place your left hand on the Bible. Do you swear to tell the truth, the whole truth, and nothing but the truth, so help you God?

THE STARLET: Yes.

THE PROSECUTION: How do you know the defendant?

THE STARLET: Harry? Every girl in Hollywood knows Harry. He's such a sweetheart. *[Waves at "Harry" and Willie waves back.]* Nicer than any of these other so-called "men" in Hollywood. It's like he just fell off a turnip truck. Nicest boy.

THE PROSECUTION: I mean, the man seated to his left.

THE STARLET: Orson? If I had a glass of water, I'd throw it in his face. *[Turning to the judge.]* May I have a glass of water...

THE JUDGE: Bailiff, can you fetch Ms. ████ a glass of water?

THE STARLET: ... to throw in his stupid face?!?

THE JUDGE: No. You may not have a glass of water to throw in his face. You will be on your best behavior today, Ms. ████.

THE STARLET: Ah, shucks. But you tell him to be on his best behavior. His so-called "friends" can be a little too handsy, if you get my drift.

THE PROSECUTION: Did the defendant, Orson Welles, ever introduce someone to you that may have a less than savory individual?

THE STARLET: Why sure! That's why I'm here right? You want me to talk about "Gunter", even though that wasn't the name he first gave me.

THE PROSECUTION: And what was it about "Gunter" that struck you as a little off.

THE STARLET: He sure was handsy!

THE PROSECUTION: Was there anything, other than being overly affectionate, that struck you as a little off.

THE STARLET: He was a Nazi spy!

THE DEFENSE: Objection. Calls for a conclusion.

THE PROSECUTION: The witness was in a personal relationship with "Gunter" and may know intimate details concerning the gentleman in question.

THE JUDGE: I'll allow it.

THE STARLET: Yeah, he was a Nazi spy!

THE PROSECUTION: How did you come about this knowledge, Ms. ████?

THE STARLET: Do I have to answer than, Judgie-poo?

THE PROSECUTION: Yes. And don't call me "Judgie-poo".

THE STARLET: He talked in his sleep.

THE PROSECUTION: The Nazi spy talked in his sleep?

THE STARLET: Yes! It was like out of some B-picture, like where archaeologists fight Nazis over Holy Grails, you know. And I know pictures. I've been in a slew of them, including some downright awful B-pictures. But no pictures with Nazis, thank God! I get enough of Nazis in real life!

THE PROSECUTION: And do you know what the Nazi spy was saying in his sleep?

THE DEFENSE: Objection!

THE JUDGE: I'll allow it.

THE STARLET: I don't know. I don't speak German.

THE PROSECUTION: How did you become aware he was a Nazi spy?

THE STARLET: Men like to brag to impress a lady, even when it'll get them thrown in the hoosgow and cooked in an electric chair.

THE PROSECUTION: He admitted to being a Nazi spy?

THE STARLET: Of course! And of course, I didn't believe him... until he started speaking German in his sleep.

THE PROSECUTION: Why did you strike up a relationship and maintain a relationship with a Nazi spy?

THE STARLET: Orson wanted me to.

THE PROSECUTION: Let the record reflect the witness has identified the defendant: Orson Welles.

THE JUDGE: So ordered.

THE PROSECUTION: And why did Orson Welles want you to date a Nazi spy?

THE DEFENSE: Objection. Calls for a conclusion.

THE JUDGE: Sustained.

THE PROSECUTION: No further questions.

THE DEFENSE: No questions for this witness.

THE PROSECUTION: The Government calls to the stand ████ ████. *[Orson Welles begins to shift in his seat.]*

THE BAILIFF: Please raise your right hand and place your left hand on the Bible. Do you swear to tell the truth, the whole truth, and nothing but the truth, so help you God?

THE NAZI SPY: *Ja.*

THE BAILIFF: In English

THE NAZI SPY: "Yes".

THE PROSECUTION: Please state your reason for being in the United States of America.

THE NAZI SPY: In service to the *Abwehr*, I was smuggled into America with an impeccable American passport, an Iowan driver's license and birth certification, with the expressed purpose of detailing the use of propaganda by Hollywood studios in furtherance promoting the war cause in the American people. The most famous example I was able to personally study the creation of was *Der Fuehrer's Face* starring Donald Duck, a cartoon fowl. The security on the Disney lot never once suspected I was a German spy. The animators on the project were very open about sharing their political views on Germany and their personal views of my Führer with many choice invectives.

THE PROSECUTION: And how did you come to have a professional relationship with Orson Welles?

THE NAZI SPY: Despite having perfected an Ioweanian accent, once I had been reassigned to the RKO's Forty-Acres, Orson Welles plucked me out as being a natural German speaker almost instantly. Having been exposed, my duty was to inform my handler and be repatriated to Germany at the earliest possible convenience.

THE PROSECUTION: Then why did you remain in the United States?

THE NAZI SPY: Orson Welles had no intention of exposing me to the American government.

THE PROSECUTION: Did he want anything in exchange for his silence?

THE NAZI SPY: Yes. He wanted to use my expert skills in espionage to his advantage.

THE PROSECUTION: What could Orson Welles have possibly wanted from a German spy?

THE NAZI SPY: Intelligence.

THE PROSECUTION: What kind of intelligence?

THE NAZI SPY: On whether or not there was a Martian invasion of the planet Earth on October 30, 1938. Whether or not there was government documentation of such an event.

THE PROSECUTION: He believed there was documentation of an ludicrous invasion from Mars made by the United States government?

THE NAZI SPY: He believed that the German government had documentation of the Martians invasion of the European theater. *And* he believed that *Abwehr*-allied double-agents within the Pentagon could access classified documentation of the Martian invasion of the America and proof of a conspiracy to cover-up said invasion.

THE PROSECUTION: He wanted proof of a conspiracy that he claims to have been an integral part of.

THE NAZI SPY: Yes. Proof. Documentation.

THE PROSECUTION: So he could release the documents to the press?

THE NAZI SPY: No. He wanted to flesh out his screenplay with information that he didn't have access to having been confined to the CBS studios that evening.

THE PROSECUTION: He was conspiring with a German spy to obtain classified documents through the unauthorized removal and retention of classified documents and material in violation of statue 18 US Code § 1924 merely to improve this Hollywood screenplay?

THE NAZI SPY: Yes.

THE PROSECUTION: What you're alleging is Orson Welles was willing to commit treason against the government of the United States of America to improve his Hollywood screenplay.

THE NAZI SPY: Yes. He didn't know what he didn't know.

THE PROSECUTION: And what did you, as an agent of the German *Abwehr* get in return for your espionage?

THE NAZI SPY: A date with █████ █████, a Hollywood starlet.

THE PROSECUTION: You were willing to expend numerous German resources to obtain classified documents merely for a date with a Hollywood starlet?

THE NAZI SPY: Have you seen her? She's gorgeous.

THE PROSECUTION: No further questions.

THE DEFENSE: I just have a couple of questions. You've admitted under oath that you committed espionage concerning the classified documents. What did the prosecution offer you in exchange for your testimony?

THE NAZI SPY: Nothing.

THE DEFENSE: The prosecution did not offer you any immunity for your testimony in this case.

THE NAZI SPY: No. Because there is nothing illegal in my interactions with Orson Welles.

THE DEFENSE: You're asserting in open court that by obtaining classified documents in exchange for a personal relationship with █████ █████, a Hollywood starlet, you did nothing illegal.

THE NAZI SPY: Yes.

THE DEFENSE: Can you exclaim this apparent contradiction?

THE NAZI SPY: Because the documents weren't classified, they were faked.

THE DEFENSE: What?

THE ORSON WELLES: What? *[Standing.]*

THE JUDGE: Sit down, Mr. Welles? *[He does.]*

THE NAZI SPY: If the *Abwehr* can counterfeit an American passport, an Iowan driver's license and birth certification, and United States currency, then it would have been too easy for me and my colleagues to fake classified documents, particularly absurd documents purporting to be part of a government conspiracy to cover-up a Martian invasion.

THE DEFENSE: For what purpose did you "fake" these documents?

THE NAZI SPY: Have you seen her? She's gorgeous.

THE DEFENSE: No further questions for this witness.

THE PROSECUTION: The prosecution calls Charles Koerner. *[Charles Koerner takes the stand.]*

THE BAILIFF: Mr. Koerner, please place your left hand on the Bible and raise your right hand. Do you swear to tell the truth, the whole truth, and nothing but the truth, so help you God?

THE RKO EXECUTIVE: I do.

THE PROSECUTION: Then please state your role at RKO Radio Pictures.

THE RKO EXECUTIVE: I'm a film executive, best known for being executive vice president of production at RKO Radio Pictures from 1942 until today.

THE PROSECUTION: What was your association with the *Invasion From Mars* motion picture?

THE RKO EXECUTIVE: After the colossal ignominy of *Citizen Kane* that cost my predecessor, George Shaffer, his job, I insisted that Orson Welles make his "War of the Worlds" radio-dramatization into a motion picture.

THE PROSECUTION: And did Orson Welles want to make this motion picture?

THE RKO EXECUTIVE: Of course not. He screamed bloody murder over the very notion that he film his "War of the Worlds" radio-dramatization. He even went so far as to go to Louis B. Meyer to buy out his RKO contract.

THE PROSECUTION: And did Mr. Meyer offer to buy his contract.

THE RKO EXECUTIVE: Yes! But only if Orson Welles adapted his "War of the Worlds" radio-dramatization for Metro-Goldwyn-Mayer studios.

THE PROSECUTION: And how do did the defendant react to this news.

THE DEFENSE: Objection. Hearsay.

THE PROSECUTION: Mr. Koerner was in the room.

THE JUDGE: I'll allow it.

THE RKO EXECUTIVE: He was furious. He wanted nothing to do with a *War of the Worlds* motion picture. Absolutely nothing. He went to Jack Warner. He even went to Walt Disney. But the only movie that everyone, quite literally everyone, from the best boys and key grips to the executives, wanted one movie from Orson Welles: *The War of the Worlds*. He was cornered like a rabid dog.

THE PROSECUTION: And when forced with the reality that he would *have* to make *War of the Worlds* as his next motion picture, what did Orson Welles do?

THE RKO EXECUTIVE: First, he threatened to quit, to leave Hollywood, and go back to his "first great love" the theater, but I still had one more movie I needed from him to fulfill that blasted and asinine contract that George Shaffer had signed Orson Welles to in the light of the "War of the Worlds" radio-dramatization publicity. Ignominy. So Orson needed to film *The War of the Worlds* or I'd sue him into poverty.

THE PROSECUTION: And did he deliver the *War of the Worlds* picture that you expected of him?

THE RKO EXECUTIVE: Certainly not. I had secured the rights to the "War of the Worlds" radio-dramatization from Howard Koch, the original script writer on the infamous "panic broadcast", but Orson Welles did not use Howard Koch's radio-script as the basis for his renamed *Invasion From Mars* motion picture.

THE PROSECUTION: What story would he tell?

THE RKO EXECUTIVE: At first I believed he was filming an adaptation of the radio-script because the young screenwriter I assigned to Orson turned in a wonderful screen-adaptation of Howard Koch' own radio-adaptation of HG Wells' seminal novel. Orson was delivering dailies of scenes that matched William Brown's screenplay, but then came the screening for his *Invasion From Mars*.

THE PROSECUTION: What was your reaction when you watched a movie clearly shot with a script you did not approve?

THE RKO EXECUTIVE: I was stark-raving furious!

THE PROSECUTION: No further quesions.

THE DEFENSE: Hello, Mr. Koerner. I have just a couple of questions. What was your reaction when you watched a movie clearly shot with a script you did not approve?

THE PROSECUTION: Objection. Asked and answered.

THE JUDGE: I'll allow it.

THE RKO EXECUTIVE: As I've already testified. I was stark-raving furious! I could have spit nails, I was so mad. Where was the picture *I* paid for? He wasted hundreds of thousands of *my* money on this... atrocity.

THE DEFENSE: So, you're saying that you did not, in fact, cry tears of joy for Orson Welles having exposed the reality of an invasion from Mars that you and your family distinctly remember hearing broadcast on the radio that cold, windy October evening almost exactly five years ago?

THE RKO EXECUTIVE: Where did you get this cockamamie notion from? Orson? That boy loves telling his stories. Harry Houdini? Ha! Manolete? Ha ha! He lies like a sociopath!

THE DEFENSE: So, you're not claiming that you and your family did not listen to the radio that October evening in 1938?

THE RKO EXECUTIVE: No. I was listening to the radio that night with my wife and children.

THE DEFENSE: So, you heard news broadcasts of news reports of an invasion from Mars interrupting an evening of dance music.

THE RKO EXECUTIVE: Yes.

THE DEFENSE: No further questions for his witness.

THE RKO EXECUTIVE: But what I heard on the radio had nothing to do with the motion picture that Orson Welles filmed. I hired William Brown to adapt Howard Koch's radio-script into a Hollywood screenplay, so we're square. He did what I hired him to do. But I hired Orson to direct said adaptation of Howard Koch's radio-drama, which is what I heard on the radio. I know what I heard on the radio!

THE DEFENSE: I said I have no further questions for this witness.

THE PROSECUTION: Rebuttal, you honor.

THE DEFENSE: Proceed.

THE PROSECUTION: Mr. Koerner, what did you actually hear on the radio on October 30, 1938?

THE RKO EXECUTIVE: I heard a character called Carl Philips interrupting an evening of dance music by Ramon Raquello, *not* Han Von Kaltenborn interrupting Guy Lambordo's evening of dance music. I heard a character called Profession Pearson *not* a real Princeton professor, Arthur Buddington. I heard fictional Martians invade Grover's Mill, New Jersey, *not* Grove Hill, Virginia. I heard the fictional Martian machines fall into the Hudson river *not* disappear in a *deus ex machina* in front of the White House.

THE PROSECUTION: You're saying you weren't frightened like millions of other Americans during the so-called "panic broadcast".

THE RKO EXECUTIVE: Of course not! The program I heard on the radio had been advertised in the *Los Angeles Times* as 'The *Mercury Theatre on the Air* presents *The War of the Worlds.*' And that's what I heard!

THE JUDGE: Thank you, Mr. Koerner, you may be excused.

THE PROSECUTION: The government calls Elda Furry.

THE BAILIFF: Ms. Furry, please raise your right hand and place your left hand on the Bible. Do you swear to tell the truth, the whole truth, and nothing but the truth, so help you God?

THE GOSSIP COLUMNIST: I sure do, sweetie.

THE PROSECUTION: Ms. Furry, you are newspaper gossip columnist commonly known under your stage-name, Hedda Hopper, are you not?

THE GOSSIP COLUMNIST: Yes.

THE PROSECUTION: And how is your professional relationship with Orson Welles?

THE GOSSIP COLUMNIST: Strained.

THE PROSECUTION: Can you elaborate?

THE GOSSIP COLUMNIST: I can't stand the boy. He made a fool of a great man. He lied to my face when I asked him, point-blank, if his *Citizen Kane* abomination was based on William Randolph Hearst. He laughed off any suggestion that his fictional publishing magnate Charles Foster Kane was even remotely portraying Mr. Hearst. He claimed then and he claims to this day that Kane was more based on *him* than Mr. Hearst. Laughable. Obscene.

THE PROSECUTION: Where you aware that Mr. Welles was filming an adaptation of his "War of the Worlds" radio-dramatization.

THE GOSSIP COLUMNIST: He wouldn't shut up about it. He screamed from the "Hollywoodland" sign that the *only* picture that executives wanted from him was *The War of the Worlds* and that he didn't want to make it. He wanted to make anything else. He pitched the life of Christ, as if written by William Shakespeare, complete in *iambic pentameter* verse, to every executive in Hollywood. But nobody bit on that apple. Louis B. Meyer wanted *The War of the Worlds.* Jack Warner wanted *The War of the Worlds.* Universal wanted to add Martians to his menagerie of horror movie icons. Even Disney wanted singing and dancing cartoon Martians. But Orson was indignant. He wouldn't deliver what they wanted. He had the "keys" the Hollywood. He could directed any *damned* thing he wanted.

THE PROSECUTION: How did Hollywood react to Orson Welles filming *War of the Worlds* for RKO Radio Pictures.

THE GOSSIP COLUMNIST: Relief! Charles Koerner, with the "help" of Meyer, Warner, and Disney, had finally reigned in the "boy-genius". But then the rumors began to circulate.

THE PROSECUTION: And what were these rumors?

THE GOSSIP COLUMNIST: Although Orson can be a Svengali when it comes to his actors and crew, his cult-leader control of his set could not completely dampen the rumors of... mischievousness. While seated at dinner with me and Joseph Cotton, his ever-present collaborator, he insisted be was filming a straight adaptation of Howard Koch's infamous radio-script, but I don't trust a blessed word that comes out of his cursed mouth. So I put my little birdies to work on the Forty-Acres to uncover the truth that Orson was so desperate to conceal through his obvious lies. What I heard back was harrowing.

THE PROSECUTION: What did you hear?

THE GOSSIP COLUMNIST: There were actors portraying "Franklin Delano Roosvelt" and "William Randolph Hearst"! He wasn't even trying to hide behind character names like "Charles Foster Kane" anymore. He was lampooning a great man with his own great name. The handful of pages of shooting script my little birdies were able to smuggle out of that Fort Knox of a set made my already graying hair go white with fright!

THE PROSECUTION: Which was?

THE GOSSIP COLUMNIST: His retitled *Invasion From Mars* motion picture claimed that the radio broadcasts heard that cold, windy October evening five years ago were *real* and that two great men, President Franklin Delano Roosevelt and William Randolph Hearst *conspired* to cover-up the reality of the invasion with Orson Welles faking the radio-dramatization on wax! The ignominy of that man! Has he no shame? It's one thing to put a man's life up on the screen for all the world to see in *Citizen Kane*, even with its exaggerations and outright lies, but it is another thing entirely to caricature two great men with lampoonery and scorn! He was a court jester biting his thumb at the king in his own court!

THE PROSECUTION: Why didn't you publicize the truth in your wide-reaching Hollywood column?

THE GOSSIP COLUMNIST: You don't think I wanted to? I wrote a blasted column exposing every little detail that I had. Everything. The filming two pictures at the same time! *The War of the Worlds* to placate the ignorant brass at RKO and *Invasion From Mars* that he truly intended to release! I had the script pages that put the most absurd and laughable dialogue on the very lips of "President Roosevelt" and "William Randolph Hearst". Sure, the "boy-genius" in his genius made himself a character. Yes, this "Orson Welles" said and did the most outlandish things like traveling through time! But lampooning himself was not going to absolve him of his sins! My column was going to expose the greatest scandal in the history of Hollywood: the mocking of great men, the literal wasting of hundreds of thousands of dollars on filming *War of the Worlds* scenes that only served to placate Koerner. But I wasn't allowed to publish it.

THE PROSECUTION: Why not? If you column exposed all this and more, why did it never see publication?

THE GOSSIP COLUMNIST: It came from on high, from the Old Man himself, that I couldn't publish my column. I had it all there, in black-and-white, what Orson Welles was trying to do, but there I was in Mr. Hearst's office, with Mr. Hearst himself seated behind his glorious desk, and he took the only copy I had of my most delicious column ever and threw it his safe. The very safe that kept the greatest secrets of Hollywood: all of the salacious photographs, all of the lewd love letters, all of the dirtiest dirt we had on Hollywood stars. He locked my column away never to see the light of day! I was indignant! Why would the Old Man censor me? Didn't I always do his bidding? Didn't I always attack those he wanted attacked? I was his best guard dog and now he was treating me like a lap dog. Like a goddamn Shih Tzu! I'm a Doberman Pinscher for Christ's sake!

THE PROSECUTION: No further questions.

THE DEFENSE: When Mr. Hearst censored your column by locking it away in his safe, did it ever occur to you that your column actually exposed the "Orson Welles' Conspiracy"?

THE GOSSIP COLUMNIST: What?

THE DEFENSE: If William Randolph Hearst conspired with President Roosevelt and my client, Orson Welles, to cover-up a Martian invasion on October 30, 1938, then by publishing your column in his 40-plus newspapers, would he not have violated his oath he swore before God and country?

THE GOSSIP COLUMNIST: Wait! What?

THE DEFENSE: You thought your column was exposing Orson Welles for "lampoonery", as you so eloquently put it, but your column was actually exposing your boss, William Randolph Hearst's involvement with a wide reaching and wide ranging government conspiracy!

THE PROSECUTION: Is there a question here?

THE DEFENSE: Did it never occur to you that he was protecting his own neck?

THE GOSSIP COLUMNIST: That's patently absurd!

THE DEFENSE: If what you claimed in your column was true that Orson Welles was wasting hundreds of thousands of RKO Radio Picture's dollars on a film, you claim, he wasn't supposed to film, then why wouldn't William Randolph Hearst want to trumpet that in every single one of his forty-plus newspapers? Wouldn't he want to crucify his most noted Hollywood rival in 144 point headlines on the front pages of his papers?

THE GOSSIP COLUMNIST: Yes! That's what I thought! But...

THE DEFENSE: But! Instead of publishing your column, he quietly filed it away?

THE GOSSIP COLUMNIST: Yes!

THE DEFENSE: For all the world *never* to see!

THE GOSSIP COLUMNIST: Yes! Oh, God! No! Orson Welles couldn't have been right! He couldn't have.

THE DEFENSE: No further questions for this witness.

THE GOSSIP COLUMNIST: No! This isn't possible. The Old Man wouldn't have conspired with President Roosevelt. The two weren't on speaking terms. They had that falling out over the Old Man's attack in the *New York American*! He accused the President of being a Socialist, Communist, and Bolshevik! That the New Deal was part of a Marxist agenda! He wouldn't have conspired with a Marxist to cover-up a Martian invasion! It's absurd! Patently absurd! Hearst would have exposed the President in every one of his newspapers! He would have trumpeted the Martian invasion in his headlines! But! But? But the headlines blasted Orson Welles for his asinine radio-drama! Wait! What? The headlines *did* blast Orson Welles as his conspiracy claims! Why *didn't* the headlines blame the President for a Martian invasion! The Old Man wouldn't have conspired to cover-up it! That's absurd. He would have exposed the President! He would have! He would have! He would have!

THE JUDGE: Ms. Hopper?

THE GOSSIP COLUMNIST: Oh! No! Why did he put my column in the safe with all the secrets? The secrets! That's where he kept the secrets. All of the secrets that nobody wants anybody to know. They are in the safe... with my column. All of the photos... with my column. Why was my column put in the safe? It doesn't make any sense. My column doesn't belong in the safe with all of the secrets. Hollywood's secrets! No! Oh! No! What secrets did I expose in my column? No! Oh! I couldn't have. I couldn't have. I couldn't have.

THE DEFENSE: No further questions for this witness.

THE JUDGE: You're excused, Ms. Hopper.

THE GOSSIP COLUMNIST: No! No! The Old Man wouldn't have. No! No! The Old Man wouldn't have. He wouldn't have. He wouldn't have.

THE JUDGE: Bailiff?

THE GOSSIP COLUMNIST: *[She's visibly shaken. The bailiff escorts a crying Ms. Hopper our the courtroom.]* No! No! The Old Man wouldn't have. No! No! Oh! No! What is happening? *[She leaves the courtroom.]*

THE PROSECUTION: The government rests.

THE DEFENSE: The defense calls its first witness: *the* Orson Welles.

THE BAILIFF: Mr. Welles, please raise your right hand and place your left hand on the Bible. Do you swear to tell the truth, the whole truth, and nothing but the truth, so help you God?

THE ORSON WELLES: Why not?

THE DEFENSE: Upon cross-examination the prosecution will, no doubt, ask why should the jury believe you, Mr. Welles?

THE ORSON WELLES: I beg your pardon?

THE DEFENSE: You swore earlier to tell "the truth, the whole truth, and nothing but the truth, so help you God", but you also assert that you swore an oath before God and country to conceal a Martian invasion for the good, honest people of the United States of America? Which is it, Mr. Welles? Your word here in this court or your Oath you swear you swore to President Roosevelt and William Randolph Hearst?

THE ORSON WELLES: My Word is my Oath and that so-called Oath was sworn under duress. Judge, you cannot expect me to except responsibility for oath sworn on the verge of interplanetary war. My Oath is not to a president or a newspaper magnate, but the people of the United States of America, a people that I personally betrayed as part in that conspiracy.

THE DEFENSE: So you admit you betrayed your oath.

THE ORSON WELLES: To the people. You see, I didn't really swear an Oath to William Randolph Hearst nor to President Roosevelt. The Old Man and I swore and oath to the Constitution. And what are the first words of the Constitution? "We the People". I swore and oath to the people of the United States of America, whom I believed I was protecting by participating in this government conspiracy I have so eloquently coined the "Orson Welles' Conspiracy". And if my Oath was to the people for their own protection, then why not let them decide if they need protection from their own government.

THE DEFENSE: Why did you choose to expose this so-called "Orson Welles' Conspiracy" in a motion picture?

THE ORSON WELLES: Unlike Ms. Hopper, I don't have ready access to over forty newspapers owned and controlled by William Randolph Hearst.

THE DEFENSE: The prosecution presented a witness who claims to have delivered to you a number of classified documents. This witness claims to have falsified these "classified" documents in a ruse to enter into a relationship with a Hollywood starlet. What are your thoughts on his testimony?

THE ORSON WELLES: I saw the documents. They could not have been falsified, even by skilled counterfeiters with the German *Abwehr*. I saw the teletypes that cold, windy October evening five years ago. I remember each and every word printed on those teletypes.

THE DEFENSE: How could you possibly know "each and every word" printed by the teletypes?

THE ORSON WELLES: I have an eidetic memory, commonly but erroneously called a "photographic memory". Every word that had interrupted an evening of dance music broadcast by CBS studios was recorded into a teletype and printed out. I to this very day can recite chapter-and-verse of that teletype.

THE DEFENSE: And this is why you do not believe ████ ████, the Nazi spy's testimony.

THE ORSON WELLES: The documents he provided me corroborated the teletypes perfectly, so perfectly they could not possibly be counterfeit.

THE DEFENSE: Unless the German *Abwehr* gained possession of the CBS teletypes.

THE ORSON WELLES: Unlikely. Those teletypes went into the possession of William Randolph Hearst and then, most likely, into the National Archives never to be seen again. And why would the *Abwehr* counterfeit "classified" documents using actual classified teletypes.?

THE DEFENSE: Why would the Nazi spy falsify his testimony?

THE ORSON WELLES: Because he is a Nazi spy and the prosecutor is a fool.

THE PERSECUTION: Objection!

THE JUDGE: Sustained. The jury will ignore the comment.

THE DEFENSE: Why did you need the classified government documents from the Nazi spy if you remembered "each and every word" of the teletypes?

THE ORSON WELLES: Because the teletypes only told a part of the story, the story of what was said on the CBS broadcast that evening. For my screenplay to expose the *true* story, I needed to know the *entire* story. There was no way I could gain access to the classified documents documenting the vast government conspiracy to hide a Martian invasion without a network of government spies.

THE DEFENSE: An *Abwehr*?

THE ORSON WELLES: Precisely. Using the Nazi spy to use his colleagues in both the United States and Germany to sure the documents was the coup that I need to complete my screenplay. And what a treasure trove of information was in those documents!

THE DEFENSE: The Defense would like to enter into evidence Defense Exhibit No. 1. *[The court officers open the rear doors to the courtroom and wheel in a barbecue grill.]*

THE PROSECUTION: Objection.

THE JUDGE: I'll allow it.

THE DEFENSE: Mr. Welles, can you identify Defense Exhibit No. 1?

THE ORSON WELLES: It's the barbecue grill from Herman Mankiewicz's bungalow in Victorville.

THE PERSECUTION: Objection! What purpose does this exhibit serve?

THE DEFENSE: Your Honor, we're getting to it.

THE JUDGE: Overruled.

THE ORSON WELLES: That barbecue grill contains the ashes of the classified documents I had obtained from the Nazi spy. Unfortunately, Willie Brown and I were forced through paranoid circumstances to burn the documents to ash to protect our skins.

THE PERSECUTION: Is the defendant admitting to the willful destruction of classified documents in violation of 18 US Code § 1924?

THE DEFENSE: Of course not. We're getting to the point, your Honor.

THE JUDGE: Proceed. But cautiously.

THE DEFENSE: Why did you burn the classified government documents in this barbecue grill?

THE ORSON WELLES: The government spooks were like Hellhounds hounding our trail. In a fit of paranoia typically reserved for schizophrenics, Willie and I started a fire in that barbecue grill and torched each and every document. I'm hoping that forensic scientists can reconstruct the documents.

THE PROSECUTION: From ashes? What kind of miracle workers in the Los Angeles Police Department can reconstruct documents from ashes? This isn't the 21st Century!

THE ORSON WELLES: Actually, your Honor, we won't need forensic scientists to reconstruct the documents from the ashes in this barbecue grill You see, Willie and I never burnt the classified documents. Instead, we needed to keep the documents close.

THE DEFENSE: The defense would like to enter into evidence Defense Exhibit No. 2, the satchel sitting under the defense's table. *[The bailiff retrieves the satchel from under the table.]* Mr. Welles, can you explain Defense Exhibit No. 2 for the court?

THE ORSON WELLES: Of course, you see that satchel does not contain a miniaturized reel-to-reel recorder as evidenced by the microphone attached to said satchel. The satchel contains the key classified documents that my Nazi spy had acquired.

THE PERSECUTION: Is the defendant admitting to the willful possession of classified documents in violation of 18 US Code § 1924?

THE ORSON WELLES: Of course. But now, the classified documents will now be entered into evidence. The government will no longer be able to hide the invasion from Mars because the classified documents are now entered into evidence. *[Orson smiles like the Cheshire cat!.]*

THE PERSECUTION: Objection, your Honor. You cannot allow the Defense to enter these documents into evidence!

THE JUDGE: Overruled. I'll allow the document into evidence. Mr. Prosecutor, in your charging documents you are prosecuting the defendant for the violating 18 US Code § 1924, or the unauthorized removal and retention of classified documents or material, which the defendant is admitting to in open court. You've proven this charge and should be grateful. The documents are key to the prosecution of this case and will therefore be admitted into evidence.

THE PROSECUTION: The prosecution dismisses all charges against the defendants, George Orson Welles and William Francis Brown. Please, don't allow those documents into evidence.

THE JUDGE: The charges are dismissed with prejudice and the defendants are likewise dismissed. Court is adjured.

Mr. Brown, you may have questions concerning whether or not Orson Welles had actually burnt the classified government documents in that barbecue grill on Herman Mankiewicz's bungalow in Victorville. Orson explained in his hand written note, provided with this 16mm film, that he *had*, in fact, burnt the documents in a fit of paranoia and that the satchel *had* contained a miniaturized reel-to-reel recorder, but when the government actually charged him with these very real crimes, he had the properties department at RKO Radio pictures produce counterfeit classified documents that would give the impression, at first glance, that they were the real deal. Orson was orchestrating another *deux ex machina* to save his hide from government prosecution for having filmed his *Invasion From Mars* motion picture. Was he willing to go to jail for possession of classified documents, even if those documents were counterfeitted? I don't know.

Now that the prosecution had dismissed the case *with prejudice* he and Willie Brown were free from any threat of further prosecution. Orson would continue on his Hollywood journey to film the films he filmed and Willie would go back to his small Colorado hometown to work at the steel-mill having ended his own Hollywood journey. The screenplay your father left you in that safety-deposit box, along with the reel-to-reel tapes that recorded my interview with Orson and the 16mm film should be all the proof you need. I don't know what form that will take, a documentary or a book, but please, for the love of God, expose once and for all the "Orson Welles' Conspiracy!"

Milton Keynes UK
Ingram Content Group UK Ltd.
UKHW051835231024
450027UK00012B/105